LOST
MAN'S
LANE

ALSO BY SCOTT CARSON

The Chill

Where They Wait

LOST MAN'S LANE

A NOVEL

SCOTT CARSON

EMILY BESTLER BOOKS

ATRIA

NEW YORK ■ LONDON ■ TORONTO ■ SYDNEY ■ NEW DELHI

EMILY
BESTLER
BOOKS

ATRIA

An Imprint of Simon & Schuster, LLC
1230 Avenue of the Americas
New York, NY 10020

First Emily Bestler Books/Atria Books hardcover edition March 2024

EMILY BESTLER BOOKS/ATRIA BOOKS and colophon are trademarks of Simon & Schuster, LLC

Simon & Schuster: Celebrating 100 Years of Publishing in 2024

For information about special discounts for bulk purchases, please contact Simon & Schuster Special Sales at 1-866-506-1949 or business@simonandschuster.com.

The Simon & Schuster Speakers Bureau can bring authors to your live event. For more information or to book an event, contact the Simon & Schuster Speakers Bureau at 1-866-248-3049 or visit our website at www.simonspeakers.com.

Interior design by Dana Sloan

Manufactured in the United States of America

1 3 5 7 9 10 8 6 4 2

Library of Congress Control Number: 2023951776

ISBN 978-1-9821-9145-0
ISBN 978-1-9821-9147-4 (ebook)

Thinking of Stewart O'Nan, August Derleth, Keith Robertson,
and a magical place called Bloomington, Indiana, 1999.

AUTHOR'S NOTE

A CONVERSATION about earthquakes made me decide it is time I tell the truth.

Let me explain the lying first. That started in 1999, when I was sixteen years old, and became the coconspirator of a murdered man. I turned forty last summer, staring down the barrel at middle age, and much that once seemed as distant on the horizon as a mirage now feels welcome. Professionally welcome, anyhow. Nobody's referring to me as the "next" anything these days, no more wunderkind talk—though it's already been a long while since I heard that one. Maybe I'll miss those predictions someday, but I'm not sure, because the predictions were born of the truth that I refused to tell.

I had my reasons to avoid the truth. Ego was one of them. It was nice to be viewed as a natural talent. When it comes to motivators, though, I don't think anything trumps fear.

"Vain and afraid" doesn't have the same flair as "talented and hard-working," does it? But you could make your peace with it.

What about lying, though? Could you make your peace with that?

Probably not.

Is refusing to tell the truth different from lying? Most would tell you it is.

I'm not so sure.

All I know is that when it comes to telling ghost stories, people tend to regard the storyteller as a liar or a fool. Except, of course, for the hard-core believers. In nearly two decades of book tours, I've determined that there's a disconcerting correlation between ghost stories, close talkers, and halitosis. Keep the skepticism close and the Listerine closer before you tell someone a ghost story, I recommended on one television appearance. It's always easier to make a joke of the experience.

Now I'm going to find out what it's like on the other side. I'm going to find out what it's like to be the wild-eyed man with the hushed voice and the hand on your arm to prevent you from turning away, imploring you to listen, please, *really listen*, because this is how it happened. *This is the truth!* You believe me, don't you?

With a ghost story, it's always easier to turn away than it is to believe.

I've done all right telling the made-up ones. I've published a dozen books, made a living, even had a couple movies made. The people who liked the books hate those movies, but most of the people who watched the movies never read the books, so I guess it's a wash. The books that sell the best aren't the novels about ghosts. The bestsellers are the true crime stories. They please the critics, who sometimes use words like "prescient" and "perceptive" to describe my reporting. They never use those words with the ghost stories, which amuses me on my better nights, and keeps me awake on the bad ones.

I've made it this far with my secrets. I could keep going. But here at the proverbial crossroads of midlife—supposing that my body holds off illness and my truck's tires hold on to the pavement—I'm at that point where you're supposed to look back. You charge forward in your twenties, you strategize in your thirties, but somewhere in your forties you're supposed to look back. To develop a taste for nostalgia that you didn't have before, as you realize that you're going to have plenty of occasions to stare into the past whether you want to or not. Time has a way of forcing that. Sometimes the looking back is sweet and sometimes it's bitter, but in my experience it is almost always involuntary.

The past calls you, not the other way around.

I can hear it knocking now. Can feel it beside me on the porch on this unseasonably warm spring evening, with that glorious humidity that clings even into darkness, like summer is sealing winter out and taping the seams. We're bound now for the sun and the heat, the swelter of dog days, and then the first crisp night when a cool wind rustles brittle leaves and reminds you that it was all a circle, dummy, and there's only one way off this ride, so stop wishing that time would pass faster.

All of this brings my mind back to 1999, as did that conversation with the geologist. He told me there are twenty thousand earthquakes around the globe each year, or fifty-five each day. Think about how common that is. How natural. It got me to thinking about an old crypt, and what lies beneath, and what had better stay buried.

What *must* stay buried, if what I've heard is the truth, and I'm confident that it is. Dead men tell no tales, they say, and they are wrong. Dead men tell plenty of tales.

But they do not tell lies.

CHAPTER ONE

DRIVER'S EDUCATION

February 1999

"I said, 'What you wanna be?' She said, 'Alive' "

OUTKAST
"DA ART OF STORYTELLIN', PART I"

1

I GOT MY DRIVER'S license on February 11, 1999. This would be easy to remember even if I didn't have the speeding ticket with the date on it.

But I do.

My mother drove me to the BMV that afternoon, which was a Thursday, and she talked about the weather the entire way there. It wasn't idle small talk; she was a meteorologist, and that day was closing in on a February heat record in Bloomington, Indiana. We'd had snow only a few days earlier, but we drove to the BMV with the windows down, welcoming the 70-degree air like a gift, which is the way those days feel in a Midwestern winter, a jump start for your draining battery.

My personal battery was running high already—this day had been a long time in coming. If you didn't take the formal driver's education course, you needed to wait six additional months to apply for a driver's license. This was the state's way of bribing teenagers to take driver's ed—and my mother's way of buying time before releasing me to the world in a "two-thousand-pound killing machine."

Finally, the wait was over.

I wasn't worried about the written portion of the test, and while I expressed high confidence about the driving portion, let's all admit that our heart rates picked up at the phrase "parallel parking" when we were sixteen. I took the driving portion first and passed without trouble. Even nailed the parallel parking—no small feat in the Oldsmobile Ninety Eight my mother had given me, which was the length of a hearse. On to the written test—twenty-five questions, multiple choice, fill-in-the-answer bubble on a separate Scantron sheet with a No. 2 pencil. I cruised through twenty-three before a male voice boomed out, "It's Miller Time!"

I heard my mother's laugh in response. Melodic, practiced, unsurprised. When you're Monica Miller the meteorologist, you can't go long before some dimwit producer decides to affix a famous beer slogan to your segments. People often recognized her, and they loved to indicate it by shouting out, "It's Miller Time!" When you're sixteen and this is the way the community responds to your mother's presence, it's not a great deal of fun.

Particularly when your mother is beautiful, and it's mostly men shouting at her.

I didn't bother to turn around at the exchange, so I never saw the cheerful citizen who recognized my mother, only heard him, and then my mother's on-cue laugh, but the distraction was enough that when I filled in my test circle, I missed the twenty-fourth line entirely, and filled in the twenty-fifth blank on the accompanying Scantron sheet. I then dutifully answered the next question in the twenty-sixth line, stood, and handed my exam to the bored clerk.

"You are allowed two mistakes out of the twenty-five questions," she intoned in a voice that said she could—and maybe did—recite this in her sleep. "You may return no sooner than tomorrow to retake the examination."

"Great—gives me extra time to figure out a way to cheat," I said, a remark designed to make her smile. It did not make her smile. She lined her answer key up beside my test and peered through the top halves of her bifocals as she scanned the results. Her red pen made little taps of contact with each correct answer, a nice, steady rhythm.

Slow ride, I hummed softly, *take it easy* . . .

The clerk's red pen paused. Hovered above the test.

I leaned forward, frowning, and immediately saw the mistake. There was no answer to question twenty-four.

The clerk's mouth twitched with a barely concealed evil smile.

"Mr. Miller," she said, in a voice exponentially louder than she'd used previously, "you have missed question twenty-four by failing to answer it."

"I did answer it. I just got out of order."

"You have also missed question twenty-five," she continued. "And it is my duty to—"

"What happened was I filled in the wrong—"

"*It is my duty*," she snapped, glaring at me over her glasses with a look that effectively severed my vocal cords, "to inform you of the correct answer. Question twenty-five reads: 'If you encounter a law enforcement officer whose command differs with the signal at an intersection, what do you do?' "

The easiest question on the whole damn test. A question that half the kindergartners in the county would answer correctly.

The clerk smiled at me.

"The correct answer," she said, still loud enough for the room, "is option C: 'Obey the command of the law enforcement officer.' You selected option B: 'Honk and proceed with caution.' "

Laughter erupted. One man repeated my answer for his wife. Another woman snorted and clapped. I didn't dare turn around to look at my mother. I stood there imagining the responses from my friends when I informed them that even after a six-month wait, I still didn't have a driver's license. I was so lost to my horror that it took me a second to realize the clerk was still speaking.

"You have missed only two questions, which means you have passed the test. Please follow me over to the back of the room so we can get a photograph for your driver's license, Marshall Miller."

I'd passed.

I also spent four years carrying a driver's license photo in which my face was so red, it looked freshly sunburned.

When I finally looked at my mother, she was smiling that 100-watt, television-approved smile of hers.

"Honk and proceed with caution," she said, and handed me the keys.

We laughed about it then, and we laughed even harder in the car on the drive home. If we'd had any idea how much of our lives would soon be lost to my interactions with law enforcement, we wouldn't have cracked a smile.

I dropped my mother off at home, knowing that I wouldn't see her again until breakfast the next morning. She'd been offered the prime-time broadcasts on numerous occasions when I was younger, declining them each time, but when I turned sixteen, she agreed to move from days to nights, guaranteeing a better paycheck and a larger audience—and requiring a hell of a lot of trust in her teenage son. I was determined not to screw it up. I was the only child of a single mother, and if you can make it to sixteen without disaster in that dynamic, you're carrying at least a little bit of extra maturity. Extra concern, anyhow. I did not want to disappoint my mother.

I also genuinely did not believe that I would.

There's no confidence like a sixteen-year-old's confidence in the future.

I dropped her off in the driveway of our simple two-story colonial on its tidy lawn. We lived on Raintree Lane on the north side of town, west of what was then State Road 37 and is now Interstate 69. It was a neighborhood of modest but well-kept homes and mature trees and I appreciate it more now than I did then, but I suppose that's true of a lot of things.

I made about a thousand assurances that I would be careful, gave my mother a one-armed hug without relinquishing control of the steering wheel, and then pulled out of the driveway, headed for the Cascades Golf Course, intending to hit a few buckets of balls at the driving range on this strangely warm day, but mostly ready to experience my freshly minted freedom. I put the windows down, and that unseasonable warm air flooded in. The ancient Oldsmobile didn't have a CD player, so I had a Sony Discman resting on the bench seat beside me, connected to the stereo through an auxiliary cord that ran to the tape deck. Badass. With my mother out of the car, I turned the volume up on Tupac's "2 of Amerikaz Most Wanted." Badder-ass.

Beside the Discman rested not one, not two, but three massive binders of CDs, divided into three categories: rap mixes, rock mixes, and make-out mixes. The former two, unfortunately, saw more airplay than the last. I let the Oldsmobile's speakers blast all the bass they could handle and bobbed my head in rhythm, and had Pac still been alive, he'd have no doubt laughed his ass off at me, but in that moment, alone behind the wheel, I didn't care about the old car or the shitty stereo. I was a free man, no chaperone required.

Life was good.

I made it four miles before the colored lights came on behind me.

It was more frightening than it should have been, maybe. I'd never been pulled over; hell, I'd never been alone in a car. Police were the ultimate authority figures, like principals with guns.

In the adrenaline rush of the moment, I forgot a key rule from the BMV study guide: when one is pulled over by police, one is to pull off the road on the right-hand side. I opted instead for what struck me as the clearest area: the wide expanse of grass that ran between the road and the fairway of the thirteenth hole of the golf course. This required crossing a lane of oncoming traffic, a maneuver that I executed without so much as a turn signal.

The siren went on. A single, bleated chirp that chilled my blood.

On a normal day in February, the course would have been empty and even the driving range closed. Because we were chasing that heat record, it was busy, packed with cabin-fever sufferers taunted by new sets of Christmas clubs. Wonderful. I had an audience.

Four miles as a free man. A good run while it lasted.

I parked the car and waited while a muscled-up officer with a crew cut approached. The window was already down, and he leaned in and studied me, seeming torn between anger and exasperation. His stiff uniform shirt strained around his chiseled chest and arms as if determined to escape it. His name tag identified him as CPL. MADDOX.

"Son, what in the hell were you doing, crossing over here?"

"It seemed safer for both of us," I said. This was up there with *honk and proceed with caution* in terms of poor answers.

"Safer? On the wrong side of the road?"

"There was lots of room to park."

"Are you trying to tell me that I'm *wrong*, son?"

"Not at all, sir, I'm just . . . the thing is, it's a big car."

"Does it steer itself?"

"Pardon?"

"Does it steer itself?" His eyes were the same dark blue as his uniform shirt, which was pressed against pectoral muscles that looked like they belonged to a creature from *Jurassic Park*.

"No, sir."

"So let's stop blaming the car for your decisions."

"Yes, sir."

"It is not a 500 Benz," he said without a hint of emotion.

"No, sir. It's an Oldsmobile."

"Do you think the district attorney is really a ho?"

My lips parted but I didn't offer any words. I was stunned and confused—and then, oh-so-belatedly I realized my music was still playing. Tupac's "Picture Me Rollin'." Pac was describing his Mercedes and expounding on his theories about the personal lives of the law enforcement members who'd put him in custody.

I am going to jail, I thought as I punched the stereo power off just as Tupac offered a few words to the "punk police." I wondered how handcuffs felt.

"It's a song," I said. "I mean, not a . . . you know, the lyrics aren't mine. They do not represent my views."

"Oh. I was confused. The voice sounded exactly like yours."

When I looked at him this time, I thought I saw the barest hint of a smile. Then it vanished as he said, "License and registration, please."

Shit.

"I, uh . . . I only have this." I showed him my temporary license. The real one would be mailed. And now, no doubt, dropped directly into the garbage disposal by my mother.

Maddox eyed the temp. "You got this *today*."

"Yes, sir."

"Off to a heck of a start."

"Yes, sir. I mean, no, sir."

He lowered the temp license and fixed the steel-blue eyes on me again. "Registration?"

I found the registration, wondering how long it would take for my mother's insurance rates to soar. Teenage males were more expensive to insure even *without* points on their licenses.

"Please wait in the vehicle," Corporal Maddox said, and then he returned to his cruiser.

I wanted to punch something—mostly myself. I hated the tight-throated sensation and the rapid heartbeat and the echoing words of my ridiculous exchange with the state trooper. All of it so stupid. All of it something a kid would do. I did not feel like a kid either.

At least, I hadn't until those colored lights had come on.

I looked in the sideview mirror, trying to make out what Maddox was doing. I deserved a ticket. But he'd smiled—almost—when he made that remark about confusing my voice for Tupac's. Was he smiling like a jerk—or someone who'd give a kid a break?

The driver's door of the cruiser swung open, and Maddox stepped out. It was only then that I realized someone else was in the car. Not another cop, but someone in the back, behind the grate. A blond-haired girl wearing a teal polo shirt with a white logo and script over the left breast. Her hair was tied up loosely in a bandana that matched the teal-and-white shirt. The combination was immediately familiar to me: the uniform of the Chocolate Goose, a local ice-cream shop that had been in business for generations and was a townie staple in summer. The logo on the polo shirt would show a version of the Mother Goose character, complete with reading glasses and a babushka and a chocolate ice-cream cone held jauntily in one wing. It was strange to see the outfit in February. The Chocolate Goose was strictly seasonal, opening on Memorial Day weekend and closing on Labor Day. The girl, who looked about my age but wasn't familiar, seemed to stare directly at me as if searching my face in the mirror. She looked the way I felt: frustrated and foolish and a little frightened. Maybe more than a little.

Then Maddox swung the door shut, and my attention returned to him, the girl's face relegated to a faint outline seen through dark glass.

Maddox approached, holding my license in his right hand and a ticket in his left.

"Mr. Miller," Maddox said, passing me the license and registration, "this is not an ideal day for you to receive a traffic ticket, is it?"

"No, sir."

"Points on your license before you even get started. Not good."

He gazed down at the golf course, seeming to follow the descending slopes down to the dark wooded valley that traced Griffy Creek into the heart of downtown Bloomington. His big chest swelled. I wondered how much he could bench-press with those arms and that chest. I wondered if he was as intimidating to that girl in the back of his cruiser as he was to me.

"What's your father going to say when you show him this?" he asked.

I didn't answer. He shot me a hard look.

"What's he going to say, Mr. Miller?"

"He's dead," I said.

I was afraid that he would ask how it had happened. It was hard to explain that I didn't know. Harder to explain that he might not be dead at all. He was to me, though. That's the way it feels with a father who bailed before you were born. Closer to dead than alive, but more hurtful than a dead man could ever be.

"I see," Maddox said. He seemed to mull over something, and then he separated the two halves of the ticket—one original, one carbon copy on pale pink paper. He handed me the copy.

"I clocked you at 39 in a 30," he said. "That's the first violation on the ticket. The second is for improper lane movement. These are lessons you shouldn't have to learn the hard way."

I couldn't come up with anything to say and didn't see the point in trying. The consequences were already in hand, and that question about what my absent father would say sizzled in my brain, temporarily as troubling as the ticket itself.

"That copy is yours. This one is mine, property of Corpo*real* Maddox, until it is filed with the court."

He'd drawn his rank out in an odd Southern drawl, as if enjoying the flavor of it. I kept staring at the ticket. His thumb had left a grimy print on the bottom corner, probably from the carbon paper. It looked like ash, though. Appropriate, for the document that would burn my freedom down.

"Sometimes," Maddox said, "I forget to file them."

It was as if the ticket in my hand had gone from traffic citation to lottery winner. He was granting me mercy.

"*Thank you*," I said, looking up from the carbon-stained ticket.

"For what?"

His broad face was empty, the eyes still cool, but I was sure he knew exactly what I meant. He was giving me a break.

"For the second chance. I won't screw it up."

"Did I say you have a second chance? I said sometimes I forget to file paperwork with the court. I made no fucking promise of it. Where the *fuck* did you hear the words '*second chance*'?"

I was so shocked I couldn't even begin to answer. I'd heard adults swear, but I'd never had an adult swear *at* me. Not like that.

"You make assumptions," he said. "That's a dangerous way to live, Mr. Miller. It is a better way to die."

A better way to die?

I glanced at the golf course, this time *hoping* that I had an audience. Everyone had their backs to me, heads bowed over their balls or tilted to watch them in flight. I suddenly felt alone and afraid.

"Do you know what I hear when you say *second chance*?" Maddox snarled. For the first time, I was aware of the gun and baton on his belt.

"No, sir." I managed to murmur this.

"I hear a little prick who thinks the world owes him kindness."

A police officer had just called me a prick. No one was listening to us and there was no one I could call for help. I didn't have a cell phone. I had only a few friends who did, and they weren't with me. I was alone. The only person who was still paying attention to us was the girl in the back of the police car, and she was also alone—and worse off than me.

For now.

Maddox let the silence spread out like his massive shadow. He hadn't asked a question, and I didn't know what to say, so I didn't speak.

"Driving a car down a road filled with strangers who are just trying to get home safe," he said at last, "is *responsibility*, Mr. Miller. Not a joke, not fun, not a privilege. It should feel damn serious to you. Nobody is promised a second chance at getting home safe. You will learn that."

The ticket was trembling in my hand now.

"Go on your way," Maddox said. "Now."

He turned and walked away. I sagged in the driver's seat, the carbon copy in my hand. Right then, I didn't care if he filed it or not. I felt as if I'd glimpsed the chasm between the kinds of consequences that existed in the world. There were tickets and there was violence.

He wouldn't have hurt you, I told myself.

Right? No way a police officer would have hurt me. There were people not far away and . . .

What if there hadn't been?

I looked in the mirror in time to see him settle back behind the wheel. In the half second before the driver's door swung shut, I saw the girl in the back seat again.

She'd started to cry.

I would have remembered her face even if I never saw it on a MISSING poster.

2

I DIDN'T GO TO the driving range. I went home, watching the mirror the whole way, fearing another burst of colored lights.

I hear a little prick who thinks the world owes him kindness.

I was on my street when it occurred to me that I didn't want my mother to see me, because I was returning way too quickly for her not to suspect trouble.

That was fine, though. My best friend in the world lived just down our street, tucked in the back of a cul-de-sac at the end of Raintree Lane. I'd known Kerri Flanders since the crib—literally. She lived four houses away, the only kid in my class on our street, and her parents had embraced my mother like family when she moved into the neighborhood. They weren't much older than she was, but they always acted as if they were, as if a single mother were perpetually less wise than her married peers.

When we were in elementary school, Kerri and I were together from the moment we got off the bus. Summer was even better, when fireflies were chased and water balloons busted and bike brakes blared in protests of peeled rubber. She was the smartest kid in our class by a mile, and in a way I owe my career to Kerri—well, Kerri and a private investigator named Noah Storm. He played an essential role, but we'll get to that.

My love of books is a gift from Kerri. She read *everything*, and when we were very young, I was motivated by a sense of envy—and stupidity—watching her churn through chapter books while I struggled through picture books. I'm sure my mother played a role, but to be honest, I don't remember that. What I remember was Kerri sitting in a lawn chair with her feet swinging beneath the seat because she was too short to touch the ground, finishing *Little House in the Big Woods* and setting it on the grass with one hand while she plucked *Little House on the Prairie* out of the stack to her left. She was five years old then.

Even Kerri's parents were perplexed by her intelligence, unsure of what exactly to do with her. At one point, the school suggested she should skip a grade. Jerry and Gwen Flanders resisted that, concerned about the social impact, probably, but also aware that Kerri wasn't unhappy or bored, just brilliant. Her father accepted that with a laugh and a shrug the way some dads might acknowledge that their Little League player was a switch hitter. Proud, sure, but not motivated to push the kid because of a gift. Jerry was a good old boy, as townie as they came, a fourth-generation Bloomingtonian, and the third generation in his family to work as a tool and die maker at Otis Elevator. Also the last. Otis was one of several major manufacturing plants in Bloomington when I was born—along with RCA, General Electric, Thomson Consumer Electronics, and Westinghouse, those plants employed thousands—and not one remained by the time I graduated from college. I heard a lot of competing theories as to why the relentless rounds of closures were happening, but I was too young to understand. For a long time I thought NAFTA was a curse or a slur because I only heard it muttered by Jerry Flanders when he had a beer in his hand and a faraway look in his eyes.

When he was still employed by Otis, Kerri and I found it hilarious when he'd begin carrying on about the "simple genius" of the elevator. He played it for laughs back then, everything said dryly and with a wink. After the layoffs began, the winks stopped, and he spoke of the simple genius of the elevator with earnestness that made you uncomfortable.

The other plant shutdowns ultimately affected many more people, but the first round of layoffs at Otis stands out in my mind because it struck closest to home. We were two weeks into the fourth grade when Jerry was laid off. Kerri cried, and a kid named Danny Neely made fun of her tears at recess and I threw a handful of rocks into his freckled face and earned myself an afternoon in the principal's office. On the bus ride home, Kerri kissed my cheek. Neither of us spoke. I was terrified that her family might move.

They didn't move, but Jerry Flanders was on his sixth job in seven years. He kept bouncing around, avoiding any of the obvious choices, like Thomson, the massive television plant, or GE, where the world's best-selling refrigerators were made. He couldn't stop imagining doom for any of the large factories, so he was always moving on to the next small-time hustle. With each job change, a little more tension seeped into the house.

Gwen, Kerri's mother, always said she was "in academia," which means something to some people in a college town, but she was staff, not faculty, which I learned meant even more to some people in a college town, the kind who genuflect at the word "tenure." Gwen was an administrator for event programming, a part of the campus infrastructure but not an *academic*.

She desperately wanted Kerri to be the real deal, a professor competitively courted by elite schools. It was Gwen's decision to send Kerri to the gifted-and-talented program—"GT," as we called it—which meant in fifth grade she was pulled out of our elementary school and bused with the high schoolers, sent off to a single classroom of Monroe County's best and brightest.

That broke my ten-year-old heart.

It also made us closer friends, though. None of the classroom cliques infected our relationship, because we were still neighbors, still had the weekends and the summers. Those were special days. The gifted-and-talented program returned its refined minds in junior high, a day I'd learned to dread, aware by then of the vulnerability of our private friendship, afraid it wouldn't stand up to the stress test. The cul-de-sac summers felt like a lost paradise. At thirteen, I was already nostalgic.

Our friendship held up, though. We were always closer out of school than in the building, but we didn't pretend to be strangers. Different social circles, that's all. Looking back, I think we realized that the friendship was better in a bubble and took steps to protect that without ever discussing it. As our social circles diverged, we found classes to take together, and no weekend passed without my dropping by Kerri's house or vice versa. The only time it changed was when one of us began dating someone new; at that point, the other one drifted away to offer space and watch the result, like a basketball player clearing out for a teammate on a fast break. The depth of our friendship had been private for so long that it felt like the right kind of secret, and it was an unspoken understanding that whenever something significant happened, we returned to Raintree Lane to share it.

That's how I ended up pulling into the driveway alongside Jerry Flanders's battered Chevy S-10 on the day that I was called a prick by a police officer.

He opened the door when I pulled in, wearing jeans and a flannel shirt open over a *1992 Big Ten Champions* shirt, a pack of cigarettes in the pocket of the flannel. The shirt made me wince—that team, starring Calbert Cheaney, Greg Graham, and Damon Bailey, should've won at least one national championship if not two, prevented from titles by fluke injuries and a referee named Ted Valentine. I'll never forgive "TV Teddy."

Jerry Flanders was a muscular guy with sandy hair and what seemed like an all-seasons sunburn. I loved Jerry, but after my encounter with Maddox, the sight of any authority figure rattled me, so I promptly put the Olds in park and shut the engine off. I saw him grinning as I stepped out of the car, and only then did I realize that in my effort to avoid coming close to his truck, I'd left the ass end of the Olds hanging into the street.

"Go ahead and bring that old boat all the way up to the dock, Marshall."

"Yes, sir." I climbed back behind the wheel, started the car, and nudged it up almost to the garage door of the split-level house. Jerry came down to the landing of the front steps and lit a cigarette. He was always trying to stop smoking, but that spring the effort wasn't even getting lip service. He was drinking a lot more on the weekends too. I didn't mind that; he was a funny drunk. When you're sixteen, that doesn't seem like a bad thing. It takes a few years to see the whole.

"Finally got the license, chief?" he asked.

"I did."

"Parallel parked and everything?"

"No problems there." That wasn't a lie, at least.

"Well, congratulations. What a day for it, right? Feels like spring." He exhaled smoke and nodded at the house. "She's in the basement."

I thanked him and walked inside a house that was nearly as familiar as my own. Jerry and Gwen had a beautiful, manicured lawn, but inside, everything was chaotic and cluttered, as if they were unpacking from a move. I jogged down the steps to the basement, which was one of my favorite places on the planet, outfitted with a pool table, two leather-upholstered beanbag chairs, and a wall of stereo equipment featuring speakers that were nearly as tall as me. There was a small bedroom and a separate bathroom, and Kerri had moved from her childhood bedroom into the basement, an act of independence that her parents tolerated with shrugs and smiles.

She was curled up in one of the beanbags, dark brown hair bouncing to the chimes of the Smashing Pumpkins song "Disarm" as she worked on calculus homework. She was two full years ahead of me in math.

"Did you remember to put it in neutral and rev the engine before the test like I told you?" she asked without looking up.

"No. But I've already been pulled over and called a prick by a police officer."

That got her attention. She stared up and pushed her hair back from her face. She had Jerry's dark complexion and hair and Gwen's petite build and fine-boned features, and when she laughed, her entire body got in on the act.

"You're serious?"

"Yep." I flopped into the beanbag beside her, feeling safe for the first time since I'd seen those colored lights. Except I hadn't really felt in *danger*, had I? That was too extreme.

Then I remembered Maddox's voice biting off the words: *Where the fuck did you hear the words* "second chance"?

"I was scared," I told Kerri, the only person in the world I'd admit that to so readily, and then I told her the way it happened: how Maddox had loomed over me, biceps bulging, profanity popping; how alone and afraid the girl in the back of his car had looked.

She closed her math book and put the notebook on the floor and listened without saying a word, those dark, hyperfocused eyes of hers locked on me.

"Are you going to report it?" she asked when I was finished. She extended her slim, tan legs and crossed her feet at the ankles. Her calves were laced with scratches from trail running. Outside of practice, she refused to run on the track, much to the coach's chagrin when she inevitably sprained another ankle.

"Call the police on the police? That's crazy."

"They might not think so. It's a bad look for them, having such an asshole out there. Getting the report might help. You know, for an internal affairs investigation."

"Internal affairs?" I laughed. "I don't think they've got that department in Bloomington."

"Sure they do. There's oversight. Someone's in charge. Someone has to be, right? It's an institution. There are checks and balances."

I gave that a grudging nod. "He was a corporal, though. Pretty high up."

"Well, there are higher ranks than corporal."

"Yeah, I'll find an admiral, right? Put something else on; I got sick of that album in seventh grade."

"By which you mean put Nas on. Gag." She hit the remote and the disc changer hummed and clicked. Beyond the stereo, hanging above the door to Kerri's bedroom, red light glowed from an exit sign. She'd found it at a yard sale and hung it above her bedroom door the day she moved into the basement, a way, she explained, of reminding her parents that she was growing up.

"Visual cues are important prompts," she would say. "At sixteen, each day I'm walking toward the exit." Jerry and Gwen would roll their eyes and grin.

The CD shifted and the intro of *I Am . . .* rippled through the speakers.

"It's so good," I said.

"It's no *Illmatic*." She was goading me, but I couldn't resist the bait.

"It's a progression. He's not doing the same thing on repeat."

"Eminem is better."

"You're high. He's a character, not a rapper. All shock, no substance. I guarantee you, no one will remember Eminem in twenty years."

She smirked and we sat without speaking as Nas rapped on. The simple swagger—or rage—of hip-hop put a welcome, false confidence in my bloodstream, bravado that helped me forget the fear I'd felt when Maddox glared down at me.

"Are you going to tell your mom?" Kerri asked, and the bravado faded fast. Nobody rapped about running to their mother after a cop scared them.

"Why would I do that?"

"He called you a prick! Cops are supposed to be observant, granted, so he'll get credit for that, but it's not the proper approach as a public servant."

I had to laugh at that.

"It's not worth it," I said. "This will just make her wig out even more about me driving. I'll end up right back on the bus."

Kerri nodded sympathetically. She knew how my mother felt about my driving. "Did you get the two-thousand-pound-killing-machine lecture again before you left?"

"Not really. We were laughing about my test answer, and she was in a good mood."

"What test answer?" Kerri asked.

Damn it. Unforced error.

"Marshall Miller," Kerri said, leaning forward, spotting the high-value secret with a practiced eye, "you tell me this instant."

So I did, and by the time I finished, she was laughing so hard she had tears in her eyes.

"You actually guessed that. 'Honk and proceed with caution.' " She could scarcely get the words out.

"I didn't guess it! I . . . selected it."

Now I was laughing too. When she repeated "Honk and proceed with caution" in the voice of someone saying a sacred prayer, as if she simply couldn't believe how sweet it was, we both cracked up, and when Jerry poked his head in to ask what was so funny, Kerri insisted on telling him the story. Jerry had a beer, which should have stood out to me on a Monday afternoon, but it didn't. It felt good, laughing with them. Maddox's empty eyes and the frightened face of the girl in his back seat seemed far away.

When the song changed to "I Gave You Power" and Nas explained that he'd seen cold nights and bloody days, Jerry groaned and headed for the stairs.

"I don't need to hear that crap. Never mind the filthy lyrics; he's ripping off Eric Gales."

"It's called sampling," I said.

"It should be called felony theft," Jerry shot back.

Kerri waved him off. "Get out of here, then. Radon doesn't mitigate itself."

"Not until I'm done with it," he said with mock seriousness, and then he was gone. I looked at Kerri quizzically.

"Radon?"

"Some kind of poisonous gas that leaches up from limestone."

"I know what it is. Why were you talking about it, though?"

The humor left her eyes.

"His new next job," she said. "Sales for some company that installs pipes in your basement that, I don't know, drain the radon? Wait, you don't drain a gas. Use your brainbox, Kerri!"

She was trying to recover her humor, but I knew her too well to miss the undercurrent of sadness. *His new next job.*

"He quit the dealership?" I asked.

She nodded wearily. "And my mother is going to be *bullshit* about that. Whatever. On to the next one."

"Right."

There was an awkward beat of silence before she said, "The good news is that radon, being a gas, rises." She lowered her voice and went wide-eyed, dramatic. "And do you know what else rises, Marshall?"

"Elevators," I whispered. "They're simple genius, I tell you."

It sounds mean, laughing about Jerry's beloved job, but the jokes were a comfort, a reminder of the good days when he'd been in on the joke. You can't patch up a parent's pain no matter how badly you want to, and if you absorb too much of it, you'll drown alongside them. Part of being sixteen is laughing at things that hurt. Hell, it might be the most important part.

We would do a lot of laughing that year.

When we concluded with the simple-genius giggles, Kerri said, "You didn't recognize the girl in that cop's car?"

"No. Couple years older than us, maybe? Not much. She was dressed like she'd just come from work at the Chocolate Goose."

"They're closed."

"Exactly. That was weird. That's what she was wearing, though. She looked frightened at first, and she was crying by the end."

Kerri was quiet, thinking about it. "That would be so scary. Imagine being in the back of that guy's car, with him swearing at you, and he's wearing a gun and he has the steering wheel and you've got nothing, just along for the ride, and nobody even knows where you are."

Should I report Maddox's behavior? Maybe. Or maybe I should suck it up and not be intimidated. I didn't want to be the very thing he'd assumed I was: a scared kid with a mom to report to. I was about to articulate a version of this when there was a click and hum as the garage door started to rise. Kerri grimaced.

"Your mom?" I said.

"Yeah. And guess who hasn't heard about the lucrative world of radon mitigation yet?"

"Shit. Sorry. You want to hang at my house for a while? Mom will be in Indy."

"I'm going to Jake's."

"Ah." Jake Crane was Kerri's new boyfriend, who'd moved from Colorado the previous semester. He was a nationally ranked rock climber, making him instantly unique in Indiana. He was a senior and wore a lot of flannel and flip-flops and was unfailingly friendly—so authentically good-natured that nobody even busted his balls for it. The shredded rock-climbing physique probably helped with that. His father was a philosophy professor at IU, and Jake was like Kerri, a reader of everything. While I had no reason to dislike him, I couldn't pretend I was rooting for him either. Kerri and I had never discussed the idea of dating and had never so much as kissed, as if we were both aware that it was the easiest way to screw up the longest friendship either of us had. At least Jake would graduate in a few months and go on his way.

"Should I stay and say hi to your mom or just bail?" I asked, rising.

"Today you might want to duck and slide."

It was another inside joke, the same as "simple genius," this one ripped from a Nas lyric and already turning into a regular phrase between us when someone needed to leave. If she wanted me out of the house, it was a clear sign of the blowup she expected when Gwen Flanders learned the news of Jerry's latest job change. I gave her a fist bump and headed out. I was halfway up the stairs when she called after me.

"Oh, crap, Marshall, there's one thing I forgot to tell you!"

"Yeah?" I looked back, saw her face was wide-eyed and concerned.

"Honk and proceed with caution, okay?" she said gravely.

I flipped her the bird as her laughter filled the basement once more.

Outside, the warm, humid air was fading with the oncoming night, a chill sliding in. A few fat raindrops fell like scouts. I ran for home ahead of the storm the way I had thousands of times before.

"Marshall!" Jerry Flanders barked.

I stopped short and turned back. Jerry was smoking another cigarette on the front steps, leaning against the wrought iron railing. He gave a wide grin and extended the cigarette in the direction of my car.

Oh, yeah. My car. I didn't need to run up the street anymore.

"Gotta get used to that!" I said, and we both laughed as I crossed the lawn and slid behind the wheel. A few more raindrops plunked off the glass, and I searched for the windshield wiper controls. I still had to look for everything; nothing was reflex yet.

When I looked back up, Gwen Flanders faced Jerry on the top step, dressed in a black skirt and red blouse, pretty and professional. Her hands were turned palms up, and she was looking down at her husband with the obvious, weary bearing of someone waiting on an answer that was sure to disappoint.

I was glad to have the excuse to look in the rearview mirror as I backed up and headed for home.

My mother was gone, a premade meal waiting in the fridge. I sat at the table and stared at my copy of the traffic ticket, remembering the way Corporal Maddox had barked that he saw a little prick. His thumbprint was still visible on the bottom of the ticket. Now that I was indoors and under bright lights, it seemed even clearer, and even more like what I'd thought it was originally: ash. I held it up and to the light and frowned. It looked as if it had been singed, as if someone had held a match just beneath the paper.

I lowered the ticket and eyed the trash can. Would I need to keep my copy, or could I just show up at the county clerk's office and pay it? I certainly didn't want my mother to stumble across it, so I went into the living room and picked a DVD of a movie I knew she wouldn't watch—*The Rock* with Nicolas Cage—and tucked the folded ticket inside the case. With any luck, I could burn it in a month.

I warmed my dinner up and ate alone at the kitchen table while I watched the evening news. My mother told me that I didn't have to watch her, and I joked that I liked to see how frequently she was wrong with the forecast because it made my own grades look better, but the truth was that I liked to hear her voice in the empty house.

Kerri passed in the rain, honking twice as her Civic blew by, headed for Jake's house. The Oldsmobile sat in the driveway in the rain while my mother told her TV audience that the near-record warmth in Indiana coincided with Pluto crossing Neptune's orbit, making it the ninth-farthest planet from the sun after twenty years in eighth place. Some scientists, she said, wanted Pluto to be demoted from planet status entirely.

"On February 11, between 11 a.m. and noon eastern time, the universe literally changed," she said with a broad smile.

I would reference this at breakfast, proof that I'd watched. She didn't get home until after midnight, but she was always up by six to make breakfast before I left for school. It was many years before I realized how little sleep she got in those days.

A lot of the most important things occur to you too late.

We saw each other before 6 a.m., though, and by then we had a lot more to talk about than Pluto and the changing universe.

3

THAT NIGHT I DREAMED of a weathered red barn with a high center beam
and steep rooflines, one of a thousand along lonely Indiana highways, but
there was a twist to this one—it had no doors.

The doorless barn stood alone in a field of dry summer grass browned
beneath a withering sun. No one worked in the field; no driveway led in or
out. It was the most isolated place I'd ever seen, and yet I walked toward it
the way you must in a nightmare.

As I advanced, the building grew larger and larger and the sky behind it grew darker and darker. I crunched across the grass and reached
the wall, then placed my palm on the worn wood. The relentless buzz of
crickets or cicadas haunted the air. The barn wall was warm, though the
sun was hidden by the storm clouds. A rasping sound came from the other
side, and the wood shivered against my palm. I jerked my hand away.

The rasping sound continued, moving away from me now. I put my
hand back to the barn wall and walked in sync with the sound. It moved
quicker and quicker, and I chased it, walking at first, then at a half jog,
then an all-out run. The wall was no longer warm to the touch but *hot*,
like a grill lid. The weathered boards tore at my fingertips, splinters lanc-
ing my palm, but for some reason it seemed crucial to keep my hand up,

to try to hold contact with whoever—or whatever—was on the other side of the doorless, windowless place.

Because they were trapped. I understood that much clearly.

Beyond the barn was a field of waist-high wheat whipped by warm winds, and the sky to the west roiled with dark clouds, a crimson sunset fading beneath the black cloud wall. A big storm was coming on fast, and I was alone in the field and there were no houses, roads, cars, or people in sight. I knew that someone was inside the barn and searching for escape, that the rasping sound was from fingernails scrabbling over the rough wood.

The wind blew harder and the clouds massed darker and I moved faster and faster, the search growing more desperate, my fingertips rubbed raw as they scoured the barn walls seeking a door that didn't exist. The heat intensified with each dizzying lap of the barn, and the wind brought only more heat, as if vented from some terrible furnace.

I woke when the heat and the sound of the frantic scraping from inside the barn reached a crescendo that seemed unbearable, a point of no return. I was soaked in sweat and gasping, and outside a chill rain rattled the windowpane, February returning with a cruel edge, as if angry that it had slept through its work for one day.

I was so disoriented that I will never know whether I woke before or after the smoke detector went off.

CHIRP.

Damn it. I knew the sound meant the battery had to be replaced, and I threw back the covers with a groan. I was wearing gym shorts and a T-shirt, barefoot. I stepped out of the bedroom and into the dark hall. My TV was muted but still on, the flickering images of some old movie throwing blue-and-white bursts on the walls, just enough light that I didn't reach for the wall switch. I could see well enough to make the stairs, and once I was on the stairs, the warm glow of the light I'd left on for my mother in the kitchen waited.

My bare feet slapped off the shadowed steps, pale against the dark wood. It is an image I've never been able to shake, one that can still make me shudder twenty years later. I made it down the stairs in the dark, guided by the kitchen light. I was vaguely aware of an additional, out-of-place sound, a soft whispering that was so low as to seem inconsequential against the piercing, demanding *CHIRP* from the smoke detector. When my feet touched the cool tile floor of the foyer at the base of the stairs, I looked left, into the living room, where the suspected smoke detector waited. The room was dark and silent.

CHIRP.

The sound was coming from the detector by the mudroom between the garage and the kitchen. I headed toward it, my bare feet moving from tile to carpet and back to tile, cold to warm to cold, hard to soft to hard, the familiar transitions that guide you through the darkness when you're walking in the only home you've ever known. No need to glance at the floor. One dim light was plenty.

I made it to the kitchen and into the light and stood beneath the offending smoke detector.

CHIRP.

I pulled open the junk drawer beneath the kitchen island and sifted through the AAAs, AAs, and even a few loose Cs. No 9-volts.

Perfect.

Did the detector shut up if there was no battery? They had to. Cut off the head and the body would die, I figured, and then I went into the garage and found the stepladder.

CHIRP.

When I carried the ladder back into the house, I finally turned on another light. With the rest of the kitchen and the dining room now illuminated, more light bled into the dark corners of the house. I climbed up the stepladder, unsnapped the battery compartment, and pulled the battery free, silencing the detector ahead of its next harsh beep.

I was there, at the top of the ladder, with an elevated view, when I heard a new noise intrude in the restored silence of the night. The subtlest of sounds, a whisper beneath a whisper.

But enough.

I looked left, a reflexive turn toward the sound, and with the height of the ladder and the additional light in the dining room, I was able to see the snake on the stairs.

It was five steps from the top and slithering down in an undulating S, wedge head raised like a hood ornament riding in front of a body that was sleek and thick and at least four feet long. The colorations were unlike anything I'd seen before, a blend of ivory and black diamonds. As the snake slipped from step to step, it reminded me of the slinky that I'd had as a kid, lengthening and shortening and lengthening again as it descended with soft *thump, thump, thumps.*

I stayed frozen on the ladder until the snake was almost to the ground floor. It was that moment of imminent arrival that finally shook me into action—that, and the first clear *BUZZ* from the rattles on its tail, which were the length of a dollar bill and as black as oil.

I shouted then, a short yelp of terror that was aborted because there wasn't enough breath in my lungs to really let loose, and the stepladder fell sideways as I jumped from it. When the ladder smacked against the wall and collapsed to the floor with a clatter, the rattlesnake's buzz intensified, and I had the terrible feeling that I'd put myself on its radar, hastening its path across the floor toward me. I don't know what direction it did take; once my back was turned, I bailed out fast, first into the garage, pounding the opener as I passed, then ducking under the still-rising door and sprinting out into the street, running over the rough concrete to rougher asphalt.

I stopped in the middle of the street, heart thundering, every nerve alive and electric, and stared back at the house as the garage door nestled into its elevated position and then went silent. I looked up and down the shadowed street. Every house was dark. I had no phone and no idea when my mother would be home. What was I supposed to do?

Open the door and let it out.

I couldn't make myself step back toward the house.

Sack up. Be a man and go open the door. You can wait for it to leave.

I looked down at my bare feet, then back at the house, and right then the light from the garage door clicked off, plunging even more of the property into darkness.

Hell no.

I crossed the street in a hurry and pounded on Kerri's front door. It stayed silent inside, so I knocked louder, then heard someone mutter with confusion.

"It's Marshall!" I shouted.

Footsteps on the stairs, the click and rasp of the opening lock, and then Jerry Flanders was staring at me, bleary-eyed.

"What's going on? What's the matter?"

"There's a snake in my house."

Jerry exhaled. "Okay. Relax. I'm sure it's not poisonous. Probably just a—"

"It's a rattlesnake. I'm positive."

"Fuck *that!*" Kerri said from behind us. Both Jerry and I turned to look at her. She was wearing pajama pants and a tank top, and her hair flew as she shook her head emphatically, as if to refuse the news.

"I doubt it's a rattlesnake," Jerry said, almost hopefully.

"It is," I said. "I saw it, and I heard it. It was coming right down the stairs and it has rattles and it is not small."

"Nope, no, thanks, now close that door," Kerri said.

Neither of us responded. Jerry looked from me up to my house and his Adam's apple bobbed as he swallowed.

"All right," he said. "I suppose I'm gonna need a shovel."

When I think about the definition of what it means to be a grown man, I can't come up with a better visual than Jerry Flanders on the night I ran to him with news of the rattlesnake. Jerry, wanting nothing more than to go back to bed but knowing he couldn't. He was no less afraid of snakes than I was and hardly enthused about the prospect of leaving his house in the night to find one, but I'd run to him for help, and he had nobody else to turn to. The difference between boy and man. Some night you're going to need to be the one who carries the shovel.

I didn't have to be yet.

Instead, I stood in the street with Kerri, holding a bright flashlight aimed at my porch as Jerry, wearing his tallest work boots, unlocked my front door and let it swing wide, the shovel held high, blade poised to strike.

The foyer was empty.

Jerry deflated, lowered the shovel, and wiped his brow.

"Damn it," he said, and we both exactly knew what he meant—it would've been far better if the snake had been waiting right behind the door so Jerry could deal with it without having to cross the threshold and venture deeper inside, unsure of where it waited.

"Marshall, bring me that light, would you?"

I brought him the flashlight.

"I'll go find it," he said.

"I can go with you." Words that I absolutely didn't want to utter but felt had to be said.

Jerry shook his head.

"You stay outside."

"But you'll need someone to hold the light."

"I can hold my own light. But I'll need someone to keep an eye on my daughter, okay?"

I nodded, ashamed of how enthusiastically I handed off the light and retreated. Jerry took a breath and then stepped inside. He left the door open behind him. We saw glimpses as he passed back and forth, searching the ground floor, and then he disappeared from sight.

My mother came home while Jerry was inside. Kerri and I stopped her in the street and we were all talking over each other in rapid, wild words when Jerry stepped back onto the porch. There was a long yellow ribbon dangling over the blade of the shovel.

"He got it!" I yelled.

Jerry shook his head unhappily.

"Can't find it," he said. "But this was in the pantry."

That was when I saw that it wasn't the snake but only a snakeskin— thin and brittle and very long. More than four feet.

My mother said, "The pantry." Her voice was calm and almost pleasant, the tone she used to announce a sunny spring day to her viewers. If you didn't know her, you wouldn't have understood how she went to that voice when she needed to calm herself.

"Yep. Down along the baseboard. I've checked everywhere, but I don't see the damn thing. I expect it's down in the crawl space by now."

"The pantry," she said again, still in that sunny-day voice.

Jerry looked up at her, squinting against her car's headlights.

"Yes."

"It has been too long since I've stayed in a hotel," my mother said. "Let's do something about that, shall we, Marshall? And in the morning, I'll call"—she paused and looked at the snakeskin—"the National Guard."

She called an exterminator, who went through the house three times the next day and reported nothing.

"Looks to have moved on," the exterminator reported.

"Let's be sure," my mother said, and then, probably because he recognized her from TV and her smile made him blush, he went through the house a fourth time, sealing any gap he could find with caulk. He left traps in the crawl space and the attic and told us to try not to ignore any unusual sounds.

"I don't think we'll be able to ignore unusual sounds for quite some time," my mother said.

"Had to be the heat that brought it out," the exterminator said. "Yesterday's temperature spike must've confused it."

When he was gone, my mother and I finally went back into the house—hesitantly. She replaced the batteries in all the smoke detectors, and while we talked plenty about the chaos the low-battery alarm had led to, neither of us voiced the obvious question.

What if it hadn't gone off?

CHAPTER TWO

A WHIPPER AND
A CORPORAL

March–April 1999

"Miscommunication leads to complication . . ."

LAURYN HILL
"LOST ONES"

1

AGAINST ALL ODDS, WE slept again. No snakes appeared. Winter returned. March arrived. We got a week off for spring break. I watched the first round of the NCAA tournament with Kerri and Jerry Flanders. Indiana put up 108 points on George Washington in the first round only to lose to St. John's two days later. Bob Knight's incoming recruits gave Jerry hope for bigger things.

"Turning a corner," he said. "Bobby is turning a corner, mark my words."

I don't think there was anyone in the state who would have guessed that Bob Knight had won his last NCAA tournament game at Indiana.

Gonzaga won the first, second, and third NCAA tournament games in its history. Nobody knew how to pronounce the school's name. In between games, the announcers commented on the opening of a new hotel and casino in Las Vegas that had kicked off with concerts featuring the Blues Brothers and Bob Dylan. It was supposed to be the most luxurious resort on the strip, with a construction budget of nearly a billion dollars. Jerry Flanders couldn't believe that.

"Gamblers get a billion-dollar playpen and workingmen get NAFTA," he said, opening a fresh beer and shaking his head. "It's a beautiful world. Wonder whose elevators run in that place. Otis's, that's whose. Guarantee ya."

Kerri and I looked at each other and didn't say anything.

The resort did look magical.

It was called Mandalay Bay.

March came and went and no letters arrived from the court, no notice of a summons or a missed hearing date. It didn't seem that Maddox had filed his ticket. After thirty days, I stopped worrying about it, believing that, despite his meltdown—or maybe because of it—he'd decided to give me a break on the ticket. I wasn't losing sleep over it. I'd failed an algebra test, I was crushing on a girl named Leslie Carter, and I was trying to break 80 consistently enough for the varsity golf team. There was too much going on to wonder about Maddox's motivations, let alone the girl in his back seat who was dressed for a summer job on a February day. We were on to April in a blink, and the month arrived with high anticipation.

Sean Weller was having a kegger.

Weller was a senior and star linebacker at Bloomington South and I was a mediocre junior golfer at Bloomington North—not exactly a shared social circle—but party invitations in Bloomington were more like a virus than a formality—you could acquire one with many degrees of separation from the source.

Weller's party was taking on more substantial status than most because his older brother worked for Better Beers, a local distributor whose drivers had a tendency to lose a keg or three along the route. These "spill sheet" casualties have probably been lost to modern technology. A shame.

As the week drifted to its close, the question "Are you going to Weller's party?" was ubiquitous. For most, the planning involved formation and corroboration of excuses for their activity that night. This was a problem I no longer faced—my mother would be gone until nearly one in the morning herself. There were no Arlo or Ring cameras, no phone tracking apps, few cell phones, period. Parental monitoring required either trust or suspension of disbelief.

Those were, as they say, the good old days.

Weller's party was of particular note to me because of the pending presence of Leslie Carter, an ethereal blond beauty who'd made the mistake of speaking to me on enough occasions to give me hope for a date. I'd spent weeks cultivating the potential of this relationship via long conversations on AOL Instant Messenger. AIM was the dominant social media of our generation, although the term hadn't yet been coined. That was still to come, the baby of my generation. We had a chance to change the world and we gave you Facebook and Twitter.

Sorry.

Can't say we didn't change it, though.

In those Stone Age days of 1999, AIM was the only game in town, and you logged in with a screen name, had a "Buddy List" that showed which friends were logged in, and maintained private chats. You had to be sitting in front of your desktop computer to use it, meaning that it couldn't infect every waking second of your life or record your missteps for eternal public consumption. It could command your attention but it could not follow you out of the house, making you pass through the world with your head down.

All this is to say that AIM remains the superior social media achievement in history. By 1999 it was becoming the dominant source of conversation that wasn't in person, largely because parents didn't use it or understand it. When your phone rang, they knew who was calling. Worse, they could potentially eavesdrop. AIM was private, our thing.

My favorite of AIM's incredibly limited feature list was the Away message. This was an auto response that would appear to anyone who messaged you when you were, ostensibly, away from the computer. However, this was a tragic waste of its full potential. The Away message, properly deployed, could signal your current emotional state, beg for attention, or host bullshit of all forms. The teen audience responded best to the amusing.

Example: the standard Away message would say "track practice, ugh" or some such. Boring. It was far more crowd-pleasing to deliver the unexpected or absurd, such as "At 7-Eleven shoplifting a stick of deodorant and a Slim Jim" or perhaps a simple "clipping toenails, back soon!"

You couldn't be a one-hit wonder, though; you had to deliver time after time. The audience was fickle, their attention fleeting. Thus a "clipping toenails, back soon" needed to be followed by a "can't find toenail clippers, looking for knife, back soon" and then "need a Band-Aid" and "oh, no, there is so much blood!" and "tell my mother that I loved her," et cetera. This was what the audience demanded: increasing stakes and Mencken-like wit. I was capable of one of the two, although I certainly believed that I delivered both.

It was at this stage in life that I began to write my first original stories, though I certainly didn't consider it that way at the time. What started as a pursuit of silly laughs became more thoughtful, and soon I was planning messages in advance, considering the progressions, aware that none of them would be worth a damn if I couldn't wrap it up properly. You needed to set a strong hook, build the emotional investment, and then nail the ending.

It was a few years before I realized this could also be called "plotting."

When my mother began working nights and I could tie up our computer for hours on end, my Away messages became ever more elaborate, and I began to draw a substantial following, with numerous strangers sending messages to get the latest installment. On the week of Sean Weller's party, I was deep into a narrative in which being two dollars short for a Noble Roman's pizza had led to a hostage situation involving a blind man and his service dog at Old National Bank on Kirkwood Avenue. I was concerned about how to bring the story to a close, but Leslie Carter was enjoying it so much that I felt required to sustain at least a few more installments.

I would love to tell you that during the weeks after my encounter with Corporal Maddox I was distracted from the trivial immaturity of all this by thoughts of the girl in his back seat, haunted by her face, the way her eyes had locked with mine, tears on her cheeks, as I stared into the sideview mirror. But I've promised to tell the truth, and in truth I don't remember thinking of her in those days. I did think of Maddox when I was driving, though, the same way I thought of the rattlesnake when I walked through the house at night. I kept my eyes on the mirror more than I should have, probably. I became aware of pull-offs, areas screened by trees where his police cruiser could lie in wait. Whenever I was alone behind the wheel, I thought of him.

But I did not call to report him, and I did not wonder about the outcome for the girl in his back seat. Not until the night of the party, at least.

My friend Dom Kamsing was driving, and I was happy with that plan, both because his car was cooler and because I wanted to have a couple beers and there was *no chance* I would get behind the wheel after drinking. Maybe there would have been before those colored lights found my mirror—I'd like to believe not—but bad choices are often the result of a failure to appreciate the potential consequences. Maddox had shown me something about consequences.

When the fuck *did you hear the words* "second chance"?

In truth, my taste for beer was a thespian achievement. Holding the red cup around the keg was a better way to blend in, that was all. Dom never drank, and he handled hassling about that in an easy, indifferent way that I never could manage. Part of that was probably a size factor— Dom had hit puberty in about fourth grade, it seemed, and had the stature of a grown man—but part of it came from a place I'd never understand, a reservoir of calm that ran deeper than most and possibly came from a Buddhist faith that I knew very little about. Dom was Thai—his full name was Duangphet—and his father was the first Asian-born firefighter in the Bloomington department's history. That background wasn't overly unique among kids in Bloomington, which is one of the great benefits of growing up in a college town. My high school had kids from around the globe; my graduating class alone spoke two dozen languages. There was bigotry in Bloomington—I won't deny that for a minute—but I think it ran at a lower volume in that town in those days than in most of the country around us. Or at least it seemed that way.

Things would change over the summer, but I'll get to that.

Friday dawned warm and humid, feeling closer to summer than spring, as if the universe were aware of the potential of our weekend. There was something special in the air—and my mother sensed it.

"What's your plan tonight?" she asked that morning as she scrambled eggs on the stove, as alert as if she'd gotten a full night's sleep, though she was probably running on four hours.

"Hanging with Dom."

"Hanging where?"

"Not sure yet."

"Let's be sure," she said. "If you can't figure that out before I leave, you don't need to be anywhere but here."

"Why?" I asked, parrying rather than lying about our plans. I hated lying to my mother; we were too close, it was just the two of us. I rarely wished for a sibling, but it would have been nice to have someone else in the house to screw up now and then.

She used the spatula to transfer eggs from the pan to a plate, looking so drawn and serious that I thought she'd heard about Sean Weller's party somehow and knew there would be booze. Then she clicked off the burner and turned to me, the plate in her hands, eggs steaming.

"There are going to be storms," she said.

"Tornadoes?" I asked. They were her great fear.

"Maybe. I don't know what's going to happen, obviously. It's just . . . eerie today."

I looked out the open window. The trees were beginning to bud but not in full leaf yet, and the branches tossed and swayed as if stretching out after a long winter.

"You think about the weather too much," I said. "Like it's personal. Everyone has to deal with the same thing."

"No they don't," she said. "Weather *is* personal, Marshall. You remember the tornado I covered two years ago, where one house was completely destroyed, nothing left but pipes and pink insulation, and the neighbor's place was untouched except for a few shingles blown off the roof? Tell those people that it wasn't personal."

Her mood made me wonder what else was going on, what problems existed in her life that I wasn't privy to.

"What's wrong?" I asked.

"Nothing. I'm just saying that we don't all deal with the same things. Snow on a road across town can be black ice under your tires."

She looked out at my car. The tires on it were new. Not much else was, but she'd replaced the brakes and tires before grudgingly entrusting me with the keys.

"Relax," I said. "We'll be fine. Come on."

She set the plate down in front of me with a tight smile. "I know. We can't police the wind, can we?"

It was an odd phrase, and the reference to police made me think of Maddox, those dark blue eyes that matched the tight uniform shirt that showcased his size and intimidation.

"I'm sorry," my mother said, running a hand through my hair. "I'm freaking you out."

"Trust me," I said, "Dom and I will be fine. You're talking about the son of the meteorologist and the son of a firefighter. I've got that whole disaster-lurks-around-every-corner thing down, Mom."

She gave a distant smile and nodded. "Of course you do."

I think there is a voice in the world that whispers only to mothers. We understand it is there when we are young, but the older we get, the less seriously we take it. I was floating somewhere in the middle that year, torn between childhood and adulthood, between eye rolls and full faith.

I watched her watching the tossing oak trees that lined the front lawn, and the too-warm-for-morning air filled the room, rippling my oversized T-shirt against my body, making a *pop, pop, pop* against my back.

My mother shut the window.

"I don't like being gone so many nights," she said.

"I'm fine. Trust me."

She searched my eyes. "Sure," she said. "You're fine. And alone. And a good mother would not—"

"Stop it," I said, and my voice was so authentic that she did. I won't pretend that she thought of me as an adult, but she listened to me more like one than most of my friends' parents did. We had grown up together. She'd been only twenty-three when I was born, fresh out of school, bright future ahead, and then she met a man with a nice smile and a small heart. He bailed as soon as he heard the news that she was pregnant. My mother refused to tell me his name.

"When you're eighteen, if you really have to know, we can talk about it," she would say. Always that qualifier, "if you really have to know," nearly begging me to put him aside the way he'd put her—put *us*—aside.

Her parents hadn't wanted her to have the baby. That much she'd told me when I was ten and I wondered aloud why we didn't visit them more the way my friends went to see their grandparents. Mine lived in Atlanta and I hadn't seen them in years. I didn't mind that. All I really knew about them was that they'd hurt my mother, so why should I want them around? Of course, this also held true for my father, and yet I felt that absence more acutely. At least I knew where my grandparents were.

Some people—Kerri and Dom included—thought that my mother should tell me more.

"It's too big of a thing to hold off on," Kerri would say. "It's your identity."

There were times when I agreed. The older I got, the less I spoke up about that, though. When I thought of the man, it filled me with a vast and impotent anger. I had nothing but hate for him by my sixteenth year.

And I had never wanted more desperately to find him.

Sometimes I thought it was to ask why he'd left. Other times it was to confront him. Punch him, smack him, drag him by the collar to a bank and demand that he mortgage whatever he had and give the money to my mother. I fantasized about laughing at him, spitting on him, ignoring him. How would I show contempt and disinterest at once? The emotions were genuine, but the motivation beneath them was not.

I wanted to *know*. That was all. The rest, from the displays of rage to the earnest questions, shifted from day to day. The desire to know his name never did.

I had stopped asking, though, because I could see how much it hurt my mother.

"Please," I told her as we sat there in the kitchen on Raintree Lane on that windy Friday, "don't say anything about what a good mother would do, like you aren't one."

She seemed both touched and pained. She leaned down and kissed the top of my head and said, "Prove that I am, then, and make good choices tonight."

"Of course," I said, and then I ate my breakfast and thanked her and left the house feeling about two inches tall. Make good choices: *Which way to the kegger!*

I knew better. I really did.

Then I was behind the wheel of my car, feeling mature once more, and thoughts of Leslie Carter filled my mind, and thoughts of my mother faded. By the time I got home from school, the breakfast conversation was forgotten and my mother was gone, the house stuffy, the windows sealed tight against that restless wind.

I cracked them and let the spring air fill the house as I showered and set to work crafting the Leslie-slaying machine that was needed to mow through Sean Weller's party: hair gel and cologne, check and check. Unbuttoned blue shirt over white T-shirt paired with baggy carpenter's jeans complete with a hammer holder, check and check. Beaded necklace, check. All the rest was what I had to bring along for the ride whether I wanted to or not: dark brown hair; bright blue eyes that I disliked only because they were so obviously my father's contribution; dimple on right cheek that some girls told me they found cute; zit on tip of nose that no girl would identify as cute. I added another spritz of Perry Ellis cologne as if it might balance out the zit, and then, properly fermenting, I went downstairs to wait on my ride.

Dom arrived at six and pulled the Beast to a chugging stop in my driveway. The Beast was a 1976 Ford Bronco, bloodred with a white top, that Dom and his father had restored from a wreck and built into one of the strangest vehicles in history. It had the height and tires of a monster truck, the headlights of an old DeLorean—they were supposed to rise when a switch was pulled, but that never worked—and an extra exhaust pipe that ran vertically up the side of the car and looked like something that belonged on a tugboat. It had no power steering but did have a custom JBL stereo. The driver's seat didn't match the passenger seat. The steering wheel was repurposed from a 1950s Cadillac and had one of those little knobs you were supposed to clutch to turn the massive thing, like a ship's wheel. The clutch was moodier than an emo band and the exhaust belched, choked, and smoked, but the four-wheel drive ran flawlessly. It was the strangest, ugliest, least efficient vehicle I had ever seen, and I will never love a car more than I loved the Beast.

Dom arrived wearing baggy jeans, untied Timberland boots, and a white T-shirt. It was his uniform that year. The color of the T-shirt changed, but the jeans and untied Timbs almost never did unless we were playing basketball.

"It is going to be a big night," he predicted, the Beast shuddering beneath him.

"No doubt." I climbed into the passenger seat without opening the door. This was not an attempt at macho behavior; the passenger door had never opened. The roof was off on the Bronco, and Dom saw me eye the overcast sky.

"It'll be fine," he said.

He pulled away from the curb just as Jake Crane's Volvo purred past en route to Kerri's house. Jake waved. He was a big waver, that guy. I half lifted a hand in response. The Beast jolted forward, hesitated, shimmied as if shaking itself awake, and then banged into second gear. Dom cranked the volume on the stereo, and Big Pun's "Still Not a Player" blasted loudly enough to be heard over the muffler.

"Onward," he said.

We tapped fists and rolled away from Raintree Lane beneath the roiling clouds, and only when we reached the highway did I realize that I'd forgotten to close the windows at the house before leaving.

Oh, well. You can't police the wind, right?

2

THE MUCH-ANTICIPATED WELLER PARTY was located in a remote field in the northern part of the county, not far from the state forest, down a winding road called Lost Man's Lane. The road dead-ended in front of an old farm gate, but tonight the gate was open, and rows of cars were parked in front of three kegs of beer resting in tubs of melting ice, surrounded by kids holding red Solo cups. There was no visual attraction to the field other than those three kegs and a bonfire that kept smoldering out on damp wood. Someone had parked a pickup truck up near the kegs and speakers mounted in the bed rattled with the driving drums of Korn's "Got the Life."

"This is sweet," Dom said as we approached.

"Hell yes," I agreed, trying not to cough when the wind shifted and blew that punky smoke in my face.

We'd attempted a fashionably late arrival, twenty minutes after the designated start time, and there were already at least fifty kids in the field and more coming in behind us. There was no fear of parental intrusion. Weller's father was a developer, and we were standing in a massive tract of farmland he'd acquired to build a subdivision. I scanned the crowd, searching for familiar faces. Everyone had drifted into little clusters.

"Your girl's here," Dom said.

"Where?" I said, pretending indifference, but I'd already seen Leslie

Carter standing beneath a white-barked sycamore that swayed in the night wind. She was tall and blond and tan and, bless her, wearing a pale blue tank top that just *barely* reached the waistband of her shorts. I caught her eye and lifted a hand and she gave me a little fingertip wave and smile but didn't move away from the group. I would have to come to her.

"Don't choke," Dom said helpfully.

"I'm not going to choke. She likes me. You've read her messages."

We pored over AIM exchanges with girls as if we were working with Alan Turing on cracking the Enigma code.

"Those are messages, though. You have time to think. That's your secret weapon: the time. Or maybe the thinking." He pondered that. "I'll give you credit and say it's partly the thinking. Regardless, she's over there right now in human form, and you're standing here, picking your nose."

"I'm not . . ." I lowered my hand, which had drifted up to check the status of that threatening zit. "Let's get a beer. I don't want to, like, rush to her."

"Let's get you a beer," he said agreeably.

We approached the kegs, Dom walking with ease as I put my hands in my pockets and tried to match his natural calm. I was taller than him, but Dom carried himself with the confidence of an inherent leader. He exchanged handshakes and fist bumps with the guys, hugs with a few girls, while I went straight to the keg. There was a stack of Solo cups in the grass and an empty two-liter bottle filled with bills, mostly ones. I jammed a few bucks into the bottle, grabbed a Solo cup, stepped up to the keg, and began to pump the tap. I hadn't checked it before pouring the beer, and it would sadly be several years before I realized that you didn't actually *need* to pump the damn thing before each pour, and if you insisted on doing that, you were dooming everyone to four inches of foam for every ounce of decent beer.

I pumped it a half dozen times, which seemed like the right amount for the half beer that I intended to sip while pretending it was my fifth or sixth, and then brought the nozzle to the lip of my cup.

"The fuck are you doing?" a deep voice said.

I looked up to see Sean Weller staring down at me. He was an all-conference linebacker and didn't need the pads and helmet to look the part. He was well over six feet tall and built about like the Beast, although he moved better. His crew cut gleamed almost white in the firelight and he wore a beaded necklace much like my own, except his hung over the thick chest of a weight lifter.

"Hey, Sean."

He squinted. "I know you?"

"Yeah, man, we've met. I'm Marshall."

"I invited a Marshall? I don't think so." He took the nozzle of the beer tap out of my hand.

It had fallen quiet, all the people around us now listening. This was the nightmare scenario—being thrown out of a party. Even worse, Leslie's group was in earshot.

"Who'd you come with, bro?" Sean Weller said.

"Uh, Dom and I were told . . . you know, that we should be here."

I looked wildly around for Dom, who finally arrived, oblivious to the situation. Weller didn't look any more delighted to see him, but he at least *knew* him.

"What up, Kamsing? This guy is saying he knows me. I don't know him."

Dom shot me an *oh, shit* glance but played it with a relaxed smile.

"Man, you know Marshall."

"People keep saying that, and yet I *don't* know him," Weller said.

"Marshall Miller," I offered pointlessly. He was literally taking the beer tap out of my hand in front of an entire party of onlookers, and I was attempting to dissuade him with my full name?

But he stopped. Cocked his head.

"MarshMan25."

It was my AIM screen name.

"Uh . . . yeah. That's me."

A smile crept over his face.

"Dude," he said, "I like your Away messages."

There was a pregnant pause and then the high, shrill pierce of Dom's laugh, which always sounded like a crow's scream.

"Thanks," I said to Weller.

"It's hilarious shit," he said, looking around as if to convince others.

"He's writing this whole thing about a bank robbery. Only he's the bad guy and he doesn't realize it yet. It is funny as hell. Seriously."

Sean Weller, the keg-party-throwing linebacker, had just solved my story. I had never even considered that I was the bad guy, but it was all right there. The chaos I'd created in my fictional encounters with everyone from the pizza deliveryman to the bank teller to the blind man and service dog . . . yes, I was the bad guy. Son of a bitch, he'd cracked the code.

"Here," he said, and pressed the beer tap back into my hand.

"Thanks. Hey, which screen name is yours?"

"TheWeller. I keep it simple."

I remembered seeing it now.

"You only send random letters or numbers."

"I'm not there for conversation, just the story. Get on with it. And finish your beer. It's Busch Light." He said this as if announcing the keg were filled with a thirty-year-old single-malt scotch.

"Awesome," I said.

"Keep writing those things," he said. "They don't suck." He slapped me on the shoulder and then moved on.

He was the first critic to give me a pass, and no *New York Times* review ever mattered more.

I depressed the nozzle on the beer tap and it splattered an inch of foam into the bottom of the cup. The speakers made the truck's tailgate rattle as Ice Cube joined Korn, spitting angry rap verses over their hazy guitar riffs and whisper-screamed rage.

"So you're the bad guy in the end?" an amused voice said, and Leslie Carter stepped up beside me. She had a half smile on her lips and a full one in her eyes and life was as promising in that moment as it ever had been.

"We'll see if he's right," I said. "Could be I'm innocent."

"Boring," she said, laughing as the wind swirled eye-watering smoke around us.

"Villains are more interesting to you?"

"They are to everyone."

"Fair point." I took a sip of beer foam. "Speaking of villains, the police are holding paper on me right now."

"Holding paper." She snorted.

"It's a villainous term for a warrant, you know."

"Oh?"

"Yeah. He's seen it." I nodded at Dom. "Tell her about the warrant, man."

"Oh, I've definitely seen it." He widened his eyes and looked side to side, then lowered his voice and nudged me. "No narcs here; you're good. Go on, tell her how it went down."

"Somehow I don't think you can make it up as well on the fly," Leslie Carter said to me, a teasing challenge that eerily echoed Dom's jab from earlier in the night.

"Don't need to make it up," I said. "I legitimately was stopped by police within the first five minutes of my first day with a driver's license. The 'warrant' might just be a ticket—fine—but it felt about the same when it was handed to me."

She covered her mouth with her hand. "You're serious? In the first five minutes?"

"Sadly, he is," Dom said.

She threw her head back and laughed, and then two of her friends joined her, and suddenly I was recounting my encounter with Maddox, step by step, only this time I was playing it for laughs. The details were right but the context was different. It was closer to the way I'd told the story to Dom the day after it had happened. Each time I told it, I moved further from the version I'd given to Kerri right after it happened, when I admitted that I'd been scared.

Further from the truth.

But it killed for laughs. The scares had all been internal, my own trapped fears, harder to convey without feeling vulnerable, the emotion I loathed above all others in the spring of 1999. And who needed the truth when the audience was happy? It was fun and the energy was good and the night felt alive with hope. The air was warm, the fire had finally caught, and summer felt within reach.

Leslie extended her empty red Solo cup. "Fill me up?"

"No problem. Let me pump it first, though. It's still foamy."

She stood close to me while I poured the beer, and when I handed the foam-covered cup back to her, our fingers touched, the lightest of grazes with the most electric of possibilities.

"You're very good," she said. "I could almost believe that story."

"Well, that one actually happened."

"Yeah, right." Her blue eyes were bright and dancing in the firelight. "You might fool ninety-nine out of a hundred girls with that one, but their dads aren't cops."

"Your dad is a cop?" The electric promise of that grazing touch sparked with a glimmer of threat.

"You scared of me now?"

"Nah. I'm the villain, remember?"

She smiled and then said, "Do you know what you screwed up?"

"What do you mean?"

"In your story about being pulled over. There's only one detail wrong."

"I seriously did get pulled over."

"Not by Bloomington police, you didn't."

"Back that up with a bet," I said. "If I can show you the ticket, you have to take me to dinner and a movie. And not some action movie with a lot of explosions either. I want something with heart and passion."

We shook hands, and the physical contact held all my attention until she said, "You keep calling him Corporal Maddox. That's your mistake."

"He *was* Corporal Maddox."

"Wrong," Leslie said, and made a *buzz* sound. "You lose. There are no corporals in Bloomington. Only the state police have that rank."

She was still smiling. I wasn't, because she was confident, but so was I, and there seemed to be a serious problem in that chasm.

"You're sure," I said. It wasn't really a question.

She nodded. "He was state police, that's all."

"No. The ticket says BPD. I'm positive. Unless a state trooper would use a BPD ticket?"

Now it was her turn to frown. "I don't think they do that. Do you remember the badge?"

I shook my head. "Just that he had one. The badge and the car, how they were marked . . . I don't remember. The lights were all I really needed to see, you know? And the siren. That was official enough for me. But he called himself 'Corporal.' I think it's on the ticket."

"Weird," she said. "You said he was screwing with you, though? Like the stuff about Tupac, and then the yelling and everything . . . Maybe he was cutting you a break but decided to really put a scare into you."

"Maybe," I said. "He seemed like that kind of guy."

It was quiet for a moment, then she nudged my shoulder playfully.

"Good news is, he's definitely not filing a fake ticket, so you have extra money to pay off that bet."

I tried to recover the smile. It wasn't all that hard; Maddox's stop had happened weeks ago. Sixteen-year-old life moves in dog years. He was gone and Leslie was here.

I got back to the party.

One keg was killed and then a second was laboriously tapped, with Sean Weller barking out instructions like a surgeon supervising a heart transplant. He threw an arm around my shoulders and tapped his cup off mine, then let out a loud belch, fragrant enough to penetrate both my cologne and the mossy smoke of the bonfire, which was no small feat.

"Next party is for graduation, Marshmallow Man."

This was not a nickname I sought, but his quarterback-crushing hand was close to my throat, so I nodded.

"Awesome."

"Hard to believe, dude. *Graduation.* Shit. You'll be here?" Checking as if I were a valued guest and not the kid he'd almost used as a tap handle.

"For sure."

"Better be. We're getting Keystone Ice for that one. Don't fuckin' sleep on the 'Stone, man."

"Never."

He slapped me on the back hard enough to make me spill some beer and then moved on. Graduation, he'd said. It seemed like a distant dream. Like about everyone else in my class, I had only one clear plan for college: leaving Bloomington. Every fall, thousands of kids from around the globe arrived wanting to be in our town; naturally it worked the other way on the townies. We were always promising we'd leave, even if we wouldn't.

Leslie Carter approached with her friends, a disappointed expression on her face. "I've gotta go. Curfew."

"Come on, it's early."

"Curfew from a cop dad," she said.

"Ah, yes. That would be different." It wasn't even eleven yet; my mother still had a broadcast to get through before she could begin her drive home.

"We parked up by the road," Leslie said. "Walk with us?"

"We can drive you," Dom said, appearing from behind me. Dom never missed an opportunity to drive people in the Beast. I'd never appreciated the bastardized vehicle more than I did that night, when Leslie's friends, Sarah and Beth, insisted on climbing into the back together and Leslie rode on my lap in the passenger seat, relaxed against my chest, laughing as Dom intentionally found any and every available ditch, rut, pothole, or root. The warm wind was still blowing and I could smell her hair. She shifted on my lap, her slim back arching as she prepared for Dom to blast through a deep ditch, and I issued urgent commands to my body: *Think about baseball, or grandmothers, or grandmothers playing baseball, but do not stand at attention, my friend . . .*

It was maybe two minutes from the bonfire to the road, but it was a glorious ride.

We dropped the girls off at Sarah's car and said our goodbyes, and Leslie scribbled her number on a scrap of paper for me with the words PAY UP, BUDDY!

"I'm a serious debt collector," she said. "Check the ticket when you get home. It's going to say state police."

"Then I'm paying." But the ticket was not going to say state police.

"Better be." She winked and waved.

"That seemed to go better than your traditional attempts," Dom said as we sat in the shuddering Beast and watched the taillights of Sarah's Toyota disappear down the road.

"Wasn't the worst of them. Considering the start of the night . . ."

"Dude, Weller was two seconds away from kicking you out!"

"I know."

"He likes your Away messages." Dom let out that crow-scream laugh again. "Unbelievable. A win for the Marshmallow Man."

Shit. He had caught that one.

He drove me home, and when he pulled up in front of my house, I suddenly wished I'd left a light on. It was past midnight and the street was dark. At least it hadn't started to rain yet. I still had time to close the windows. My mother's forecast had been wrong. No storms tonight. But it was too warm, and that reminded me of February and the night of the snake.

"Wanna come in and hang?" I asked.

"I'm already late."

"All right." I climbed out of the Beast and waved as he executed a tight turn, exhaust smoking, and clattered back up the road. I unlocked the front door and went into the living room, turning on each light that I passed, and found the DVD case where I'd hidden the ticket.

It was still there, complete with the undeniable Bloomington Police Department logo and the *Maddox* signature, no first name, no rank. He'd written my violations and he'd signed his name and he'd smeared the ticket with that odd ash-colored stain.

And yet I was positive he'd said "Corporal."

That was the first night in a long time that I really paused to think about the girl I'd seen in the mirror and how the tears had run down her cheeks when he closed the door.

I didn't have any proof, though. Leslie Carter was right, and I was wrong, and that would work out fine for me.

I closed the DVD case and was returning it to the shelf when red-and-blue lights lit up the front window. I froze like a guilty man replacing a murder weapon in a knife block, caught in the act. For a moment, my terror was simple selfishness: this had to be about me.

Then I remembered Dom, and that odd, clattering contraption he called a car, and I slammed the DVD onto the shelf and ran out of the house and into the unsettled spring night, looking up Raintree Lane to where I knew Dom had to be waiting, his Bronco pulled over on the side of the road just as my Olds had been on that awful February day.

A police car idled at the curb three houses away, but the Bronco was nowhere in sight. No other vehicle was in sight, in fact; other than Jerry's work truck, Raintree Lane was a garage-users street. The police car sat in disturbing silence. The siren hadn't been engaged and no one moved. The engine surely hummed but I couldn't hear from where I stood. From my vantage point, the car was known only because of the lights. The yards and porches illuminated by the colored strobes were still and soundless. There were no police officers visible on foot, no sign of a human presence at all. The car was facing my house, but it had hung back, remaining close to the intersection, as if unwilling to commit to the path down our cul-de-sac, and in the darkness I had the strange sense that it had chosen that spot because of the escape opportunities, as if the car itself, and not the driver, were something feral.

Crazy. There was a human behind the wheel, I knew that. So what were they doing?

Maddox? It can't be.

But I knew that it was.

I backpedaled slowly, refusing to turn my back to the police car, slipped into my house, closed the door, and locked it. Then I stood at the window, holding the blinds apart with two spread fingers, watching with breath held, waiting for something to happen.

A porch light went on up the street, where the Redfearns lived. Mrs. Redfearn was coming out to investigate the trouble. I felt myself exhale for the first time, and right then, the police car's overhead lights went out, as if I'd snuffed them with that long release of breath. The car reversed, turned, and drove away. I could see a license plate but had no hope of making out the identifiers on it, not from here, hiding behind the closed door of my safe home.

Maybe I should have stayed on the porch, alone. I had a better view out there. Maybe I should have walked toward the car, showing the casual courage that Mrs. Redfearn had. I felt childish and afraid and shook my head as if to deny an accusation.

What answers would have come from walking up the street alone in the darkness? None. The license plate was unimportant. The car was a random neighborhood patrol, that was all, and I hadn't retreated because I was afraid, but because I was smart.

I let the blinds fall shut, checked the dead bolt again, and went to bed.

3

IN A MOMENT WHEN I should have been genuinely concerned about the disconnect between my memory and the police reality, I was instead blissfully distracted by daily life, riding with as much confidence as I'd ever had, the kind a date with Leslie Carter could instill. It was perhaps because of this confidence—or because of the pending date—that Kerri appeared on Saturday afternoon and announced she was taking me to Hoosier High Ground, the new indoor climbing gym where Jake was an employee.

I tried to beg off, feeling no desire to watch Jake spring around like a ninja while we clapped from below, but Kerri wasn't having it.

"I desperately need to get out of the house," she said, "and you're coming with me."

And so I found myself in her Honda, bound for Indiana's replicated Rocky Mountains.

"It's mostly amateurs who go," Kerri assured me. "Rock climbing is just catching on here. You're not going to be any worse than anyone else."

Since Jake was working, it would be just Kerri and me goofing off, making each other laugh, no different than the monkey bars at Hollinger Elementary School all those years ago. I secretly didn't mind the idea of Jake watching us from the desk down below, held at bay from our private laughter.

This image lasted for about thirty seconds. The facility was in a massive old warehouse that had once been part of the RCA manufacturing empire. My only experience on a climbing wall had been at a YMCA camp when I was ten, and that had been maybe fifteen feet high. The walls at Hoosier High Ground were at least seventy, and in the filtered light from the old factory windows, they looked as imposing as Half Dome. There were hand- and footholds strategically placed along walls that varied in pitch, ropes hung from bolts and pulleys, and the floors were lined with thick wrestling mats. The room smelled of sweat and effort and strength and, I was afraid, even of skill. Yes, I thought I could smell the skill in the same way prey smells a predator's advantage.

"It looks busy," I said. "Maybe we should come back another time."

Kerri looked from me to the gym, where a grand total of three people were currently scaling the walls, two more standing below.

"Busy?"

"I don't want to get in Jake's way. I'm sure he's got paperwork and stuff."

On cue, Jake bounded up. He was wearing a sleeveless shirt that showed his chiseled arms, and shorts that were straight out of the Daisy Dukes era of 1980s basketball. In the age of baggy everything, those shorts should have made him a target of derision. Since his quads looked like two-liter soda bottles and his calves were like softballs, not much derision was thrown his way.

He swept Kerri up with one arm, lifting her off the floor, and kissed her. I looked away, then had to turn back when he slapped me on the arm.

"Good to see you, dude!"

"Yeah," I said. "Right on."

He beamed. "This is *so much* fun, Marshall. You're gonna dig it, I promise."

"Oh, for sure. I mean, I can tell that already, but I also really don't want to be in your way, so we can come back another time when you're not working."

"Teaching guys like you is my job! That's the best part. Working with rookies, bro."

Guys like me. Rookies. Terrific.

"Cool," I managed. "Thanks."

"There are locker rooms over there, so change up and then we'll hit some rock."

I stared at him. "Change?"

He frowned. "Uh, you're not . . . climbing in the jeans, right?"

I looked down at my jeans, which billowed around my skinny calves in the badass style with which they'd been designed. Tommy Hilfiger didn't make mistakes.

"I was planning on it. But if I need basketball shorts, then I'll totally come back—"

"It'll be fine," Kerri cut in. "We're just doing the training wall anyhow."

Jake, still displeased with my wardrobe, nodded grudgingly.

"Yeah, it'll be fine for the Kitten's Cradle, I guess."

"Kitten's Cradle?" I echoed.

"It's our nickname for the training wall." He pointed behind me, and I pivoted to see a wall that was exactly what I remembered from day camp.

"I think we can skip that one."

"Well, the protocol is we start with—"

"I've done stuff like that since I was a little kid, Jake."

He cocked his head. "I didn't know you were a climber."

"He's not a climber," Kerri said. "I don't know what—"

"I went to a camp where we did stuff a lot more intense than that," I snapped.

"Wasn't that at the Y?" she said. "When we were, like, nine?"

"They had some serious walls."

"Serious walls? We played dodgeball and Marco Polo."

"I've been to a lot of camps, Kerri. You weren't at all of them."

Jake nodded, thoughtful. "You've bouldered, then."

I had no idea what boulder meant as a verb, but it seemed obvious enough—a boulder was large and round and not tall or steep. Kid stuff. I wasn't taking Jake's bait.

"Sure, but I'd rather try one of those walls." I gestured at a midsize apparatus beside us that looked like a sheer slope but was not particularly tall.

"That is the bouldering wall," Jake said.

Interesting. I was about to suggest that perhaps a bouldering refresher was exactly what I needed, but then I caught a glimpse of a smile on Kerri's face. I flushed and pointed at one of the floor-to-ceiling monstrosities.

"I meant those."

"Top roping," Jake said. "Right on. You're a lead-climber kind of guy?"

I hadn't the faintest idea what lead climbing meant, but I was committed now, and so I could only nod as Jake led us to the base of the towering wall and slipped into a harness, then tied a rope onto the front of it.

"Security belay. You've used them?"

"Belay is be *lame*," I said, and Kerri leaned forward and stared at me as if I'd lost my mind.

Jake frowned. "It's required, Marshall. Nobody should free climb this sort of pitch."

"I was only kidding."

"I know, but we don't joke about it. Amateurs without your camp experience can get legit hurt on these walls if they're not roped in."

He handed Kerri a free end of rope. She had already slipped on a harness and buckled it, and the familiarity she had with the gear made me acutely conscious of how much time she'd spent here with Jake.

He pointed at the wall I'd selected for my debut.

"Great choice. We call it the Terminator Tower. This wall is righteous, Marshall. Most people work their way up to it, but since you've got climbing camp experience, let's not waste your time. I've still got to do a little demo first or I'll get in trouble. You understand."

"Sure." I looked longingly back at the training wall, good old Kitten's Cradle.

"Best things about the Terminator Tower are the approach options," Jake informed me. "You can route plan and free climb in real-world scenarios. Score-wise, anything between a 2 and an 8 is possible." He glanced over his shoulder at me. "That's the French system, of course."

"Of course."

"You'll see some tape markers that score it Yosemite-style, though. Americans, right?"

"We should just go metric." I pretended not to see the look Kerri shot me.

"Have fun with it, be creative," Jake said. "On the Terminator Tower you can use the dynamic, explosive moves—you know, it's all fast-twitch muscle."

"Sweet." My voice cracked.

Jake dipped his hands into a pouch tied around his waist and they came out covered in chalk.

"Don't want to grease off the wall. I'll do a quick scramble myself, just to check the 'instructor' box, and then get out of your way. Got me on belay, babe?"

"Got you," Kerri said.

With that, Jake crouched and sprang and suddenly he was on the wall, legs and arms spread wide, muscles taut. The only thing missing was the Spider-Man suit.

"There are some jugs early, but then the features get tighter. Color-coded routes are established, but you can feel free to rainbow it, Marshall," he called down as he exploded up the wall, caught himself by one hand on a thin ledge, and then swung his feet expertly into place on the narrow plastic-rock features beneath him. He hung easily, right arm dangling free, and looked down to see if I was following.

"Sounds good," I said.

"Once you reach the various problems, you can work on edging, stemming, or smearing," Jake called, continuing his lemur-like scamper up the face of the wall. I tilted my head to keep him in view and felt a cramp in my neck. "There's obviously a crag and a chimney; you can see that."

"Sure!" I yelled it because he was so high now that he seemed out of earshot.

"Marshall . . . ," Kerri began, and I lifted a hand to silence her. She sighed and gave up.

"Reaching the top, you can mantle if you choose," he continued. "It's a tricky one, though, so if you try it and miss, you can take a good whipper. Remember to yell that out, bro. Whippers are fun, but screamers are righteous."

"Excellent!" I shouted, clueless.

"They hung a bell up here so the rookies can smack it if they make the top." He was already at the top, which seemed utterly impossible, and he smacked the bell casually with his right hand. It rang and echoed through the old warehouse. Everyone in the gym looked over and then broke into applause. "But it's not about the bell, bro, it's about the problem, you know that."

"Hell yeah."

I heard Kerri sigh again.

Jake lounged at the top of the wall, holding on to some invisible grip point. It seemed as if he had suction cups for fingers. His smile was wide and delighted.

"It's not the real deal, but it's not bad." He paused, then yelled, "Take!"

Kerri stepped back and pulled the rope tight, bracing herself to absorb his weight. Jake pushed off the wall and slid gracefully down as Kerri paid out the rope, which ran through the belaying device on her harness and was clipped to a sandbag behind her to provide extra weight. I made a mental note to remember this crucial step so that I seemed experienced when I reached the top of the wall. Jake had thrown out a blizzard of terms, but "take" seemed to be a cue that you were prepared to retreat. Or was it rappel? I didn't need to know all the terms. Just enough to prove my proficiency from the climbing camp I'd never been to. What was the other one he'd said to yell?

"Whipper"—that was it. *Remember to yell that out,* he'd said.

Why?

Before I could sort it all out, he landed beside me with a soft thump.

"You're gonna dig it," he said.

"Absolutely."

He unclipped his harness and slipped it off and handed it to me. I stuck my feet through and pulled it up and over my baggy jeans. Jake watched, frowning.

"That one might be a little big for you, bro. Kerri, why don't you give him yours?"

Talk about emasculation! All this time, I'd thought that Jake was a good guy, albeit it a little overly friendly, but I'd never seen him as someone to take passive-aggressive shots.

"This is fine, Jake," I snapped. "Trust me."

He shrugged, face still furrowed with concern. The harness was loose around my waist, but there was enough bulging denim to hold it in place so I could keep my dignity and not have to trade harnesses with Kerri.

Jake handed me the rope.

"Tie in."

I had not the faintest idea what to do with it. There were webbed loops on the front of the harness and carabiners on the side. I glanced surreptitiously at Jake's harness to determine that the rope went through the loops and not the carabiners, then tried to guess in a glimpse exactly how he had tied the knot that secured him. I made a couple loops, fed the free end back through the middle, and pulled the rope tight. It flattened out, not a single knot achieved.

"Just go with a figure eight," Jake suggested. "No need for the complex hitches."

"Got ya."

It was when I was making bunny ears, like a child with shoelaces, that Jake cleared his throat and said, "Ya know, they require us to tie clients in. It's stupid, but I should do it or I'll get in trouble."

Five seconds later I was secured to the belay rope with a complex knot he'd seemingly tied with one hand.

"Chalk up," he said, offering his bag.

"No grease, no peace," I said, dipping my hands into the bag and then clapping them together. Chalk blew into the air, and I sneezed violently. Jake and Kerri leaned back, blinking dust out of their eyes.

"Just have fun," he said. "Get back into the groove. Even when you've climbed before, it takes a while to warm up. Don't worry about speed. Don't worry about the bell."

Immediately, I looked for the bell, which was so high up, it made me dizzy. I put one hand on the wall to steady myself, and Jake interpreted that as a signal.

"Climber on!" he shouted.

Shit.

I reached for the first foothold, missed it, and then tried again. Success.

I was climbing—except for the foot that was still on the floor. I found a thin ledge above me and discovered that it was pocketed on the inside, providing a solid grip. I pulled myself up and found a brace for my right foot. Then I reached with my left hand, fumbling for another hold. This time the grip wasn't as solid, but it worked. I moved higher. Left hand, left foot. Right hand, right foot. My legs were beginning to quaver from strain, and my fingers ached. Left, right, left, right. Higher now. Looking down proved to be a mistake, as I immediately felt a wash of dizziness. Lesson learned: keep eyes on the wall.

"Doing great, bro!" Jake called. "That's a complex rainbow, man, you're going bold, no surrender!"

His enthusiasm—and my aching hands and trembling legs— convinced me to go faster. If I looked down, I was dizzy; if I looked up, I was dizzy. Best to go as quickly as possible, then. I was secured by the rope above and protected by the mats below. I needed only to scramble to the top, smack that bell, and yell out that I was no rookie, I was a lead climber or a topper or whatever he had—

My left foot slipped off the hold and my face pounded the wall.

"Marshall?" Kerri called, sounding uneasy.

"Fine!" I shouted back, my cheek pressed to the rough synthetic rock. "I'm just . . ." I sought for a Jake Crane–approved term. "Chimneying!"

I heard Jake mutter something indistinct that suggested I was doing no such thing. Oh, well. Technique didn't matter at this point. What mattered was ringing that damn bell. It had to be close. I chanced a glance up.

The bell gleamed at me as if to taunt, still far out of reach.

I was fifty feet in the air, and the shaking that had begun in my legs was now working its way through my torso. My fingers and wrists ached. There was no clear option for resting, but I *had* to rest. Maybe if I found better foot support, I could remove one hand at a time, the way Jake had. Perhaps he hadn't been showing off but merely giving his hands a break.

I eased away from the wall far enough to see above me. There was an assortment of minuscule grips and one good-sized lip of false rock. I didn't trust the tiny grips to provide the proper opportunity for rest, so I leaped for the larger lip. It had seemed well within reach until I was in the air, at which point it seemed to retract teasingly, like a girl pulling her hand away at a dance. I got my outstretched fingers clutched onto it—barely— and swung above the mats, both feet dangling free.

"Oh, hell, yeah! Love the aggression!" Jake called, clapping his hands.

I was going to fall if I didn't get my foot on something in a hurry. I scrambled in all directions, searching frantically for a foothold, and almost lost my handholds in the process. Finally, I got my left foot on a solid brace, but this one was almost level with my head, giving me the sensation of being fully reclined yet precarious, like a cat stretched out on its back on the arm of a La-Z-Boy.

I reached up with my left hand, couldn't find anything to grasp, and felt myself beginning to slip. I scrabbled again with my feet in search of a more secure hold and located one with my right foot, but this one was actually *above* my head. I was now upside down, performing what appeared to be a handstand, and staring directly into Kerri's apprehensive face. Even Jake looked somber, and his encouraging clap was soft and slow.

"You got it, you got it," he said.

That was when I felt my jeans slide over my hips.

Oh, no. Oh, no, no, no!

The too-large harness was tugging my jeans right off my ass. I tried to adjust, then slipped, making the harness devour more denim. This was no good. It was time to abort. What was I supposed to yell?

"Whipper!" I shouted.

Jake frowned and cocked his head, as if he didn't understand. My jeans were still slipping—and now taking my belaying harness with them.

"WHIPPER!" I screamed. "*WHIPPER!*"

The whole gym went silent. Everyone was staring. Meanwhile, the harness had managed to catch a stretch of boxer shorts beneath the denim. My chalked palms were sweaty and my forehead dripping beads of perspiration, but the top of my ass was now alarmingly cool, greeted by fresh air.

"RETREAT!" I shouted. "RAPPEL!"

Jake turned to Kerri. "Take!" he said.

That was it.

She was already braced, fortunately, because in the next second I lost my right-hand grip. I fell, letting out a cry that was cut short by the piercing pain of the harness jolting against my testicles, and then I swung free, the rope guiding me in a long pendulum arc out over the mats, affording me a bird's-eye view of Kerri fighting the rope like she'd just harpooned a whale. Then the pendulum reversed and I whizzed past them and smashed back into the wall.

I was dimly aware of Jake asking Kerri for the rope, and then he was paying out slack and I was descending smoothly, albeit upside down. At this point I'd have accepted the shame of being dropped on my head, but the upside-down position offered more pressing threats: my harness and jeans were now well below my ass, and the possibility of sliding right out of my pants and underwear and being deposited butt naked onto the mats below was very real.

I lurched and twisted, searching for the rope. Missed. The harness slid another two inches. I could feel cool air across the crack of my ass, a sensation so inspiring that on my next wild reach I was able to grab the rope. I hauled myself upright just as Jake dropped me to the mat, at which point I stumbled, knees pinned together, and fell on my face, my red Indiana University boxer shorts a bright crimson bloom above the harness and jeans that were now snarled around my calves, my underwear shining like a baboon's butt as I presented myself to the gym.

Laughter echoed through a warehouse that seemed designed to amplify the sound.

"NO!" Jake Crane bellowed, lifting both hands. "Come on, guys! We do not laugh at effort in Hoosier High Ground; we applaud it!"

And so the applause began just as I pulled my pants up, as if that had been a singular and surprising achievement.

Jake dropped a comforting arm around my shoulders and leaned close. "Bro," he whispered confidingly, " 'whipper' is not a command. It is a fall. You scream when you take one to show that you're not scared."

"Well," I said, "I was scared and I was screaming and I was, evidently, whipping. Checked some boxes."

Jake hit me with a double thumbs-up.

"The journey begins," he said.

"Are you okay?" Kerri whispered.

"Fine." The pain in my testicles was so intense that I could scarcely breathe.

Jake dropped into a squat beside me like a helpful Little League coach.

"That was a good leap you had early. Seriously. I did *not* think you were going to make that one. Like, no way. But you did it."

"Yeah," I gasped. "It was a real master class."

"I'd been thinking about trying the boulder wall," Kerri said. "Maybe we can walk over there? Or literally anywhere else?"

Jake and I agreed that someplace out of the center of the room was a good idea. We walked together to the sanctuary of Kitten's Cradle, the two of them going slowly so as not to draw attention to my limp. The pain from my groin was now radiating into my stomach, and it felt like a heroic effort to avoid doubling over and vomiting on the mats. A few soft chuckles still echoed around the cavernous space, but either Jake Crane ruled with a resolute hand or the members of Hoosier High Ground took the moral implications of their name seriously, because there were none of the hysterical howls that I'd have heard in the halls at school.

I leaned against Kitten's Cradle, grimacing, and went to remove the harness. Only then did I realize I was still trailing the belaying rope and that Jake held the free end as if he were walking a dog on a leash. He reached toward my waist and freed me. The oversized harness dropped to the mat with a jingle, like the gun belt falling from a fighter who has surrendered after having his pistols shot out of his hands.

"You'll get back into the groove soon," Jake said.

I didn't even bother to nod. My lies about climbing experience had slipped away even faster than my pants. Jake looked at Kerri, exchanging some unspoken thoughts, and then he said that he needed to go check the locker rooms and he'd catch up with us later. He clapped me on the back once more and went striding off across the matted floor. Then it was just Kerri and me. She slipped off her ponytail holder and then retied it, buying time as I got my breathing steadied. Finally, she looked me in the eye.

"No honk," she said. "No caution."

"Can we go home?"

We didn't speak again until we were in her Honda and she had the AC blasting in our faces and the White Stripes, her new favorite band, on the stereo. Then she turned to me and said, "Which camp was it that had the serious walls?"

"Just drive, Flanders."

She drove to the edge of the parking lot, then hit the horn twice.

"Proceed with caution?" she said, and then checked to see if I was laughing. I stared straight ahead, trying to channel my embarrassment into anger, as if any of the debacle in the climbing gym had been her fault. She turned north, a thoughtful look on her face, and then punched a button on the stereo. The CD changer she'd had installed in the console hummed and clicked as the discs exchanged. A few seconds of silence passed before DMX's signature growl filled the car.

I looked at Kerri, suspicious. She was struggling for a poker face. As DMX informed us that to live is to suffer but to survive requires finding meaning in the suffering, she put her sunglasses on to shield herself from my gaze. Her jaw trembled with suppressed laughter. She thumbed the volume louder.

"*I'm slippin', I'm fallin', I can't get up!*" DMX raged, and then Kerri fell apart. The laughter wracked her whole body, and she swerved off the street and into a parking space and then laid her forehead against the steering wheel and laughed until there were tears on her cheeks, and by then I was laughing, too, despite myself—laughing so hard that I slid down and slumped into the footwell of the passenger seat of Kerri's Honda, damn near in the fetal position. Then she asked me if I was "chimneying" down there, and the laughter started all over again.

Somehow, throbbing balls and all, it was the best day I'd had in a long time.

If you'd asked me how Kerri was doing that afternoon, I'd have said everything was terrific in her life. She was laughing and she was happy and it never occurred to me to ask why she'd wanted so desperately to get away from her house.

4

I PAID OFF MY bet with Leslie Carter the next weekend. Dinner was gourmet fare—chicken fingers and fries at Macri's Deli—and the night was perfect. I got a lot of laughs, only one kiss, but that one held the promise of more.

"You really doubled down on that ticket," Leslie teased. "You were white-on-rice with that. *'Oh, I've got proof. I've got evidence.'* "

I almost asked her to do me a favor and see what her father thought of Maddox. The guy had been such a prick, and he'd seemed almost dangerous, and then there was the girl in the back seat . . .

But I didn't ask. I was on a date, and it was more than two months after the incident. Emotions fade, new ones rise to replace them. Memories move like tides. Maddox's rage was never gone from my mind, but it had definitely receded.

Tides always wash back in, though.

We went to see a movie, *The Matrix*, which was unlike anything I'd seen before. It was about a futuristic world after humanity had lost a war with intelligent machines. Keanu Reeves looked fierce in sunglasses and a long black trench coat, a gun in each hand. Leslie loved it, and she let me sit with my arm around her shoulders. At one point she rested her hand on my leg. I didn't follow much of the plot after that.

I dropped Leslie off just before 11 p.m. and spent a few minutes talking with her parents, trying to seem respectful and harmless. Her father told me to call him Bruce, but I stuck with "sir." He was a member of his department's CIRT, which stood for "critical incident response team," Bloomington's version of a SWAT team. I did not want to appear to be a critical incident requiring response from Bruce Carter.

I said my goodbyes and then drove back across town, holding the speed limit with the caution that Maddox had instilled in me, and pulled into my own driveway a little before midnight. I headed for the front door, then stopped on the steps and frowned. There were two sheets of paper stuck to the door with a single strip of tape across the top, leaving the bottoms free so the sheets rose and fell and fluttered in the wind like teasing fingers waving goodbye.

I tugged the pages down and held them close enough to my face to make out the two words scrawled in marker across the top page: CALL ME.

It was Kerri's handwriting. I let out a breath, reassured that my nocturnal visitor had been a friend, then unlocked the door and flipped to the second page.

It was a flyer, printed in black and white, the headline MISSING across the top above a photograph of a smiling girl. I recognized her immediately. I'd seen her only once before, and only reflected by a mirror, but the memory was vivid, and there was no room for doubt.

5

MEREDITH SULLIVAN

Date Last Seen: February 11, 1999, 1:15 p.m.

Place Last Seen: Corner of 7th and Elm Streets, Terre Haute, Indiana

Age: 19

Race: White

Height: 5'6"

Weight: 125 lbs.

Hair Color: Blond

Eye Color: Blue

Distinguishing Marks/Features: Two piercings in left ear, one in right

Clothing When Last Seen: White sneakers, white shorts, teal polo shirt with "The Chocolate Goose" ice cream shop's logo and name

Personal Items: Necklace with thin gold chain and cross

Any and all information is requested. Reward offered.

Noah Storm, Private Investigator, CLI, CFE

I read it three times, faster each time and with rising panic.

I'd seen her in Maddox's police car on February 11 at 4:15, give or take a few minutes. The ticket should have the time—but the ticket didn't seem to be worth much. I retrieved it from the DVD case in which I'd hidden it, and the ticket confirmed my suspicion: I was apparently the last person to have seen her. Last one but Maddox, anyhow.

"Holy shit," I whispered. I'd seen her on the day she went missing. But what in the hell was I supposed to do? The flyer was from a private investigator, and that didn't make sense to me. If a girl went missing, the police were in charge, right? It was after midnight, and I wasn't about to call a private investigator in the middle of the night and tell him I'd seen a missing girl in the back of a police car driven by a fake cop.

My mother had a cell phone, but what I had to explain felt like something that needed to be said in person, not while she was driving down Highway 37 in the dark. It was too late to call Kerri at home, but that didn't mean there was no option to speak to her. After she'd moved into the basement, her bedroom was accessible from the sliding door that led to the backyard. If she was awake, she'd see me.

I had a feeling she was awake.

I walked to her house with a flashlight in one hand and the flyer in the other. It was an uneasy night, spring storms passing to the north. I cupped my hand over the flashlight to dim the beam in case Jerry or Gwen was awake, then cut through the lawn, their perfect grass spongy underfoot, and slipped around one of the planter boxes that would hold tomatoes in the summer, following the slope down to the walk-out basement, where a single red light glowed—the exit sign was on.

Kerri was up.

I let my hand slip off the flashlight lens and angled the beam toward her window, then thumbed the light on and off, four long blinks that were supposed to indicate four dashes for my initials in Morse code. This is what happens when you go to second grade with a kid on your street.

There was the soft sigh of a window unsealing as Kerri cranked open the old basement window in her room, which rose in the shadows like a drawbridge.

"Stay there, I'll come out," she whispered. "And turn the light off. Dad's up."

She slipped out a moment later, wearing old cotton shorts and a tank top, flip-flops held in her hands as she crossed the grass barefoot, a silent escape.

"Hollinger?" I asked.

"Yeah."

Hollinger Elementary School was behind Kerri's house. It had been closed in a round of school consolidations, but the old playground remained and the swing sets that had been our refuge as little kids still drew us more frequently than we'd ever admit to others. We pushed through the row of pines at the back of the yard and Kerri opened the gate on the old fence and then we were on the playground. A single security lamp cast white light over the empty parking lot, the rest of the property lost to shadows, but we knew every step. We crossed in silence, Kerri pausing to slip her flip-flops on before we left the grass for the woodchips that covered the playground. She had her glasses on, and I knew without needing to ask that she'd been up reading and waiting for my response.

Depending on when Jake Crane had dropped her off, at least.

Maybe I didn't know as much as I thought.

Kerri dropped onto the seat of one of the old swings, the chain creaking in protest, and faced me in the darkness.

"Is it her?"

"Yeah."

"You're sure."

"Yeah."

"Holy shit."

"What I said."

Lightning flashed in a harsh sheet, then returned the night to us. I saw her face clearly for a blink, the concern and shock in her eyes, and wondered what she saw in mine.

"Where did you get that flyer?" I asked.

"They were all over campus. I went to the Student Union with Jake—we were going to go bowling—but I saw that, and I made him bring me home so I could try to find you."

I looked at the flyer again. Meredith Sullivan's face was hidden in the darkness.

"I don't understand why it's a private investigator. Shouldn't it be police?"

"That's what I thought. But she's over eighteen. It's different when an adult goes missing. Maybe the police don't think she's really gone, or if she is gone, then it was of her own free will."

I pictured the girl in the back seat of the police car and shook my head. It hadn't been her free will.

"I can't believe we hadn't heard about this before."

"She went to Indiana State. A missing girl in another town isn't quite like one in Bloomington."

"Right," I said, but suddenly I thought that I *had* heard about it—part of a broadcast I'd ignored while waiting for my mother's weather segment, just another tragedy in the nightly roundup of other people's problems.

"Do your parents know about this?" I asked.

"No. I wasn't sure . . . I thought you might look at it and say it wasn't the same girl."

"It is."

More lightning. The wind rising, the pines rustling.

"You've got to tell someone," Kerri said.

"I know it. But—"

She was already shaking her head. "No, Marshall, you can't worry about the other cops or your mom or anything like that. This is real, that girl is missing, it is real and—"

"*He* isn't, though."

She stopped talking. Twisted the swing to face me. The first raindrops fell.

"Who isn't?"

"The cop who pulled me over." My voice cracked. "I should have asked more questions earlier."

"What do you mean?"

I told her what had happened at Sean Weller's, the way Leslie had confronted me on my story with such confidence, and how I'd lost the bet.

"She's not wrong," Kerri said softly. "I should've thought of that. They all have different ranks, you know. The sheriff's department has deputies and the state police have troopers and whatever, but the city doesn't have corporals."

With any other peer, I might have said, *How do you know that?* but when Kerri said something, she was sure about it. And Leslie's dad was a cop. I could feel the truth like a shackle clamped around my ankle, binding me to all the things ahead—wherever it would lead.

"I am *positive* he said corporal," I said. "It's a weird word and he said it in a weird way. I didn't imagine that."

"But it's not on the ticket." Unlike with Leslie, there was no judgment in Kerri's voice, no sense of having to prove my memory.

"No. So that's not worth anything."

"Sure it is. You have his handwriting."

That jarred me, a reminder of how much the evidence I had might matter.

"I guess I need to call this detective?" I said, looking at the flyer.

"Want to talk to my dad? He's up. If not, I'll wake him up."

"Yeah," I said. "If you don't mind . . . that sounds like a good idea."

Kerri stood, leaving the swing to sway in her wake, and gave me a quick, impulsive hug.

"It'll be fine, Marshall. It's *good* that you saw her. You can help."

Right, I told myself. It was good, and I could help.

We ran back to her house together as the rain opened up on the forgotten elementary school playground.

6

JERRY FLANDERS WAS AWAKE, wearing gym shorts and a Rik Smits jersey, watching *SportsCenter* with a beer in his hand. When he saw me, he said, "Oh, shit, another snake?"

"Maybe worse," Kerri said. "Tell him, Marshall."

Jerry listened patiently and calmly. It felt good to tell an adult. He got out the phone book, found the number for the Bloomington Police dispatch, and called. We listened as he explained that we might have some information about the missing girl who was on the flyer, and then there was a pause, and Jerry asked me for the flyer and the ticket. I passed them to him and he read off the description.

Another pause.

"Not aware of it, huh?" Jerry said into the phone.

Kerri and I looked at each other, puzzled.

"Okay," Jerry said. "Yes, his name is here. It is Noah Storm. Then it says CLI and CFE. I don't know what those mean. You don't, either? Okay. Yes, I got it. Thank you. I appreciate that. Hang on one moment, please—do ya'll have an officer named Maddox?"

His sunburned face creased with a frown. "All right. Thank you."

He hung up, looking thoughtful.

"They said the flyers are news to them, and that the case belongs to

Terre Haute city police and Vigo County sheriff's department." He turned to me. "Said they don't have an officer named Maddox either."

I held the ticket up as if in protest.

"I know, Marshall." His voice was calm, soothing. "Something's wrong, for sure, but . . . I don't know what. You're sure it was a squad car, not a personal vehicle?"

"It was a police car."

"They were overhead lights, though? Not inside the car?"

"Yes. I'm sure."

Jerry's frown deepened and he rubbed his jaw. "That's one hell of a prank."

"Prank?" I looked from him to Kerri, seeking support. "It was a real police car, and he had a real gun, and that girl on the poster was in his back seat!"

"I hear ya, bud, calm down."

I took a breath. Jerry took a drink.

"The police said we could give this private detective a call, because they don't know what the flyers are about," he said. "I guess that's as good an idea as any right now. We might wait until your mother's home to do that, though?"

I nodded. "That's fine."

Jerry watched me with kind eyes. "Why don't you stay here until she's home?"

I thought that was a grand idea. I sat up with Jerry and Kerri and we watched highlights of that night's NBA action while I kept one eye on our dead-end road, watching for my mother's car. It was just the three of us in the living room, and I assumed Gwen Flanders was asleep and nobody wanted to wake her. When I think back on that night, I remember the way neither Jerry nor Kerri betrayed any problem worth discussing except for mine, and I'm both struck by that kindness and ashamed of it.

It's so easy to fold into your own troubles.

And so wrong to allow that to happen.

When my mother's headlights finally brightened the dark street, Jerry said he'd walk down to the house with me. He squeezed my shoulder as we walked, then spoke in the low, encouraging voice that I always associated with coaches.

"You'll be a help to that girl's family. We'll get it sorted out."

My mother was calling my name when we reached the house, her voice high and tense. She'd already cracked my bedroom door and discovered that I wasn't asleep in my room. We caught her just before the tension bloomed into panic. Jerry took the lead in explaining things, showing her the flyer and talking her through the call with police.

"I've heard about her," Mom said, studying the picture. "We did a segment or two, although most of it has been focused in Terre Haute."

My mother looked at me. "You're sure?"

"Yes."

She touched my cheek with a cool palm and gave a gentle smile. If you didn't know her well, you'd have believed she was unconcerned. The only visible fear was in her eyes.

"It's one in the morning," she said. "Why don't you get some sleep, and I'll give him a call tomorrow. Even a private eye is probably asleep at this hour."

"I'm not tired. Try him now and see what happens. Please."

She didn't argue with that, and Jerry stayed in the house while she called the number listed for Noah Storm and verified that, as predicted, there was no answer at this hour but the machine. She left a message identifying herself and saying she would like to speak to him about the flyers left on campus. She never mentioned me.

"All right," she said when she'd hung up. "Get some sleep, Marshall."

I still didn't feel tired, but I knew there was no point in arguing. We both thanked Jerry, then stood together in the doorway watching as he jogged up the street in the blowing rain. The lightning was gone but thunder lingered, and the soaked grass smelled distinctly of spring. My mother closed the door and turned both the thumb lock and the dead bolt.

"Are you really okay?" she asked. "All this doesn't have you shaken up?"

I told her that I was fine, and I really was, right then. She was home, Jerry was nearby, adults were aware, and the police had been called. My tiny role in things seemed more intriguing than frightening. Then again,

I was also adamant that I wasn't tired, and yet I fell asleep within minutes. The things we believe don't necessarily overlap with the things that are true.

That night I dreamed of the lonesome red barn once more. I felt the warm weathered wood beneath my palm and I heard the scratching from the other side. As I searched for an opening, frantic, the heat rose from broiling to unbearable, and when I opened my mouth to scream, steam poured from between my lips and a terrible laugh came with it.

While I slept, the phone rang, and my mother answered it and spoke with Noah Storm. It was the first time he called our house, and somehow it feels appropriate that I was lost to a nightmare at that moment.

By the time I woke, the sun was angling in the window, and I realized I was still in my clothes, and that weird, fire-heated dream made more sense. I was cooking in the bright light. I rolled out of bed and headed groggily for the bathroom. I was in the hallway when my mother's voice floated up the stairs.

"Good morning. I'll make some breakfast while you take a shower. We've got an appointment with the private detective."

I rubbed my eyes, still groggy, and stared over the banister to where she stood in the foyer, watching me with a gentle smile. It was only eight, but she was already dressed for the new day, looking as refreshed as if she might have slept more than a few hours.

"He called?"

"Yes. He'll be in his office, waiting for us."

"I'm ready."

I started down the stairs before she waved me away, wrinkling her nose.

"Shower first and put on clean clothes. You smell like a campfire and too much cologne. Trust me, kiddo—I don't care how old the girl is, we appreciate a less-is-more approach to cologne."

"There's no girl."

Her smile called my bluff on that, and I flushed and looked away.

"Get ready," she said. "It's poor form for a meteorologist to keep a Storm waiting."

I groaned, and her laugh chased me down the hall.

It was almost exciting right then. That's an awful thing to say about being a witness to a crime, but it was also the truth. I can't deny that I was more excited than scared. That day exists in a perfect time capsule of memory for me, the details heightened by the emotion, the anticipation— and the overriding certainty that my cameo role in a small-town horror story was finished. I had met Maddox once and I would not see him again.

The moments immediately before you make a mistake have a way of lingering, I think. It's as if the mind archives the last chance you had to turn the right way before you went the wrong way, imprinting that memory in a hope that you won't make the same mistake the next time around.

Of course, we don't always get that next time. As the man who'd called himself Maddox told me, nobody is promised a second chance at getting home safe.

CHAPTER THREE

IN A TOWN LIKE OURS

April 1999

"I never sleep, 'cause sleep is the cousin of death."

NAS
"N.Y. STATE OF MIND"

1

I HAD NO CONCEPT of what a private investigator's office should look like, but I wouldn't have conceived of a place like Noah Storm's headquarters, which was a Gothic limestone house on Lockridge Lane, a few blocks northeast of the downtown square. The home was three stories of stately stone flanked by massive shade trees that were beginning to bloom.

"Those are beautiful elms," my mother said as she cut the engine on her Oldsmobile Bravada. We were strictly an Oldsmobile family—an unsexy choice, to say the least, although my mother was inexplicably certain that they were reliable cars, a conviction that somehow wasn't shaken by any of her numerous visits to mechanics. "I haven't seen any that nice in years. The Dutch elm disease killed almost all of them. I wonder how these made it."

I had no interest in the trees. The house held all my attention. Everything about it was imposing, slab after slab of thick limestone massing upward like a monument. Southern Indiana was limestone country, and townie kids dutifully learned that the great buildings of Washington, DC, and Manhattan were built from our very own stone. It was a yawn-inducing topic to a kid, but I've never walked down Lexington or Park avenues as an adult without inventorying the Indiana product towering above me.

"This is his office? It looks like a house."

"Number 712—that's him." She opened the car door. "It was a house at one time, I'm sure."

"There's no sign or anything."

"Let's just ring the bell, Marshall."

I heard the trace of tension in her voice, a reminder that she was bringing her only child to the home—or office, or both?—of a stranger to talk about the sighting of a missing girl, and I belatedly realized she had to be stressed. She stepped out of the car and smoothed her dark blue dress. The ticket was now paper-clipped to the flyer and tucked inside a manila envelope.

We walked beneath the majestic elms and up the limestone steps, each one wide enough to require a full stride before you reached the next. My mother's heels clacked and echoed. Even as I walked forward, I was tilting my head backward, gawking at the strange wrought iron bars mounted on the high windows that made the house look like a prison. On the top of the mansard roof, a weather vane in the shape of a clipper ship wobbled in the breeze. It was surrounded by iron rods that rose at least six feet above the shingles, each capped with small glass globes.

"What are those?" I asked, pointing.

My mother was a stride ahead, but she stepped back and shaded her eyes. "I don't see anything?"

I was about to explain when a male voice said, "Lightning rods."

We turned back to the door as a lean man in jeans, a crisp white shirt, and a black blazer stepped out. He had dark hair brushed back from his forehead and his smile was relaxed and warm, one of those rare first impressions that puts you at ease. No small thing when your business is always related to trouble.

"I'm Noah Storm," he said, extending his hand.

"Hello," my mother said. "I'm the one who called. Monica—"

"Miller, of course. I recognize you."

I waited for the dreaded Miller Time joke, but none came. His dark eyes shifted to me, and he leaned past my mother to shake my hand.

"Noah," he repeated.

"I'm Marshall."

"Good to meet you, Marshall. Nice eye, catching the lightning rods. They're classics." He studied me with what felt like real interest, then added, "It's a shame how many people walk right by and don't see them."

I felt my chest swell a little, having been complimented by a PI on my powers of observation.

"It's an exquisite building," my mother said.

"Thank you. I'm still settling in."

"Oh?"

"Only moved to town four months ago," he said. "Bought this place in February. I was lucky to find it."

"Why is the weather vane a ship?" I asked. "We're a long way from the ocean."

"What weather vane?" my mother said, but Noah Storm's warm smile widened.

"I like your mind," he said, and again I felt that flush of pride. He pointed southwest. "The ship is supposed to catch the fish. The man who built the house ran for mayor several times."

I actually understood this bizarre explanation. The Monroe County Courthouse was—and still is—topped by a massive weather vane in the shape of a fish. There are many competing theories as to why it is a fish, but as far as I know, there's no definitive answer.

"Who built the house?" my mother asked.

"Daniel Stuart. He owned a lot of quarries in the area. Never did catch the fish, though."

He opened the door and motioned with his free hand. I followed my mother into a foyer. A steep staircase rose dead ahead, and a hall extended past it, deeper into the house. Bloodred runner carpets lined the hall and the stairs, and the woodwork was a dark walnut, making the interior seem gloomy. Noah Storm opened the first door on the left and led us into a simple office with a large central desk in front of a massive case filled with books. There were two burgundy leather chairs facing the desk, and the office rug matched the bloodred runner carpets.

Kerri would love this place, I thought. It was a room that reeked of secrets and stories.

"I'll confess that I didn't know there were any private detectives in Bloomington," my mother said.

"There are exactly five of us. One is a bail bondsman who holds the PI license because he thinks it will impress women at bars, another is a house investigator for Joe O'Brien's law firm, and the other two are retired police officers who want people to believe they're doing anything other than playing golf in their golden years. Then there's me."

"The only real deal in town, evidently," my mother said, and he grinned. His face was all hard angles but not unappealing. There was a peppering of gray in his hair, but his skin was unlined. I didn't know if he was thirty-five or fifty. He was lean but his shoulders were broad.

"Honestly, I really am the only real deal in town. It's a small market, and that's why I chose it. I was in New York, got tired of the city."

"Why on earth did you pick Bloomington?" my mother asked.

I looked at her pointedly, wondering why on earth *she* was asking questions when we were here to discuss a disappearance. She ignored me.

"I was here for a couple semesters of classes during my Air Force days," Noah Storm said. "Loved it. I was in the Air Force intelligence service, so I moved around a lot, but Bloomington stuck with me. A town like yours is special. I don't need to tell you that; you're here for a reason. What is it?"

"A safe home for my son," my mother said without hesitation.

"There you go. Also, the beer's cold and the pizza's good at Nick's, which never hurts," he said, and my mother laughed. "Are you from town originally, Mrs. Miller?"

"Monica. And, no, I'm from Georgia. I came here for school. Lived in a rental house not three blocks from here."

"Were they good days, being here for school?"

"Lovely days."

I shifted in my chair. We were here on a mission, my mother didn't seem to care, and Noah Storm was acting with all the urgency of a man who'd bumped into two new neighbors while watering his lawn. This was the detective who was supposed to find a missing woman?

I tried not to show my irritation, looking away from them and studying the bookshelves. They looked like fat textbooks, all with grim titles:

Practical Sex Crimes Investigation; Practical Homicide Investigation; Advanced Forensic Civil Investigations. There was a stone trophy on one shelf, about ten inches tall, with a curved top that gave it the shape of a small gravestone, and there was writing chiseled into it.

EVERY STONE HAS A STORY.

The letters suddenly seemed to swim and retreat, a piercing pulse flared in my temples, and I blinked and looked away. My mother missed it, but Noah Storm gave me a quick glance. I forced a smile: *All is well! Let the small talk flow!*

"So you came for school and then stayed," Noah Storm said. "Nice." He looked at her as if uncertain about his next question, and then, with a hint of embarrassment, said, "I love a phrase you use in your segments, by the way."

Here we go, I thought. *It's Miller Time.*

"You say that you're 'interrogating the storm.' I love that."

My mother blushed. Flat-out blushed, her cheeks reddening.

"I can't claim that one," she said. "It's an academic term for studying the data. Radar, pressure changes, all those things."

"But it's the perfect phrase for the task of warning the audience," he said. "If you can't get them to look up, you can't warn them, and if you're hyperbolic, they're not going to trust the warning the next time you give it. That's when people get hurt. By saying that you're 'interrogating the storm,' you also remind the audience that the storm has secrets. You can't guarantee what it will do. The storm is in control."

It was quiet for a moment. When my mother said, "That is an excellent description," her voice was soft, touched by his attention to detail.

In a way, I was too. Most people didn't give her that kind of credit, seeing only a pretty woman pointing at a weather map.

"I was going to steal the phrase, but it doesn't work as well for me," he said. " 'Interrogations *by* Storm' doesn't have the same ring to it."

My mother laughed too loudly, then shifted in the chair and crossed her legs, smiling at him. As I watched, I had a horrifying realization: she was attracted to him.

I wondered if I could ask her to go wait in the car.

"So, uh, the missing girl," I said. "That's why we're here, right?"

Noah Storm swiveled to face me, and I had the unsettling sense that he knew exactly what I'd been thinking, and the twinkle in his eye was there to tell me that he meant no harm.

"Down to business," he said. "Excellent. You'll do well on billable hours, Marshall."

He leaned forward, grabbed a pen from a canister on the desk, uncapped it, and pulled a yellow legal pad toward him. He jotted the date, time, and my name on the top of the pad, and when he looked at me again, I understood the small talk had been intentional. He was assessing us, determining the best way to talk to us, and putting us at ease.

"What information do you have for me?" he asked.

"Well, I don't know the first thing about it," my mother said. "I know only what Marshall told me, and . . . it's confusing."

Seeing my injured look, she lifted one hand and said, "Not *his* story. Marshall can explain that to you. What confuses me is why we're talking to a private investigator. That's extremely unusual if the girl is missing, which is a police matter."

"It *is* a police matter, but Meredith is a legal adult living away from home and there are indications that her disappearance might be of her own accord."

"Do *you* think she left of her own accord?" my mother asked.

"I don't think anything yet," he said, lightly but firmly. "It's too early."

"Why are you searching in Bloomington?"

"Because the Chocolate Goose is in Bloomington," I said. "She was wearing that uniform."

Noah Storm gave me a half smile, and again I had the feeling that I'd impressed him.

"Marshall said he saw her in a police car," my mother said. "Does that make any sense to you? Based on what you do know?"

I was getting annoyed by her now—we'd come here so I could share my story, and she was doing all the talking, falling back into mom mode, as if I were a little kid. I was about to speak when Noah Storm beat me to it.

"How about I hear it the way Marshall remembers it? Always better to remove as many degrees of separation as possible from the eyewitness and the report."

Thank you, I thought. He leaned forward, pen poised above the notepad, and gave a faint, encouraging nod.

"I saw her on February 11 in the afternoon and she was in the back seat of a police car," I said. "She was wearing that uniform, the one from the Chocolate Goose. When they left, she was crying. The cop was named Maddox and he said he was a corporal, but he gave me a ticket from the Bloomington Police Department and they don't have corporals. They also don't have anyone named Maddox."

It was quiet for a moment. My mother shifted and recrossed her legs again. Her hands were squeezed together in her lap. I realized how afraid she really was and why she hoped I had made a mistake. It would be easier on her if I'd confused the missing girl for someone else.

But I hadn't.

"We're going to walk through this a little slower," Noah Storm said, and his face was all business. "I need to hear the whole story, from beginning to end. Don't invent anything to fill a gap in your memory; just tell it the way you remember it."

I told the story. He didn't jump in with any questions, just listened and took notes, his eyes alternating between the notepad and my face. When I got to the part about Maddox swearing at me and telling me that expecting second chances was a good way to die, he stopped taking notes entirely. He didn't interrupt, but from then on he only listened.

"You don't know where they went after he pulled you over?" Noah asked when I was done.

"No. Well, I saw the direction. He went past the clubhouse, down the road that winds toward Griffy Creek and Cascades Park."

Noah made a note. One of my mother's knuckles popped as she squeezed her hands together, and the loud sound seemed to surprise her. She flattened her hands on her legs.

"And you have the speeding ticket?" Noah asked.

I hated how my mother produced it, as if it were a permission slip.

"You can see how he filled it all out," I said. "He even put his name on it—or *a* name, because we were told there is no Maddox with the Bloomington Police."

"There's definitely not a corporal," Noah said as he scrutinized the ticket, "and I haven't heard of a Maddox. If Dispatch told you there isn't one, I believe them."

"If this man had a police car and was in a police uniform with a badge and a gun, that is absolutely terrifying!" my mother said, her steady TV voice gone, but Noah Storm didn't look up. He was studying the ticket as if he were alone in the room with it. I half expected him to produce a magnifying glass and examine it like Sherlock Holmes.

"What is this stain?" he asked.

I knew without asking that he meant the charcoal-colored smear.

"That's from his hand."

He looked up with sharp interest. "He was barehanded?"

"Yes." The importance of that hit me for the first time—I might have a fingerprint.

Noah Storm nodded at me as if I'd voiced the thought aloud. I felt an intense private connection between us, as if he understood me perfectly and didn't need to put everything into words. It was both eerie and comforting.

"Anyone other than you handle it since?"

"I wore gloves when I put it in the bag," my mother said, sounding proud of herself.

"Jerry held it last night," I said. "I don't remember if Kerri did. I don't think so. I handed it to Jerry."

"What's Jerry's last name?"

"Flanders."

Noah made a note. "You've told other people about this traffic stop and the girl in the car." Not a question.

"Yes."

"How many?"

"Not many. A couple friends. Then Jerry. He was the one who called the police."

"And Dispatch told him there wasn't a corporal with BPD?"

"Uh, no. A girl named Leslie Carter did."

"When did that conversation take place?"

"Last weekend."

"Did anyone else overhear that?"

"Maybe? There were others in the area, you know. We kind of made a bet about it. People heard that."

I didn't understand why this mattered. Once again, Noah seemed to read me.

"The police may want to control the release of this information," he said. "It's valuable to the investigation if it's not widely known. If people are talking about it, though, the calculation changes, and it might be more valuable to release your account widely and promptly."

"Oh, I get it. You mean Maddox—the guy who called himself Maddox—might not know that his cover is blown."

"Correct. But you did have a public exchange about his name and rank?"

"Not *public*, but a few people definitely heard it." I felt disappointed in myself for this, even though I'd had no idea of its importance at the time.

"Where was this?" my mother asked.

I didn't want to lie, but I also did not want to talk about Sean Weller's party. I was getting a pass from my mother on hiding the speeding ticket only because there were bigger concerns from that traffic stop.

"I was with Leslie, Dom, and some friends," I mumbled.

"At his house?"

"No, we were . . . it was just around some kid's yard."

She frowned. "What kid?"

I was cut off by the loud *ding-dong-ding-ding* chime of a doorbell.

"I'm sorry," Noah Storm said, rising abruptly. "That's UPS. I ordered some file cabinets. I'll be right back." He started for the door, then half turned, as if in afterthought, and said, "Marshall, may I borrow your strong young back? I need to sign for these and pull them inside."

"Sure." I was happy to escape an exchange with my mother that was already floating between a lie and a confession.

I followed him out of the office and down the hall toward the back door. He stepped out behind me and closed the door. We were in the alley, and there was no sign of a UPS truck or filing cabinets. I looked around, puzzled, and Noah Storm spoke in a low voice.

"Were you drinking when you told the story about Maddox and made the bet?"

I blinked at him, surprised and nervous.

"I'm not reporting it to your mother," he said. "I just need to know."

"I was around beer," I admitted. "But I only had a little. Honest."

He lifted a reassuring hand, indicating he wasn't about to sweat me over it.

"Okay. How many kids heard you tell the story, roughly?"

"Maybe a dozen, tops? But I was talking more about the cop than the girl. I said she was in the back seat but I didn't describe her. Well, I guess I mentioned the uniform from the ice-cream store. I brought that up because . . . well, back then, because it seemed funny, in a way."

I felt awful, saying that, but Noah nodded.

"Got it." His eyes searched mine. "Were you drinking on the day you saw her?"

"No! I'm not some big drinker. Jeez, I barely even had a whole beer the night of the party. When he pulled me over, I was absolutely—"

He cut me off with a soothing gesture, like someone patting a nervous dog.

"I need to be clear on what I'm getting into here, that's all. One more question that stays between the two of us?"

I waited.

"Did you try to burn the ticket?"

I frowned. "No. Why?"

He was watching me with his head at an angle and the first hint of skepticism in his eyes.

"Maybe you wanted to hide it from your mother. I would have at your age."

"Well, I didn't."

"The mark that you said was left by the cop's hand looks like a scorch mark. As if you—or someone—held a match to it, then pulled it back before the paper caught fully. Had second thoughts."

"I know what you mean," I said. "It does look like a burn mark. But that's not from me."

"Was it possibly there from the beginning, then?"

I tried to remember. When did I notice that strange scorch mark? I'd been distracted.

"It could have been," I said slowly, but I didn't think it had been. He'd touched it and left the mark.

Noah Storm nodded. "He grabbed a book of them somewhere. Could have snagged them from a burn barrel or something. Who knows? It got close to a flame. I'm sure of that."

"I mean, that's what it looks like, but . . ."

"But?"

I was about to say that I was certain the mark had been left by Maddox's thumb, but that didn't make any sense. Noah had to be right.

"It does look like someone tried to burn it, that's all."

He let out a breath and his eyes took on a faraway stare.

"Here's what matters: you saw her; you can describe her; you can describe him; you can say when and where it happened. Yes?"

"Yes."

"All right. Let's go back in. I'll keep the booze out of it in front of your mom."

"Thank you," I said, but I had my doubts that he'd be able to distract her from the unanswered questions she already had loaded in the chamber.

He opened the door for me, and I was halfway through when I paused.

"You made the doorbell ring," I said, realizing how he'd rescued me. "You have a button under the desk or something?"

He flashed a half-amused, half-chagrined smile and winked at me. "Tricks of the trade. You'll learn them soon enough."

At the time, I thought that was a reference to maturity, to picking things up as I went through life, the way any adult can patronize a kid with "soon enough" promises. Only later, when I was in another room with another kind of detective and the stakes were much higher, would I realize that, even during our first meeting, Noah Storm believed I was going to be around his office in the days ahead.

I hadn't applied, and no job existed, but he'd already hired me. I just didn't know it yet.

When we returned to where my mother waited, Noah never gave her the chance to resume her own line of questioning.

"Well," he said as soon as we entered, "we are going to need to speak to the police."

"Jerry Flanders tried," my mother said. "Last night he called and was told they knew nothing about it."

"We're going to receive a very different response today," Noah said. There was a calm but rising energy to him, like a battery hitting full charge. "You're of course under no obligation to have me present, but I think I may be an asset to you. It's entirely your decision."

He looked at my mother. Her hands were squeezed tightly together.

"That's fine," she said tentatively. "That may help."

"They're going to separate the three of us, of course," he said matter-of-factly. "You'll be able to stay with Marshall, and you should. While they speak with you, I can head out to the golf course. There probably aren't any security cameras, but you never know."

I hadn't thought of cameras. His mind was quick.

"When your story checks out," he said, betraying total confidence that it would, "there will be media attention. That's a good thing. People need to know about this man who pulled you over."

"Yes, they do!" my mother said, but she squeezed my leg protectively. She knew about media attention. For the first time, I realized how many people would hear my story. A man impersonating a police officer, with a missing girl locked in his back seat? That would be big, and not limited to local news.

"You can handle it, Marshall," Noah said. "You'll do fine."

Once again I was struck by that sense that he'd heard my private thoughts as clearly as if we were in conversation.

"Okay," I said. "Let's do it."

He was reaching for the phone when I said, "May I ask you a question?"

"Shoot."

"Are you working for her family?" I was thinking that I didn't want to talk to them directly. I couldn't imagine that pressure, being the last person who'd seen their daughter.

"It's a good question," my mother said, and I felt as if she wished she'd asked it herself.

"It is," Noah Storm said. "And I can't disclose that. I apologize. It's a confidential business. You understand."

He had a way of saying things that made you nod in agreement. That's what my mother and I did, anyhow. The phrase was "private investigator" for a reason, right?

He picked up the phone and called the police.

2

THINGS MOVED QUICKLY after that call.

The first meeting was in the Indiana State Police post on the bypass and Fee Lane. Noah Storm led us in and then separated from us before the police had to request it. He had an effortless style, so slick that you didn't realize how he took charge until after it had been done. Even the police followed his lead, because he explained everything clearly and with deference, as if agreeing with decisions that hadn't even been made yet.

"Let me know when you're ready to issue the media statement and I'll come back immediately," he told the trooper who met us at the station. "I want to direct calls to the right place, which is your office, not mine."

The trooper agreed to this, but I wondered if he would have included Noah Storm at all if Noah hadn't explained it as if he were doing the police a favor.

The rest of the day was like skiing into a blizzard. I spoke to the trooper, then a lieutenant, and then there were three more cops in the room. It became hard to keep track. Tape recorders and video cameras were produced. The speeding ticket was photographed and then placed into a plastic bag by an officer wearing latex gloves. A state police detective named Ron Walters arrived from Vigo County, where Meredith Sullivan had disappeared. He was introduced as "running point" on the investigation.

"Mrs. Miller, you're more familiar with television news than any of us," he said to my mother. "Are you comfortable with Marshall appearing on camera?"

She glanced at me. I nodded.

"If I'm with him," she said.

An hour later I was standing on the courthouse lawn in the center of downtown with three television cameras trained on my face. The state police spokesman took over after me, explaining that there was no officer by Maddox's name, that the rank was wrong, and that no police cars had been reported missing in the state. They were seeking any and all information, he said, and public response would be crucial.

Noah Storm didn't appear on camera, but he stood behind the reporters. He reminded me of a coach watching from the sidelines as the game plan he'd orchestrated took shape. He gave me a smile and a thumbs-up when the press conference was done. I felt better for the approval.

I'd started to follow my mother away from the courthouse when a newspaper reporter asked to speak with me. Donita Rickert was the police beat reporter from the *Bloomington Herald-Times*. I recognized her name from the byline in lots of front-page stories.

"Have a water first," Noah said, pressing a cold bottle into my hand and producing another for my mother. "She can wait. The presses aren't running yet."

I was grateful for the moment to gather my thoughts. I sipped the water, watching as the cameraman from my mother's network took a wide shot of the downtown square and the reporter spoke into a boxy cell phone, the antenna extended well above her head, the mouthpiece flipped open. Everyone seemed flushed and breathless. I heard their conversations in soft snippets that seemed to blend with phrases I'd already heard and committed to memory.

There are no corporals with Bloomington Police.

Nobody is promised a second chance at getting home safe.

Above us, the six-foot-long fish on the weather vane atop the courthouse dome swung gently in a strong southern wind. Somewhere out of sight a few blocks away, the clipper ship above Noah Storm's limestone office—or house? Did he live there too?—was shifting to match.

He never did catch the fish.

Noah was talking to my mother in a voice so low, it was inaudible to me, and she was nodding, and I could tell that she was grateful he was there. We'd met him only a few hours ago, and yet he no longer felt like a stranger. I watched him, thinking of how quickly and effectively he'd saved me from having to explain Sean Weller's party. He'd disarmed my mother easily, too, speaking about her weather segments with a detailed interest and respect that few people offered.

"Interrogating the storm." It's the perfect phrase.

He was right, I supposed. I hadn't heard her say that phrase often, though, and I watched nearly every broadcast she made. She saved it for supercell thunderstorms, the systems that could spawn tornadoes. If Noah had moved to town only a few months ago, it was even more surprising that he'd registered and remembered it. As I finished my water, I thought that I should ask my mother when the last time she'd said that was.

Ron Walters, the state police detective, touched my elbow.

"Marshall, Donita with the *Herald-Times* would love a few minutes with you. Are you okay with that?"

I nodded, and then I was escorted toward a woman who was waiting with a notepad in hand, and everything else was forgotten. It was a long time before I remembered to ask my mother about the phrase "interrogating the storm."

Too long.

3

THE TELEVISION INTERVIEWS aired Saturday night, and I began hearing from people soon afterward—including Leslie Carter, who told me that her father was impressed by how much I'd noticed and remembered.

"He said that most witnesses don't do that well even when they knew they were seeing something out of the ordinary," she said.

That made me feel good.

Meredith Sullivan's parents went on TV and implored the public for help. They were much older than my mother, gray-haired, and with lined faces that looked even older because of their fear. They stood on the porch of a weathered home in Huntington, Indiana. A dog barked in the background in high, nervous yips. They were red-eyed and weary and held photographs of Meredith in which she looked young and energetic and unafraid. It was hard for me to square her expressions in those photos with the one I'd seen in my sideview mirror.

In high school, she'd been an honor student and a volleyball star. She'd gone to Indiana State in Terre Haute to study geology, and she had a dream of working in the West, Yellowstone or maybe Alaska. She'd told her roommate that she wanted to save enough money from her part-time job at a grocery store to take a summer off and hike as much of the Appalachian Trail as possible. She'd become a fan of the beat writers Kerouac, Kesey, and Ginsberg. She spent hours on the internet, chatting with strangers about her desire to experience what she termed "real life." Her roommate and friends had speculated that maybe she'd decided to take off in pursuit of these dreams. Wanderlust was the prevailing theory for her sudden disappearance—until a sixteen-year-old kid in Bloomington named Marshall Miller claimed he had spotted her in a police car.

There were no explanations for Maddox, or at least none expressed on the evening news.

The attention to my story accelerated on Sunday, when the print articles appeared. Bloomington was still a newspaper town in 1999. The TV networks were in Indianapolis, and while there were a few nascent internet news sites, there was no social media to spread the stories. That was the spring when Larry Page and Sergey Brin were recruiting angel investors for a company that would become known as Google—one of those investors was a guy named Jeff Bezos—and in New York, Mark Zuckerberg was attending eighth grade and playing video games. We were on the verge of a seismic shift, but when my account of seeing Meredith Sullivan appeared, local news was obtained via a walk to the end of the driveway to collect the daily edition of the *Herald-Times*. Print moved the needle. That was made clear to me by noon Sunday, when Donita Rickert's story hit the Associated Press wire service and local became national.

Our phone didn't stop ringing that day.

My mother managed the media interest—with Noah Storm's help. She called him several times, and he called her to give us a heads-up that police would announce they were looking for a man who'd purchased an old, wrecked police car from an auction in Fort Wayne two months earlier. The man had given a fake name and his check had bounced. His description, however, sounded nothing like the man I'd known as Maddox. Noah relayed this to police, and that evening I met with a sketch artist who came up with a rendering of Maddox.

"Close?" Ron Walters asked.

I stared at the sketch. Close? Maybe. But helpful? No. If they arrested the man who'd called himself Maddox, people might look from him to the sketch and nod, but would anyone spot him *because* of this? I couldn't imagine that.

"It's . . . realistic." I offered a word that wouldn't show the sketch disappointed me.

"They're good at this," he said, "but they need good witnesses. You're the one making the magic happen, Marshall."

Walters gave me his home phone and cell phone numbers, with instructions to call at any hour if I remembered anything new.

I had plenty of memories, but they were the old ones on loop. I did have one new question, though.

"Did she ever work for the Chocolate Goose?"

"No."

"Then why was she dressed like it?"

"She was wearing that when a security camera caught her in Terre Haute. We're not sure where she got it or why she was wearing it."

It wasn't much of an answer, but I thought it explained why a private investigator in Bloomington was involved. It was our town's local ice-cream shop, even if the missing girl had vanished in another town.

There was something about that out-of-season uniform that creeped me out more than any other aspect of the story. I couldn't explain why, and I didn't try.

They aired the sketch on television Sunday night, and Walters called me with a question not long after.

"Did you try to burn that ticket?"

The same thing Noah Storm had asked.

"No, sir. That mark was on it."

"And you're sure he wasn't wearing gloves?"

"Positive."

"Well, he handled it carefully. The only fingerprints belong to you or your neighbor Jerry."

I tried to recall the moment when Maddox had passed the ticket through the open window. I could picture his eyes and his arms but not his hands. Still, I was certain he hadn't been wearing gloves. It was almost the absence of the memory that made me sure of that. Gloves would have stood out, I thought. I would have noticed them.

Wouldn't I?

I didn't sleep well that night. Too much adrenaline, sure, and when I did sleep, dreams came on fast and frightening, the same nightmare of the old red barn in the lonely field. I'd had recurring dreams before, always variations on a theme—showing up to school unprepared for a pop quiz, or one where I was falling and from which I always woke with a gasp just ahead of impact. These dreams of the barn were different. It was the same setting, the same action, the same sensation of doom. The same helplessness. She was right there, reaching out for me, and I couldn't get to her because there was simply no way in.

Monday morning was overwhelming. Everyone in school wanted to ask me about what I had seen and how I'd felt and what I thought would happen now. I tried to pay attention in class, but I found myself imagining questions from reporters and framing my answers, trying to come up with ways to sound savvy, older than my years. Ways to make the reporters appreciate my observation in the way Noah Storm had when I'd asked about the lightning rods.

Nice eye . . . It's a shame how many people walk right on by and don't see them.

I wanted to talk to him again, ask what he thought of my performance at the press conference, what I might do better the next time around. Did it even matter, or was that simple shallowness on my part, believing that anything I said or did could help? I wasn't sure. My friends all acted as if I had a role in things, but the police seemed done with me now.

On Monday afternoon, a billboard went up near Miller-Showers Park, Meredith Sullivan's smiling face ten feet high:

LAST SEEN ON FEBRUARY 11. REWARD OFFERED.

"I wonder how much the reward is," Dom Kamsing said as we sat in the Beast, studying the billboard. He'd picked me up for school when I told him the Olds was broken down. The truth was, I didn't feel like driving. I couldn't suppress the creepy sensation that Maddox was out there, watching the news, remembering both me and my car. He might not be a real cop, but that didn't mean he couldn't find me. I suspected he hated himself for letting me go.

"They haven't told me."

"You're going to be on the news every day until they find her," Dom predicted.

"Hopefully it's not long."

But in my gut I felt as if it would be.

Meanwhile, I was famous. Kids I barely knew approached me to ask about Meredith Sullivan and how it had felt when I locked eyes with her in the mirror. Everyone wanted to know if she'd looked scared. I wanted to go back to writing my silly AIM Away messages, but that chance was gone. There were no jokes now that the girl in the police car had been made real. Strangers messaged me and asked me for details. I thought most of them simply wanted to say that they'd talked to me directly, thus putting themselves closer to the crime story.

Horror trumped comedy for holding the audience, I guess.

"The craziness will end soon," Kerri told me while we walked between classes on Tuesday morning. "It's too hard for a guy pretending to be a cop to hide. They'll find the car, they'll find him, and they'll find her. Then the media will stop calling you."

It turned out she was both right and wrong. No one found Maddox, but the media calls stopped less than forty-eight hours after they'd started.

On Tuesdays, Kerri and I shared the final period of the day together, working as library aides. The first person Kerri sought out in any school was the librarian. At our school, that was Mr. Doig, a cerebral and dryly hilarious man with a dignified, formal bearing that seemed more appropriate for an Ivy League college than a public high school in the Midwest. By the end of September of our freshman year, Kerri had already formed a bond with him. He also taught a creative writing workshop that met after school, an extracurricular club of sorts, and Kerri had convinced me to try it once. We started with first sentences: *Write the opening of the story you most want to read,* Mr. Doig instructed. *Or write the last one. Some writers have different methods. There is no wrong approach, only your own approach.*

I tried to take it seriously because the others in the group were. I couldn't imagine writing the last sentence first—how did you know the ending before you started?—and I had no original ideas, so I tried to focus on that idea of writing the story you most wanted to read.

I wrote: *The father was crying when he left the boy.*

Only when I realized that we would be asked to read them aloud did I draw a line through "The father" and replace it with a generic pronoun. When I read it to the group, I said, *He was crying when he left the boy.*

They were all supportive of the potential for a story to emerge from that opening, and Mr. Doig was particularly encouraging, other than telling me to try it in active tense: *He cried when he left the boy.*

Hear the difference? he asked, and I did. It was more immediate, closer to the heart. There were reasons I didn't like that sensation, though. Passive was safer.

That was the last time I went to the workshop.

It's just not for me, I told Kerri. *I'm not interested in writing.*

But I did love Mr. Doig, and being in the library was a wonderful way to end the day. We sorted and shelved books and wrote the occasional brief essay on some piece of reading that Mr. Doig would assign out of the blue. He was one of those rare adults who never talked down to you. He challenged you by treating you as an equal, making you want to keep up with him. I began reading the newspaper every day simply because I didn't want to see that look of disappointment pass over his face if I didn't know what he was talking about when he asked me for my opinion on a matter of the day. His ability to connect current events to historical ones was remarkable, and he always seemed prescient, as if he'd read enough about the past to have a better handle on the future than most.

It's so easy to know so much, he would tell us, gesturing around the library. *It's all right there, and it's free.*

On the Tuesday after the press conference, Kerri and I walked into the library with the sound of the bell and saw Mr. Doig standing in the AV supply room with his back to us, his attention on one of the old televisions that were mounted on rolling carts so they could be brought into classrooms. A grave-faced news anchor was on the screen.

"Oh, great, he's watching the news. Maybe I'll have a rerun appearance."

"You need an agent," Kerri said.

"I'm not giving you ten percent."

"You're right. I'm not taking less than twenty."

We were both laughing when Mr. Doig turned and we saw that his patrician, gentleman's bearing was wracked with grief.

"They are killing children with guns and bombs in a school just like ours," he said, and then we stepped up beside him and watched a helicopter circle above a high school in Littleton, Colorado, where preliminary reports said there were at least two active shooters in the building.

It wasn't the first time I'd heard of a school shooting. I had memories of one in Kentucky and one in Arkansas and maybe Minnesota. They had not looked like this, though. Kids covered in blood ran through a parking lot while a SWAT team with bulletproof shields crouched low and approached the school, moving like a military unit. More students walked out of a side door with their hands clasped behind their heads as if they were all being arrested. Paramedics unloaded stretchers and rushed them toward the building—or loaded them back into ambulances with wounded students hidden beneath bloodstained sheets. An armored car approached, flanked by police with rifles. The thrum of the helicopter provided a steady beat in the background, the bass line to a series of soprano sirens.

"This is a rampage, this is a massacre," the news anchor informed us. "This is an unprecedented moment in American history."

It was April 20, 1999, and while Kerri and I had walked, laughing and joking, into our high school library in Bloomington, Eric Harris and Dylan Klebold had already walked into their own high school library, also laughing and joking as they tossed pipe bombs toward their teachers and fired bullets from semiautomatic guns into the bodies of their classmates. More than twenty students had been shot by the time we saw the first report from Colorado.

No one from the national media called for Marshall Miller that night.

Kerri and I stayed in the library after the final bell rang to end the day. Thirty minutes passed, then an hour. A dozen teachers and maybe twice as many students gathered with us. Ms. Rivas, the Spanish teacher, cried audibly. That was the only sound I remember other than the sirens and the staccato chop of the helicopter blades and the breathless voices of the news anchors.

The camera cut to a girl who spoke with a detached, almost woozy calm: "They came into the library and they were shooting everyone that they could, and we were all under the tables, and the girl who was right next to me was shot in the head. Blood was going all over everyone. And I witnessed that. I was still under the table in the library and they were walking back and forth and laughing and shooting and killing."

The screen shifted again, this time a cut to a parent standing behind a police barricade, tears streaming down his cheeks. Then the television screen went black. There was a frozen moment as we all waited for it to come back on, assuming there was some technical glitch, and then I saw that Mr. Doig held the remote in his hand.

"That is enough for me right now," he said in his soft but deep voice. "Go home, kids. Go home, stay safe, and love each other."

It was the kind of earnest exhortation that usually draws eye rolls or laughs from teens. We didn't laugh. Not then, not later.

Go home, stay safe, and love each other.

It should be that simple, shouldn't it?

We went home. Kerri drove, and we rode in silence, and when we reached her house, her father came out to greet us before we made it to the door. Jerry had just gotten off work, dressed in dirty jeans and a dusty denim shirt that bore the logo of his new employer, Eliminator Inc., across the breast pocket.

He took one look at us and said, "You already know."

Then he hugged his daughter tightly, and Kerri allowed it without objection. He shook my hand and squeezed my arm and we went into the house and saw that the television was already on and the news was still playing. It probably was on in most American homes.

"We have a report that on the second floor a student is trying to escape," the newscaster said, and just like that, we were back at Columbine.

A boy in a white T-shirt dangled out of a shattered window. He was soaked in blood. His left arm hung uselessly. He made frantic waving motions with his right.

I heard an echo in my mind then, Maddox's voice, deep and furious: *Nobody is promised a second chance at getting home safe. You will learn that.*

An armored vehicle had pulled up beneath the boy, but it looked like a long way down. Officers in riot gear reached up for him as he leaned out of the window, dripping blood onto the broken glass. He was desperate, trying to escape from a terrible place with a body that would no longer obey his brain, and his efforts and the police efforts were out of synch— they saw each other but didn't understand each other, couldn't match the right need with the right response.

We watched, stunned, as the boy tumbled out of the bullet-busted glass and down the wall, trailing a bright smear of blood before he smacked onto the roof of the armored vehicle and lay still.

Kerri covered her face with her hands.

"No more," she said. "No more, please, turn it off."

Her father turned off the television and then looked back at us. His face had that same stricken angst we'd seen from Mr. Doig. Jerry Flanders was desperate to make it better. We were kids; we shouldn't have to see this tragedy. Out in Littleton, Colorado, they were kids; they shouldn't have to live through this tragedy.

Or die in it.

"I'll tell you one thing," Jerry said in a voice that sought the ring of authority but couldn't find it, "it'll never happen again. Not in a school. Not after this one. We will not let this shit happen again."

He was grim and sincere and we believed him. The bodies of children lay in their cooling blood inside a high school library, and police in an armored truck tended to a boy who had a bullet lodged in his brain, and it was the United States of America in the year 1999, and, yes, we absolutely believed that people with power would make it stop.

Those were different times. You couldn't fool today's kids the same way.

CHAPTER FOUR

THE BYSTANDER

May 1999

**"Listen, you hear the difference between
science and science fiction..."**

REFLECTION ETERNAL
"GOOD MOURNING"

1

I'D LOVE TO TELL YOU that we came together for coalesced grieving after Columbine. I don't remember that, though. It was a conversation topic, sure, and chatter about Eric Harris and Dylan Klebold and the Trench Coat Mafia and other facts and fictions swirled in the halls at school, but it didn't dominate our lives the way it should have, maybe. There were adults in charge, adults and institutions who weren't going to let it happen again. We were sixteen years old and learning a lesson about tragedy: the one that lingers longest is always the one that's closest to you.

Meredith Sullivan was closer to us.

Everyone had a theory about her disappearance. It seemed as if everyone in Bloomington suddenly knew someone who knew someone who'd heard something about her. Much of what people claimed to hear was derogatory to the victim. She was using drugs at work; no, she was selling drugs at work; her boyfriend was an abusive asshole; no, she'd cheated on her boyfriend with another abusive asshole. Her parents were poor white trash; no, her parents had taken out a massive life insurance policy when she went away to school. And what was she doing wearing those shorts and that top in February? Begging for attention, and she got it.

I inhaled each story. I wish I could pretend otherwise, that I floated above it all, dismissive of the human vultures. I didn't, though, and I heard more stories than most because I was the last person to see her. Meanwhile, my role was being lauded by the media. Several commentators suggested that I'd narrowly escaped being a victim, myself. That should have been terrifying—and it was, when I was alone at night, remembering Maddox's venomous voice—but during the day, among my peers, a near escape was only more cachet.

What if?

I'd touched tragedy and stepped clear. People were fascinated by that. Everyone loves a survivor story.

While I told my story, again and again, I didn't tell anyone that at night the strange dreams still came for me, that I found myself facing that weathered red barn in the overgrown wheat field beneath the dark, coiling clouds, and that I could hear fingernails scraping over the boards on the other side as I chased an unknown presence.

Except she *was* known to me by then. I was convinced that the sound from inside the barn was Meredith Sullivan. I never saw her in those dreams, but I knew her. Each night I chased her, the dizziness swirling, the heat rising.

Talk, I wanted to scream. *Say something!*

But there was no sound save for the whistling wind and the frantic fingernails on warped wood.

On the first Monday of May, I returned to driving after three weeks of leaving the big Oldsmobile parked in the driveway. The joy I'd felt alone behind the wheel on the first day had been extinguished by Maddox, but I couldn't go much longer before my mother began to worry that something was wrong. So I drove, but I was overly cautious, pegging the cruise control at two miles per hour over the limit and always watching the rearview mirror.

That week my mother went to work early and stayed late. A storm cell over the plains swelled and burst and tornadoes rippled out like bees swarming from a nest. Over the course of the week, 154 tornadoes touched down, including 72 on one day alone, one of them an F-5 in Oklahoma with some of the highest wind speeds ever recorded. By Friday, fifty people had been killed across four states, and the damage estimates exceeded one billion dollars, even more than the construction cost for the new Mandalay Bay resort in Las Vegas.

It was terrible, but it was a break from some of the Columbine coverage.

That was also the week that Kerri told me her parents had separated.

"Mom says he's drinking too much and not serious about work; he says she just wants to be with someone who has a better job. They're both right."

We were in her basement, watching my mother "interrogate the storms" that thus far had spared Indiana. I was stunned by Kerri's news. Jerry and Gwen felt like family to me, and while I knew they had their arguments, I had never imagined them separating. Breakups felt like kid stuff to me; adults hung in there together.

Then again, I'd never known more than one parent.

"Where will you live?" I asked.

Kerri shrugged. She looked exhausted, numb.

"For now, he's here, and she's at a friend's house. She talks about getting an apartment near campus so she can walk to work. I don't know."

"They just told you?"

"It's been a few weeks."

"What?" Now I was beyond stunned—I was betrayed. It was huge news, and she'd withheld this long?

"You've had a lot going on," she said.

"Not like this, Kerri! This is personal."

She shot me a look that said, *Exactly, dummy,* and I understood then. There's a difference between saying that people feel like family and actually being family. It still hurt, though. Kerri and I had shared so many secrets for so long.

"I'm sorry," I said.

"I know. It happens, right? I mean, how many of our friends have divorced parents? But I always thought . . ." She shook her head. "Everyone always thinks it's going to be someone else's family." She pointed at the TV. "Or someone else's apartment getting leveled, someone else's school getting shot up, someone else's daughter disappearing. We don't have twenty-four-hour news because we need it; we have it because it's easier to stare at other people's lives than look at our own."

I didn't know what to say to that, so I stayed quiet. She gave a little laugh.

"How's that for deep thinking? Yeah, right. The point is they're splitting up, and it's going to suck, but I'll be okay. And if it's any consolation, you're the first person I've told."

I was embarrassed by how much that mattered to me.

"Do you know who you're going to live with?"

"No. That hasn't come up yet. It will, though. There will be 'A Big Talk.' That's how my mother describes every damn thing now. We are in a series of Big Talks."

"What will you say?"

She sagged back in her beanbag chair, looking skyward, her dark hair spilling over the gray leather, and let out a deep breath.

"I don't know."

It was quiet except for the sound of my mother's voice describing a rising pressure system that was heading east. Kerri flicked her eyes over to me.

"You got nothing for me? No life advice? Come on, Coach."

She was trying to joke, but the smile didn't reach her eyes. I had *no* idea what to say. I wanted to tell her how much her parents meant to me, too, and how sad I was to hear this, but that would make it all about me. I wanted to tell her it would be fine, but it wouldn't be fine, it would suck, just as she'd said. It was a life-altering event.

"Honk and proceed with caution," I said.

For an instant, I felt like a fool, but then the smile reached her eyes.

"That's the wisdom I was waiting for."

"Words to live by," I said.

"Absolutely. Life's an elevator, Marshall. Sometimes it must go down before you can send it back up."

We laughed. It wasn't much of a laugh, and it didn't last long, but it felt good, and it mattered.

Then Kerri stretched and stood. "I've got to head out."

"Off to see Jolly Jake Crane?"

She arched an eyebrow. "What does that mean?"

"Nothing. He's very friendly. Big waver. I appreciate that."

"He's polite."

"Exactly."

She studied me for a moment, then turned away as she said, "Give my regards to Lovely Leslie Carter."

"And what does *that* mean?"

"Nothing. She's very beautiful. Big laugh. I appreciate that."

"I'll let her know."

She picked up the remote without looking at me, then turned the TV off as she said, "If she needs clothes, by the way, I've got some old ones she can have."

"*What?*"

"I just notice that the poor thing doesn't have many shirts that go all the way to her waistband. That seems chilly."

She looked at me then, and her smile was so wide and pleased that I had to laugh. I threw a pillow at her, which she caught with one hand, and then she squeezed the pillow to her chest and turned serious.

"Thanks for listening to me."

"Thanks for telling me. And I'm sorry."

With the TV off, it was quiet and dark in the room. She'd said she needed to go, but she didn't make a move to leave. It was silent and still and somehow felt electric. I wanted to hug her—no, hold her. But I didn't know what *she* wanted. I didn't move and I didn't say anything, but then she nodded as if I had spoken. She flicked the lights on, stepped toward me, still hugging the pillow to her chest, and extended her fist.

"With caution," she said, mock formal.

I bumped her fist with my own.

"With caution," I agreed. It was already part of our routine, this inside version of an inside joke, the shorthand language of our friendship. There were a hundred things like it, words that wouldn't make sense to anyone else in the world but would always make us smile.

I left her there in the basement, and by the time I got to my car, I could see the red light of her exit sign, and I could hear the shower running through the open window, and as I looked at her house and realized that she might not be there by summer, I felt a lump in my throat. She'd hung the exit sign to prepare her parents for life on their own when she left for college, and I knew that she had pictured them in this house, and together.

I went home and put on the TV and watched the cameras bounce between Oklahoma and Colorado and people who had it worse.

2

THE HIGHLY PUBLICIZED witness account of Marshall Miller in Bloomington, Indiana, didn't produce a damn bit of progress in the investigation of
Meredith Sullivan's disappearance.

As the weeks passed and no leads panned out, regular police brief-
ings on the case dissolved into "No comment" responses. The posters
multiplied while the articles dwindled. My friendly police contact, Ron
Walters, now took his time responding to my calls, and he didn't offer
anything resembling an update when he did. People stopped asking me
to describe Maddox. They'd heard it by then, and nothing was changing.

Old news.

Spring moved along.

My brush with the big story reminded me of when I'd stepped over
the rattlesnake, blissfully unaware, then left with nothing but memories
and a story to tell. No consequences.

I was dating Leslie Carter, while Kerri was usually off with Jolly Jake
Crane, who would make his cheerful, waving way down the street. His
silver Volvo was equipped with a feature I'd never seen before: little windshield wipers on the headlights, ostensibly to clear snow or road spray,
and certainly to drive up the sticker price. He liked to flick them on when

he was departing even in dry weather, so his car itself looked like it was waving at me.

Sometimes he would pull into my driveway with Kerri and we'd all talk. It was okay. He was a nice guy, and I couldn't hate him, but I wasn't comfortable asking Kerri questions about her parents in front of him, and I couldn't get past the irrational sense that he was intruding on the conversation. Graduation loomed for Jake. I wouldn't be sorry to see him head back west.

Jerry Flanders was still working for the radon-mitigation company, Eliminator, driving a battered white panel van filled with pumps and hoses and compressors. The company let him drive it home, which was a good thing, maybe, but I struggled to see it that way. It felt like a mobile billboard advertising his disappointment. Gwen was almost never around.

One night toward the end of May, Leslie and I walked down Kirkwood Avenue and got ice cream from White Mountain, across from Peoples Park, where the skateboarders and protestors hung out. A college town is never short on protestors. The causes change but the energy remains. I think that's probably a good thing.

The park was near the beautiful Sample Gates that mark the western perimeter of Indiana University's campus, twin spires of limestone above brick sidewalks, looming over Kirkwood Avenue like sentries. While they were a small marker of a massive campus, they felt like the formal entryway. They also conjured a sense of separation: college on this side, town on that side. The IU semester was done, the chaos of graduation and move-out and raucous parties giving way to overflowing dumpsters and couches abandoned on sidewalks. Shoes hung from telephone lines in all directions, tied together by their laces and then flung over the lines in a bizarre farewell ritual of unknown origin.

It was a change that townies looked forward to—you could park anywhere you wanted!—but always struck me as eerie, how the lifeblood drained from the town so quickly. Everyone knew it would be restored in the fall, so they enjoyed the low-key tone of summer, but there was an element of a lost city to it, the purposelessness of a place built to support something that was no longer in action. It made me think of Otis Elevator and RCA and Westinghouse, leaving empty buildings behind like oversized gravestones.

"It's weird without the students," I said as Leslie and I walked through the quiet campus.

"In a good way," Leslie said. "Summer."

She held my hand lightly in hers. She was wearing white shorts and a pale blue tank top and her skin was bronzed with the early stages of a deep summer tan.

"I know. But the emptiness is only nice because people know it's temporary. Imagine if they closed the school for good."

"You're cheerful." She let go of my hand.

We followed the winding brick path beneath the tall oaks and beech trees of Dunn's Woods, then traced the banks of what was then called the Jordan River. It was little more than a meandering brook, but it was pretty, cutting right through the heart of campus, and in a hard spring rain it could thunder with whitewater. We walked past Bryan House, where the university president lived, and then the Lilly Library, where some of the rarest books in the world were housed, from an original Gutenberg Bible to the first printed collection of Shakespeare's works to George Washington's handwritten letter accepting the presidency. It also housed the collections of the Mystery Writers of America, which were about to become important to me, though I didn't know it yet.

On past the Lilly Library and the Showalter Fountain, the Arboretum waited, eleven acres of pristine landscaping that featured trees from around the world, a pond, a meadow, and a stone gazebo. Numerous perfect spots to sit beside a beautiful girl on a warm evening. We settled down on the soft, new grass, listening to the quiet brook. I put my arm around Leslie and she kissed my neck, her lips cold from the ice cream. Her hair fell across my cheek as she kissed the base of my throat and gave my collarbone a teasing nip with her teeth.

"Has your dad heard anything about Meredith Sullivan?" I asked.

Leslie pulled back. "*What?*"

"I was just curious if he'd heard anything new. I know the FBI was supposed to have a profiler working on—"

"You need to stop," she said, gentle but firm.

"I'm sorry," I said. "My mind wanders back to it a lot. To her. And . . . him."

The carillon was sounding, the big bells playing the song of the hour as the clock struck eight. Leslie gazed off in the direction of the sound and her expression softened.

"I can't imagine what it feels like to be the last one who saw her," she said. "It has to haunt you. And I know you've had all those people calling you, and everyone asking about it, but . . ." She took a breath and faced me again. "You think about it too much. I mean, we're sitting here together, and I'm *kissing* you, and you interrupt to ask what my dad has heard? It's not your job to worry about that. You were a bystander, that's all. Don't let it take over your life."

"I'm not doing that."

Her face showed how unconvinced she was.

"Summer's almost here," she said. "I want us to work out in summer, beyond summer. I want us to last."

I sat up. "Me too. Of course."

"What will you be doing while I'm out at Camp Amherst?" she asked.

She was going to be a counselor at a summer camp in Brown County, which was thirty minutes away, or roughly a thousand miles if you're sixteen and your girlfriend is going to live there for two months.

"Thinking of you, of course. Writing sad poetry. That kind of thing."

"Seriously."

I shrugged. "Hanging out. Working. Sleeping. You know . . . summer."

"I might be able to get you a job there. My dad knows the director."

It should have been appealing—making money, the two of us working together by day, sneaking off by night . . . it should have been exactly what I wanted from the summer . . . but something about the suggestion made me uneasy.

"Why do you want me there?" I asked.

"Why do I want you to be with me? Isn't that obvious?"

"Is that the only reason?"

"It's the major one."

"What's another one?"

"I just . . . want you to be occupied, you know? It's good to stay busy. Keep from dwelling on the missing-girl thing."

The missing-girl thing?

"I'm not dwelling on it," I said, "and I've already got a job."

"I'm sure they can find another umpire for the Little League games."

"It's Babe Ruth League," I said defensively, as if the difference between calling balls and strikes for twelve-year-olds or eight-year-olds were that significant. "I'm supposed to help Dom mow lawns too. If he can get that trailer fixed, we'll be able to tow the mowers all over and make some real money."

"So you don't want me to ask about Amherst?"

I wanted the carillon to play again, to give me an excuse to look toward the sound the way she had. Why was I angry with her? She was offering me a chance to spend the summer with her. She wanted me there.

You were a bystander, that's all.

"Maybe," I said. "I'd have to talk to my mom."

It wasn't much, but it was enough to make her smile.

"Great," she said. "Do that! Imagine what it would be like if we had the whole summer together. You haven't even seen Amherst yet. It's so beautiful out there; the sunset on that lake is amazing. We could swim out to the raft together . . ."

She kissed me, lips no longer cold from the ice cream, and I kissed her back and told myself to listen to my body and not my brain, which is a very simple order for a sixteen-year-old male to follow. It was a nice night, after that. It was mostly a very nice night.

Keep from dwelling on the missing-girl thing . . .

I got Leslie home late, and her father came out and pointed at his watch and I nodded and lifted a hand in apology. I should have gotten out to speak with him, but I didn't, and not because I was afraid of the lecture about getting his daughter home on time.

I was afraid that I wouldn't be able to keep from asking him questions.

Bystander, Leslie had said. I'd spent the semester studying root words for the SAT, immersed in Latin and Greek derivatives, and while nothing so sophisticated rose to mind in this case, the origin felt clear enough to me: "by" as in "goodbye."

So long, see you.

The story of Maddox had started with me—started *because* of me, from the media perspective—but now it continued, and I'd been left behind. That was good, of course. That meant I was safe.

But I couldn't shake the memory of the girl's face in the mirror, or Maddox's voice. My girlfriend didn't want to hear about it; the girl who might want to hear about it was off with her own boyfriend; my mother would be gone until late in the night, and I certainly didn't want to tell her about my nightmares. The people who might listen were gone; the people who were available were tired of listening.

Maybe it was time to embrace the idea of being a bystander. My mother would not only support my taking the counselor job at Amherst Woods, she'd be delighted by it, because it meant fewer nights home alone with the potential to get in trouble. I'd make good money and I would be with my girlfriend. The "missing-girl thing," as Leslie had termed it, would fade into the past where it belonged. I promised myself that as I turned onto Raintree Lane.

But I didn't talk to my mother about Amherst Woods over breakfast the next morning, and when school let out that afternoon, I went to visit Noah Storm.

3

WHEN I WALKED UP the massive limestone steps beneath those looming lightning rods, I realized I should have called. I hesitated at the door, almost losing my nerve, then rang the bell.

Noah greeted me with a smile and no trace of surprise, as if my visit had been expected.

"Marshall! How are you?"

"Fine." I parted my lips to offer some reason for my visit, but he was already walking away from the open door as if expecting me to follow. His office was one room in a large house, but it felt as if it were the only place that mattered. I wasn't even sure if he was the only tenant or if he lived there.

"No leads," Noah Storm said, leaning back in the leather chair behind his desk and propping his feet up, answering the unspoken question casually. "No *promising* leads, at least. Everyone has a theory, you know. But in terms of helpful evidence?" He shook his head.

"That's the way I feel," I said, and then flushed, embarrassed by equating his professional work with my high school experience. "About the theories, I mean, that everyone claims to have heard something."

He nodded. "With a sensational crime, the problem is never silence. I'm checking it all out, and obviously the police are running their own investigation, but . . ." He spread his hands.

"Nothing yet."

"Nada." He loosened his tie and took a breath, his chest filling under the crisp white shirt. He was dressed almost exactly as he had been when we first met. This shirt had a faint blue pinstripe, but the difference was negligible. I felt as if he would look this way if you woke him in the middle of the night.

"How are you holding up?" he asked. It seemed like a genuine question.

"Okay, I guess. The reason I came by was . . . well, I don't know, I just . . . in the beginning, I was part of it." I leaned forward, flustered. "That doesn't make sense, but—"

"Sure it does," he said. "You were helping. You were active. Now you've been relegated to a spectator role, and that's frustrating."

"Yes! I couldn't have said it like that, but you're right."

I appreciated that he knew I'd been more than a bystander.

"I guess I had an unrealistic expectation. I thought people would let me know things that . . ." I searched for the right idea, and he provided it for me.

"That weren't public. Of course. You weren't merely part of things; you were the protagonist."

"It felt that way, anyhow."

"Sure it did. That's being a detective, Marshall. The story doesn't move without you."

"It's got to be a cool job," I said, gazing around his office.

"It is nothing like the movies, but there's also nothing I'd rather do. No day is the same, and for a curious man? Well, it's the dream job. A good detective is a perpetual student." He grinned. "That might not sound like fun to you."

"I was surprised by all the books in your office," I confessed.

"You were looking for guns and bourbon bottles, eh?"

"I knew it wouldn't be like *that*, but I wasn't expecting this either." I hesitated, then plunged ahead. "Is there a way to learn the business without having to be a cop or in the military or whatever?"

"Sure," Noah said. "But to be any good, it takes time and it's humbling.

Anything worth doing in life meets that criteria. Detective work has one essential requirement: a willingness to admit that you might be wrong. Being observant and quick on your feet is nice, but self-doubt is mandatory. You *will* make mistakes, you *will* go down the wrong road with the best of intentions and the soundest of reasoning, and then you *must* acknowledge the mistake and start over. Think you have that in you?"

"My mother forecasts the weather," I said. "I understand what it's like to get it wrong more often than you get it right."

His rich laugh boomed through the room.

"Not bad, Marshall." He smiled and nodded at the bookcase behind him. "Borrow any book you want, if you're curious about the profession."

I shifted in my chair. "Are there any good ones about how to find people?"

His smile faded. "You're not going to find Meredith Sullivan by reading a book, you understand that?"

"I'm not talking about her." As his eyebrows rose, I spoke hurriedly. "I'm not talking about anyone in specific. I'm just interested in how it's done."

He studied me for a moment, then rose and withdrew a volume as thick as a dictionary. The cover said: *The Sourcebook to Public Record Information.* When he passed it to me, I needed to use two hands to accept it.

"You don't have to read it all," he said with a grin.

"Thanks." I looked from the book to him. "Do you ever have anyone work for you? You know, part-time or an internship, like that?"

"I haven't. It's a small shop, Marshall." He tapped his chest, indicating that he was the shop.

"If I could help in some way, summer is coming up, and I've got time."

He rubbed his jaw. "It's a highly confidential business. Everything I do is under a nondisclosure agreement." He lifted his hand before I could speak. "I know you won't tell tales out of school. But you're under eighteen, so there are legalities involved that I've never had to consider."

"If there *is* anything that I could do, I'd take it seriously. I promise."

He looked at me without speaking. I couldn't read his face.

"Let me think on that topic," he said at last.

"Okay. Thanks. It's like you said earlier: I don't want to be a spectator. I'm not saying that I think I can solve this—I'm not an idiot—but I'd
rather understand what's happening than just wonder about it like everyone else."

He twisted in his chair and pulled open the door of a mini fridge.
There were bottles of water and two bottles of Upland beer inside. Upland
has sold tens of millions of beers in the years since, but it was new to the
Bloomington scene that year. Noah tossed me a water and took one for
himself.

"I shouldn't be bothering you," I said, even as I opened the water and
leaned back in the chair, the fat sourcebook to public records resting on
my lap.

He waved that off, putting his feet back up on the desk.

"You caught me at a good time. My eyes are tired. I'm going through
email tips, looking for any that feel legitimate."

"Are there any?"

He shook his head, and right then he did look very tired.

"I expected to have so much more by now. I thought I'd be putting
together a pattern that might have brought her together with this guy,
and instead . . ." He ran a hand over his face. "Hell, I dream about her. It
sounds like some bad cop cliché, but it's the truth."

"So do I," I blurted. "All the time."

He looked at me over the tips of his shoes, one eyebrow cocked, waiting. When I didn't offer anything, he said, "Is it always the same dream?"

How had he known to ask that?

"Marshall?" he prompted.

"Yeah." My voice was scarcely audible.

He took his feet off the desk and pulled his chair up closer. His eyes
were so intense that I had trouble meeting them.

"Me too," he said. "And I don't usually do that. I dream about similar
things, sure, but . . ."

"Not in the exact same way?"

"Never. In these dreams, I'm in the same field, looking out at the same
farm, and I'm close, but I can't see her."

I felt my muscles go loose and watery with fear and, oddly, relief. The sense of not being alone dulled the fear of the surreal shared nightmare.

"It's a farm?"

"I think so. Fields, fences, and a—"

"Barn?" I blurted.

He stopped and stared at me.

"You too?"

"Yes."

We were both quiet then. He took another drink of water. The thick limestone walls blocked all the street noise. There wasn't so much as an engine's purr or a bird's song. It was only Noah Storm and me—and our nightmares.

"We could scare ourselves with the similarities, but any good shrink or rational investigator would point out that our unconscious minds are filling in the blanks," he said. "We don't know what happened to her, but we do have a visual of what's between our town and hers—a lot of farm country. It makes sense."

"Right," I said, though I wasn't as sure.

"Your dreams are none of my business," he said, "but do you mind if I ask another question?"

I shook my head.

"Are you inside of the barn or outside of it?"

Immediately, I envisioned the weathered red wood painted with shadows from the turbulent clouds, fingernails moving across the other side of the boards like a whisk broom.

"I'm outside but she's inside."

He dropped his feet from the desk and leaned toward me. "You see her?"

"No. I just . . . know she's in there."

"Does she speak?"

"No."

"Then how do you—"

"I hear her fingernails. I can move around from the outside, and she can do the same from the inside, but there are no doors or windows. We're together, separated by this thin wall, but . . ."

"You can't see her and she can't talk."

"Right."

"Do your fingers bleed?"

What an odd question. His eyes were blazing with the concentration of someone who felt he was close to a breakthrough, though I couldn't imagine why.

"They don't bleed, but it seems like they're about to."

"And she can't talk and you don't?"

"No."

"Have you *tried* to speak?"

I frowned. "It's a dream. I don't know how I could try."

"Since it's a recurring dream, I didn't know if you ever . . . prepared for it. You know, psyched yourself up, set a goal."

He was so intense that I felt uneasy. I wet my lips, started to answer, and then settled for shaking my head again. He deflated a little, then nodded and leaned back in his chair.

"What about you?" I asked.

"I can't see her, and I can't hear her, but I know she's nearby. I never get close to the barn. You're ahead of me, I guess. I'm always stuck up on a hill, looking down at it." He gave a short, harsh laugh. "That's why I asked you about getting psyched up. The last couple of nights, I've told myself, *Tonight, I will walk down the hill.* But that doesn't make a bit of difference."

He offered a 50-watt version of his usual grin.

"Some detective, right? No leads, just dreams."

"What about Maddox? I know they were looking for the guy who bought that old, wrecked police car . . ."

His mouth twisted with distaste.

"Neither the car nor the man matches the description you gave, never mind that it would take a master mechanic to restore that heap into anything resembling a functional police car in two months, let alone without anyone remembering the purchase of police lights, sirens, all that. I largely disregarded that one based on the description of the man. I suppose he could have been in one hell of a disguise at the auction, but . . ."

"It's not the same guy," I said.

He looked at me with renewed interest. "Your memory of Maddox is that vivid."

"Yes. And the sketch artist didn't do a good job."

"Oh?"

"I'm sure he's good at the art of it, but I felt like the man I was describing didn't come through, you know?"

He nodded slowly. "Can you articulate what was missing?"

"No. They were asking all the right questions, and I was trying really hard to give the right answers, but the result . . ." I shook my head. "Not even close."

"Have you tried doing it yourself?"

"Drawing him? No way. I'm terrible at art."

"You might be surprised."

I had to laugh. My high-water achievement in an art class was drawing a decent woodpecker. The only problem was that it was supposed to be a swan.

"I don't think so."

"No, really. A good evidence sketch is all about specific shapes and details. You don't have to be Monet to highlight those things."

My face must have showed my skepticism. He pointed at me and stood up.

"We're trying it. An experiment in the name of deductive science! To the basement, Watson!"

"The basement?"

"This place used to be a surveyor's office. There's a pile of old drafting equipment down there. Come on, humor me. It's certainly not the worst idea I've had on this case."

His tone was light, but I read some darkness in it—some guilt—that made me follow him. He wasn't any closer to solving the case than he had been when we met, and if I could help him, I wanted to. Like he'd said earlier, I didn't enjoy being the spectator. It was so much more satisfying to be active.

We left his office, walked down one of the bloodred runner carpets, and descended into the basement, side by side.

4

THE BASEMENT WAS DRY, but the limestone walls trapped the smell of old water, like an archive of floods. Ancient shelves held crumbling cardboard boxes, and mousetraps lined the uneven stone floor, poised to snap even though the bait had either been stolen or rotted away.

"Are those all case files?" I asked, looking at the boxes overflowing with dusty old documents.

"None of them are. Those are all documents about the Stuart family, their quarries, the building of this house. I'm sure it has historical value but I'm not sure who in the world would want it. I can't bring myself to pitch them, though. Someone saved it for a reason, you know?"

He was moving across the room, pulling short chains beneath bare light bulbs that illuminated one at a time. There was a gun cabinet in the corner of the room, and he saw me looking at it and seemed dismayed.

"Locked," he said firmly, "and largely unnecessary for PI work."

I tried to look indifferent, even though I was both scared of guns and fascinated by them. Along the far wall was a drafting table coated in dust and littered with triangles, T squares, and stencils. Noah swept the drafting tools to the side and then blew at the dust, sending it into a swirling cloud that made him sneeze violently.

"Need to do some straightening up down here," he said, eyes watering. "But there's plenty of paper."

He unrolled a sheet of blueprints across the old drafting table, using a straight edge and a T square to hold the edges down and keep them from curling back up. The sheets themselves were blank. He picked through the loose pencils in a fruitless search for one that was sharpened, grabbed a fresh one, and turned to a sharpener mounted beside the doorframe. When he cranked it, spiders scattered. His black blazer was now laced with white cobwebs.

"Believe it or not, I've taken a course in this kind of thing," he said, turning back to me.

"Sketching?"

"Not exactly. More like the art of . . . talking someone else through a sketch."

He came back to the drafting table and stood over it, pondering the bright white sheet.

"Do you need a stool?" he asked, looking around the cluttered room.

"It won't make a difference if I'm sitting or standing. I can't draw anything resembling an actual person."

"No problem, because you aren't going to draw. You're going to . . ." He hesitated. "Remember, that's all. You're just going to remember."

"I'm not having any trouble with that part."

"Then we're in good shape." He stepped back from the drafting table and motioned me forward, handing me the pencil. "It's not about the picture, anyhow. It's about engaging the subconscious. Your conscious mind holds what you *think* is a clear picture. But your subconscious—or unconscious—mind has details you're not even aware of. There are incredible stories of what people can remember when they're properly guided. One detective in an abduction case got an eyewitness to recall a full license plate number."

I took the pencil. Beneath the bare bulb the blank blueprint was a white square above the dark floor, like a trapdoor. Dust motes shivered in the air. The smell of damp stone and decaying cardboard sealed my sinuses and put a pulse between my eyes.

"If the sketch is nothing but a jumble of lines in the end, that's fine," Noah said. "The process that matters is recall."

Recall wasn't my problem—I could picture Maddox's face just fine, it was the translation to the sketch that was the trouble—but before I could object, Noah told me to close my eyes and draw a single line.

"Concentrate on feeling the tip of the pencil against the paper," he said.

It was amazing, how much of a difference it made to simply shut my eyes. To this day, when I'm struggling to paint the scene properly for a reader, I'll close my eyes. The imagined place becomes real. The camera clicks on and clarifies and there are details to the scene that I simply could not envision with my eyes open. The truth is there in the dark, and if you trust that, you'll be able to see it.

"Come into calm contact with the pencil and paper," Noah said, "and move right to left, left to right, right to left, left to right."

Calm contact. A strange phrase, yet one that felt perfect for the task. Like "interrogating the storm." The words mattered. Calm contact was exactly what I felt as I slid the pencil along, drawing meaningless lines. Because I couldn't yet see the outcome, though, they didn't *feel* meaningless. There was a sense of clear purpose in the work if not in the result.

As I listened to Noah's soft, steady voice telling me to draw to the right and then to the left and to concentrate on the feeling of the pencil against the paper, I relaxed, my shoulders loosening, aware of the weight of my head on my neck. The pencil slipped off the page with a soft click, and I brought it back on without opening my eyes. I was still aware of Noah's voice and of the smell of dust and dampness and the sinus pressure above the bridge of my nose, but with each long, whispering stroke of the pencil across the paper, I felt more detached from my surroundings. The soft *whisk, whisk, whisk* of the pencil reminded me of the sound of the fingernails on the barn walls in my dream, but it wasn't frightening.

Not yet.

"Good, good," Noah said. "Now . . . are you ready to think of Corporal Maddox?"

I started to tell Noah that, yes, I was ready, but I felt as if speaking would break something crucial to the process, so I gave the faintest of nods.

"I know you can recall his face. Let yourself do that now. See the whole face. Draw what you'd like of it."

I tried.

"Now recall his eyes," Noah said, voice soft and soothing. "Recall his ears, his nose, his chin. Recall it all clearly and draw what you wish."

Eyes, ears, nose, chin—all these features had been mentioned by the police, and yet there was something different about this experience. I wasn't being asked a question that demanded an answer; I was being given permission to think. Noah wasn't asking for anything, and that made a difference. I felt returned to the scene in a way I had not before. The clarity of the memory seemed to change.

I could see the hint of fine dark stubble that swathed one cheek, as if Maddox had shaved hurriedly and missed a stroke. I could see that while his eyes seemed narrow, that was from the expression, the way he was glaring down at me, and not the reality of his face. His face was broad, eyes were set wide above prominent cheekbones, very different than the way the sketch artist at the police station had rendered it.

"Recall his jaw, recall his mouth," Noah said. "Draw what you wish."

I felt the pencil sliding in a circular pattern as if it had a will of its own, like a Ouija board pendant—no, not pendant. What was the word? Parlay, perchance, pendulum . . . planchette? I was no doubt making meaningless squiggles, but it didn't matter, because I could see Maddox's face, I could hear his voice, I could feel the weight of the car shift as he leaned on the doorframe.

I was there again. I was behind the wheel and Maddox loomed above my left shoulder and I couldn't see the girl in his back seat because Noah hadn't told me to think of her yet, so it was just me and Corporal Maddox—

He said it wrong.

The memory rose rapidly. Corporal Maddox. That was what he'd been, but it was not what he'd *said*, he had stumbled on the word he had said—

Corporeal.

I'd heard him but it hadn't registered, seeming so much less significant than the ticket. Not *Corporal* but *corporeal.* Close to the right word but *not* the right word.

Corporeal Maddox.

"Recall his chin, recall his cheeks," Noah said.

I scribbled on.

"Recall his teeth," Noah said.

The pencil lead broke. I felt it snap, and the feeling triggered an impossibly loud sound in my brain, a thunderclap from deep in an infinite space. I parted my lips as if to shout but my mouth merely went slack-jawed. I tried to open my eyes but the eyelids resisted, like a quarrelsome window shade.

Bright colors, blackness, a rush down a tunnel of rising heat.

Burst of white lights.

Clarity.

Maddox was still there, but he was no longer standing beside my car. He was in farmland—*we* were in farmland, because I was there with him, though he didn't seem to know it. We were standing in a field of dry grass and humid air hung over us like a shroud and everywhere was the sound of buzzing insects, a piercing trilling noise that wouldn't cease, and then thunder rolled over it, a rippling boom that made the earth shudder. Maddox responded to the sound, casting a wary eye skyward. When he did it, I saw nothing but the coiling black mass of clouds overheard. It was as if I'd put my eye to a viewfinder that was locked into his vantage point, the sensation intense and claustrophobic.

He did not know I was there because I was him.

The shrill insect buzz grew louder. Maddox pivoted, looking from sky to earth and taking my eyes with him once more, a dizzying, disorienting feeling, like following a falling camera. We panned over the field and the dense green woods beyond and I knew the barn would be there even before his gaze settled on it.

The barn from the dream stood before us with its high peak and steeply angled roofline and red paint. It was the same barn but there were crucial differences: there were doors now, doors and windows, and the doors were thrown wide, and inside the barn I could see hay scattered across a bare floor. There was a metal pail with its rusted handle stuck upright, and a trail of dark water drops led from the pail to the open doors. The warm wind rose and scattered pieces of straw across the barn floor and swirled them out into the farmyard. They blew at him—or me, or us?—and suddenly it was like staring into a dust storm, the air abrasive, as harsh on the eyes as the droning hum was on the ears.

Maddox lifted one big arm to shield his face and then he ducked his head and turned away and I saw his uniform clearly from his own eyes, the navy blue shirt buttoned tight against his broad chest, the metal name tag glinting bright beneath the shadowed sky, everything as I remembered it but clearer now, and I understood at last what I had not understood in the adrenaline of our first meeting.

The uniform was old. Very old. The fabric showed the weight and texture of an age when the cotton had been milled beneath some smoke-stacks in a New England river town, stretched and dyed and cut, nothing synthetic in the blend, nothing that allowed it to stretch or breathe, and this mattered because of the oppressive heat of the farm and because of that *buzz, buzz, buzz,* why did the buzz matter, what was that insect, what was—

Maddox turned again, away from the wind and toward the sound, and my eyes traveled with his and together we saw the snake.

The black-and-white rattlesnake rose from the trampled grass not far from our boots—boots of old dusty leather, brass eyes, and square laces—and as it retracted its wedge-shaped head, Maddox stepped back. The snake's head separated into two, became twin heads that turned and faced each other, and then the snake itself pulled apart, seeming to peel inside out and then curl back together before separating again, and only then did I realize that there were two snakes, locked in battle.

They were intertwined like a girl's long braid, and their muscles bunched as they struggled against each other. They rose higher as they uncoiled and pressed and sought leverage, surging skyward in some terrible dance. For a moment they paused, heads some four feet above the earth, thick bodies frozen as they assessed each other through dark slanted eyes fixed above widespread jaws. Then they thrashed together with sudden, horrible speed and strength, driving each other down into the grass, twisting and writhing only to elevate again, those two diamond heads facing off, wicked forked tongues flashing as they opened their jaws and swayed and the tips of their tails hammered the air with the shrill *buzz* of their warning rattles.

Maddox looked away from the rattlesnakes, taking my eyes with him, and I wanted to shout at him not to do that, because I didn't want to turn my back to the snakes.

But he took my eyes and fixed them on the open door of that barn with the bright red paint, then panned across to where the pail stood, its rusted handle trapped upright, and then along the dark beads of water that dotted the boards between the pail and the door. Why was he so interested in the damn pail? Behind us, the snakes danced and thrashed and rose and fell, buzzing, buzzing, buzzing, and they were closer now, I knew that, I could hear them rustling in the grass at our feet, each of them as thick as Maddox's arm, but he would not turn, and why did the pail matter more to him than the snakes?

The wind blew again, shearing through the open doors with a high whistle, scattering straw across the barn floor. This time a fine piece of straw contacted one of the water droplets and stuck, and finally I understood why Maddox was looking at the barn floor with such interest.

They were not water droplets.

They were dark splatters of drying blood.

BUUUZZZZZ . . . .

SNAP!

5

"MARSHALL? MARSHALL, are you all right?"

I heard Noah Storm's voice a fraction of a second before I struck the limestone wall with my elbow.

The world boomeranged back to me—the basement, the drafting table, Noah looking at me with worried eyes in the dim light.

"It's just the bulb," he said.

I stared at him.

"Marshall?"

"Yeah." My voice cracked, but it was still good to hear it. It had been a long time since I felt as if I could speak at all.

"It was only the bulb blowing out, kid. You're fine."

I looked up at the bare bulb above the drafting table. It was dark now, and an ash-colored smear was visible inside the glass. The light in the basement came from behind us, leaving it dim but not dark. The house was real, I could speak, and my eyes were my own. Progress.

I looked at my hands as if unsure that they, too, belonged to me, and saw that I was still holding the pencil. The broken lead jutted sideways, torn through the thin wood, like an exposed bone in a compound fracture. My elbow throbbed from where it had clacked off the stone wall. I rubbed it with my free hand.

"The bulb blew?" I asked in a weak voice.

"Yeah. And you jumped like I'd shot off a cannon under your balls. Sorry." He lifted a hand. "Didn't mean to say that, but . . . *damn*, kid! You were so scared, you scared me!"

"Sorry," I said, a strange response, considering the visceral terror that I'd experienced, but in that moment, still dazed and trying to understand what in the hell had happened, the only clear emotion I felt was embarrassment. It was like the time in fourth grade when I'd had a fever and fainted in the hallway while walking to the nurse's office. When I woke up, everyone was clustered around me, worried as hell, and all I felt was confused and ashamed, desperately wishing that I could be alone long enough to figure it out. This was the same except I was still standing and apparently Noah was oblivious to the fact that I'd fainted at all.

Except I *hadn't* fainted. What would you call it? A seizure, a trance? I thought of the snakes again—the two from the vision and the real one from my house—and I shivered.

"Hey, hey, you're fine," Noah said, squeezing my shoulder. "Let's get upstairs, huh?"

"Hang on." I blinked and swallowed, feeling my ears pop as the pressure in my sinuses subsided. "I want to see the drawing."

Noah snorted. "Didn't go so well."

I stepped up to the drafting table. My shadow blocked the light from behind us, but even in the darkness I could see that there was nothing on the blueprint but a series of mad squiggles and nonsensical shapes.

"Told you I couldn't draw," I said.

"Told me you couldn't draw," he agreed affably. "Didn't tell me it would look like you were holding the pencil with your left foot. But what the hell, we tried."

I struggled to smile. He leaned closer, face concerned.

"I've never hypnotized anyone before, or even tried, but I swear there was a moment when it seemed like I had with you. You sure you're okay?"

"Yeah. I kind of . . . spaced out, that's all."

"Well, that's what we were going for. I didn't count on the damn light bulb blowing out like in a John Carpenter flick, but I suppose it suits the house. Let's go upstairs."

"Sure." I started to follow him, then turned back. "Can I have it?"

He looked at me as if I'd lost my mind.

"The picture?"

"Yes."

"By all means."

I went back to the drafting table and tore the blueprint free from the rest and then rolled it tightly. When I got to the stairs, Noah was watching me with a rueful smile.

"Still want to study the art of detection from this master?" he asked.

I nodded, the blueprint clutched in my damp palm. "Yes."

He clapped me on the shoulder and we walked out of the basement. My legs were trembling the way they would after a series of hard sprints— suicides, my old basketball coach called them—and I hoped Noah didn't notice. I wasn't sure what in the hell had happened down there, but it wasn't something I wanted to talk about—not yet.

Maybe not ever.

"Let's get you a bottle of water," he said as we stepped into the hall. The long red runner carpet extended before us, and I thought of the piece of straw stuck in the drop of blood on the barn floor.

"Nah, I'm good. I need to get going."

"You sure? You look pale. I wish I hadn't tried that little game with the sketch. It was a bad idea."

"It's fine. All the dust down there got to me, I think." I rubbed the bridge of my nose. "Can't say I didn't warn you about my artwork."

He laughed, sounding a little more like himself.

"Your disclaimer was accurate. Hey, don't forget the book I was going to lend you. If you actually want it."

"Yeah, I do."

He ducked into his office and then reappeared with the massive *Source-book to Public Record Information* in his hands. He extended it with mock solemnity, like a priest offering a Bible.

"The keys to the kingdom, sir."

I took the book, pinching the blueprint between my arm and my side. When he opened the front door and daylight flooded in, I felt myself exhale from deep in my core.

"Sorry to bother you today," I said, "but thanks for the book, and your time."

"Always, Marshall. And good luck with the dreams. It's nice to know I'm not alone in that foxhole."

This time his laugh was strained.

I walked down the wide stone steps and beneath the towering elms whose survival had astonished my mother, and then I had to set the book on the hood of the Oldsmobile while I fumbled the key out and unlocked the door. It took me a couple tries. My hands were not steady. I tossed the book and the blueprint on the back seat, slid behind the wheel, and started the engine. Something moved in the mirror, and I jerked my head up to see Noah's frame throwing a long silhouette across the lawn. When he lifted one hand in a farewell, his arm seemed to join the outstretched branches of the elm trees. I lifted my own hand and then pulled away from the curb.

I would not tell my mother what had happened. I would not tell Leslie, or Dom, or even Kerri. Putting a story like that into the world felt decidedly risky, like announcing you didn't trust your own mind. As far as the world was currently concerned, I was Marshall Miller, the observant young eyewitness—or bystander—and that was how I wanted it to remain.

When I got home, the phone was ringing. It was my mother.

"I just hung up with Noah Storm," she said.

Shit. He was so freaked out by my episode in the basement that he'd called my mom.

"It's nothing to worry about," I began.

"I know," she said. "I wouldn't mind it if you talked to me *before* you ran around town asking detectives for office jobs, but it's a lot better than other options."

"He called you about a job?"

"Of course. He's a professional, Marshall; he's going to consult the parent. I'll tell you the same as I told him: I'd rather have you answering phones and shredding papers in an office for a few hours every day than just wandering around all summer. But we'll need to talk about the details. Your jeans are *not* going to cut it in a professional environment. I don't know why you insist on wearing clothes so baggy that—"

"Wait—he's giving me a job?"

"Yes, if I approve. Isn't that what you wanted?" Now she sounded as confused as I felt.

"I guess. I mean, yeah. It's why I went over there, anyhow."

"It sounds like mundane office tasks, but I suspect with your imagination, you'll be able to turn it into a far more exciting role when you explain it to your friends."

"Sure."

"It'll be good for you to stay busy this summer," she said, and I thought of Leslie, realizing that I had taken Camp Amherst off the board before I'd even intended to.

"Sure," I said again.

"Okay, kiddo, I've got to get to the soundstage. There's lasagna in the fridge. And please bring in the cushions from the patio furniture—it's going to rain tonight."

"I will. Hey, Mom?"

"Yes?"

"What does 'corporeal' mean?"

She chuckled. "Still working on the SAT prep, eh?"

"Right. Do you know what it means? Not 'corporal' but 'cor-por—' "

"Of the body," she said. "A human form. It's the difference between a ghost or spirit and a real person. Does that make sense?"

"I think so."

"Okay. Then take your corporeal butt outside and grab those cushions before they get soaked. And congratulations on your summer job. I'm proud of your initiative."

"Thanks."

She hung up, and I went outside and sat down on a patio chair and stared at nothing, thinking about what had happened in Noah Storm's office until it started to sprinkle. It wasn't a heavy rain yet, but I didn't like the way the drops looked on the porch boards. When I went back inside, I forgot the cushions.

It was that kind of day.

CHAPTER FIVE

A PANTHER AND A PUNCH

June 1999

"I'm in the game now
Brought a couple of cats from the way down"

MEMPHIS BLEEK
"STAY ALIVE IN NYC"

1

OVER MEMORIAL DAY WEEKEND, the state police used the massive national draw of the Indianapolis 500 to expand the push for information about Meredith Sullivan, distributing hundreds of thousands of flyers with photographs of her, as well as the sketch that police had made of Maddox. As part of their efforts, my mother grudgingly allowed me to participate in a national interview on ABC. It wasn't a long interview, so I didn't know why she was so nervous. The race's sportscaster, Al Michaels, conducted the interview, which I thought was cool and my mother thought was odd. Ron Walters sat beside me, ready to answer any questions—and share one new revelation.

For the first time, the police told the public that they had evidence from Meredith Sullivan's dorm room computer suggesting that she had been solicited as a model by a man who identified himself as a photographer from upstate New York.

"The internet is a new and wonderful thing," Ron Walters said, "but we need to remember—and need to be sure our children understand—that it can also be a predatory place."

"The dynamics with this police car are unsettling," Michaels said. "That alone feels extraordinary, even in the light of an extraordinary story. And it raises a question: Is it possible that an active-duty officer was involved?"

I looked to Ron Walters. He paused, then said, "Based on the story provided by Mr. Miller, that is of course an avenue that we have to consider."

They put the awful sketch of Maddox's likeness on the screen then.

After the interview concluded, they gave us tickets to the race. My mother was delighted to learn that the winning car had an Oldsmobile engine.

"What did I tell you?" she said, as if my ancient Olds had anything in common with the Aurora racing engine. "Maybe you'll appreciate that car a little more now."

My television appearance helped generate thousands of tips.

None of them led to the identification of the cop who'd called himself Maddox.

I couldn't stop from searching the web, night after night, for any reports or rumors. How was he hiding so well? The sketch wasn't great, but the man had driven a police car and pretended to be a cop! Someone had to know *something*.

School ended on the first Friday of June, and graduation was on Saturday, which meant one thing of interest to a junior: parties. Specifically, Sean Weller's second kegger of the year, to which I actually *was* invited this time.

It was also Leslie's last weekend at home before a summer of teaching tennis lessons to ten-year-olds, and our parting was supposed to feel like one usually reserved for predeployment farewells. My failure to join the staff at Camp Amherst had been offset by my acquisition of what was undeniably the most fascinating summer job among our peers: working for a private detective who was investigating a case of national notoriety. My mother was right in her prediction that I would pitch the gig as more intriguing than answering phones, shredding papers, and emptying wastebaskets. By the time the bell released us on the last day, I'd adopted a noncommittal response as to whether Noah Storm would train me in weapons and high-speed chases.

"It's a confidential business," I would say, a verbatim Noah Storm quote, although I offered it with a flourish that suggested the summer ahead might be similar to Ethan Hunt's. In reality, I hadn't seen Noah since our eerie sketch session. I'd spoken with him by phone once, agreeing that I would arrive at 9 a.m. on the first Monday of summer vacation.

"It might not be high adventure, but it will be an authentic glimpse at the business," he said. "What did you think of *The Sourcebook to Public Record Information?*"

"Uh, it's kind of dry." So far as I could tell, the sourcebook was little more than a list of courthouses and assessors and auditors.

He laughed. "See you in June, Marshall."

And that had been that. He didn't mention the surreal sketching session, and neither did I. I wasn't worried about it, though, and I wasn't worried about working with him. In fact, I wasn't worried about much of anything, mostly because the lasting impact of that terrifying time at the old drafting table was positive: the dreams had stopped.

I waited for the inevitable return of the nightmare, but nothing happened. It was as if, in his attempt to conjure a deeper memory, Noah had inadvertently purged me of trauma. I still recalled the vision of the barnyard, from the weaving rattlesnakes to the straw stuck in the drop of blood. Snakes were a logical nightmare for me that spring. I believed the one true achievement of Noah's effort had come in the moments prior to the nightmarish hallucination—it was the word "corporeal," the way Maddox had stumbled over it, or into it, while trying to say "Corporal." While it was evidence, I didn't see what help it would be to the police, who already knew that Maddox wasn't anyone's corporal, and who cared if he'd mispronounced the word once?

I was less sure about the old uniform shirt. That memory felt useful; it could target a search for the costume he'd donned before climbing behind the wheel. I called Ron Walters once and left a voice mail explaining that I'd been thinking about it and suspected maybe Maddox had been in an old-fashioned police shirt. Walters didn't get back to me.

I was fine with that. I was having fun, hanging out with friends, playing golf and pickup basketball, dating Leslie. I was even able to keep my mouth shut about the case when I was with her, shifting to a total focus on her, a technique that paid dividends. I was allowed to put my hand up her shirt, then to remove her shirt, and then, on the last weekend before the end of the school year, the bra finally fell, a revelatory experience from which I hadn't properly recovered in time for final exams, leaving more than a few grades uncertain. On the night of Sean Weller's grad party, Leslie and I were supposed to leave early for a romantic hour on the boat ramp at Lake Monroe, an encounter that would solidify our commitment across the months of summer, and I had visions of belt buckles parting at last.

The party was held in the same field as before, and I still couldn't fathom that there would ever be houses on that old farmland bordered by forgotten quarries, let alone the sidewalks and stormwater grates and manicured lawns that exist there now. They're lovely homes, fetching seven figures these days, and I loathe all of them.

Sean Weller had upgraded—his term, not mine—the beer selection from Busch Light to Keystone Ice, and people were duly excited by that nice, crisp dishwater flavor. I had no intention of drinking because I was driving, so I parked in the back of the field.

"Nice car, Grandma!" Aaron Corbett hooted as he bounced up in a Jeep Wrangler, his red hair and freckled face lit by the dash.

"Remember when you chose, of your own free will, to play the piccolo in seventh-grade band?" I asked. "Because I do."

"It was the flute, and my mom made me pick it," he snapped, and the Wrangler rolled on. I was halfway across the field, able to smell the bonfire but not see it, when two thunderclaps cracked behind me, followed by an aggrieved bellow that could come only from the Beast's exhaust. I turned to see Dom pulling up with Nadia Langley riding shotgun. They were a serial off-and-on couple. I liked Nadia and never understood why they couldn't figure out their relationship status for more than three weeks at a time.

"Put your thumb out like a hitchhiker and I'll let you ride in the back," Dom said.

I put my middle finger up. He laughed and pretended to pull away, then stopped so I could clamber into the back of the Beast.

We bounced along across the recently mowed field, which had a sweet, summertime smell I'd always loved. It reminded me of what my mother said about freshly cut grass: "It smells like a kept promise." The low valleys were filled with fireflies, and the breeze that stirred the air was the right kind of humid, the kind that told you most of the summer still lay ahead, with all its potential.

I could have sat back there and been pleasantly lost to the perfect evening, but Dom was shouting at me and blasting the "No Scrubs" song from TLC that Nadia favored. His big summer plan was the installation of a periscope in the Beast. Nadia was convinced that was not only insane but likely illegal, but Dom was undeterred.

"It's safer than having *only* a windshield," he said. "Last winter, when my hood latch broke off, the hood flew up and I couldn't see anything. I'm lucky that I remembered which side of the road you're supposed to pull over on. If I'd pulled a Marshall Miller, I might have been killed. But with a periscope, the situation is a nonissue. The hood flies up, covers the windshield? No problem: I pivot to the periscope." He mimed the head shift with both hands framing his face, like a dance move. *"Boom-bam,* solved it, ma'am!"

Nadia groaned, I laughed, and we blasted to the fire through a cluster of low-lying thornbushes that lesser vehicles had skirted in favor of the clear path.

The crowd was large—at least twice the size of Weller's April blowout—and I recognized most of them, but when my eyes landed on Kerri, I was surprised. She rarely showed up at a party like this, seeming to float above them—not in a haughty way, but as if she simply understood something about the spectacle that the rest of us didn't. I started toward her, then stopped when Jake Crane returned to her side with a cup of beer in hand and slipped his arm around her waist. He caught my eye, smiled, and lifted his beer in a wave.

"Yeah," I muttered to no one, giving him a lackluster salute and turning away. He'd graduated and would be gone soon, and while that shouldn't please me, it did. Usually the keg or the fire drew people, but tonight everyone seemed to be focused on something behind the fire. A high scream broke the night, one that raised the hairs on my arms.

"The hell was *that?*" Dom said.

"No idea," I said. The back of my neck was prickled with gooseflesh, but everyone who could see the source of the noise reacted as if it were either hilarious or impressive, not scary.

We walked forward, slipped through the crowd, and discovered the origin of the excitement.

There was a circus cage on the ground between two pickup trucks, lit with work lamps clamped onto the tailgates, and inside the cage was a live cougar. Strung above it was a banner that said: *Panther Class of 1999, Bitches!*

"Is this for real?" Nadia asked, frowning.

"Kenny Glass's uncle owns that, and Kenny's right there." Dom pointed him out for her. Kenny was a big guy who'd played on the offensive line for South after transferring from North. North had lost nearly every football game we'd played that season, and South had won all of theirs, so it wasn't much of a rivalry. My knowledge of Kenny, who'd ended up in our class after being held back in the fifth grade, was limited to his fondness for making "Miller Time" jokes about my mother. He was disappointed that he couldn't get under my skin with them, but I was battle-hardened to that shit.

"He *owns* a cougar?" Nadia said. "That's illegal."

Dom looked to me, questioning.

"It should be," I said. I wasn't sure.

Inside the cage, the cat pinned its ears back and paced—or, rather, tried to pace. The cage wasn't large enough to allow that. The cat could turn, take a step, and then turn again. That's what it was doing now, whipping back and forth, crouched low, muscles coiled beneath almond-colored skin. It wasn't a big cat, really, all paws and tail and incredible gleaming eyes with an intimidating quality that was undermined only by the bars of the cage. Some people were laughing and some people seemed disgusted and Kenny Glass smirked with satisfaction.

A huge hand slammed down on my shoulder, and beer-scented breath blew into my face.

"Well, Marshmallow, what do you say to this? A *panther*, man! Think anybody else has one of those at their grad party?"

Sean Weller in host mode.

"It's statistically unlikely," I said.

He laughed as if that were the funniest thing he'd ever heard and slapped me on the back.

"Where's your beer?"

"Getting it soon. Whose cat is that?"

"Glass's uncle owns it, for some reason. It's cool, right?" He sounded vaguely unsure.

"I guess."

It didn't feel cool, though, even if it was legal. It felt sad.

"Man, you need to update your Away messages!" Weller barked. "You never finish shit. It's like a good movie with no ending."

"Sorry."

"The Weller hates to wait," he said.

The Weller?

"Sorry," I repeated.

"You gotta learn how to wrap 'em up." He drained the rest of his red Solo cup. "I'll keep reading, though. You'll get there. Besides, you were the one who saw that kidnapped chick. It's probably not smart to be making jokes right after that."

He belched and lifted his empty cup. "Gotta replenish the Weller," he said, and vanished in the direction of the keg.

I turned to speak to Dom and saw that he and Nadia had walked off to join a group of kids who were smoking in the trees, passing a lighter that threw sparks as amateurs snapped at the wheel in search of a flame. I knew Nadia would smoke a little weed and enjoy it, and I knew Dom both wouldn't smoke it and wouldn't care who did, impervious to peer pressure in that effortless way of his. I was standing there, hesitating halfway between the bonfire and the smokers, when Leslie called my name. She jogged up to greet me, her smile wide, eyes bright in the firelight. I kissed her.

"You look amazing," I said, and she did. She was wearing a black skirt and dark red top and generally looked far too good for a bonfire in a field.

"Do you really want to stay here?" she asked.

"No."

"Great. I want to say hi to, like, five people, and bail. Then . . . the lake?"

The skirt seemed suddenly far more important.

"Definitely," I said, and my voice was a little hoarse.

She smiled, and for a moment everything was just right.

"Check it out," Kenny Glass said loudly. "I'll make her scream. That shit is wild."

I looked back to see him approaching the cougar in the circus cage. Kenny had a three-foot-long piece of rebar in his hand, and the cat flattened her ears and hissed.

"Oh, shut up," Kenny said, and gave the cage a whack with the rebar. The metal shuddered, and the cougar crouched lower and showed her teeth. Some onlookers murmured and pulled away; others rushed closer. When Kenny ran the rebar across the bars, the cat growled from deep in her chest. Then he ran it back with a flourish, like a pianist playing from one end of the keys to the other, and the cougar threw her head back and screamed. It was an awful sound, even knowing that it was coming.

"He's an idiot," Leslie said with disgust.

"Yeah."

"Let's get out of here. I don't want to watch him torment that cat, and it's stupid to have a party like this on graduation weekend when the police are already looking to bust them."

Lieutenant Carter's daughter wasn't wrong about that. I took her hand and turned from the scene, and we'd gone about five steps when I heard Kerri's voice.

"Do you actually think that's funny, you ignorant prick?"

I stopped walking while Leslie continued, and her hand slipped from mine.

I turned back and saw that Kerri was right in Kenny Glass's face. Jake Crane was nowhere in sight.

"Relax, PETA," Kenny said, and a few people laughed. "It's not abuse. No animals were harmed in the making of this party."

"The hell it isn't abuse! You think she's *enjoying* this? What is the matter with you?"

"Get out of my face, bitch," Kenny said, his voice a dark warning.

"Marshall," Leslie said, "let's go."

"Hang on."

"No. Marshall, he's an asshole, and he always want to fight. Let's—"

I started toward the fire without the faintest idea of what I intended to do. Kenny Glass was built like a man—a strong man—but he wasn't going to hit Kerri. Not in front of a crowd, at least. Even at that age, I understood that what he'd be willing to do when no one was watching might be worse than when he had an audience. The only sure thing was that he would *always* be happy to hit *me*. Kerri wasn't backing down from him, though, and nobody was helping her.

"Have someone get this poor cat out of here or I will call the police," Kerri said clearly and calmly. She hadn't budged an inch. Kenny towered over her. He reminded me of Maddox in that moment; a muscled-up bully trying to intimidate through size and anger. If Kerri were intimidated, she sure as hell wasn't showing it.

"Did you seriously just threaten to bust our party?" Glass said.

"Take that cat out of here or I will call the police," Kerri repeated. "I will say that only one more time."

"Blow me slowly," Kenny Glass said. "And I will say *that* only one more time."

I was five paces away. I heard Leslie call my name, but I didn't stop.

"Get the fuck away from her," I said, and my voice sounded strong, and that was good. Then Kenny turned and looked at me, and that was less good.

"It's *Miller Time!*" he shouted gleefully. "That's what I shout out when I'm—"

"Banging my mom. Yeah, Kenny, always hilarious. Your jokes from fifth grade still working in senior year. That's impressive. A lot of guys come up with fresh material after their balls drop. Wonder why you haven't."

Kenny's face darkened, and I heard a collective murmur of anticipation that exists only in childhood or sports arenas.

"Step to me, bud," he said. "Do it."

In his eyes I saw the promise that I'd already understood: he wouldn't hit Kerri, but he would be thrilled to hit me. In fact, he *needed* to hit anyone who was acceptable, and here I was, putting myself on a tee for him.

"Just stop being an asshole," I said, and my voice was not strong this time, and he grinned with savage delight.

"Marshall," Kerri said, "don't."

"Yeah, Marshall," Kenny said in a falsetto, striding toward me. "Don't."

I had never been in a real fight before. Nothing that escalated beyond what young kids do, which typically begins with shoving and clumsy jabs and ends in an awkward wrestling match before someone breaks it up. You might get hurt, but never badly, and the pain is fleeting. In my mind, Kenny Glass and I would end up in some similar clench, grappling on the ground, and then people would break it up—and while it would surely hurt, it wouldn't be *that* awful.

This was my hope.

When he punched me in the face, I didn't even get my hands up.

Dom Kamsing swears that my feet left the ground on impact. I believe him, though I don't remember it. The pain seemed to come from the inside out, as if my skull had exploded rather than absorbed a punch. The only thing I remember clearly was the delight in Kenny Glass's face, the horror in Kerri's, and that incredible cannon blast of pain. Then I was tumbling backward and down the hill, my shoulder digging a divot out of the earth, my face slapping the grass.

2

WHEN I OPENED MY EYES, I was upside down and looking up into the cougar's face.

The big cat stood over me, white teeth gleaming, eyes lit like emeralds, and for a moment, as the world reeled and my nose filled with blood, I thought that she looked almost concerned for me.

Then she peeled her lips back, dipped her head, and growled, and I could smell beef mixed with my own blood, and the cougar looked anything but concerned. I was too dazed to remember she was caged, so I scrambled away with fright.

I heard laughter then, and someone yelled, "Oh, *shit*, he got his bell rung!" and the world came back to me. I was crawling away from the cage and Kenny Glass was circling me, taunting me, a chorus of *"Get up, bitch. Thought you were tough. Let's have some Miller Time now, bitch,"* when a deep, enraged voice boomed out.

"What the fuck did you do to Marshmallow?"

Sean Weller was striding down the hill, staring at Kenny with a blend of astonishment and building fury, as if he both couldn't believe this development and was already considering how many tackling dummies would be required to pay for it.

"He's a little prick," Kenny said. "I'm not taking shit from him or her or—"

When Sean Weller hit Kenny in the stomach, he drove the punch up from his thick thighs, putting the whole force of his rising, twisting body into the blow. Kenny doubled over and clutched his midsection with both hands, then retched out a geyser of beer. His eyes were wide and white. Weller grabbed a fistful of Kenny's hair with his left hand and his belt with his right and then ran him downhill and toward the fire.

"He's gonna burn him!" someone yelled wildly.

I rolled onto my shoulder in time to see Weller give Kenny a final heave with an extra lift, just enough altitude to send him up and through the flames instead of down and into them.

As he flew through the fire, Kenny made a high screech that was almost like Dom's laugh. He landed with a bone-jarring crack on the opposite side of the fire, then rolled and batted frantically at his clothes, although they were not burning.

Weller walked around the fire and Kenny curled up tightly, cowering.

"Get up, get that cat, and get out of here," Weller said. "I never liked your dumb ass and I don't have to pretend to in practice anymore. There's no coach watching out for you here. And the chick's right. You're being a prick to that cat. I shouldn't have let you bring it."

With that, Sean Weller turned away from Kenny and looked at the crowd as if searching for another gladiator to challenge him. None did. He walked back around the fire and looked down at me with grim eyes.

"You okay, Marshmallow?"

"Yeah," I said, or tried to say. My mouth filled with blood and when I moved it felt as if sand shifted in my skull.

"You'll want ice on that," Weller said.

On cue, someone pressed a cold package into my palm.

I looked up and saw that it was Jake Crane. He'd taken off his shirt and filled it with loose ice from the keg bucket. His rock-climber-muscled torso was exposed now, and his eyes were kind, as if he wanted to wave.

"Good man," Sean Weller told him approvingly, clapping Jake on his strong, bare back.

Dom and Jake helped me sit up. Around us, people murmured about how hard Kenny Glass had hit me, how they'd never seen anything like it before, exchanging words like "concussion" and "skull fracture."

Leslie pushed through the onlookers, and while there were tears in her eyes, she looked angry.

"You need to go to the hospital," she said.

"He only hit me once," I said. It came out like "He onthly hith me onth."

A couple guys snickered. I spat blood and tried to clear my nose. Jake Crane helpfully moved the ice pack to accommodate.

"You'd be dead if he'd hit you more than once," Dom said.

"I'll be fine," I said, this time a bit clearer. I could breathe through my left nostril. That was nice. Jake's T-shirt smelled of Abercrombie & Fitch cologne. Lovely. I tilted my head back and tasted blood. Over by the fire, two guys lifted the cougar's cage into the bed of a truck while Sean Weller reviewed a checklist of threats with Kenny Glass. It began with broken limbs and concluded with unfavorable futures for Kenny's unborn children.

"You won't go to the hospital?" Leslie said.

"It's a bloody nose," I said. "I'm fine."

She shook her head, disgusted.

"Get him home safe," Leslie said to Dom, rising.

"Where you going?" I asked. I didn't understand why she was so angry.

"I'm leaving. You made your choices."

"Made my choices? That asshole hit *me*! I didn't start a fight. What're you so mad about?" My words came clearer, though each one deepened the pain. "You *agreed* with Kerri!"

"I'm not leaving because I disagreed with her; I'm leaving because you're in love with her, you asshole!" Leslie shouted.

It went silent. The circle of kids around us seemed more stunned by this exchange than by the punch. I looked away from Leslie, saw Kerri staring at me, and then looked back at Leslie.

"Just grow up and admit it," Leslie said. A tear broke and ran down her cheek, and she wiped it away furiously. "It's fine. I mean, it's not fine, it absolutely sucks, but at least . . . be honest. That's not asking too much."

Now *I* was getting mad. I was in pain, and I was embarrassed—both for getting my ass kicked with a single punch and for having my girlfriend call me out in front of the group. In front of Kerri, most of all.

"You were jealous of an abducted girl," I said.

Leslie's tear-filled eyes widened.

"*What* did you say?"

"I could never give you enough attention. That's the only real problem. It always has to be about you."

She folded her arms under her breasts and gave a sad laugh.

"I don't need that much attention," she said softly. "I only need to be real about things. And in reality? My boyfriend is hung up on another girl—one who has her own boyfriend, by the way—and he likes the attention he got from a tragedy a little too much, and I'm somewhere down the list. That's not being jealous; that's accepting the truth. And it sucks. And . . ."

She started to say more, stopped, and shook her head.

"And I'm done," she finished, and her voice broke, and then she turned and walked away.

The pregnant pause that followed felt worse than Kenny Glass's punch. I couldn't look at anyone.

"Um . . . here, dude," Jake Crane said, and brought my hand up to hold the ice to my own face so he could stop doing it.

"Thanks, Jake."

He stepped away and looked at Kerri and made a questioning head tilt, as if asking her if they should leave. She looked at me sadly, and if we were alone in her basement or on the swings out at Hollinger Elementary, I would have known what to say to her.

Out here, with everyone watching, I didn't.

"I'm fine," I said.

She didn't say anything.

"Proceed with caution," I added.

This time it didn't bring the smile to her shimmering dark eyes. It just seemed to deepen the sadness. Jake put out his hand and she took it. They walked toward the fire, and I leaned back and stared into the darkness while the ice melted out of Jake's shirt and onto my swelling nose.

3

ON THE NIGHT I'D HOPED to lose my virginity, I got drunk in a hayfield with a linebacker.

Leslie had gone, and Jake and Kerri hadn't been far behind. Dom and Nadia tried to take me home, but I refused their best efforts and started drinking beer fast as my nose swelled up to the size of and color of a McIntosh apple. The ice melted and I threw Jake Crane's T-shirt into the woods, then felt bad and went to retrieve it and crammed it into the hammer holder of my jeans, which were stained with mud and blood.

I drank another beer. Keystone Ice wasn't so bad. You just needed to acquire the taste.

Kids came up to ask me how I was, and I made dumb jokes in response, telling them how it had been a sucker punch.

"Problem was, he knew right where to hit me—the face. That's the only weakness I've got. It's what kept me out of the Golden Gloves. Maybe the Olympics. Coulda been a contender, but . . . glass face."

They howled with laughter. They were drunk teenagers. It was not a tough crowd. The laughs made me feel better. They brought me more beers and then they brought more friends with more laughs, and I drank all the beers and enjoyed the exchanges, as if they were laughing with me and not at me.

The party began breaking up. A lot of people left early, worried about the police showing. Between the fighting and the cougar in the cage, that was a valid concern.

"Man, I gotta get home," Dom said. "Just come home and sleep it off and we'll tell your mom that I elbowed you in the face playing basketball or something."

"I can't go home yet, I'm still thirsty," I said, trying unsuccessfully to balance a full Solo cup on my head. When it fell and doused me with beer, the handful of idiots who'd gathered around me laughed uproariously, and I smiled as if this were a good thing.

Dom sighed, exasperated. Sean Weller caught his eye and said, "I got him, Kamsing. Go on, get out of here. I'll stay with him."

Dom spread his hands, giving me a *Last chance* look, and I accepted a fresh beer from a stranger. Dom nodded and then he and Nadia walked away and I heard the Beast roar to life and watched its taillights recede.

"He's gonna put a stethoscope in that Bronco," Weller told the small group that remained around the dying fire.

"That's not right," I said. "It's gonna be a . . ." The right word had disappeared, spirited away by alcohol. "You know, the one that helps you see."

"A microscope?" Weller suggested.

"Maybe that was it."

An hour passed, or maybe two, and I was in the middle of a nonsensical rant about how Leslie Carter was cocky because her dad was a cop when I realized it was just me and Weller and the fire was going out.

"Where'd everybody go?"

"Home, you drunk fool." He punched me lightly on the shoulder, and the impact made my skull pulse with fresh pain. "Your girlfriend is long gone."

"I don't think she's my girlfriend anymore."

"Too bad. She's hot. So is Pita, in her own way, but I guess she's got a boyfriend?"

I stared at him. "Pita?"

"The one with the attitude. Got all upset about the panther."

I remembered Kenny Glass calling Kerri "PETA" then. I thought about explaining the insult to Weller, then decided against the effort.

"Yeah, she's got a boyfriend."

"He seems like a good dude."

I did not want to talk about Jolly Jake Crane's many wonderful attributes. I touched my nose gingerly.

"You think my mom will notice?" I asked.

"Notice what? Your face?"

"Yeah."

"Dude, it's gonna be a long time before anyone *doesn't* notice your face."

"Oh." I was dimly aware that this wasn't good. I lifted my beer and realized it was empty. I had never consumed remotely this much alcohol. It had been fun for a while. Everything had been funny and the pain had receded. Now it was coming back, and my stomach was swirling ominously. When I leaned back into the grass, the world tilted and spun.

"Will your dad be pissed that you got in a fight?" Weller said. "Or does he understand guy stuff?"

"Don't have a dad," I muttered. The earth beneath me rose and fell like the open sea.

"What do you mean, you don't have one?"

"I don't know who he is."

I never volunteered this story. I usually settled for saying he'd died when I was a baby. Most people stopped asking questions then.

He cried when he left the boy, I thought, because that was so much better to imagine than a man who was laughing, giddy with relief, making a clean getaway.

"Shit, man," Weller said. "That's messed up."

"It happens."

"I could never get away from my dad. Sports, hunting, hiking around land like this that he was looking to buy—he was always right there."

"Must be nice."

"I guess. But he's trying to make up for something."

"What do you mean?"

"He cheated on my mom when she was pregnant. That's some bull-shit, right? They act like it's water under the bridge now, but I think it's always there. I mean, they both told me about it at different times, all secretive and confessional. So nobody forgets."

"Sorry."

"Think it was with your mom?"

"What?"

"Maybe he cheated on my mom with yours." He was drunkenly serious. "What if we're brothers? Wouldn't that be crazy?"

"Yes. Crazy."

He studied me, then shook his head.

"You're not a Weller. The way you flew around when Kenny hit you? That's not our family stock. No offense, but we've all got a solid trunk, you know?" He pounded his quads with his fists. "A good base. It would be hard to knock us around like that is all I'm saying. It's nothing for you to be ashamed of, just biology." He considered, then added, "And physics, I guess."

"Then we're probably not brothers."

"Crap. Would've been wild."

"Wild," I agreed.

Sean heaved himself upright, staggered to a truck that was parked beside the keg, opened the door, and rooted around in the glove box. When he came back, he held a bottle filled with amber liquid.

"Tell you what you need for the pain in your face," he said. "A little sweet syrup."

"I don't like maple."

"Not real syrup, Marshmallow. SoCo! Southern Comfort. It's a premium whiskey." He unscrewed the cap and took a long swig. "Back in the American Revolution? Soldiers would drink whiskey as medicine because there wasn't any morphine. No antibiotics, no Pepto, no *nothing*. But what happened?"

He pressed the bottle into my palm and looked at me gravely.

"We won the fuckin' war," he said.

It seemed like sound logic.

Ten minutes later I was on my hands and knees, vomiting into the weeds.

Holy shit, I thought as the axis of the earth shifted beneath my grimy palms. *Never again. I will never drink again, not once, not ever.*

Then the smell of the whiskey hit my nose, a fresh surge of vomit hit the back of my scorched throat, and I sagged into the weeds and weakly purged whatever was left in my gut. When it was over, I was sweating, and my nose was bleeding again.

"Weller," I called. "Can you bring me some ice?"

The only response was a loud, lingering snore, a peaceful, almost mellifluous sound.

"It has not been a good night," I told the weeds. They stirred as if in acknowledgment. The sour smell of my SoCo offering rose in the wind, and I turned and pushed myself upright. I made it three steps before my feet tangled and I went down again. It hurt but it made me laugh.

"Try again," I said to no one. "If at first you don't succeed . . ."

This time I crawled. It was easier to keep hold of the tilting and pitching planet from all fours. The fire was down to embers, faint glimmers deep within the smoldering wood. Sean Weller sat watching me from the shadows, his big silhouette even more imposing in the darkness.

"Thought you were asleep," I mumbled.

He didn't speak.

"Not gonna drink again," I told him.

"What is it," a deep voice answered, "with you and second chances?"

I looked up from the embers and saw that it wasn't Sean Weller waiting for me.

It was Corporal Maddox.

He was wearing his uniform, and a police hat with a high crown rested on his lap, the brim touching the handle of the revolver in his service belt.

"You were told," he said. "Were you not?"

I was too scared to scream and too drunk to move. He stared at me with contempt in the faint red-orange glow as the dying fire flared. Then he drew his gun.

"Don't," I said. "Please."

"Please," he echoed, shaking his head as he spun the cylinder out from beneath the short barrel of the revolver. He watched it twirl, the metal flashing in night, and I could see the brass caps of the bullets inside.

"How I love hearing that word after the mistake has already been made. The *choice.* It is a choice, damn it. How do you fail to understand that? You pick your fate!"

He snapped the cylinder shut and looked up again, his face twisted with rage.

"Don't blame the snake when you choose to walk off the path," he said. "I won't listen to that shit. I simply will not. The snake has no role here. Your choices are all that matter."

Then he lifted the gun, leveled it at my chest, and squeezed the trigger.

The world rode away on a bullet.

Blackness and pain.

Impact.

Gray fog parting swiftly, and then I was at the farm from my nightmares again, that terrible, sun-scorched farm. The bullet had blown me into the side of the barn, and I slid down the wall, the coarse wood rasping over my back, and landed on my ass in the dust. It was bright and hot and in front of me the severed head of a rattlesnake snapped its fangs. The head swayed left to right, a frantic, futile effort to engage the body from which it had been separated. It wriggled forward, inch by inch, and the forked tongue flicked, and the jaws clacked at the air beside my bare foot. When it finally died, the slanted eyes on the side of its wedge-shaped head were fixed on me, filled with hate until the end.

4

I WOKE WITH THE SUN full on my face and Sean Weller's massive hand on my shoulder, shaking me.

"Gotta roll, Marshmallow. I'll get the rest of this shit cleaned up later."

I pushed myself upright and looked around. It was morning, and we were alone. The fire was out, and red Solo cups dotted the grass like fallen soldiers on a battlefield. My skull pounded. I lifted a filthy hand and touched my nose. The flesh was spongy, and there was a crust of dried blood beneath my nostrils and above my lip.

"You got your keys?" Weller asked.

I patted my pocket and found the Oldsmobile keys.

"Yeah."

"Go on, then." He looked at the carnage around us wistfully. "It was a good party, right?"

He sounded more than hopeful. Needy.

"It was wild," I reassured him, and nodded, a gesture I promptly regretted as the sand that seemed to fill my skull shifted and lodged in the front of my face, making my nose throb. When I stood, the effort seemed unbearable. After a few seconds the dizziness cleared, and I looked at my car, parked in the far distance, and thought that if I made it there, I would be a hero. It was the Oregon Trail.

And my mother, not the Pacific, waited at the end of it.

"See ya, Sean."

"Later. Here, take a water."

He gave me a water bottle, and I made the trek to the Oldsmobile, pausing once to throw up in the trees, and then dumped myself into the driver's seat and adjusted the rearview mirror to see my face.

Both eyes were black and my nose looked like a conch shell. I could smell vomit on my clothes, and when I assessed the damage, I saw that my jeans were fine but my shirt had taken the damage. Jake Crane's shirt, on the other hand, was tucked in the hammer holder of my jeans, still clean.

I climbed out, peeled off my own shirt, and pulled his on. I put my shirt in the trunk, then rinsed my face and hands with the water Sean Weller had given me. I wondered if my mother had called the police already, or if she was simply calling every friend who might be able to account for my presence. I drove home slowly, my brain seeming to float behind the car at its own pace. I had flashbacks of the night—Leslie's tears, Kerri's sadness, Kenny's delighted rage—but all those memories felt less significant than the dream.

Maddox had shot me.

I shivered. It had been a booze-fueled nightmare, that was all.

But you saw his uniform clearly. It's like Noah said: the unconscious mind remembers. His uniform was old and the hat was old and the gun on his belt was a revolver, not some modern handgun. Maybe that matters.

Sure—the gun a ghost had shot me with in a drunken dream was a revolver. Maybe I wouldn't call police with that big break in the case just yet.

My house was quiet. I parked and gazed around the car, knowing that I would never drive it again. Up the street, Kerri's Honda was gone; the only vehicle in the driveway was Jerry's work van. I didn't mind that. I wasn't sure if I was ready for Kerri yet.

I damn sure wasn't ready for my mother. I took a deep breath and got out and went up the steps and into my house.

My mom wasn't waiting inside the door. I walked into the kitchen. It was empty, but there was a bouquet of fresh flowers on the table. I read the card:

Get Well Soon—From Dom Kamsing and Family

"Marshall?" My mother walked into the kitchen, and when I turned, she gasped and put her hand to her mouth. "Oh, my goodness. I knew it was bad when Dom's family sent *flowers*, but . . . Oh, come here."

Before I was entirely clear on what was happening, she was wiping gently at my face with a wet rag and muttering about doctors and concussions.

"He said he didn't mean to do it," she said. "When he called, he said that it was just basketball and things got out of hand. But you tell me the truth. Was it more serious?"

"Dom said he hit me?"

"Of course." She frowned. "Did you not know he left the message?"

"No."

She went to the answering machine on the counter. A lot of our friends had switched to voice mail, but my mother hated that, said without seeing the blinking light, how did you know you had a message waiting? She pressed Play and I listened to Dom doing a credible impression of a chagrined kid as he told my mother we'd gotten into it on the basketball court and he'd hit me in the face but it wasn't intentional and I was okay, although Dom and his parents didn't think I should drive in the dark.

"We're going to observe him. He'll call you if he wants to come home. I'm really sorry."

I looked at the floor, remembering the way I'd refused Dom's best efforts to get me home, and feeling about one inch tall.

"The flowers made me nervous," my mother said with a laugh. "I was, like, *How bad does my kid look?*" She assessed me and grimaced. "Maybe I *did* deserve flowers. I think we should go to the ER to make sure there's nothing more serious."

"We don't need to do that. I just need to lie down."

"You're sure?" She was looking at me closely.

Oh, yes, I was sure. If I didn't lie down soon, I was going to dry heave on the kitchen floor.

She let me go upstairs. I turned on the shower. Once it was running, providing cover noise, I grabbed the phone and called Dom.

"Thanks," I said. "You saved my ass."

"It was Nadia's idea. You owe me for the flowers."

"I'll pay you double."

"You doing okay?"

"Feel like crap, but I'll live, thanks to you."

I hung up and walked to the bathroom, then stood in the shower until the water began to lose its warmth, got dressed, and headed back to my bedroom.

When I opened the door, I saw that my mother was sitting on the edge of the bed, head bowed, wearing shorts and the old denim shirt she always wore when she was gardening. Her hair was tied back in a ponytail and she looked about sixteen years old herself—until she lifted her head.

Then she was a mom again.

An angry one.

"Did you honestly believe that you could fool me with flowers?"

I knew better than to speak.

"No, no," she said, as if I had answered, "it was a brilliant idea. How am I going to spot a hungover sixteen-year-old when there are *daisies* in the house? Impossible! And then you walked in, saw my worry, saw my fear, and lied to my face."

I swallowed and looked away.

"I'm seeing two options here," she said, her voice cool and clinical. "I can call Dom's parents and thank them for the flowers and ask for the details of the night you spent recuperating at his house after the basketball game, or you can tell me *your* version of the night. In one choice, your friend suffers. In the other . . ."

"Don't call them," I said. "Please."

She nodded, as if that response was both unsurprising and disappointing, which is a terrible blend of emotions to feel from your own mother.

"It is not easy," she said, "for a woman to raise a man. I have always understood this. I think we've done all right, in large part because of trust and open dialogue. You deserve some of the credit. I will be the first to admit that. I will also admit that I am very afraid of the age you've reached and the freedom you have. The choices. I am going to need to figure out how to handle all the fresh risks in this world for you, Marshall, and to do that without our historic levels of trust? That's going to be difficult."

I was suddenly very close to tears.

"I'm sorry," I said.

"For what?"

"All of it. Dom didn't hit me. He tried to take me home but I didn't let him. I slept in a field." I was blathering now and tried to get my words under control. "It was a stupid grad party, and I didn't even want to drink, but then Leslie broke up with me, and so I did drink, and then things . . . got away from me."

It was quiet. She stood and withdrew a package of Alka-Seltzer tablets from her pocket. She tore it open and dropped two tablets into the glass of water she'd put on my nightstand. She was watching them fizz when she spoke again, in a low voice that held the trace of a tremble.

"The worst mistakes of my life . . . I guess I mean the worst days of my life . . . all came after too much drinking," she said. She still did not look at me. "I don't do much of it now."

I knew that. There was maybe one bottle of white wine in our house, gathering dust. I'd never seen my mother have more than two glasses of any alcohol, ever. The idea that she'd had terrible days because of booze was jarring.

"I know what's out there, waiting for you," she said. "I get it. And I'm trying to be ready for it, because we've done too well for too long to become a house of secrets now."

I had to wipe my eyes then before the tears ran down my face. Her disappointment was so much worse than her anger.

"Here's what I know right now," she said, still watching the fizzing glass. "You will get a cell phone. You will pay for your cell phone. Your opportunities to sleep in fields after illegal drinking will come to an end, because you will use your cell phone if you make a bad choice, and I sincerely hope you will not make a bad choice. But if you do, you will call *me*. Not Dom, not Kerri, *me*. Because you trust me, damn it. Because I have earned that."

Now she sounded on the verge of tears, and I nodded, unable to speak because of the lump in my throat.

She took a breath.

"It will be many weeks before you're going to have a free night to demonstrate your maturity again. I don't know how many, but I'd make yourself comfortable in here. You'll be allowed to use the car to drive to your new job. That's it. I'll alert you when things change. If you lobby for privileges, you'll wait longer for them."

"Okay. Yes. And I'm sorry. I really am."

Her eyes searched mine, and then she nodded faintly and handed me the glass.

"Drink that and then get some sleep."

I drank the water, sipping down its bitterness, and then I put my pounding head on the pillow and stared at the ceiling and wondered what experiences my mother had with drinking and why she had caught herself in midsentence to adjust from calling them the "worst mistakes" to the "worst days" of her life.

5

THAT AFTERNOON I MOWED the lawn even though the grass wasn't very high. Any gesture of goodwill would matter. The aroma of freshly cut grass—that smell of a kept promise, as my mother called it—couldn't hurt.

I was done with the cutting and about to fire up the weed trimmer when Kerri came up the street. I set the trimmer down and sat on one of the patio chairs. She touched each of my black eyes very gently.

"He didn't honk first," I said, "and there was no caution when he proceeded."

"None. And then he hurt your honker," she said somberly.

We both smiled a little. Then she sighed and eased down onto the ottoman in front of my chair. She was dressed for a workout but hadn't broken a sweat yet.

"Was going to see if you want to go for a run with me," she said.

We'd done that in middle school before she became all-state caliber and I got tired of chasing her.

"Would if I could," I said.

"I'll go slow."

"Thanks, salt-in-the-wound, but I meant that I'm not allowed to leave the hacienda."

"Uh-oh. Your mom knows?"

I gestured at my face. "It was hard to hide."

"So you told her the truth?"

"Not right away."

She winced. "How long are you grounded?"

"Remains to be seen. The word 'weeks' was used, and I was discouraged from—how did she put it?—lobbying for privileges."

"I'm sorry. Really. I feel as if it was all kind of my fault."

I shook my head. "It was Kenny's fault. He was an asshole, and you called him on it."

"And if I hadn't, you wouldn't have gotten your nose broken, and you and Leslie would have gone off happily into the night."

Leslie's accusation that I was in love with Kerri floated between us. I didn't take the bait. It wasn't as if I'd thought I might win her over by confronting Kenny Glass. She'd left with Jake, and that was that. I wasn't upset with her. I wasn't upset with anyone. Sometimes you earn the punch in your face.

"So you've got to sit at home all summer?" she asked, changing the subject once it was clear I didn't intend to talk about Leslie.

"I'm allowed to go to work."

"You're working?"

That was how little we were speaking in those days. I hadn't even had a chance to tell her about my summer gig. I filled her in, and she smiled.

"I love it," she said. "The rest of us are bussing tables or sitting in lifeguard chairs, and you're the Indiana Op."

"What?"

"The Continental Op was Hammett's character."

"Shakespeare wrote about detectives?"

"Hammett, not Hamlet." She sighed and shook her head. "I'll bring you the books."

"I have plenty of reading time ahead."

She looked guilty at that. "You said Noah's office is downtown?"

"Pretty close."

"Come to the Encore for lunch. I'll sneak you some carrot cake." Kerri worked at the Encore Café on Sixth Street. It's been gone for almost two decades now, and I still miss their carrot cake.

"Thanks," I said. "How's it going with you, anyhow? The . . . family stuff."

She looked reflexively in the direction of her house and the light went out of her eyes.

"It's a grind."

I expected more than that, but she got to her feet instead. "Look, I've got to get my workout done. I really am sorry, though. And I appreciate it."

"Anytime you need a face punched, you let me know."

I walked to the sidewalk with her.

"Since when do you run in the neighborhood, anyhow? Thought you were committed to the forest."

The Morgan-Monroe State Forest was not far from where we lived, thousands of acres of dense timber, including some old-growth trees from the days when Indiana was still wilderness.

"Oh, my dad got all paranoid," she said, grasping the toe of her shoe in one hand and bringing her heel up to meet her butt, stretching her quads.

"Because of Meredith Sullivan?" Lots of parents were paranoid in Bloomington that spring.

"No."

"What, then?"

She sighed. "Snakes."

"Seriously?"

"Yeah. I'm not sure the one you had in your house didn't freak him out more than you. He's talking to snake hunters."

"Snake *hunters*? That's a real thing?"

"Yeah, it's gross. The DNR has someone who does an inventory of timber rattlesnakes. Well, for some reason my dad went to talk to the guy, learned they have dozens of rattlesnakes in Morgan-Monroe, and all of the sudden I'm supposed to stick to the track or the road."

She shook her head, exasperated, as she stretched the other leg. "It's not like they're attacking people. They're eating mice. I mean, I don't want one in my *pantry* like you guys, but I'm not freaked out by their existence in the world."

I remembered the way the black-and-white snake had come down the stairs with its head raised, the soft thumps its body had made as it descended. I felt bad, knowing that Jerry was so worried now. At least he hadn't seen it, though. That was worse.

Wasn't it? Then again, he'd gone into the house in the dark, looking for something that was both frightening and in hiding. That could get into your head too.

The man who called himself Corporal Maddox knew something about that.

6

THE NEXT MORNING was Sunday, and my grounding evidently didn't preclude me from participating in our Sunday morning ritual golf game. My mother was the only reason I played golf; I preferred basketball and baseball but wasn't good enough at either to play at the varsity level. Golf was my game simply because she'd started me on it so young. Her father had been a wonderful golfer—and, she'd told me, miserably disappointed that his only child was a daughter and not a son.

The one area he could make peace with that was on the golf course, she'd said. *Mostly, he left me to my mother and didn't show much interest. But we shared golf.*

And now so did we. It was always odd for me to think about her own childhood, playing with the grandfather I hardly knew in a place I'd visited only a few times, and there were moments when she'd go silent during a round and I would wonder if her mind was back in Georgia, in a childhood that never sounded like much fun. They'd had money; I knew that. My grandfather was a successful stockbroker. Once, I'd made the mistake of asking whether they would help with my college tuition. That was the last time I ever brought up the idea of my grandparents playing an active role in my life, financially or otherwise. They weren't missing, like my dad, but they were almost as absent.

My mother had been a member of the Bloomington Country Club for a few years, back when I was young enough that she'd leave me at the pool with other kids and under the lifeguard's watchful eye while she played a round, but when I was old enough to play with her, she cut costs and dropped that membership for Cascades, the public course, which was closer to our house. Every Sunday that it was open, we went together and played eighteen holes no matter the weather. She always walked and carried her own bag, scorning carts. We went out early, usually the first group off the tee. She said she liked the way the grounds awakened alongside you, and while I knew that was true, I'd also observed another reason she wanted to play early: if we played late, some of the men on the course had been drinking, and then they were more likely to talk to her, or wolf whistle, or simply stare. Once, a balding man with his belly hanging over his belt had winked at me while he watched my mother bend to pick up her tee and said, "Lemme know if you need a stepdaddy, kid."

I had never seen my mother look as angry as she did that day. She turned with a three-wood clenched in her hand and walked close to him and spoke in a voice so soft I could make out only a few of the words. I was young enough that I thought the phrase "redneck peckerhead" might actually be a bird.

The man tried to grin and chuckle his way through it, but I could see color drain from his face, and his boozy buddies kept their distance. When we reached the fairway and I turned back to see if they were teeing off, I realized they'd skipped the hole and moved on.

After that, we mostly played at first light.

On the Sunday after Weller's party, I was relieved by this, because I didn't want anyone to see my battered face. My mother liked match play, although we'd complete the full round regardless of whether the match had already been decided. This morning we played a couple holes in silence, other than the occasional "Nice shot" or "Tough lie." I was typically good off the tee, long and accurate, because driving was all I practiced with diligence. I wanted to have a power game. My mother, on the other hand, had a metronome's rhythm to her swing, never missed a fairway, threw darts with her wedges, and had a better short game than anyone on my team. Nothing pleased her more than a sand save or a perfectly lagged chip. She liked to scramble to success when observers thought the odds were against her.

We were on the third green when she said, "Why didn't you tell me the way the fight started? The kid with the cougar and all of that?"

I looked up from my putter. "How'd you hear that?"

"Kerri stopped me when I was driving. She wanted to claim responsibility for some things, although she's too smart to take credit for your drinking. She also told me about her parents. I had no idea."

She looked stunned by the divorce news, the way I'd felt when I first heard.

"It sucks," I said.

"Stinks," she corrected automatically. "Yes. Kerri told me that she needs you now more than you need her, and I think she meant it."

I hit my putt too firmly and it rolled by on the right. My mother then curled in a tricky six-footer, putting her three up after three holes. I thought she was determined to beat me as badly as she could following my Friday night activities, a subtle way to deepen my punishment.

"It is so sad about Jerry and Gwen," she said as we walked to the fourth tee. "Is she staying at the house for now?"

"I don't think so."

She seemed unsurprised. She teed up, then stepped back for a few fluid practice swings.

"I have decided that you may see Kerri as often as you wish, so long as it occurs on our street. Or as far as you can run with her." Her mouth twitched with a little smile. "She warned me that it was risky to let teenage boys sit idle for too long. You need to release endorphins, she informed me, to maintain your limited quantities of willpower and self-control. She said that she understood that might sound counterintuitive but insisted she stood by the biological argument. That girl is something else."

"Yep."

She shot me an intrigued look. "Anything you want to talk about?"

"Not really." I wasn't being terse on purpose. I wasn't sure of my own thoughts and feelings for Kerri, let alone how to voice them. It had been a confusing couple of days. I had a memory of Sean Weller, drunk in the field, asking me if we might be brothers, and suddenly I had an overwhelming desire to ask my mother one more time who in the hell my father was.

I said nothing, though—simply watched as she launched another arcing tee shot into the center of the fairway. My turn. There were some tall trees on the left, plenty of room on the right, but on a good day I could carry the trees and turn it into an easy birdie hole. I hammered it with everything I had and promptly hit a snap hook into the trees.

"Ugly," my mother observed. "If you humbled yourself and played the course instead of your ego—"

"I know, I know." I trudged after my ball, pretending not to see her satisfied smile.

She was five up at the turn, but I managed to halve the first three holes on the back nine, stemming the bleeding, which didn't please her in the least. She wanted me to bleed this morning. On the thirteenth, my most consistent hole on the course, with a long, open fairway that played well for a distance hitter, I couldn't stop from staring at the place where Maddox had pulled me over, remembering the way Meredith Sullivan had looked in the mirror. Distracted, I hooked another tee shot.

"Good luck getting out of that," my mother said cheerfully. "The rough is high over there. Looks about like our lawn has this spring, although I saw your guilt-induced efforts yesterday."

Zing. I almost told her the truth—I was letting the grass grow longer than normal because every time I mowed it, I found myself freaking out over memories of the rattlesnake that had invaded our house. Instead, I said, "A riding mower could be a lot faster."

The look she shot me made it plain this was the wrong day to make such a suggestion.

"If I need a groundskeeper, I'll pay one. Until then, I've got a reliable push mower and a less reliable son."

By the eighteenth, the sun was high, my nose throbbed, and I was down eight holes, the match play long over except for the humiliation. We both found the bunker on our approach shots, but my lie was clean, and my mother's ball was plugged and short-sided. I'd win the last hole, anyway. Moral victories.

A gleam came into my mother's eye as she selected her 60-degree wedge.

"Closest to the pin for your freedom," she said. "End your summer of solitude with one swing."

"Yeah, right."

"I'm serious. Never make a bet you don't intend to honor. I'll honor it; I'll even light your cigar for you."

These were the moments shaped on a Georgia golf course from her youth, echoes of a chauvinist father who didn't know what to do with his daughter.

I looked at her ball, which was buried behind the steepest ridge of the bunker. Mine was sitting cleanly, with a look at the flag, and plenty of green. She was counting on me to choke.

"Deal," I said, and then I dug my heels into the sand, eyed the flag, and found the focus that had eluded me all morning. I swept the ball out of the sand and onto the edge of the green, where it tracked a straight line toward the pin, stopping two feet away, easily the best sand save I'd had all year.

Freedom restored from a single swing. I tried to hide a smug smile.

"Impressive," my mother said in a tight voice, not looking at me as she adjusted her stance. She was so short-sided in the bunker, the pin located so close, that simply getting the ball up and keeping it on the green wouldn't be easy. A great save would still travel well past the hole. A bad one would roll off the green. This was the problem with counting on me to collapse under pressure. I hadn't, and now she was out of options.

She opened the club face, intending a flop shot right at the flag stick, her only possible play. If she caught the ball fat, she'd chunk it into the sand, and if she bladed it, the thing would be thirty yards past the green before it landed. I grinned, watching as she released the tension from her shoulders and arms and then took a full swing, accelerating through the ball, which burst out of the sand at an impossibly steep angle. The ball popped straight up, such a sky-high miss that I almost laughed. It was going to land right at her feet, and she would be livid.

The ball plummeted back down but avoided the bunker—barely. It caught the top of the ridge by an inch, rolled onto the fringe, and then kept creeping, one painfully slow revolution at a time as it passed my ball, trickling with excruciating pace until it came to rest six inches from the cup.

My mother's smile was positively radiant.

"The summer of solitude continues, my son."

She loved to compete more than anyone else I've ever known. And while she'd bettered my best shot, and that stung, I knew from her smile that the lectures were over. Or I thought so, at least, until we were back in the Bravada. Before she put the car into gear, she looked over at me and said, "One last thing before we leave this weekend in the past."

I braced myself.

"Do not ever send flowers to a woman you've lied to," she said. "I know those were Dom's idea, but I don't care. Lies and flowers were your father's favorite pairing. I will be damned if I raise a son who follows suit."

It was the most she'd ever told me about him. It was also an open door for questions. I couldn't speak, though. I was too stunned, and she was too serious. We rode home in silence.

There was a book waiting for me on the porch, a dog-eared paperback from Kerri's beloved Caveat Emptor, a used bookstore on the square that was owned by a guy named Janis. The book was a collection of the Continental Op stories by Dashiell Hammett, and I read it for most of the afternoon.

The protagonist had no known name. His identity was his role. He was an "operative" of the Continental Detective Agency, and Hammett told the story as if the only thing that mattered was the case, even though you quickly felt as if you knew the character. I liked that. It felt like a gimmick but wasn't; what mattered most to knowing the guy wasn't what people called him, it was what he said or did. Like my mother—who made bets and backed them up.

I thought about my "fight" with Kenny Glass. Fine, my ass-kicking by Kenny Glass. You could call me Marshall or you could call me Marshmallow and that seemed to matter to the story, but it didn't. Sean was the one who called me Marshmallow, and he'd acted like my friend. The name was irrelevant. What mattered about me, I decided, was that I'd stepped up to Kenny.

But it probably also mattered that I'd lost to him.

Badly.

It felt as if Dashiell Hammett was hinting at something bigger. The difference between a name and an identity *was* significant. So why did I care about my father's name? It didn't matter what anyone called him; I already knew what he'd done. He'd bailed. And, apparently, he'd paired lies with flowers. His actions spoke; his name didn't mean a damn thing.

Except it's never that simple, is it? Not with matters of blood.

I read into the evening, went to bed early, and in the morning I reported for work at the office of Noah Storm wearing khakis and a polo shirt at my mother's instructions. My face somehow looked worse after a night of sleep, the bruises deepening under my eyes and yellowing at the edges, but Noah took one look at me and grinned.

"I wasn't going to send you out on process-serving jobs because it seemed like rough work for a kid. Now I won't send you because I don't want people to run in fear before you can hand them the documents."

I didn't understand what process serving was, but I got the gist.

"It was a bad night," I volunteered as he led me inside.

"Looks that way."

No interrogation. It was exactly what I'd expected from him—treating a kid like an adult. We went into his office and he sat on the edge of the desk and considered me.

"I've never had an intern. I've never even had an employee. But I like your mind, Marshall. You're inquisitive, and that's good. It is, in fact, the quality I find most lacking in older people. It's a damn shame to go through life without curiosity."

He went silent, gazing at me with fresh scrutiny, then said, "You're not going to be much use to me unless I can trust you."

It felt oddly similar to the conversation I'd had with my mother.

"You can trust me."

"We'll find out, won't we?"

This was a hell of a welcome.

"I could have you answer phones, but they don't ring often enough to warrant that," he said. "I either put you to work as a genuine help or drive us both crazy finding busy work. So let's get to it. I've got one case that's the utmost priority, and you know which one it is."

Meredith Sullivan. The only case I wanted anything to do with.

"I'm going to ask you to do some work on that," he said, his eyes never leaving mine. "It won't be exciting work, but I assure you that it could matter."

"Yes, sir."

"Drop the 'sir,' Marshall. It's just the two of us." He reached into his pocket, withdrew a key on a silver ring, and tossed it to me.

"To the front door."

It's hard to explain, even now, how momentous that key felt. It was the first time an adult had given me a key as a gesture of trust in me rather than trepidation for me.

"We'll get a confidentiality agreement in ink, but signatures aren't worth a damn," he told me. "I want your word that you will not share any details of our investigation outside these walls. A man's word means everything in a partnership, Marshall."

His easygoing nature faded, and I saw the hardness that was beneath, a trace of a life that I knew nothing about.

"I understand," I said.

"I hope so," he said. "Now let's get to work."

CHAPTER SIX

THE INDIANA OP

June–July 1999

"Driven by my ambitions, desire higher positions . . ."

TUPAC SHAKUR
"UNCONDITIONAL LOVE"

1

A PRIMER ON THE art of private detective work: it's tedious until it's not. You stay attentive during the endless hours so you don't have to pause to think during the crucial seconds. It's an endurance game, a concentration challenge, and nobody can focus for you. Self-starters required; all others need not apply.

These were central themes I learned from Noah Storm during the summer of 1999. He was a great teacher, probably because he'd never stopped thinking of himself as a student. I also felt as if he had no concept of how to talk to a kid—and I loved that. Most people have no clue how badly a kid wants to be treated like an adult.

On my first day at the agency, he gave me a legal pad to take notes, but not before he'd scrawled a few words across the top:

$$Success = Humility + Curiosity + Effort$$

"Don't lose sight of that," he said. "And don't laugh at it. It might seem like a cheesy locker-room slogan, but it's the way you solve cases."

I assured him that I'd remember it, and I always have. Despite all the horrors of that summer, I've kept Noah Storm's mantra taped to my desk for more than twenty years now.

On my first week at the agency, Noah had a singular focus: Meredith's uniform.

"It's the tie to Bloomington," he said. "We've got to account for what's in our backyard. It begins with employees, but it doesn't end there. People give the shirts away, donate them, grab swag for a friend, a souvenir for a tourist. People like that silly logo. And that's good for us, because they remember those shirts. You're going to find the right one."

I felt as if he were giving me a manufactured task, a bullshit time-filler, like a teacher at the end of the semester when your grade was already decided.

"What's the problem?" he asked, reading my face.

"Well . . . it's just a shirt. I don't see how it is worth the time."

He studied me. "I need you to operate with emotional intelligence, Marshall. You're plenty smart. But if you're going to help with this, I need to count on your maturity as well."

"That's not a problem," I said, a little defensively.

"Let me ask a question: Why *don't* you think the shirt is important?" he asked.

"If you say it is, it is."

"No," he said sharply. "Use your mind. I'm here to teach you, not to hold your hand. You feel like this exercise is a waste of time. Why?"

I wanted to avert my eyes simply because his gaze was so penetrating.

"Because we know who she is," I said. "I don't see how this helps identify Maddox."

He seemed pleased. "Fair point. So I will now disclose what I've already determined: no one—not her family, friends, or roommates—remembers Meredith having that shirt. Meanwhile, your police friend from the Indy 500 interview shared some big news, didn't he?"

"That someone was recruiting her as a model. The photographer who said he was from upstate New York."

"Exactly. It's clear they don't have an identity for this guy yet, but they have his approach. What are the crucial elements of a modeling session?"

"A photographer, a camera, and a model," I said.

"And wardrobe," Noah added.

He thought she'd been given the uniform by the man who'd pretended to be the photographer. It was sinister and sickening.

"Who would be the most interesting Chocolate Goose employee to you?" he asked.

"One who knew her."

"Sure. That's the first tier. Who else?"

I shook my head. "I don't know."

"Would you be interested in male employees with a history of violence?"

"Yes. Definitely!" I almost shouted it, as if he'd cracked the case already. I hadn't even imagined the potential of a suspect pool coming from a shirt.

"That's where we come in," he said. "The legwork."

With that, he produced an accordion folder filled nearly to bursting that Grace Castle, the owner of the ice-cream shop, had obtained from her accountant. Inside were W-2 stubs.

"A decade's worth of employees," he said. "We'll start by cross-referencing local criminal records against the names. That's tier one. Tier two is going to become your purview: find the current contact for each employee, call them, and determine whether they still have the shirt. If not, where did they dispose of it? Garbage, Goodwill, gift to a niece?"

"People won't remember that."

"Not all of them. Some will. Some always do."

I watched him remove a stack of W-2 stubs from one of the folders.

"This will take forever," I said.

"One can never waste time when the hours are billable, Marshall."

When he looked back at me, his smile faded and he turned serious.

"You're going to spend more time producing misses than hits. That's a guarantee of detective work. But something to remember? You rarely get answers to questions you don't ask."

That was how my life as a private detective began: an ice-cream shop, tax forms, and a laborious search.

And I loved it.

I loved it from the start, crazy as that sounds. It was tedious, it was repetitive, it inevitably led to conflict with people who were angry or afraid, and it produced no immediate rewards. But we were active. While the rest of the world wondered about the missing girl and the impostor cop, we were working to answer the questions. I was in the mix, and there was an intellectual puzzle in play, and you never knew what the next call might yield, what the next dusty document might reveal.

Noah seemed to like the idea that the odds were stacked against us. He never criticized the police who were working the case, but he mentioned them often.

"Five full-time detectives and twenty assisting on that task force is what I'm told," he'd say. "Three different agencies in Indiana alone. That's a lot of hours, a lot of eyes, a lot of good minds. But we are not overmatched, are we, Marshall?"

This line of conversation always replenished his energy. He didn't say we were in competition with the police, but I know that he felt it. He wanted to get there first.

Despite that, at times I felt as if we weren't rushing enough, a sense of urgency probably driven by the novels I was reading.

"Why don't you ever talk about him striking again?" I asked, then felt foolish for using a phrase that sounded straight out of a *Batman* comic. "I mean . . . whatever he did to her, aren't you surprised he hasn't done it again?"

"He will," Noah told me simply.

"You don't talk about that, though."

"Because we don't know the clock yet. He may be in a basking season. We'll know when the season shifts. There will be another victim, and that will establish some things."

All of this was clipped, matter-of-fact, with no hint of his standard self-questioning, that capacity for arguing all sides at once.

"What's a basking season?" I asked.

He blinked at me as if he'd already forgotten his own words.

"A lull. Serial predators are always dangerous but not always active."

Those felt like the terms of homicide detectives, yet we never did anything resembling the PI stories I was devouring in books at home.

No surveillance, no covert videos, no knocking on doors. If we were not working the phones, we'd walk to the Monroe County Justice Building, where the county clerk's office was, or over to the courthouse, where I learned the difference between a tax assessor and a tax auditor and which records each office kept. We went to the library to track down phone books from around the state. Yes, the physical phone books, the big old volumes stuffed with their thin pages.

The internet was a primary tool—I was only reading about Sam Spade's era, not living it—but the physical sources we used daily seem hard to believe now. The county clerk's office had two public access terminals, but the date range was limited, and a comprehensive search required scanning through massive bound volumes, deciphering the penmanship of the clerk who'd logged the case, filling out a hard-copy request form for the file, and dropping the form in the tray at the counter. The entire process seems impossibly quaint at this remove, like something from a time before my own, because I came into the business at the end of an era. It was more time-consuming, sure, but the experience of dealing with people face-to-face was invaluable in a way I didn't understand at the time. I was no one's kid or grandchild or student, and I sure as hell wasn't a cute distraction to the busy, overburdened strangers who worked there. A couple pissed-off employees in the county clerk's office did more to prepare me for real life than many of my college courses.

Noah would show me the basics on each search and then let me run. He supervised but didn't look over my shoulder. The high expectations created an oversight system of their own. He wouldn't lecture or scold, but he could turn a phrase that suggested he was considering my future and arriving at dubious conclusions.

It's a detail-oriented business.

Remember, there'll be a day when no one checks your work.

Every construction site has a guy who says "Measure twice, cut once" and a guy named Stumpy. Which one do you want to be?

And my all-time favorite: *Nobody can focus for you.*

I got better in a hurry.

Meanwhile, I was learning the document trail that a human life acquires.

Traffic tickets and taxes, misdemeanors and small-claims cases, mortgages and evictions, marriages and divorces—all of it produced a paper trail.

I was considering a list of resources from his beloved public records sourcebook when I said, "You can't be invisible. It seems like if someone wants to find you, they can always do it."

Noah swiveled his chair to face me. "Got someone in mind?"

"What? No."

But I felt as if he knew. People always got around to asking about my dad in time. Noah's silence on the topic made me wonder if my mother had asked him not to bring it up. I didn't think so, though. She withheld the name from me, but she never moved to protect me from the questions. I suspected that Noah had simply read the single-parent dynamic during our visit and made a tactful decision. Now he watched me with interest and a measure of sympathy.

"Case selection is a challenge," he said. "You can either let money rule every choice, which is poisonous, or come up with a criterion. Right case, right reasons, right time—that's my criterion. If it checks the boxes, go. If not, hold off."

"That makes sense." I felt as if he knew exactly whom I was curious about finding. A case had a client. Nobody paid you to look for someone who'd gone missing from your own life.

My days took on a rhythm: public records research in the morning, then lunch, then back to the office to work the phones, all in pursuit of a missing ice-cream store uniform. The police had said publicly that the shirt was from 1992 or later, so we narrowed our search to employees from that range. It wasn't a small list. The business ran on part-time employees in the transient world of a college town. Within one week we'd generated a list of seven former employees and two current employees who had criminal records. Most were small-time offenses such as public intoxication, but one was for domestic violence and another for burglary. We found photographs of each man. None of them looked remotely like Maddox.

"Can't rule out the possibility of a collaborator," Noah reminded me. "You saw one man. Doesn't mean he was the only man."

He was an equal opportunity detective: we also found four women with criminal records, and one of them was the most violent of the lot, a twenty-three-year-old who'd been arrested on one occasion for breaking her boyfriend's nose with a baseball bat after he smoked the last of her marijuana, and on another for shooting out her landlord's car tires when he served her an eviction notice. She was the only person I'd seen who smiled in a jail booking photo, and I realized she was the older sister of a girl in my class, Carly Potter.

"Remember: confidential business," Noah told me when I shared that detail. "I encourage you not to bring the sister up in conversation with Carly."

After reading those police reports, he didn't need to warn me.

He explained the basics of how to talk to strangers, warning that people tended to be immediately suspicious or nervous or both when a private investigator reached out.

"It's crucial to prepare for an interview but equally crucial not to turn it into a Q and A. Listening is the imperative. A bad interviewer puts too much value on the questions. In reality, it's like a quarterback reading the defense—capitalize on what they're giving you. The person with the most to hide usually doesn't indicate that by being uncooperative or hostile. They try to distract you with cooperation, in fact. If you're a good listener, you'll get them to say more than they intended."

The problem with our current quest was that no one seemed to have any elaborate story to hide or share. The amazing thing—at least to me—was how correct Noah had been in his prediction that people would remember what had happened to their old work uniforms. Only a few people laughed us off or simply said they had no idea. Most would try to remember, and many *seemed* to remember in detail. There was a woman who'd sent her T-shirt to a pen pal in Germany, for example, and another who'd cut it to fit her boyfriend's basset hound.

"Even then it was baggy," she said solemnly. "Not enough leg on that dog. Not enough on the boyfriend either."

I was on my third day making calls when I contacted a former IU student in Chicago named Jonelle Harvey. She'd heard about the case—it seemed most people had—but she had her own shirt from the shop, a dead end. I was crossing her off my list when she spoke again.

"I think the police are looking for the wrong shirt," she said casually.

I had her on speakerphone, as always, so Noah could listen. He shifted closer to the phone now.

"What do you mean by that?" I asked her.

"They said it's from the past seven years because those throwback uniforms started in 1992. That's when they brought back the old-school logo with the stupid goose in the babushka. But I was there in '92, and I remember we did a photo shoot for the local newspaper and the owner, Mr. Castle, came in. I think he's dead now, and I'm not surprised, because he looked rough that day. He was nice, though. He came in wearing one of the original shirts. We wore the new ones, the fifty-year-anniversary shirts. They were supposed to look exactly alike."

"But they didn't?" I asked. Noah was scribbling notes beside me.

"Mostly," Jonelle Harvey said. "But you can't make a *perfect* replica, you know? And when I saw the girl's photo on the news, I thought, *That's the old shirt, the original.*"

I thought of my sketching session in the basement, how I'd fixated on the fabric of Maddox's police uniform and thought it was something from another time.

"Do you mean the weight of it?" I asked. "The texture?"

"I can't really define it. They look the same, but I'm telling you, there's a difference. I mean, how did people make shirts in the '50s or whatever? It had to be different than now. But this is a random thought. I'm probably wrong."

We exchanged thanks and pleasantries and I disconnected.

"Well," Noah said, "what do we think about that? Is Jonelle on to something here?"

"Maybe."

"If she is, we've got trouble. Do you see it?"

I shook my head.

"The haystack was already plenty big for our particular needle when we thought that shirt was from recent years. If we have to go back fifty years, though?" He gave a low whistle.

I hesitated, and he saw it. "What's wrong, Marshall?"

That was the first time I told him about the reality of our sketching session in the basement. It came pouring out in a torrent, from my certainty that I'd seen from inside Maddox's eyes to my bone-deep conviction that his uniform and his boots and even the barn itself were from another time, an older time.

Noah listened with customary interest, but I felt as if he didn't hold eye contact in the way he typically did, and it was the lack of his patient, respectful gaze that finally brought me up short. I sounded foolish. He was trying his best to pretend otherwise, but he couldn't hide his response.

"So, uh, what I'm thinking is—I mean, if there is *anything* to the crazy dream or vision or whatever, maybe both of the uniforms were old, hers and his," I said.

Now he fixed his eyes on mine again.

"That's what you think? It was an old uniform?"

Did he sound hopeful or disappointed? I couldn't tell.

"Well," I said, "that's what I thought during that time in your basement, and it's what Jonelle Harvey just said about the Chocolate Goose shirt. So if I'm right—if I didn't completely hallucinate things—then maybe we have a pattern? Something that connects the victim and the perpetrator?"

For a long moment I thought he wouldn't answer at all. Then he nodded slowly and said, "That is extremely practical, Marshall. An excellent bit of reasoning, one that would explain both why the police haven't been able to ID the officer and why his rank didn't match the department he claimed to represent. Well done."

I exhaled, relieved that I hadn't blown it by sounding too crazy. Should I mention the word "corporeal"? No, I decided. Noah was pleased with my detective work now. Why ruin that with something outlandish?

We moved along.

2

THE DETECTIVE AGENCY became the center of my world. Kerri was the only friend I saw in June, and Noah's office was my only chance to leave home, but I was happy there. Each day was new, the work was intriguing, and he treated me like an adult. I started drinking coffee simply because he offered it to me. It became part of the morning ritual: we'd have our coffee, and we'd review the work ahead, and then we'd get to it. He started letting me make some runs to the clerk's office on my own.

That was when I checked the marriage licenses for my mother's name.

She wasn't in there. I wasn't surprised; I'd never believed she had lied to me.

The difference was that now I could check.

She'd had six speeding tickets in a fifteen-year span. She hadn't been a party to a lawsuit or a criminal case, and her only property transaction was the one on Raintree Lane, where we lived alone. There was no reference to a man anywhere in the public record. There was Monica Miller and her son, Marshall.

I felt guilty about even looking. I decided I would never mention the speeding tickets, no matter how tempting.

At home, I read the Continental Op stories and then moved on to Sam Spade and then to Raymond Chandler's Philip Marlowe. They were nothing like the reality of detective work, but I did notice some similarities between Noah and the fictional detectives. He saw things most people would miss, and he seemed to archive whatever he saw, so he noticed if it changed. This ranged from the mundane—*They mulched those flower beds*—to the potentially interesting—*That car has had three parking tickets in a week and yet the driver keeps coming back to the same spot. I bet the car isn't registered in his name.* I also noticed that he chose his seats with care. Always with his back to the wall, in a corner if possible, with the best vantage point of the entrance. It was like lunching with Wild Bill Hickok.

And he *did* have guns, although he never spoke of one until I stumbled across the key to the cabinet. I took out a stapler from his desk drawer, tried to staple some pages together, and failed. I opened the stapler, thinking it was empty, and saw there was a single silver key tucked inside. Noah saw me and sighed.

"Gun cabinet," he said simply. "There are very rare days in the field when I carry for protection, but that's all."

I pretended not to have any interest.

Unlike Marlowe or Spade, Noah Storm was regimented, precise, and organized. At 11:30 each morning we'd break and head somewhere near the square for lunch. Noah favored Stefano's, a café on the ground floor of Fountain Square Mall, or the Bakehouse, a coffee and sandwich shop across from the courthouse. Once we grabbed burgers at Opie Taylor's. On my third week I tentatively suggested we try the Encore Cafe, where Kerri worked. She'd been desperate to meet Noah, but I wasn't about to invite her to drop by the office. He agreed to my lunch suggestion without hesitation, and we made our way through the cafeteria-style line. Kerri was working the register, and we acted as if we didn't know each other.

Or at least I thought we did. As soon as we were seated—in the corner of the room, with Noah's back to the wall so he could see the door and the wide plate-glass windows looking out onto Sixth Street—he said, "So you know her pretty well?"

He wasn't a guy to play dumb around.

"The cashier? She's my neighbor."

"Ah. Known her a long time, then?"

"Yeah. Like, forever."

He took a spoonful of soup. "Do you want to know her better, or is the status quo good?"

He asked it seriously. It was very different than having the same question come from Dom or my mother.

"She's got a boyfriend," I said.

He nodded, keeping his eyes on me, waiting for more.

"If she didn't . . . I don't know. We've been friends for a long time, right?"

"The risk isn't worth the reward?"

"Maybe not. I don't know. I mean, it's irrelevant as long as she's dating Jake, but even then . . . I don't know if I'd make the first move with Kerri. I'd kind of want to know that *she* wanted things to change before I tried."

I stopped and shrugged, feeling a flush of embarrassment. Noah asked how my sandwich was, providing a welcome escape hatch from the conversation. Only later, when I was home alone, did I think back on it and realize that by the time the exchange was done, I'd told him Kerri's name, her boyfriend's name, and that we were neighbors, all before sharing more about my feelings for her than I'd ever spoken aloud.

He was a very good detective.

"He's hot," Kerri told me that evening when we went for a run.

"Gross. He's your dad's age."

She laughed, then said, "Is he really that old?"

"I think he has to be close. Don't you?"

She frowned. "It's hard to tell with him."

"Yeah, I know. He's kind of nondescript."

"But in a hot way."

I groaned.

"Fit, at least. I bet he runs faster than you. And . . . longer." She wiggled her eyebrows, and I made a show of putting my headphones on and cutting across the neighbor's lawn to escape her laughter.

That routine was my first month of summer. I worked and I ran with Kerri. It was easy to set up a time because we each had cell phones by then. I'd gotten mine after getting busted for drinking; Kerri had gotten

hers because her parents were divorcing. We'd each lobbied unsuccessfully for a phone all year, and now we'd have happily given them up if it
meant returning to the way things had been without them.

I'd hoped that Jake Crane would be college-bound by the end of summer, but on one of our runs Kerri shared the exciting news that he'd decided to stay in Bloomington to be closer to his family. He would start at
IU in the fall, she explained. Wasn't that just terrific?

"He's staying for you," I said, trying to hide my disappointment.

"Maybe a little bit."

"Not a little bit. The only place he ever talks about is Colorado. He
couldn't wait to get back. So it's all for you."

"There's also his father," she said.

"I thought his dad was a professor, some fancy philosopher. Why's
Jake afraid of leaving him for college?"

She gazed at me in a way that made me aware of my petulant tone.

"He's a philosophy professor, yes. He's also in a wheelchair. He has
been since a car accident that happened when Jake was six."

I'd never heard this story. I realized that I'd never really asked Jake
anything about himself. Now I felt bad.

"It's good that he's staying, then," I said, and tried to mean it this time.

We didn't talk about Jake much in the days after that. We didn't talk
about anything of consequence. We ran in the heat of the late afternoon,
before she went off with Jake or, some nights, to stay with her mother.
Gwen was living in a rental house near campus. Jerry Flanders would sit
in the yard alone on those nights, chain-smoking cigarettes. He flagged
me over whenever he spotted me, desperate for someone to talk to in his
suddenly silent home. Those talks always started out okay, but inevitably
he'd get to the layoffs at Otis or Thompson or the rumored layoffs coming
at GE, and his tone would grow maudlin, and I had no idea what to say.
He never mentioned Gwen, and neither did I. He almost always warned
me about snakes.

"That was a big bastard in your house," he said. "You can tell from
the skin. I laid it out against a tape measure, tip to tail, fifty-seven inches.
Damn near as long as my daughter is tall."

He shuddered and blew smoke. I didn't enjoy recalling the snake, but Jerry seemed unable to forget it.

"Did Kerri tell you what I heard about the state forests?"

"She said they do some kind of snake inventory?"

"Population is thriving. Timber rattlers, though, greenish black. I asked him about the black-and-white one you saw. He told me maybe it was an albino."

I could still see my bare feet on the floor, oblivious to the snake's presence so close.

"I just hope I don't see any of them, in any color, ever again," I said.

"You're going to. People don't believe this is rattlesnake country, but it always was, and it's becoming that way again. All the small farms gone out of business around here, tall grass and abandoned buildings left behind, that shit makes for a snake haven." He sucked on his cigarette. "People never want to think about the negative possibility, Marshall. Go through life expecting it to work out. Like me at Otis for twenty damn years, you know? If I'd done a better job of anticipating what might come down the pike . . . well, I probably would have made some different choices."

He had faraway eyes, and I had an uncomfortable sense that he was thinking about his marriage as much as his job. I didn't know what to say, so I settled for a nod.

"This millennium crap," he said. "Same deal. You heard about the Y2K?"

"The computers might get confused by the zeroes or something?"

"Not confused—paralyzed. They won't know whether it's the past or the present or how the hell to move forward, so they'll freeze up and die. Think *that* won't cause some problems?"

"Probably."

"Probably? Marshall, do you know how much of this society relies on computers? Think about it—not just banks and airplanes; it's the *utilities*, it's the *infrastructure of survival*. And most people are aware of that problem, but they're expecting it to work out, right? Why? Because it always has before." He spread his hands dramatically, showering the grass with ash. "But a precedent is not a promise. And this country is gonna figure that out come New Year's Eve. Your mom ready?"

"I don't know."

"I'll talk to her." He snapped his lighter with nervous energy. "Gotta get the essentials in order. Water and food and firewood. And ammunition, if you ask me."

"I don't think she'll go for that," I said. My mother hated guns.

"I figure each street needs only one guy. If everyone takes care of the basics, and every street has one guy who's *truly* prepared . . ."

He trailed off without finishing the thought, and I told him I had to get home. In truth, he was freaking me out.

Kerri had told me he'd had job offers from GE, friends who were offering him a lifeline, but he'd refused, predicting that GE was going to collapse any day now and send their jobs to Mexico. What was the point in starting work at a dying plant? he would ask rhetorically, and eventually friends stopped tossing lifelines. He spent most of his afternoons at a west side bar called the Highland Lounge, which kids in my class called the "Highland Scrounge." I could smell beer on Jerry's breath almost all the time, even when he'd just returned from work. The Eliminator Inc. van stood in the driveway like a monument to sadness, covered with mud that even a hard rain couldn't rinse clean. The back was overflowing with buckets, shovels, uneven lengths of PVC pipe, and sheets of polyurethane plastic. I tried to imagine what it must be like to go from being a union man with good benefits and a legacy job to crawling under houses owned by some of your old colleagues or supervisors.

When I thought about that, I could get angry at Gwen Flanders for leaving. I knew nothing about the interior life of their marriage, and I saw enough of Jerry's problems to grasp that they probably extended beyond what I could imagine, but it was hard for me to forgive Gwen, because I knew only what it felt like to be the one left behind. Any parent or spouse who bailed seemed like a coward to me. Maybe it was because of that sense of sad solidarity that I kept going over to talk to Jerry in the evenings. Maybe it was because I was always waiting to see his daughter and trying not to think about what she might be doing with Jake Crane.

Either way, we formed an odd-couple friendship. Two guys isolated by circumstances, both alone at night. I'd drink a Coke and he'd drink a six-pack of Miller High Life and we'd talk. I'd try to keep him on sports, but he never could drift completely away from the gloom and doom of layoffs, snakes, and Y2K.

There was only one exciting diversion for me in those weeks: Napster, a new computer program for sharing music files. To say this was revolutionary was an understatement, considering the amount of my meager income that went to CD purchases. Suddenly, everything was there. Download the songs, arrange them onto a mixed CD—which I'll still defend as an unrivaled art compared to a playlist that doesn't have a time limit—burn the disc, and expand your music collection.

All of it for free!

It was, of course, Kerri who first suggested the problem with Napster to me. We'd finished a run in the neighborhood, and I was gasping, standing on trembling legs while she casually sipped a bottle of water, a thin sheen of sweat on her forehead, as if she'd just warmed up, when she wondered aloud how much money the artists were losing with each CD I burned.

"They're not losing money," I said.

"How is that possible when you're not paying any?"

"It's like the radio," I wheezed, holding my side. "You don't pay for that either."

"Someone does."

"The library, then. Books are free."

"Only after the library bought them, and only for a limited number of people and time."

I gave a tired, dismissive wave. "You overthink everything. Meanwhile, you're missing great music."

"I'm confident that no one named 'Funny Bone' is making great music."

"Now you're just trying to piss me off. His name is Krayzie Bone."

Before she could retort, her dad's van approached. Jerry lowered the window and looked at us with a wan smile. It was 90 degrees, yet he seemed paler than he ever did in the winter. He'd lost weight since Gwen moved out, and he always looked tired, as if the stress of the separation or the new job or both was hollowing him out.

"You sticking to the streets, guys?" he asked.

"Yes, Father. My feet touch only the permissible pavement," Kerri said, sounding as exhausted as he looked.

"That's good," Jerry said, wiping his face with a rag. "Snakes are everywhere this summer. Saw one coiled up on a concrete block in a crawl space today, quiet as a church mouse. I probably would've put my hand right on it if I hadn't been alert."

I suppressed a shudder. Kerri turned away and sipped her water.

"You gonna be home tonight?" Jerry asked her.

"Nope."

"What's on your agenda?"

"Movie."

"Enjoy 'em while you got 'em," Jerry said. "Come January—"

"I know your thoughts about Y2K," Kerri snapped. "We'll wait and see, won't we?"

Kerri was never terse with her father.

"You okay?" I asked when he'd driven out of earshot.

"He's fixated on all this shit, rattlesnakes and Y2K and anything else that he can turn into a phobia." She tugged her hair out of its ponytail holder. "It might not be the worst idea in the world if he talked to someone, a psychologist or counselor or whatever."

"Does your mom know what he's like?"

"Of course. She says it's one of the reasons she can't stay with him. She keeps telling me he's a different person. Then again, she's taking ukulele lessons from a guy she met at the farmers' market, so I'm not sure if she's qualified to talk about someone else's midlife crisis."

It was quiet for a moment, and then she tried to redirect. "So when do I get to see the great detective agency?"

"It's not that exciting of a place."

"You said it was creepy as hell."

"Did I?"

She rolled her eyes. "You made a whole big deal about it. All the dark wood and shadows and carpets the color of blood, *woo-OOO-oo*."

She made a ghostly fluttering motion with her fingers, and I smiled, but I didn't remember Noah's office feeling creepy. I'd gotten used to it. I liked it.

"My mother is thinking of granting me release from house arrest over the Fourth of July. Maybe then."

"Awesome. Jake and I are going to the parade and fireworks. You could ride with us and show us the place then?"

I didn't have any interest in third-wheeling along in the back seat of Jake's Volvo, although he'd have the parade wave down. Hell, they could put him on a float.

"Maybe. I'll check with my warden—er, my mother—and see what freedom will be granted for Independence Day."

My mother did grant me a temporary release for the holiday, although she didn't tell me about it until our traditional Sunday golf game. It was a fun morning until we heard the sirens.

We didn't think anything of them at first. Only when they didn't stop did we become curious. We left the course without finishing the round, she turned on the radio, and that was when I learned that, even with my freedom restored, I still couldn't take Kerri anywhere near Noah Storm's office. The police had shut the streets down after a man named Benjamin Nathaniel Smith murdered a twenty-six-year-old IU student named Won-Joon Yoon on the sidewalk outside the church where Yoon was heading to worship.

A follower of the white supremacist Matthew Hale, Smith had briefly attended IU himself, and on July 3, less than three months after Columbine made parents all over town mutter about being grateful they lived in a safe place like Bloomington, he climbed into a Ford Taurus with a pair of pistols at his side and set off on a trail of race-based bloodshed. He shot six Orthodox Jews leaving a synagogue in Chicago, then murdered the Northwestern University basketball coach, Ricky Byrdsong, a Black man, in front of his children at their home outside the city. Next, he wounded a Black minister outside a church and shot at a group of Asian students on the University of Illinois's campus before disappearing into the night.

The next morning he appeared in our town.

While my mother and I played golf and people prepared for picnics and parades, Ben Smith completed his murder spree by firing into a crowd outside of the Korean United Methodist Church. He then fled back to Illinois with police in pursuit, wrecked his car, and ended the chase by shooting himself twice in the head and once in the chest.

Fourth of July 1999, Bloomington, Indiana.

They still had the parade that night.

That seems strange now, but I have trouble faulting the people who opted to go ahead with it. What was the right response in the face of insanity and hate? Nothing like this had ever happened in Bloomington. I imagine most mayors in the country today have a plan for just this type of occurrence. I don't think many did in 1999. As with Columbine, it seemed as if no one was sure how to react.

That afternoon, determined not to waste my holiday freedom, I met Dom for some pickup basketball at the HPER—that is, the School of Health, Physical Education, and Recreation for those of you who didn't attend Indiana University, and it is pronounced "hyper." The HPER was a big barn of a fieldhouse packed with basketball courts, weight rooms, and swimming pools, and it had once been the home of the greatest swimming and diving team in the world. In 1970 there were twelve individual world records in men's swimming, and *nine* of them were held by kids attending class at Indiana University. By 1999 the swimming and diving programs trained in another building across campus, but the HPER was still home to some of the best pickup basketball around. You had to win to hold a court; lose and you waited.

Or, on the Fourth of July, you showed up and realized the place was closed for the holiday.

"You hear about the shooting?" Dom asked as we walked back to the parking lot.

"Yeah. Insane."

"Right? My dad was out there. They asked the fire department to block off the street. Said he could still see the blood on the sidewalk."

"It's like Columbine," I said.

"It's very different from Columbine."

"How?"

He looked at me. "Because if you and I had been in Columbine, we'd have both been killed. But if you and I were on the street when Ben Smith came to town, I would've been killed and you wouldn't have been. He wanted brown skin, and I've got it."

I hadn't considered it that way. It was eerie to imagine a scope passing over me only to return to Dom.

He leaned against the Beast, then pulled back fast when he touched the metal, which was cooking in the sun.

"Are you glad about the news being redirected?" he asked.

"What do you mean?"

He held his palm above the door panel, assessing the warm metal like someone checking a stove burner.

"A break from all the talk about you and that cop and the girl. That's got to get old."

"Being grounded has its perks. I wasn't sure if people even remembered."

"They do," Dom said. "Maybe they won't, after this."

"Maybe not," I said, and then we said our goodbyes and separated and suddenly I wanted the holiday to be over so I could return to work with Noah Storm. The world felt crazy, and I wanted to restore some balance to it.

That's why we have detectives, right?

3

I WENT IN EARLY on Monday, even though it was the observed holiday. Noah was drinking coffee and reading the *Herald-Times* coverage of the shootings. It was the first and last time I remembered our local newspaper printing a special edition.

"If you're working today," I told Noah, "I don't mind helping. The holiday isn't a big deal to me."

He didn't answer right away. He took a beat, flicking his thumb back and forth over the edges of the newspaper, and then said, "It's going to be a different week. I've got fieldwork. A few leads between Bloomington and Terre Haute, out near Center Point."

Fieldwork was what I'd been waiting on. Surveillance, covert photography of a suspect, interviewing people who knew Meredith Sullivan—any of it was more exciting than the tax assessor's office.

"Sure thing," I said. "Should I meet you here, or out in Center Point, or—"

"I actually need you at the library," he said.

"The library."

He nodded as if oblivious to my disappointment.

"I've been thinking about Jonelle Harvey."

"Who?"

"She's the one who told us that the shirt didn't look right."

"Oh, yeah."

"I want to run that possibility to ground," he said. "That's a big job, and I'm counting on you for it. She referenced a newspaper photograph. I'll need you to go to the library and locate that tomorrow. We'll divide and conquer."

I couldn't help feeling betrayed, because he'd treated me as an equal, and now he was clearly dismissing me for a "big job" at the library while he went off to do the real work.

He sensed my disappointment. "What's the problem, Marshall?"

"Nothing. It's just not what I'd planned on, that's all."

He started to respond, then stopped and turned away from me.

"That's why the world needs investigators. If everything went according to plan, we'd be unemployed. Take the holiday today and then start at the library tomorrow. I'll let you know when I'm back in the office. It will probably be Friday but maybe next week."

Now the brush-off was taking on longer implications.

As I sat there, trying to think of the right way to ask about it, the sunlight drew my eye to the chunk of limestone shaped like a grave marker on his bookshelf, the one that said EVERY STONE HAS A STORY.

"Who gave you that?"

He looked up, puzzled, then followed my gaze to the stone.

"I made it," he said, and his voice was soft.

I wanted to ask him why. Something stopped me, though. Maybe it was because I was upset with him for sidelining me, maybe because I wasn't sure of the emotion that had gone into making the strange little tombstone. Whatever the reason, I decided not to press. We had a long summer ahead, and plenty of time for that conversation. So I let it go, and I left, and I forgot the most important thing he'd told me about the art of the detective business:

You rarely get answers to questions that you don't ask.

On Wednesday morning I left the house without enthusiasm for the first time that summer. I'd grown to love the routine: heading off to the office, sipping my coffee, that newly acquired, seemingly adult taste, and making small talk with Noah before embarking on a day of work. It sounds tedious now, but that summer it felt like acceptance into a world that wasn't dictated by bells and bus circles and all the trappings of childhood that I was desperate to leave behind.

It was a hell of a lot better than showing up at the library and asking to see old newspapers in search of a photograph from an ice-cream shop.

I found what I needed, though. The photo was beneath the headline FIFTY YEARS OF FLAVOR. Anthony Castle, the deceased founder of the business, had been pictured with two employees on each side, all of them grinning dopey smiles and holding ice-cream cones. He looked old and ill. He had his free hand on the counter, and his posture suggested he needed the help to hold himself up. The smile was genuine, but there was a quality of pain to his face, a look that said it had taken some effort to do this silly photo op, and somehow that made the picture better, more memorable.

Sadder.

As I studied the photograph, I became convinced that Jonelle Harvey's memory hadn't failed her when it came to the shirts. The colors and designs were identical, but there was something different about Anthony Castle's shirt, and not simply because it was older. You could tell that even from the photograph. It was the difference between modern cotton and something from another era.

A difference like Maddox's police uniform. The thing you forgot until Noah had you sketch it. Until you saw the barn and the blood and the snakes.

I felt dizzy suddenly, memories of Noah's drafting table in the basement pressing in. I printed ten copies of the photo and walked out of the library and into the humid heat of the July day, one of those Midwestern cookers that leach sweat from your pores within the first few steps. I called Noah while I stood in the sun on Kirkwood Avenue. No answer. He was gone, off on his secretive fieldwork. I had the key to the office in my pocket and figured I might as well drop the copies off on his desk. I decided to walk it, and I'd just reached the square, standing in front of Howard's Bookstore, facing the time and temperature sign on the bank across College Avenue that informed me it was already 91 degrees, when I thought of another opportunity.

I could finally show Kerri the office.

She started her shift at eleven and was probably en route to the Encore Cafe or close to it. She'd have time for a quick tour. I took out my bulky new cell phone and dialed hers. In the months and years that followed, I've wondered what might have happened if I hadn't had that new phone and if Kerri hadn't had hers. It was a damn hot day, and I wouldn't have walked over to the Encore to stand in the parking lot waiting on her. I probably would have gone to the office alone, dropped the copies on Noah's desk, and headed home.

A lot would be different now.

But by then I did have the phone, and Kerri had hers, so it went the way it went.

4

I BEAT KERRI TO NOAH'S office by ten minutes, but I waited outside. It was cool under the shade of those ancient elms, sitting on the limestone steps.

Kerri arrived in typical fashion, driving at Mach 5 and parking as if her Honda were the only car on the street. If she'd parked the Oldsmobile at the same angle, it would have blocked traffic. Jerry and Gwen had understood their daughter when they opted for the Civic. She hopped out with a grin on her face and approached up the sidewalk at a jaunty clip, almost skipping, like a little kid. Her hands were clasped behind her back.

"*Finally*," she said. "Access to the inner sanctum."

"Can you ever say anything normal?"

"I have the capacity but not the desire."

I pushed off the steps and stood, reaching for the key in my pocket, then stopped and eyed her suspiciously. Her smile was too wide. Whenever she was this pleased with herself, it meant she was up to something— usually something quite ridiculous.

"Why are your hands behind your back?"

"Because I'm prepared."

"Kerri . . ."

She brought out her left hand first, revealing a magnifying glass. I was still groaning about that when the right hand appeared with the fedora.

209

She put the hat on at a Bogart-approved angle, tried to smother her smile into a smirk, and lifted the magnifying glass to her eye.

"Let's do it."

"You're a world-class dork."

"I'm a dame with good gams looking for a private dick. If you know any—"

"Shut up," I warned. "This is where I work."

"Oh, relax. The boss is gone."

"He might have cameras."

"Yeah, right."

"He has a fake doorbell rigged up to a button under his desk to create a distraction if he needs one."

"No shit?" She lowered the magnifying glass but kept the fedora on, and there was something about her fine-boned face shadowed by that ridiculous hat that offered a glimpse of the beautiful woman who waited ahead of the girl—and not far ahead. I felt my breath catch a little, which was a sensation I was trying to avoid with Kerri.

"You're making me regret this decision already," I told her, heading for the front door.

"Relax, Marlowe. I won't shame the badge."

"Private investigators don't have badges," I grumbled as I put the key in the lock.

I smelled the blood as soon as I opened the door. I paused at the threshold, and Kerri bumped into me, unprepared for the sudden stop.

"Is he here?" she whispered.

I didn't answer. I was staring down the hall. The doors were all closed, and the overhead lights were off, leaving only the sunlight filtered through the elms to illuminate the foyer. Shadows danced on the old walnut floors. I smelled the blood as clearly as if it were my own.

Run, my brain said, and its voice was a boy's voice, a child's instinct, but some other instinct, something new—something that sounded closer to Noah Storm's voice than my own—whispered, *You have to see. You have to know.*

"Wait here," I told Kerri.

"Marshall? What is—"

"Wait here," I repeated, and then I crossed the threshold and let the heavy door swing shut behind me, and I was alone.

I had the printouts from the library in my left hand and the key in my right, held out from my waist, like a Western gunfighter. I forced myself ahead, tried to shift the key from my right hand to my left, and dropped them instead. They hit the floor, and the plush runner carpet snuffed out the sound like a breath on a birthday candle. When I bent to pick up the key, the scent of blood was overwhelming, stronger than the day Kenny Glass had broken my nose.

Run.

See first.

Run!

You have to see!

I straightened, turned the doorknob, and pushed the office door open.

Noah Storm was behind the desk, suit jacket draped on the back of the chair, maroon tie pulled loose at the neck, his eyes fixed on mine, his head cocked at that memorable, half-thoughtful, half-amused angle. It was a familiar tableau except for the large, clean bullet hole punched through his forehead. Blood smeared his forehead like an Ash Wednesday blessing, crossed the bridge of his nose, reddened his lips, dotted the cleft in his chin. His white shirt was open at the collar and it was a few stunned seconds before I realized that what I'd taken for a necktie was actually a wide ribbon of blood.

I stepped back with slow, wooden motions, and it was only because I was too scared to scream that I saw Maddox before he saw me.

He was on the high, steep staircase to the second floor and whatever waited there—I still hadn't set foot on a single step in that house—but he'd stopped a quarter of the way down and turned to look behind him as if he'd forgotten something. He was dressed in full uniform again, his big arms pressing against the tight cuffs of the short sleeves, his badge glinting in the shaft of sunlight that pierced the transom window above the front door, which was still closed, Kerri waiting on the other side. There was a revolver in his hand, the cylinder bright as the badge.

I didn't run. I didn't scream. I stood as still as I had ever stood in my life, a stillness of which I didn't even know I was capable, as if I'd succeeded in holding back my heartbeat as well as my breath. It was the posture of prey, a terrible instinct, but one that saved me.

Maddox turned, the stairs creaking beneath his weight, and walked back up to the landing, then moved away with a casual, unhurried stride. His shape was reduced to a silhouette on the wall as he walked down the hallway that was directly above me. I had begun to tremble, and the printouts in my left hand slipped from my fingers and wafted almost silently to the floor, landing on the runner carpet as softly as autumn leaves on a still pond. Above me, a doorknob turned, a latch clicked, a hinge squeaked, and Maddox's shadow vanished.

I ran then.

Kerri was standing so close to the door that she almost stumbled through it while I barreled out of it, as if she'd been about to step inside to see what was taking me so long.

"Marsh—"

I grabbed her around the waist and jerked her away from the house. She almost fell into my legs, which would've brought us both down, but her runner's grace and those wide limestone steps saved us, giving her enough room to recover her balance as I rushed us away. No one needed to speak. Real terror is its own universal language; it never lacks clarity.

We were out of sight of the house before I uttered the first word: "Murdered."

"What?"

"He murdered Noah. Maddox murdered Noah. Oh, shit, Kerri, he is in there and he—"

"Call the police," she said, and then her phone was in her hand. I hadn't even thought of mine yet. It was too new, and I was too scared.

Kerri called 911 while we huddled behind a van a block away from the house, peering up the street to where the high mansard roof with the weather vane was visible above the trees. Kerri's magnifying glass lay broken on the sidewalk; her fedora blew up the street. The jokes were dead.

So was Noah.

"Did he have a gun?" Kerri asked, shaking my arm.

"Yeah, he has a gun, it is Maddox, and he shot Noah, he shot Noah in the forehead, and—"

Kerri squeezed my arm tightly and said, "Yes, he is armed with a gun," into the phone and I fell silent again as she explained where we were and what we'd seen.

What *I'd* seen. She made the report, but it was my testimony.

The sirens seemed almost immediate, and the police cars themselves took little longer. We were less than a mile from the Bloomington police station. Kerri was still on the phone as the first squad car pulled up.

"We can see them," she said as a cruiser roared in from the wrong direction on a one-way street and blocked the road. Two cops were out immediately, guns in their hands. Farther up, another car was blocking the other side, and more sirens promised police were coming from every direction, pinning Maddox in.

I couldn't hear what the dispatcher was saying, so I didn't know that she was telling Kerri that we should stay where we were until an officer found us. I thought that I should get their attention, so I stood and stepped away from the van, one hand upraised, like a kid waiting to be called on in a classroom. The officers were looking up the street, at the place Kerri had identified as the murder scene, and so I had to go farther up the sidewalk to get their attention. That brought me back in sight of the limestone house before an officer spotted me and shouted, *"Son, get down!"*

When he shouted, the officer beside him turned, and the gun in his hand turned with him, and I was looking at the muzzle of the semiautomatic and sure that the cop was going to shoot.

"Damn it, get down!" he yelled, lowering the weapon, and I thought he was as afraid of what had nearly happened as I had been. Only when he lowered the gun did I realize that it was Bruce Carter, Leslie's dad.

"Mr. Carter, I'm the—"

"Down!"

I dropped to the sidewalk and they rushed over to me. One searched me with swift hands and both spoke together, talking over each other.

"You called it in?"

"You the kid who saw the shooter?"

"Is he inside?"

I blathered out my responses as well as I could while being searched on the pavement. By then there were even more sirens and strobing colored lights lit the street and mingled with the heat shimmer rising off the cement into the scorching summer day.

"I know him," Bruce Carter said to his partner. "Let me talk to him."

His partner retreated, gun in hand, eyes on the office where I'd spent so many happy days.

"Marshall, is the shooter in the building?" Bruce Carter asked me.

"He was when I left."

"Did he see you?"

"I don't know. I think he heard me leave, but he didn't hear me come in."

"Witness reports the shooter is in the building," Bruce's partner said, speaking into a microphone clipped near his collar. "Repeat, shooter is in the building."

"Do you know where in the building?" Bruce asked me. He was kneeling, left hand on my back, right hand on his holstered weapon.

"He was upstairs. He is in uniform."

Bruce had been looking at the house, but now he turned back to me with full attention.

"Uniform?"

I nodded. "He's dressed like a police officer but he isn't one. He's the guy who killed the girl—"

"Girl? We have two victims in there?"

"No! The victim was Noah. The cop is—" I paused with an effort, aware that I was speaking too quickly. I tried to channel a little of Noah Storm's calm. These were the crucial seconds.

"The shooter is the man who impersonated a police officer named Maddox," I said. My voice trembled but the words were clear. "That was in February."

Bruce Carter's partner stared at me. He had freckles across his nose and wasn't all that much older than me.

"How do you know that?" he said.

"Because he was the one who saw him," Bruce said softly. "He's inside right now?"

"He was."

I saw a hopeful gleam in Bruce's eyes then. They had the man they'd been searching for.

"The victim is named Noah Storm," I said. "He is a private investigator. He is my boss."

Was, I thought, picturing Noah with the bullet hole in his forehead. *He* was *my boss.*

I felt tears threatening then. Bruce helped me hold them off by asking more questions, forcing me to think. How many doors were there in the house? How many sets of stairs? Had the door been locked when I arrived? Would it have stayed unlocked behind me?

As the questions came, so did more police. There were fire trucks and ambulances, too, and curious people pouring down the street from offices, restaurants, and houses, only to be shouted back by cops. I heard the officer beside us requesting the CIRT team, the heavily armed and heavily armored tactical unit that looked more like soldiers than police officers. Bruce was a member of that. Did that mean he would have to go inside, one of the first through the door?

"I want everyone three blocks away," Bruce said. "Tell me when Mick is on scene. We're not going into that building until Mick's ready."

I didn't have any idea who Mick was, but I figured he must be the point man for the CIRT team. There was going to be shooting, I realized numbly. Right here in Bloomington, there was going to be an exchange of gunfire. Bruce Carter wasn't telling everyone to clear a three-block radius because he didn't want distractions; he was expecting bullets.

We were a lot closer than three blocks. I could still see the house.

Almost as soon as I thought this, Bruce said, "Marshall, you're going with Officer Spicer now. I need you to listen to him, all right? You've done all the right things, son, and we're going to end this. We've got it. You're safe."

I nodded numbly. The one with the freckles, who was apparently Officer Spicer, put an arm around me and said, "We're good, kid. We're going to stay low and get right over there behind the yellow house with the white trim. You see it?"

"Yeah."

"All right. When I say go, you run, okay? And stay low. I've got you."

I got into a crouch, leaning forward, like a runner waiting on the starter's pistol. My whole body was trembling. I was waiting on Spicer to tell me *go* when another voice, loud and on the edge of panic, cut the air.

"MOVEMENT! I'VE GOT MOVEMENT AT THE FRONT DOOR!"

Spicer and I both turned then, and Bruce Carter knelt and lifted his gun in a two-handed grip, and I was able to see clearly over his shoulder as Noah Storm walked out of the front door of the limestone house, his hands held high, a perplexed frown on his face, swiveling his head as if searching for the source of all the commotion.

CHAPTER SEVEN

MONROE COUNTY'S CLIFFORD IRVING

August–September 1999

"Hard to explain this
Live my life to die famous"

LIL' ZANE
"DIE FAMOUS"

1

MANY OF THE DAYS of that year are so clear in my mind that I can provide the characters and the chronology, the details and the dialogue.

The afternoon following Noah Storm's appearance on his front steps isn't among them.

Mostly, I remember the numbness. The out-of-body detachment.

I know Bruce Carter drove me to the police station. I know he did not say a word en route.

Plenty of people did offer words—some profane, even furious. The one sentence I'd most wanted to abandon in my sixteenth year was the only one I could offer: "I want my mother."

Then she was there, finally. She had her own questions. All I could tell her was that I wanted to go home.

The police had other ideas. They wanted answers.

I could not provide any.

I remember one man shouting, but he was an outlier. Most of them talked to me softly, some with pity, some with scorn. I remember that the officer named Spicer looked relieved, happy that the gunman had turned out to be a lie.

I remember that word. "Lie." It came at me directly and harshly and it floated around me in hushed tones, omnipresent.

Lie, lie, lie, lie.

"Doctor" was another word that ricocheted around the police station. Bruce Carter was one who said it—snapped it, really—and that stands out because it was directed at my mother.

"You need to get him to a fucking doctor."

She stared back at him coolly and didn't say a word and didn't look away until he did.

"I saw it," I told her, as I'd told him, told all of them. "I saw it."

And then, somewhere along the line, because it was easier, and because the words "lie" and "doctor" were so awful for such different reasons, I shifted to "I thought I saw it."

I do not recall how we got home. I assume she drove me. That would make sense, but at some point my Oldsmobile was back in the driveway, and she couldn't have driven both at once. Maybe she sent someone to get it. Maybe a cop drove it. Maybe I drove it and she followed.

I have no clue.

We sat together at the kitchen table and she held my hand.

"I worked with a man who had panic attacks," my mother told me. "It's nothing to be ashamed of. It's not in your control."

She sounded hopeful, and she seemed to be talking to herself as much as to me as she explained that hallucinations were not as uncommon as I might think and that it did not mean there was anything wrong with me.

The phone rang a lot and then not at all. Time passed the way it does, whether you want it to or not.

One thing I do remember: the rain.

The storms were terrible that night. The hazy heat built into a restless wind that fractured into a furious torrent. The porch furniture tipped and tumbled, the bird feeder fell and shattered, and hail the size of nickels hammered the house. They were the worst storms of the summer. There was no Miller Time that night because my mother had called off work after her son reported a murder that hadn't happened and the police blanketed the town to take down an active shooter who didn't exist. My mother watched her replacement, a woman who looked like she was fresh out of college, handle the breaking news.

That part is clear in my mind.

It was nearly midnight and I had gone to bed when the phone rang yet again. My mother answered it this time, probably because it was so late. I heard her say that I wasn't available, and then, in a sharper tone, "May I ask who's calling at this hour?"

A pause. Then, "Your first name is *The*?"

Another pause. "All right, Sean. I will share your message, but Marshall is not . . ."

She trailed off when I opened my bedroom door. She was standing in the hall with the cordless phone to her ear. She tipped the phone against her chest and said, "The Weller is calling?"

I reached for the phone, and she seemed uncertain, but handed it over. I put the phone to my ear. "Hello?"

"Marshmallow, what the fuck happened?" Sean Weller barked.

I didn't know what to say. I wasn't even sure how he'd gotten our number.

"People are talking a lot of shit," he said. "I just need to know if you made it up."

"No."

"I knew it." He sounded utterly convinced by my one-word denial, as if nothing more was needed. "If anyone gives you too much shit, you let the Weller know right away. Got that?"

"Uh—okay."

I could see my mother frowning at me.

"The other thing you need to do," Weller continued, talking like a coach giving the game plan, "is put on some muscle. I'm serious, and not just because Kenny knocked you around like he was swatting mosquitoes. You need to armor up. The body and the mind work together. Come to the HPER weight room in the afternoon and the Weller will get you on a confidence-building program."

"I'm grounded."

"Ridiculous. Okay. But remember, I got your back."

Before I could respond, he hung up.

"Do I know Sean?" my mother said, taking the phone from my hand.

"No. He went to South. He graduated."

"I see. Maybe we'll need to get a new number."

She tried to say it as if she were joking, but she fell short, and then we were standing there with the burden of the day floating between us. What I had said—had *seen*—was not the kind of story people would forget anytime soon.

"It is going to be fine," my mother said, and I nodded and went back into my room. I don't think either of us slept that night.

The next morning she took me to see my childhood pediatrician, Dr. Willard, the same man who'd given me pieces of candy after I endured the tongue depressor when I was six. He asked me some questions but spoke mostly to my mother and talked a lot about stress.

"There's a cumulative toll," he said. "The events of this year add up. He's been in the spotlight, of course, talking to police and reporters and even appearing on national television. That's a lot for anyone. But then there's the undercurrent."

"The undercurrent?" my mother asked.

"The world!" Dr. Willard said, making a circle with his hands. "It is a tense place right now. We've had Columbine, we had the terrible murder right here in town, we've got so much fear. Then we add the traditional fun: homework and hormones."

He winked at me when he said "hormones." I just stared back at him. When we left, he gave my mother a list of "qualified counselors."

She was paying for the appointment when I saw the newspaper on the coffee table in the waiting room. There was an article describing how "the police response prompted panic after two 16-year-old Bloomington residents reported a murder and active shooter."

Two?

For a moment, I was genuinely confused. Then I remembered that Kerri had made the call.

I had made her part of it.

The police spokesman, my old friend Ron Walters, was quoted as saying it was "an unfortunate and traumatic day for a lot of folks in town, which is particularly painful considering the very real tragedies we've all endured recently."

He declined to address rumors that one of the two unnamed juveniles in question was Marshall Miller, who had also reported the infamous interaction with a murder victim in February.

"I'm not going to comment on that directly," Walters said, "but we're evaluating the veracity of witness testimony at all times."

What Walters wasn't willing to do, an anonymous editorial was happy to do.

"If police have been relying on a Monroe County Clifford Irving for months of a homicide investigation," the newspaper opined, "it would be both tragic and illuminating. Law enforcement agencies across the country have failed to produce any explanation for how a man impersonating one of their own appeared and disappeared. We might be closer to understanding why after yesterday's troubling events."

In the car on the way home, I asked my mother who Clifford Irving was. Her jaw tightened and she shook her head and told me not to worry about that.

She stayed home again that day. We kept the phones off, although she slipped into her bedroom a few times to make calls, speaking in a low voice. I tried Kerri twice from my cell phone. It went straight to voice mail. Her phone was turned off. I wondered if that was her choice or her parents'. Her car hadn't returned to Raintree Lane, which had to mean she was with her mother.

In the evening, when my mother began to watch her replacement do the weather segment again, I went to the computer and logged onto AIM. Within minutes I had more than fifty messages, most of them beginning with "What were you thinking?"

I logged off.

Tried Kerri again. Voice mail.

It was nearly eight, the sun edging down behind the oaks in the backyard, when the doorbell rang. I answered it, hoping for Kerri, and fearing a reporter or a police officer.

It was Noah Storm.

2

HE STOOD BEFORE ME, hale and hearty, as they say, without a scratch on him. He wore a tan linen sport coat open over the white shirt. No tie. No red ribbon of pooling blood, either.

"Hello, Marshall." His eyes were calmly curious. "I wanted to reach out personally."

"We have a phone," my mother said from behind me. She was standing with her arms folded tightly, shoulders back, chin up. She looked angry, and it took me a moment to understand why.

She was my mother.

It was that simple. She was a mother and I was her child and there were threats circling the den. She was in protector mode.

"I considered calling," Noah said casually. "But that didn't seem direct enough. This was a tumultuous event and it started at my office and I take my responsibility to Marshall seriously. I promised you that. I said I was going to look after him, and I meant it."

My mother seemed to exhale slightly.

"He was confused," she said. "He was confused and he was scared and the stress around all of this is too much for any child."

I didn't like being called a child. I also didn't like being told I was confused. What I'd been able to tolerate in the doctor's office I couldn't abide in front of the man I'd seen shot in the skull. I couldn't stop staring at his forehead. Not a mark. I knew what I'd seen, though.

I knew what I'd seen.

"I wasn't confused," I said. "Was it a trick? Some sort of—"

"Marshall." My mother touched my elbow. I ignored her.

"—Thing you had planned for him? Like the doorbell, the way you make it ring? You knew something was going to happen at the office because you made me leave, suddenly had *fieldwork*, but it had to be some sort of—"

"Marshall!" My mother's voice rose with a blade's edge of hysteria that silenced me. I looked back at her, and that was the first time that I appreciated the depth of her fear. She was watching her only son, afraid he was losing his mind. That realization stopped me cold.

"That's excellent work," Noah said evenly, as if my mother hadn't screamed. "You're trusting yourself while questioning what you might have missed at the same time. Observation is only one tool, and sometimes it can fail you."

As if we were sitting at the Encore Cafe and he was giving me pointers on surveillance.

"I don't—" my mother began, but Noah cut her off, smooth and unflappable, with that voice that suggested his resting heart rate never moved above 50.

"Stress shapes experience, and fear warps memory. Nothing to be embarrassed about; it's brain chemistry. I'm afraid I might have contributed to the stress. You're so sharp, Marshall, mature beyond your years, that I probably put more on you than I should have, probably didn't appreciate the lingering effects of your encounter with Maddox, and that's on me. But don't be ashamed of trauma. I know plenty of good men who have struggled with PTSD—it's a real thing that causes real problems. Plenty of strong, smart men have had similar visions to yours. Don't let anyone tell you differently. This *is* real. And you *will* get through it. I would like to help."

He sold each of us on him in that moment, managing to deliver the right hooks for both fish in a single cast. My mother wanted to hear someone promise that I wasn't crazy and extend an offer to help. She was a single mother in a world gone mad. She knew it would have been easier for Noah Storm to call me a crazy kid and walk away, another man leaving her alone with a son to raise and whispers and rumors to contend with. Instead, he'd complimented me—which was, of course, a compliment to her—and promised to stand by me, which meant standing by her.

What mattered to me was less nuanced and more selfish: he had described my encounter with Maddox without a whiff of doubt that it had actually occurred.

We each got what we needed, and he got in the door.

He was a very good detective.

We sat at the kitchen table. Noah's eyes roved over our home in a quick, cursory way, but I knew by now how much he was taking in, how he could archive what he saw and recall it later.

I stared at his forehead. I wanted desperately to see something where once the bullet hole had been. There was nothing to see. His skin was unblemished.

"I've spoken to several police officers," he said, adjusting his jacket and smoothing his shirt, "so I have a general sense of what happened, but I want to hear it from you."

I didn't want to tell it again, but when he fixed his gaze on me, I found myself talking, taking him from my trip to the library, to the call to Kerri, to the sight of him—yes, him, the living, breathing man seated at my kitchen table—murdered in his own desk chair. I described Maddox's movements, the way he'd returned up the stairs, the way I'd fled with Kerri. It was the best job I'd done telling the story, calmer, my recall for detail stronger. I still wanted to impress him. I wanted to show him that I'd listened and learned and, above all else, that I was not insane.

I also desperately wanted him to explain what had happened.

"Do you remember our sketching session?" he asked when I was through.

"Of course."

"Sketching?" my mother said.

"It didn't go so well," Noah said. "Marshall was concentrating very hard—at my request, mind you—on the memory of Maddox. I was pressing him for visual details. And then he had a bit of . . . a jolt."

"A *jolt*?"

"A seizure, perhaps. How would you describe it, Marshall?"

"I'm not sure." I shifted uncomfortably. "But it was—"

"You didn't tell me this," my mother said. "You had a *seizure* and didn't tell me?"

"That was my fault," Noah said. "I should have followed up." He kept his eyes steady on mine. "How were you going to describe it, Marshall? You said, 'But it was . . . ' "

"It was different than your timeline."

"What on earth does that mean?" my mother said, and this time we both ignored her.

"Timeline?" Noah said. "Clarify that, please." He leaned forward, bright-eyed, eager, and I felt his old energy but something was off about it, a click different than the way I'd learned to read his excitement for the hunt.

He wasn't hunting, I realized. That was the difference. A subtle shift—the same energy and instinct but an entirely different role. He was evading, not pursuing. He was prey.

But what sense did that make?

"Marshall?" he said. "When you say 'timeline,' what do you mean?"

And, yes, now I was sure of it. He was afraid of me. Not afraid *for* me, as my mother was, but afraid *of* me. I saw it in his eyes; I felt it in the air. The most primal things are often the most difficult to describe.

"To you, it felt like a quick thing," I said. "In and out, like I got dizzy or something, as quickly as the light bulb blew. To me, it felt longer. That's all."

But that wasn't all. My experience—seizure, if that's what he wanted to call it—had taken me right out of that basement and put me down in a different time and place.

And he was afraid of that time and place.

Why?

My mother was carrying on about how she couldn't believe that I hadn't told her all this and how Dr. Willard would need to know, her voice almost hopeful, as if the new information offered a possibility that was more appealing than any she'd considered. Epilepsy could be treated. Madness couldn't.

"I want to be clear on something," Noah said. "Marshall has been an asset and a hard worker and I'd be happy to have him back when the time is right." He flicked his eyes back to me. "I don't want you to feel that this incident cost you my respect or my gratitude. But at the moment—for the two of you, dealing with the fallout—I think it would be wise if we took a break before you return to the office."

"What are you afraid of?" I asked.

They both looked at me with surprise. Noah gave the faintest of nods, a flicker of the old approval in his eyes, before saying, "I'm afraid that I might be more harm than help to your family right now. We'll give it a little time, that's all."

Bullshit, I thought but did not say. *You're afraid of that barn, the one we both dream of, but you're afraid of it for different reasons. What are they?*

"Just know that I'm in your corner, all right?" he continued. "If you need anything, call. And I want you both to know that I'm not telling you anything that I haven't already told the police. It was a bad day, but there was no malice to it. I know that. I'll keep explaining it."

"Thank you," my mother said.

Noah rubbed his jaw, suddenly looking gravely tired, then cleared his throat.

"I'm a long way from home," he said. "Probably time to hit the road."

A long way from home? It was a ten-minute drive.

"I do appreciate your support," my mother said. "*We* do."

I muttered my thanks because I knew they were expected of me, but I stayed seated while she showed Noah to the door. He turned back and looked at me over his shoulder and tipped his index finger off his forehead in a little salute, and then the door sealed him out of sight.

Just like that, I'd lost my job.

3

THAT NIGHT, I TRIED to visit Kerri. She wasn't home, but Jerry was. He opened the door and regarded me sadly.

"Shit happens," he said. "You're not a bad kid."

I felt a sudden lump in my throat and had to look away. Jerry sighed and stepped out and shook a cigarette from the pack. Neither of us spoke while he lit it and took a drag. He was pale and thin and weary, a broken man in many ways, and yet I felt better having him there, telling me that I wasn't a bad kid.

"People don't understand how easy it is to get confused at the edges," he said.

"What?"

He waved his cigarette. "Whatever you saw. Or didn't see. You walked into the place, you were tense—with good damn reason, in this world—and you're seeing things in the shadows. Hell, sometimes in a crawl space I can *feel* a damn snake behind me, and then I look and . . . well, whatever. My point is, I know you didn't make up some bullshit for the fun of it."

"No," I said. "I didn't do that."

"People blaming you for being on guard—now, *that* is crap. You think you see a threat, you better announce it. I'd rather have a million like you,

Marshall, than a million people who can't see a threat right in front of their faces."

I had a bad feeling I knew where he was going.

"Thanks," I said. "Is Kerri—"

"You know why people started programming computers with two-digit dates?" Jerry asked, peering at me through his cigarette smoke.

I shook my head.

"Convenience and money," he said. "It's easier to type two digits than four, and it uses less memory, and that means you can save money. We're in this Y2K fix because this country sacrificed readiness for convenience. Forget the land of milk and honey, Marshall; it's the land of easy money, emphasis on 'easy.' Folks want the money, sure, but they want the *easy* first. That's the friggin' North Star these days. Give me laziness or give me death, and let Mexico or China have the jobs."

I didn't speak. He smoked and sighed. Silence built.

"Two-digit dates in a four-digit year," he said, and laughed bitterly. "Half the work, kid. That's what it boils down to. People wanted to do half the work. Can't even anticipate that the joke will be on them when that's played out and there's no work left and no money either."

"Yes, sir."

My voice seemed to remind him that I was there.

"Don't let the bastards get you down," he said. "Anyone says a wrong word in my earshot, they're gonna hear about it, I promise you that."

I had a feeling there were better advocates for my cause, but I thanked him and asked if he knew when Kerri would be home. It seemed to hurt both of us that he didn't.

It wasn't until midnight that Kerri's Honda returned and the familiar pale red glow from the exit sign in the basement came on. I slipped out of my room and walked down the hall and stood before my mother's closed door, listening. It was silent. She was finally asleep. I left the house.

It was a perfect summer night, fragrant with fresh-cut grass and honeysuckle, the earth seeming recharged by the storms of the previous day. Fireflies danced in the darkness and a light breeze blew and I thought of Leslie Carter. I could have spent the summer at Camp Amherst with her on nights like this instead of interning in that limestone manor of madness.

Could've, would've, should've.

I hadn't. That was all that mattered. Your identity is shaped by your choices.

Kerri was in one of the beanbag chairs in her basement, facing the open window, a book in her hands. She seemed to sense me before she saw me, because she closed the book and then checked the window and seemed unsurprised to find me there, painted red in the exit light's glow. When she slipped outside, I had a cold, twisting sensation in the pit of my stomach, sure that she was going to be furious—that, like everyone else, she would want answers I couldn't provide.

"Hollinger?" she asked.

"Hollinger."

I followed her across her yard to the old elementary school playground. We hadn't made this same walk since the first night I'd heard of Noah Storm. Only when we were seated on the swings, the old chains creaking beneath our weight, did she break the silence.

"I would've called but my mother was supremely freaked out and took my phone."

"It's okay." I took a breath, then plunged ahead. "Look, I'm sorry. For everything. I can't explain it the way you'll want me to, but I—"

"You saw him," she said simply. "Maddox. He was in there and you saw him. I keep telling everyone that."

"You believe me?"

"Yes." She gave a short laugh and shook her head, making her hair fall forward. "That hasn't been particularly helpful for me, not with my parents or the police, but . . ."

I waited. The chains creaked.

"But I was there," she said at last. "I was there, and I saw your face, Marshall, I saw the way you looked when you came through that door, and then you grabbed me, and you were trying to save me from something *awful*. You couldn't have faked that if you tried. I didn't know what you were running from, but the way you looked and the way you grabbed me and tried to get me out of there . . ."

She pushed her hair back from her face.

"I know that was real."

I didn't say anything. I lifted my feet off the ground and kept them high, like a child, so the earth couldn't interrupt the swaying of the swing.

"The police seem to think it's a prank," she said. "A couple think you're mentally ill, but more seem to believe you planned the whole thing. Or we did together."

"And you said that I'd really seen something?"

"Not something. I said you'd seen Maddox."

"But *you* didn't see him."

"No. I believe what you told me."

Simple faith is the purest act of love, I think. It's also a hell of an easy way to get yourself in trouble.

Kerri knew that, of course. She was the smartest person I knew.

"Are your parents pissed at me?" I asked.

"Mom, yes. She thinks you're attention seeking or . . ." She gave an exhausted wave. "She has plenty of theories. Dad feels sorry for you. Jake is just worried. He told me if you need anyone to talk to, call him. He's supportive."

Of course he was. The only supporter I still had: Jake Crane, the rock-climbing psychologist in training. Oh, and don't forget the Weller and his midnight calls. My squad.

"You wouldn't lie to me," Kerri said. "Not about something like that. So you either saw it or you're crazy."

"Noah is alive," I said. "When I saw him in there, he wasn't. Explain that one."

"I can't."

"Me neither."

"But you're not crazy," she said. "And there is something wrong in that place."

I looked at her. "What?"

"The house, the office, whatever you want to call it. There's something *wrong* there, or at least there was the other day. I didn't see it but I felt it. And when you grabbed me, Marshall, you were so scared. There's nightmare scared, and then there's real-world scared. You were trying to save me from something real. Nobody else believes that, but nobody else was there."

"You never thought I was making it up?"

"No. You saw something."

"You believe in ghosts," I said. It wasn't a question. We'd had a hundred conversations on the topic over the years, most of them on October nights as the trees thinned and the Halloween decorations appeared. The most memorable had been in the summer, though, on the weekend that Kerri's grandmother died.

"Yes," she said. "Is that what you think you saw?"

"I don't know."

I was our resident skeptic, the kid who liked to puncture the balloon of possibility, arguing that ghost encounters were all silly superstition or misunderstood coincidences. The only night I hadn't held up my role was the night after her grandmother died, when I knew Kerri wanted to believe for different reasons.

"Noah came to my house," I said.

"Angry?"

"No. Still very calm, actually, which was odd, don't you think, considering I'd reported him being shot in the head?"

"It's suboptimal intern behavior."

I almost smiled, but my mind was too caught up in the memory.

"He was cool, and steady—in most ways he was himself—except . . . I felt as if he was afraid of me in some way. Not because he thought I was crazy but because he knew I *wasn't*. I can't describe it better than that."

"Try," Kerri said.

So I did. As the night crept toward dawn, we talked, and we soared on the swings, childhood present all around us like gravity, the two of us determined to push past that, deny its existence. I told her everything

I'd seen in Noah's office, and I told her everything about his visit, and for the first time I told her the story of my sketching session in the basement and the visions of the barn with the drop of blood and the snakes in the dust.

"When he was talking to my mom and me about what I'd seen in his office, he said, 'This *is* real.' Then he moved on, and I don't think she caught that the way I did. But . . . he was not questioning what I saw, Kerri, and the guy questions *everything*. He didn't push hard enough on this one, or on me. Maybe that's because my mom was there, but I don't think so. I think he knows so much that he couldn't fake the curiosity. Not even about Maddox being in his house."

"If Maddox were a ghost, it would be easier to explain," she said. "No one else sees him. Noah is a bigger problem."

Vintage Kerri—everything was intellectual and forensic, a problem to be analyzed and solved. Ghost cop: possible. Ghost boss: more work needed to prove the theorem.

"Yes," I agreed. "Noah is the bigger problem."

"Because he's not dead. At least, not in a traditional way."

A traditional way. This was the side of Kerri that I had enjoyed making fun of for so many years: the dreamer, or the romantic, call it what you wish, the girl who was willing to believe damn near anything because she wanted to. It was so at odds with her academic mind that I usually laughed. Tonight, I listened like a student.

"So what do I do, Kerri?"

"I'm not sure. People won't be able to consider this seriously, of course. They won't even listen to it. They'll shoot you full of meds and send you for counseling."

"Correct."

"So what do you *want* to do?" she asked.

I didn't answer immediately. The first thought that rose to mind was *Go back to work with him*—but that was already off the table, and even if it weren't, did I really want to go back to 712 Lockridge Lane?

"Get back to my own life," I said at last. "Forget this ever happened. That's all."

Kerri was silent for a minute, letting the swing's momentum wind down, slower and slower, returning her to earth.

"Hey," I said, "who is Clifford Irving? My mom didn't tell me, and I forgot to look him up."

"He was a writer who pretended to interview Howard Hughes. It was a famous hoax. He made up the whole story. He'd never met Hughes."

"Why did he do it?"

"Money, at first. Then he said it got away from him. He couldn't stop once he'd told the first lie."

I used my feet to push off from the earth once more and let the swing take me higher, so I could see above the tree line and find the red glow that marked Kerri's room and the distant rooflines of the houses up and down Raintree Lane. Stars shone. Fireflies flashed and faded.

A police car cruised by our cul-de-sac.

I felt my breath catch.

"Kerri, look."

But she was down lower, and she couldn't see it, and then the cruiser moved on, crawling slowly by, disappearing into the night.

"What was it?" she asked.

"A cop."

"They come by sometimes. Night patrols."

I didn't remember many night patrols. What I did remember was Noah saying that it was a long trip home and hustling out of our house as if he were late for a date.

"Let's go home," I said.

Kerri didn't object.

"It's not going to be a fun fall for you now," I said as we walked away from the playground. "People will blame you, and you didn't even do anything. I'm sorry."

"Hey, you got punched in the face for me back in June. I owed you one."

Not everyone was so forgiving. The next day Meredith Sullivan's parents were interviewed on national television. They said the idea that police had been looking for their daughter in the wrong town for months, based on a lie cooked up by a kid who wanted attention, was unbearable.

The anchor asked them if the police believed their daughter had ever been in Bloomington, Indiana, on February 11, 1999.

"There's zero evidence," Meredith's father said. "All we ever had was this kid's story. There's no reason to believe that anymore. It feels like we're back to square one. It's devastating."

CHAPTER EIGHT

LOST AND FOUND

August–September 1999

"You might win some but you just lost one"

LAURYN HILL
"LOST ONES"

1

JULY FADED AND AUGUST came and went. Those were long weeks. The purpose that I'd felt with the job was gone, and the old path of filling the summer hours with friends and foolishness had closed. I went to see a counselor at my mother's request. He was a paunchy guy with a gray goatee who told me to call him Clint and always added awkward slang in an unsuccessful attempt to seem hip.

"Right on" was his favorite.

Do you ever have daydreams? Right on. What about nightmares? Right on.

I never considered telling him the truth about anything, let alone my nightmares. I told him what I thought he'd need to hear in order to give my mother some reassurances. I'd been stressed out by the media attention, by Columbine, by scary movies. Maybe it was my diet. Maybe it was *The Matrix*. I was feeling better now. Eating right and getting sleep and avoiding violent television. No, I didn't want to try medication.

My relationship with my mother was a strained stage play. We ate breakfast together and we played golf on Sunday mornings. I didn't tell her that I slept with the bedroom door locked and the light on and she didn't tell me that she already knew, just as I didn't tell her that I knew she'd thrown out the newspaper on three occasions so I didn't see articles making me out to be the villain of the Meredith Sullivan investigation. I'd fished them from the recycling bin in the garage.

The days were long and empty. I wasn't officially grounded any longer, but I acted like it. I didn't need to see people in person to know I'd be treated like a pariah; AIM did a good job of alerting me to that. I divided my time between books and music, endless hours on Napster. For a while I spent an hour a day hitting golf balls into a net in the backyard. That was a good release until the afternoon when I reached for a pitching wedge and was *positive* that the club undulated like a snake.

I yelled and scrambled backward—but the golf bag was still, the clubs motionless. All the same, I used a rake to push the bag around a little, not trusting my own eyes, and from then on, the silver shafts and the black grips bothered me. The next day I found an old can of bright blue spray paint in the garage and used it to paint the grips. They turned the textured rubber into a tacky mess, but at least they didn't look like the snake. When my mother asked me why in the world I'd painted my nice clubs, I tried to play it off as no big deal, but I didn't like the way she looked at me as if this were another thing that Clint the therapist should hear.

Jobless, I tried volunteering for the Monroe County Humane Society to help fill the hours. When I came home and told my mother about the dogs who needed fostering, stressing that they needed only temporary homes, she was more receptive than I'd expected, considering the number of times during my childhood when she'd shot down the idea of a dog. I think she was looking for anything resembling normalcy. A boy who wanted a dog was normal.

I didn't tell her that I wanted a dog in the yard because I kept thinking about snakes.

The dogs at the shelter that I liked best were Norwegian elkhounds, Alva and Haldora, from the same litter. Their previous owner had passed away, and they were housebroken and beautiful and hilarious. Knowing that my mother would never agree to take both unless she saw them, I brought her to the shelter before I made my pitch.

"I don't think it would be right to split them up," I said. They were sitting side by side, looking up at my mother as if she were the bearer of all the peanut butter treats in the universe. I watched her try to find the resolve to say there was no chance we were taking two dogs.

In the end, we took two dogs.

I didn't try to venture out socially and didn't even log onto AIM much. Friends stopped calling. Dom came by, but that was about it.

"You know I've always got your back," he said while Alva and Haldora whirled around his legs, "but you need to explain this one. Tell people you were scared and confused, even if it makes you look like a coward."

I wasn't confused, I thought, but I didn't have the energy to try to explain it. Not again.

Kerri tried to draw me out for some activity beyond running, but I kept making excuses. Finally, she showed up at my house with Jake and said we were going to go grab dinner and see a movie.

"It's not a negotiation. You need to get out of the house."

"I do not want to crash your date."

"Shut up. Jake misses seeing you."

"I bet. Would he like to see me do the Terminator Tower again?"

"Get in the car," Kerri said.

So I did. I sat in the back seat as Jake drove to Noble Roman's, the pizza place that had the best breadsticks in town. I tried to be a good sport about it, although his stereo took us from Vertical Horizon's "Everything You Want" to the Dixie Chicks' "Cowboy Take Me Away" and I knew a make-out mix when I heard one. When Joe's "I Wanna Know" came on, I almost opened the back door and threw myself onto the road.

We had a good time at Noble Roman's because their breadsticks and deep-dish pizza demanded joy, and Kerri had big news: Snoop Dogg was coming to town. She'd bought three tickets for a September concert called Hoosier Rap Daddy '99 that was going to be held in a field outside town and feature Busta Rhymes, the Roots, Method Man, Too $hort, and Eminem alongside Snoop. None of us could believe so many big names were arriving in Bloomington.

The night was going well until we reached the theater.

Jake picked the movie: *The Sixth Sense*, M. Night Shyamalan's debut, which none of us knew anything about. It turned out to be a story of a kid who sees dead people and is treated by a psychiatrist whose previous teenage client committed suicide after a series of terrifying hallucinations.

"That was an unfortunate choice," Jake said when the credits rolled. "Sorry, guys."

"It's no problem," I said. We promptly bumped into a group of kids from North who were headed into the theater as we were walking out.

"Looking for inspiration, Miller?" someone cracked. "This one's your life story, right?"

Kerri flipped them off and Jake rolled his eyes and put a protective arm around my shoulders, which was worse than if he'd done nothing. We returned to the Volvo, and when Brandy and Monica came on with "The Boy Is Mine" I absolutely would have thrown myself onto the highway if I didn't think Jake had the child safety locks engaged in the back seat. It seemed like his style.

"We'll do it again soon, man," he said when they dropped me off. "Next time, you can pick the movie."

"Looking forward to it already," I said, and then I exchanged fist bumps with them and went into the house and turned on all the lights and cranked the music loud, letting Memphis Bleek drown out the lingering memories of Brandy and Monica.

And, yes, the lingering memories of the ghost girl, so terrifyingly real, from *The Sixth Sense*.

The movie got one thing wrong, though. The scariest ghost isn't a stranger. The scariest ghost is the one you trust.

I was afraid of Noah Storm. Why, then, did I still want to speak with him? Why was there some part of me, buried beneath the fear, that believed he could help me, or I could help him?

Maybe Clint was right. It was all the media's fault.

That was the last time I went to the movies that summer.

The Dalai Lama came to town. That was big news. My mother took me to see him speak on a panel about preventing youth violence. A year earlier I'd have rolled my eyes; this summer I was keeping my mouth shut and listening. The Dalai Lama was joined on the panel by former FBI director William Sessions. My mother didn't like that pairing.

"Let's see if he has anything to say about Waco or Ruby Ridge," she said.

He didn't. He did mention overseeing the requirement to include the phrase "Winners Don't Use Drugs" on arcade games, which presumably would solve some problems with the youth. My mother caught me smiling at that one and I cleared my throat and straightened up. The Dalai Lama, through his interpreter, said he thought that bad things happened because of "many decays."

If either of them had answers for Columbine or Ben Smith, I didn't hear them.

I saw Dom at the Dalai Lama's panel. He was there with his whole family—it was a huge deal to them, I knew—and when we talked to them afterward, I felt strangely touched by the way his parents made no mention of my summer news making and had no trouble maintaining eye contact. It was a shame they wouldn't be in class with me come September. The crowd waiting at school was more like the group I'd encountered at the movie theater.

I had not heard from Sean Weller since his midnight call, but my mind returned to it a few times. What had he called his weight-lifting approach? A confidence-builder.

That certainly didn't seem like the worst thing. And while I didn't feel as if I really knew Sean, it hadn't kept him from calling. In August, I made my way to the HPER weight room and looked tentatively around for him. He was nowhere to be seen, but I didn't want to simply walk in and walk back out, so I decided to lift on my own. I remembered the punch from Kenny Glass that had slammed me into the summer, and Maddox's massive arms, and the way Jake Crane had gone up that climbing wall ju before I slid down it with my pants around my knees. Yes, I wanted to a armor.

I was straining on the bench press when Weller sat down besid He looked at me sorrowfully.

"Your form is putrid," he said. "I'm not even sure what you're to achieve here, Marshmallow. Is that supposed to be for your che shoulders? Why are you arching your back?"

"It generates power."

"It generates slipped discs. You look like you're experiencing an exorcism."

"I'm doing more weight than the last set," I said defensively.

"That's the problem," he said. "You shouldn't be."

He stood and removed the collar from the forty-five-pound bar and then slid off the five-pound plate and the thirty-five-pounder behind it. I was trying to get up to the 135 pounds that almost everyone else used as a warm-up set.

"You need to be honest," Weller said, sliding a single, twenty-five-pound plate on each end of the bar. "If you're not, you're only going to get to hurt. And don't flex in the mirror, either. That's for pussies."

With that, a routine took hold for summer's final weeks. Run with Kerri, lift with Weller. Get faster, get stronger. I didn't have a conscious plan, but it would have been obvious to an outsider. There are a couple reasons you try to get faster and stronger. Survival is one of them.

Fear is another.

School started. Senior year. I hoped everyone would be distracted and that Marshall Miller's hysterical murder report would feel like old news. Not the case. The jokes were relentless. It didn't help that the biggest movies on the planet were *The Sixth Sense* and *The Blair Witch Project*. I tried to take the jabs in stride, to keep my head down. As the days wore on, I adopted that approach more literally. I began to bring a book with me wherever I went, and I spent lunches in the library. I read everything Mr. Doig recommended. I appreciated that he didn't take a cautious approach with me, as if I were mentally fragile. The first book he handed me that year was Stephen King's *It*, which felt like a test, as if he was assessing my willingness to confront fear. I loved the book. I asked for another like it, he gave me Robert McCammon's *Boy's Life* and then *Summer of Night* n Simmons. I devoured those and moved on to Peter Straub's *Ghost*

ou're a good storyteller," Mr. Doig said. "I always wished you'd with our creative writing workshop. Your first sentence was excellent: 'He cried when he left the boy.' There's an amazing story waiting behind that one."

It had been three years since I'd written that, and I was astonished that he remembered it.

"I'm no writer," I mumbled.

"You are someone who has not yet written. Maybe you should try. 'He cried when he left the boy.' It's a wonderful opening. We begin with emotional conflict and characters in action. There are questions, of course: Who is the man, who is the boy, why are there tears, why is the man leaving, and where will he go?" He paused, thoughtful, then added, "I suppose the boy could be leaving. That would be a twist from expectations."

The boy isn't leaving, I thought. *He stays behind. And, yes, there are plenty of questions.*

"Write from that place and see where it goes!" Mr. Doig urged. "Let the story lead the way. Could be fiction, could be fact. That's up to you."

He was right about most things, but he was wrong about that. Fiction or fact is actually up to the reader. The right novel at the right time might tell a deeper truth than a biography.

I hung out with Kerri alone when I could, which was rare, and with Kerri and Jake when I couldn't, and tagged along with Dom and Nadia at other times. Always a third wheel. More girls knew me by name than ever before, but not because they wanted a date. I saw Sean Weller more than almost anyone outside of classmates. He was always at the HPER, even though the college football season was well underway.

"I'm on a redshirt year," he said when I asked. "They have too many seniors playing my position. It wouldn't make sense for them to waste me."

I thought that a redshirt was still allowed to work out with the team, and said as much, but Weller cut me off.

"It's very complicated shit, Marshmallow. You don't know the first thing about the NCAA."

I didn't press him. It was none of my business, and besides, I liked having him around the HPER. He was someone to talk to, a nice source of distractions, keeping my mind from my struggles at school, from ghosts, from snakes, from a dead man who'd arrived on my front porch.

He wasn't enough of a distraction, though. Nothing was. Even the one great distraction I'd counted on that September—the ballyhooed Hoosier Rap Daddy '99 concert —didn't deliver. Monroe County officials canceled the show after some people in Bloomington protested that the rap concert was too big, too dangerous, too violent. Nobody said too Black, but the county had just held a large concert in a similar field for Kid Rock in the spring, and if local hero John Mellencamp had wanted to play in the same space, he'd have been greeted like the pope. A homeowner's association filed a legal challenge of the concert, and the county commissioners said their hands were tied because the temporary permit code limited acceptable events to such things as yard sales, carnivals, and religious tent services.

"You have got to be kidding me," Kerri said. "We can have a *tent revival* but not a rap concert? Isn't this supposed to be a hip college town?"

Eminem gave an interview to the *Herald-Times*, which pleased Kerri to no end.

"The people who protested are probably just old people who don't know what's happening," he said.

They still had the show, but it was moved to Indianapolis, and my mother wouldn't let me make the drive. Too dangerous, she said of the same drive she made five nights a week.

So much for Snoop Dogg.

I turned seventeen. September ended. The long nights were fading, and I had to run earlier, and run alone, because Kerri was in cross-country season. Once, I'd been excited about my mother working nights because she wouldn't know what friends I was out with; now I was relieved because she didn't know that I was never out with any. I'd blast the stereo while doing homework, then head to bed, door locked, lights on, grateful to have the dogs in the house with me now. I did not see Noah Storm, and I did not dream of a weathered barn in an empty field. For a time it seemed the past was escapable. I would change what I could about myself, and I would trust time to do the rest.

It's good that we can fool ourselves.

Sometimes it's the only way to move ahead.

The problem is that the past calls you when it's ready, not the other way around. And so it seemed all too appropriate that when I most desperately wanted everyone to focus on the future, the same librarian who'd told me what was happening at Columbine High School in April brought me a note that said Noah Storm was trying to reach me with urgent news.

2

I WAS STACKING RETURNED books on the shelving cart, alone in the library office while Kerri put up a sign on the front wall, when Mr. Doig entered with a note in his hand.

"Marshall? Do you know a Noah Storm?"

I set the books down slowly. "Yeah. Why?"

"He called the office trying to reach you. There's a number here."

I didn't need the number, but I took the note anyhow. I was trying not to look scared, but Mr. Doig saw something in my face.

"Do you want me here or would you like some privacy?"

"Privacy. I mean, it doesn't matter, I guess. I don't know what's up."

Mr. Doig studied me, then pointed at the phone on his desk. "I'll be out here if you need me."

He slipped out of the office and shut the door behind him. I held the note, which was nothing more than Noah's name and phone number, but somehow it reminded me of the speeding ticket that had gotten it all started. Part of me wanted to throw it in the trash and return to shelving books.

But I called. Of course I did.

He answered on the first ring. "Storm Agency."

"It's Marshall."

"Marshall! I'm sorry to trouble you at school, but I wanted to give you a heads-up before you heard the news from anyone else."

I glanced at the door. Mr. Doig was hovering just outside. "What news?"

"Meredith Sullivan's body has been found."

I stiffened. "Where?"

"Lake Griffy, not three miles from where you saw her last."

I didn't respond to that because I couldn't speak. It felt as if something were loosening deep inside me, unknotting.

"The police are on the scene now," Noah said, "and I'm sure the media won't be far behind. I wanted to let you and your mother know so you weren't blindsided."

"Okay. Thanks. Was she . . . I mean, how did . . ."

"I don't know the cause of death yet," he said gently. "I anticipate the autopsy results take a few days."

"All right. Sure." My mouth was dry, my heart racing. The news was both awful and validating. I'd wanted to be proven wrong by Meredith Sullivan appearing healthy and well and with her own story to tell, but I'd never believed that would happen. I'd known she was dead longer than almost anyone, I think. I remembered her face in the mirror, the tear on her cheek, the rage in Maddox's eyes. I closed my eyes, my hand tight on the phone receiver.

"Do you know how they found her?" I asked.

"A private company using side-scan sonar." For the first time, Noah seemed rattled. "It's sophisticated technology but it's . . . it's a slow process. She was in twenty feet of water and there's heavy timber on the bottom out there."

I opened my eyes, saw Mr. Doig watching me through the transom window beside the door, and tried to force a smile onto my face. He turned away.

"How did they know where to look?" I asked.

Pause.

"A tip, I understand. One that I supported because it was in the direction where Maddox was taking her the last time you saw them. I knew the police hadn't searched the water with divers, so I . . . nudged a little with the sonar approach."

He'd believed my story. Kept believing it. I remembered him the last time I'd seen him in the office, blood on his face, bullet hole in his forehead.

My reputation had been cleared by a dead man.

"All right," Noah said. "I've interrupted your school day long enough. I needed to tell you she was found and that you pointed people in the right direction. Remember that. I'm sorry it took so long, and I'm sorry it ended like this, but it's . . . it's some kind of progress."

"Sure."

"If you need me," he said, "you know where the office is. You've still got a key."

"Sure," I repeated, thinking that I both badly wanted to return to his office and never wanted to see it again.

"Take care of yourself, Marshall," he said without waiting for my answer, and then the line was dead and he was gone.

I put the phone back onto the cradle and methodically folded the note Mr. Doig had given me and put it in my pocket.

She was in twenty feet of water and there's heavy timber on the bottom out there.

It's some kind of progress.

I walked out into the library. Kerri was standing on a stepstool, stretched up on her tiptoes, taping up the last letter of a sign that said BOOKS ARE PORTABLE MAGIC. She heard me approaching and turned without lowering her hand and saw something in my face that froze her. She stayed on her tiptoes and kept her hand extended when she said, "What happened?"

"They found her," I said. "They found Meredith Sullivan. It's done, Kerri."

Of course, only half of that was true.

That night, Kerri and I sat with Jerry Flanders and watched the news report from Lake Griffy. The Sullivan family offered a statement but did not appear on camera, and I was glad for that. The end of the search meant different things for different people.

They aired the police sketch of Maddox again that night. It was the first time I'd seen it in months. It hadn't gotten any more accurate.

"I hope they catch the bastard," Jerry Flanders said. He was only half watching, though. He was distracted by the roll of heavy, clear plastic that he was trimming and taping across the top of a fifty-gallon drum, part of a homemade cistern that he was using to trap and store rainwater. We were only three months away from the millennium New Year, and as he told us frequently, he had no sympathy for anyone who'd been told that Y2K was coming and didn't prepare for it. His latest project was something called a "pit house," which he promised would be an emergency shelter warm enough for survival during the worst of the winter.

At his feet was a coiled bright blue static line that Kerri had told me was an extremely expensive rope. Why did Jerry need an expensive rope? Because you had to prepare for the unknown.

There was always more gear and always more fear. One fed the other.

While the Y2K stuff sounded crazy, another branch of his growing paranoia had been validated. General Electric, Bloomington's last large-scale factory, had announced they would be cutting the workforce by at least half. A double-door refrigerator called the Millennium Model that was supposed to save the plant would be manufactured in Mexico. The layoffs were the town's third gutting: first at Otis, then Thomson Electronics, and now GE. It was, Jerry claimed, precisely the reason he hadn't looked for a job at any of the big plants. What was the point of picking up a grenade, he said, when you knew the pin had already been pulled?

Now I watched him seal another layer of plastic across the big drum, his craftsman's hands moving nimbly and surely. It was almost as bad as looking at the sketch of Maddox.

Almost.

"I hope they catch him too," I said, staring at that awful depiction of the man I'd seen twice—once behind the wheel of the police car that had driven Meredith Sullivan to her death, and once inside a limestone house in the heart of town, where he'd murdered Noah Storm.

The same Noah Storm who'd just located Meredith Sullivan's body.

The news segment didn't mention Noah. They gave full credit to the police, who in turn referenced an anonymous tip. The private detective who'd delivered results went unnamed.

"Will you talk to him again?" Kerri asked.

I shook my head.

"It's done," I said. My mantra for the day. Repeat something enough times and you can make it real, right? It worked all right that day, and the next, and the next. It stopped working on the fourth day, when I came down for breakfast and saw my mother reading the newspaper with a horrified expression.

"They released the autopsy results," she said in a soft, sickened voice. "I don't even want to know exactly what happened to that poor girl, Marshall. I truly don't."

"What do you mean?"

"She was killed by snake venom," my mother said, pushing the paper away as if she could no longer bear its presence on the table. "They don't know if it was from a true bite or some kind of poisoning. They just know that it stopped her heart."

3

IF NOT FOR THE SNAKES, I might have been able to move on.

Things were better at school. Validation helped stem the tide of mockery. Part of my story had been proven true—a small part, sure, but it was something—and people took note. Even Leslie Carter sent me an instant message.

Looks like you saw Meredith after all.

Yes, I had seen her.

What did that mean about Maddox, though? About Noah Storm? I didn't know, and I told myself that I didn't care. I tried to be the bystander that fall.

The problem was the snakes.

They formed a bridge between things real and imagined. The vision—or nightmare?—I'd had of the battling snakes in front of the old barn merged with the very real snake that had entered my own home in the spring. I couldn't dismiss Meredith Sullivan's cause of death as a reasonable coincidence.

But I also couldn't do a damn thing about it.

I kept to my routine: school, running, lifting. I'd gone from 140 pounds at the start of summer to 152. Still thin but not skinny. There was a difference. One day Sean Weller slapped two ten-pound plates on beside the forty-fives, watched me do a set on the bench, and said, "You can *finally* lift more than you weigh."

He'd been teasing me, but the observation lingered. I could take all my weight and push it away. I liked that.

Kerri stopped teasing me about my running times and told me that I should consider track in the spring.

"I don't want to be on the track team."

"Then what is the point, Marshall?"

"Exercise. Maybe you haven't heard, but it's healthy."

She didn't smile. "You're kind of OCD about it. I just figure there must be a goal?"

There *was* a goal, but not one I could articulate—certainly not in front of her.

I wanted to be a different person. One who was less afraid. The physical challenges were easier to meet than the mental. I could force myself to do an extra rep, or sprint when I felt like jogging, or jog when I felt like walking. I couldn't force my way to an explanation of Noah Storm's continued existence.

I also couldn't forget him—or the snake, or Meredith Sullivan's face in the mirror. She'd been found but Maddox was still out there.

In October, I parked the Oldsmobile below the dam at Lake Griffy and walked the trail that ringed the water. The leaves were starting to fall, not yet in the beautiful peak colors of red and orange, but more browns and greens.

Snake colors.

I walked to the place where Meredith Sullivan's body had been found. It was at the far end of the lake, closer to the boathouse than the dam, and on a summer day the stretch of trail between the two would have been busy and there would have been boats on the water. Today, on an overcast weekday edging toward fall, it was a lonely place. There was a single canoe on the water, a man and a woman paddling, and I could hear their voices but not the words. I'd made it about a quarter mile, walking along the shore trail with my head down, focused on my feet because of all those leaves, when I heard a soft whistle behind me.

I stopped and looked back. No one was there. A light breeze stirred the branches overhead and sent a single oak leaf pinwheeling down at my feet. I was about to turn when I heard the whistle again, a low double note. A man in a blue shirt appeared far down the trail, descending the same hill I'd just come by, with the dam on his right and the woods on his left. He had his head down and tilted and was peering behind him. He whistled again and tugged on something in his hand, then turned and watched as something rustled past him, and I let out my breath, realizing it was just some guy walking a dog on a long leash.

I was scared to be alone out here—scared to be alone anywhere, almost—and I hated that.

I watched as the man with the dog walked, head down and whistling occasionally, the way you do when you're both following the dog's lead and trying to guide it simultaneously—*no don't sniff that, let's go, buddy.* Out on the lake, the couple in the canoe laughed, everyone able to enjoy their day except for me. Why had I even come here? I knew only that I wanted to see the spot, as if it might tell me something.

I turned and walked ahead. I wasn't sure of the exact place to look, of course, but the newspaper photos had given the general area. The trees packed tightly around the narrow dirt path at the top of a shallow rise that gave me a decent view. I stared into the dark water and saw my reflection and was pleased by it, maybe for the first time ever. The weight room work was evident. I was an inch taller and fifteen pounds heavier than I had been in the spring. When reflected in the ripples and dimmed by the shadows, I could almost be confused for a man.

This is what I was thinking when I heard the rustle in the leaves behind me. I nearly cried out and spun toward it. So much for manliness. I managed to hold my ground, well aware that the sound was simply the man with the dog approaching. I could hear his footsteps behind the dog's rustling, and that low two-tone whistle broke the stillness once more. I was standing just off the trail, giving them plenty of room to pass by. I'd keep my back to them, I decided, because the last thing I needed was for anyone to recognize me out here.

The wind gusted and dropped off, and an acorn fell into the water with a splash that seemed too loud. Ripples spread out from where the acorn had vanished, and I had a sudden, terrible image of Meredith Sullivan waiting below, hair fanned out in the water, eyes upturned at the surface, staring through the expanding ripples and right at me.

I shivered. Behind me, the rustle continued, but the footsteps did not. A prickle crawled along my spine.

You're fine, I told myself. *You are just fine. Let them by.*

The sound behind me wasn't one of approaching feet, though. Not a man's, not a dog's. No one could walk this quietly. There was no more whistling, nor any panting from the dog. The only sound was a soft whisk, like fine-grit sandpaper rubbed very lightly and slowly over rough wood.

And it was not stopping.

I turned and saw the snake.

It was coming right down the trail, following every bend, moving with a strange formality down the middle of the path, utterly fearless. Its black-and-white body slid over the dirt, arched over a root, and undulated across the scattered leaves. There was something hypnotic about its motion. It was fifteen feet away, and if it held to the trail, it would soon head uphill—and right toward me. My back was to the lake, and the brush was thick around me, so running away meant going down to the trail, temporarily closing the gap with the snake.

I looked back at the water. The canoe was out of sight, its paddlers silent.

Jump, I thought. *Get in the water!*

But Meredith Sullivan's body had been pulled from this water, and I could not will my own into it.

I shifted as far from the trail as I could, the loose soil on the bank beginning to crumble beneath my shoes, and looked to see where the snake was.

It had stopped in the khaki-colored dust, as if to showcase its own coloration. Its head was up and bobbing gently, as if tasting the wind. I saw for the first time that there was something looped around its neck. A thin, olive-colored cord ensnared the snake's neck just below its head and trailed away. As I watched, the slack cord drew slowly taut. I followed the cord right to left, back up the trail, just as the man holding the opposite end of it rounded the bend and came into view.

Maddox lifted his head, locked eyes with me, and smiled.

"We meet again. What brings you this way, Mr. Miller? And why is it that every time I encounter you, you've left the path?"

I could not draw a breath. The soil continued to crumble beneath my heels, whispering down the embankment and into the water. Maddox looked exactly as he had the last time I'd seen him, except he was wearing a long-sleeved uniform shirt this time, and there was no badge. No gun, either, at least none that I could see. Just the snake on that long leash.

Maddox looked down at the snake and his smile widened and warmed. It was just the way my mother would look at the dogs some evenings, delighted simply by their existence.

The snake did not move until Maddox gave that low, two-tone whistle. Then the rattles burst to life with a shrill shudder.

I ran.

I ran straight through the thicket of brush to my right, thorns ripping my flesh and branches whipping my face, and Maddox laughed as the snake's rattle rose. I was too scared to scream. I ran through the brush and pushed past a small pine and found the trail again, and there I began to sprint, an all-out, desperate dash. Up ahead, the boathouse waited, and through the woods beyond that, Headley Road and humanity—if I could make it there.

I did.

I burst out of the trees and onto the pavement just as a car passed. The horn blared and I heard the driver shout with fear and anger. Then the car was around the corner and gone. I stood in the middle of the road and looked back across the lake.

There was no one in sight.

I took my cell phone out with a shaking hand, then stopped. Who was I going to call? My first instinct was the police. But I had tried that once before with Maddox and it hadn't ended well. My mother? Kerri?

I lowered the phone. Pocketed it. Stared back at the woods. No pursuer was in sight. The laugh was gone and the rattling with it.

I walked all the way back to my car on the road. It took a long time, adding miles that the trail would've eliminated, but there was no way I would ever walk that path again. When I finally reached the parking lot below the dam, I was soaked with sweat, bleeding from a half dozen scratches, and my car sat alone.

I got behind the wheel and drove to Lockridge Lane. I did not know how to explain anything about Noah Storm or what had happened in July, but I was certain that Noah would listen to my latest encounter with Maddox and offer guidance. I knew he would.

But he did not even answer the door.

I sat on the wide limestone steps, with those oversized lightning rods casting long thin shadows across the lawn, waiting for him to return home, and wondering if what I'd seen at the lake was real or imagined. The house stayed silent and the driveway stayed empty. I left when the sun began to set, and all my unasked questions traveled with me.

Maybe something more than the questions did.

That night I was awakened by police.

4

THE SOUND OF SIRENS woke me, and my first thought was of the smoke detector and the night of the rattlesnake. I was afraid to get out of bed, afraid to let my feet touch the floor. The snake could be anywhere.

Then I realized the sound wasn't from a smoke detector. It was from outside, *WOOP WOOP*, the double note of an abbreviated police siren, like the one Maddox used to pull me over. One that now called to mind the soft whistle he'd given to the snake.

I wanted to stay in bed, but the dogs barked and whined at the closed door, and I thought of my mother, who should be almost home.

I turned on the light and checked the room. No snake. When I opened the bedroom door, red and blue lights painted the wall. I walked through the guest bedroom, pulled the curtains back, and looked out to see police cars lining the street. Four of them—no, five.

They were massing outside Kerri's house.

I ran across the street in my shorts, barefoot, the way I'd run on the night when the rattlesnake had appeared and I'd gone in search of Jerry's help. Kerri's Honda was gone because she was with her mother for the week, and the only vehicle in the drive was Jerry's work van. The only clear thought in my mind was that he must be hurt.

It never occurred to me that the police weren't there to help him.

Then I got a glimpse of the interior of the house through the glass storm door, and I saw that they had Jerry Flanders in handcuffs.

I pulled up short, the rough pavement slicing my feet, and stared into the house, where Jerry stood bare-chested, his hands cuffed behind his back. At least a half dozen police officers were inside the house, and flashlight beams pierced the darkness at wild angles.

"Son, please get out of the street."

An officer was walking toward me, flashlight in hand.

"What are you doing to him?" I said.

"Step back."

I ignored him and started forward just as Jerry turned and looked out. He saw me, and our eyes locked, and the fear in his face chilled me. He looked like a child, terrified and helpless. He looked, probably, very much the way I had on the night I'd run to his door after finding the snake.

The police officer's palm touched my chest, firm contact with warning behind it. I stopped walking and looked at him. I didn't recognize him from the street outside Noah's office and was glad of that.

"What are you doing to him?"

"I can't discuss that. This is a law enforcement matter, and I am going to have to ask you to go back in the house."

"Why is he in handcuffs?"

Up and down the street, doors were beginning to open as neighbors roused from sleep came out to see what was going on.

"Go back home," the cop said. "Now. We've got it under control."

"Got *what* under control?"

He didn't answer. In the end, I stood in my yard, shivering in the sharp autumn air, and watched while they brought Jerry Flanders out of a house that was almost as familiar as my own and put him in the back of a police car and took him away. The rest of the cars stayed behind. One group of police stretched yellow-and-black crime scene tape around the yard while others searched inside. A man in a black windbreaker passed in front of the living room window, the letters FBI clear on the back of the jacket.

When I saw that, I sank down into the grass.

That's where I was when my mother came home. She ran to me, and I explained what I could, which wasn't much.

"They took him away," I said. "They arrested him, Mom, and the FBI is in there."

It was closing in on one in the morning, but still I called Kerri's cell phone. No answer. Did she know? Surely, she did. Was she with her father right now? I was lost in wondering when the voice mail began recording, and so I stuttered out a message, halting and circular. How do you ask your best friend if she knows that her dad is in custody, and why?

I didn't know Gwen's new number. My mother didn't, either.

"Go to bed, hon," she said. "We can't solve it tonight."

"It was the FBI!" I shouted. "You go to bed! I can't!"

She gave me the measured look that was her favorite way to defuse a tantrum, but her eyes didn't have the usual steel to them. She was as shaken as I was. Jerry was family.

Troubled family, of late. We both knew that.

We just didn't know the extent of it.

We found that out the next afternoon when the police held a press conference to announce the arrest. When my mother heard that from a colleague at her station, her response was immediate.

"They're going to say he had something to do with Meredith Sullivan's death, Marshall." She looked numb.

"That's impossible," I said.

"What else is there?" she said. "What else has happened in this town that merits a press conference to announce charges?"

I didn't have an answer for that. We had spent the entire day waiting for news. I had not heard a word from Kerri. TV trucks were parked outside our home, shooting video of Kerri's house, and police were stationed there, but no one had explained what in the hell was happening.

We turned on the TV and waited, watching Antwaan Randle El put up historic numbers as the IU quarterback until they cut away from the game to go live to Bloomington, where the state police announced that Jerry Flanders was being held on a $100,000 bond, charged with criminal trespass, destruction of private property, and a federal charge for violation of the Lacey Act.

There was no mention of murder or kidnapping or Meredith Sullivan.

"What's the Lacey Act?" I asked.

"I don't know. I think we're about to find out."

Ron Walters, the detective with whom I'd done the Indy 500 interview, spoke from a podium in front of a projector screen. At first, the only image on the screen was the ISP logo. Walters took his time, explaining that the criminal trespass and destruction of private property charges were based on Jerry's creation of an elaborate underground bunker in the Morgan-Monroe State Forest. Walters said that police had found a collection of supplies ranging from ropes and chain to guns and ammunition inside the bunker. The projector screen filled with images of these items, and while they looked terrible, like Waco or Ruby Ridge, I knew the place wasn't threatening, it was just sad.

"It's his pit house," I said, feeling sick to my stomach. "He thinks he's going to need a shelter because of Y2K. He thinks we *all* are. It's crazy, but it's not criminal!"

"Just listen, Marshall. Please."

So we listened as Walters showed photographs and diagrams of Jerry's pit house. He never used the phrase "pit house," though, or "shelter"; he used "compound" or "bunker." They lingered on photographs of the weapons and ammunition.

"Mr. Flanders has maintained a false identity for many months," Walters said.

False identity? He'd spent every night smoking cigarettes on his own front porch and talking to anyone who'd listen! What was false about that? Jerry Flanders, for better and worse, was the most open man I knew.

"He's even gone to such lengths as creating a fraudulent employer," Walters said. "Since late winter, he claimed to be an employee of a company called Eliminator Inc. that specialized in radon mitigation. There is no such company."

My mother put a hand to her mouth. I couldn't even draw a breath.

"He outfitted a van with the company name, and he purchased clothing with a company logo. He has maintained this fiction while spending his days constructing and arming his bunker in the woods," Walters continued. "We are seeking help from the public in identifying times and locations that Mr. Flanders and his vehicle have been seen."

The projector screen behind Walters shifted to a photograph of Jerry's van, emblazoned with the Eliminator Inc. logo. A tip line number was positioned beneath it.

Walters shuffled some papers on the podium. Cleared his throat.

"The final charges, which involve appropriate federal agencies, are violations of the Lacey Act. The Lacey Act is a national wildlife protection statute." He paused, and his jaw flexed as if he were clenching his teeth, biting down his anger. "Mr. Flanders has been charged with illegal collection and confinement of a protected species."

"What is he talking about?" I began, but then Walters looked directly into the camera, and I fell silent.

"Upon executing a search of the illegally constructed and heavily armed bunker in the Morgan-Monroe State Forest, we discovered that Mr. Flanders was in possession of no fewer than twenty-four rattlesnakes."

He paused again while the projector screen behind him shifted to a new image: a fifty-gallon drum filled with writhing snakes.

There were so many that they looked like a single, massive knot—until you saw the ones with lifted heads and widespread jaws, or the tips of rattle-lined tails. My mother made a small sound of horror and pressed her now-closed fist against her mouth.

"The eastern timber rattlesnake is a protected species under federal jurisdiction," Walters said, "and that is the only comment we will make on the matter of the snake at this time."

He concluded the press conference without saying Meredith Sullivan's name, but when he opened the floor to questions, the first one was about her.

"Our investigation is ongoing and we have identified persons of interest," Walters said, moving on to the next question, which was also about Meredith Sullivan. Time and again, Walters declined to comment. He used the phrase "persons of interest" with great care. The current charges against Jerry Flanders, he said, were not related to the abduction and death of Meredith Sullivan. He could not comment as to why the police wanted information about the van. He could not speculate. He could not correlate. He could not elaborate. For all the things he supposedly could not do, though, he took his sweet time speaking, and he left the image of the barrel full of rattlesnakes on the screen behind him all the while. A picture, they say, is worth a thousand words. Ron Walters might never have called Jerry Flanders a suspect in Meredith's murder, but the photograph behind him did plenty of talking, and he knew it.

"They don't have the evidence to hold him and they want to hold him," my mother said. "When the police call media instead of the other way around, it's a strategy, not a mistake."

"He can explain everything," I said. "He's messed up but not a psycho."

She looked at me with sad eyes.

"You think he can explain the van?"

I hesitated. "I don't know what that's all about. Maybe he was lying to Gwen because he didn't want to admit he was unemployed." This struck me as a hopeful path, and I charged down it. "You know how he always was talking about wanting to start his own business, Mom. How he never wanted to be an employee again. Maybe he was trying to start the radon business and didn't want people to know it was his own idea—not until he'd proved it could work."

"They said it was a fiction. I doubt they're confused on that point."

"Well, they have to be! Jerry isn't grabbing girls and putting them in a van. Meredith was with Maddox, not Jerry. *I saw her.*"

She looked away when she said, "How can he explain the snakes, Marshall?"

Even in that awful moment, I understood that her looking away was an act of kindness. She didn't want me to have to face an audience while I considered the possibilities . . . and while I wondered whether I should tell her about the snake I'd seen at the lake just yesterday, being walked like a dog on a leash by a man no one but me ever seemed to see.

Silence grew. On the TV, they cut away from Walters and that awful image of the rattlesnakes and returned to Antwaan Randle El carving up the Northwestern defense. The elated announcers and cheering crowd felt like they belonged in another universe. I turned off the TV and looked outside, where a police car was still stationed on the street. My mother watched me, wordless, while I called Kerri again.

There was no answer.

The next day was Sunday, and Kerri did not come home or answer her phone. I couldn't force myself to eat the toast and soup my mother offered. She didn't press. She looked wan herself, and she kept going to the window. Television vans came and went. Police never left. At some point in the night, my mother had posted signs on our front door, garage door, and mailbox that said *Private Property, No Trespassing, No Interviews, Please Show Respect.*

The doorbell still rang five times that day. We never answered it. We didn't even talk much ourselves. I think we were each afraid of an argument over the question of what was possible and what was not. The "matter of the snake," as Ron Walters had termed it.

Once, I heard my mother's voice, very soft, and thought that she was talking to me. When I looked at her, though, she was wiping down a perfectly clean kitchen counter and talking to herself under her breath.

"That poor girl. That poor, poor girl."

I didn't know if she was thinking of Meredith Sullivan or Kerri. Maybe both. I went upstairs and called Kerri again. I did this every fifteen minutes, all day long. The phone never rang. A message told me that the voice mail inbox was full. I logged onto AIM, saw that Kerri wasn't online, and ignored the immediate bludgeoning of messages from friends asking if I'd heard the news, if I'd talked to her, what I knew.

That afternoon, I called Hoosier High Ground and asked for Jake Crane. He always worked on Sundays.

"I haven't heard from her, Marshall," he told me. "I'm trying to give her space. I can't imagine what she's processing."

Give her space? All I wanted to do was be with her.

"Tell me if you hear from her," I said. "Please."

"Okay. But, Marshall? This is serious, serious stuff. The FBI is involved."

"I know that, but all I want is to—"

"My point is, she might not be *allowed* to talk to anyone without a badge for a while. They will want to know what she has seen in that house."

I almost lost my patience then, almost shouted that I knew about detective work and didn't need a rock-climbing coach to explain it to me. Then I remembered that he was right. She might be with the police.

Tell us about your dad. Tell us about his van.

"Just let me know if you hear from her," I said, and Jake promised that he would.

I put on my headphones and played music—not my usual rap diet but Kerri's music: the White Stripes, the Red Hot Chili Peppers, Mary J. Blige, the Dixie Chicks (they still had the Dixie back then). I listened to her favorite songs and stared at the ceiling, trying to imagine where she was and how she felt. I tried to imagine a plausible reason for Jerry's behavior, something that wasn't criminal, just eccentric. He was prepping for a threat he believed was real even if most other people didn't. He was trying to *help*.

Explain the fake job, then.

Explain the snakes.

It was around three in the morning, and I was tossing restlessly, checking a phone that never rang, when I thought of something I should have realized earlier. The image of those snakes intertwined in the barrel, their knotted, tangled bodies forming an indistinct mass, had reminded me of something, but in the moment of horror, I hadn't been able to recognize it. Now, in the depths of a sleepless night, the image returned to me, and I knew why it was familiar.

I got out of bed and found the blueprint from Noah Storm's basement, put it on the bed, and unrolled it, revealing the sketch I'd drawn while in a trance, a sketch that was supposed to represent the face of the man who'd called himself Maddox, but looked nothing like a human face at all, a meaningless mass of squiggles and short, jagged lines.

They were snakes.

So many of them, drawn so poorly, that neither Noah nor I had noticed it at the time. We'd been searching for a man's face, after all. The result looked nothing like a man.

It looked an awful lot like the writhing knot of rattlesnakes they had shown on the TV news.

I could now see that the short slashes were snake eyes, the random triangles were wedge-shaped heads, and the jagged squiggles were rattle-tipped tails.

I'd been wrong when I told Noah I couldn't draw.

We just didn't know what we were looking at.

CHAPTER NINE

MATTERS OF THE SNAKE

October 1999

"Best friends and money: I lost 'em both."

DR. DRE
"THE WATCHER"

1

I DIDN'T WANT TO go to school on Monday, but I did, for only one reason: if Kerri was there, she would need me.

She wasn't there. A thousand kids with questions were. Questions about predators and pedophiles, kidnappers and killers, psychopaths and snakes, and oh, yeah, had I heard from his daughter? She had to know something, right? How much was she hiding? Would she be back? She had to be back; she was going to be our valedictorian. I didn't remind anyone that Kerri was so far ahead of the rest of us with credit hours that she could graduate in December if she wanted to.

Imagining the building without her overwhelmed me. I left my precalculus class with a bathroom pass in hand, then walked out of the building and into a cold autumn rain. I was soaked by the time I got to the car. I started the engine and ran the heater as the windshield fogged and the stereo thumped with Wu-Tang's reminder that cash ruled everything.

Jerry Flanders was in jail until he came up with $100,000.

Maybe Wu-Tang wasn't wrong.

Or maybe Jerry Flanders deserved to be where he was.

I put my forehead on the steering wheel and let the tears come for the first time. I cried for Kerri and I cried for Jerry and I cried for myself. I was still crying when the passenger door opened and Kerri slipped inside, accompanied by a fresh gust of wind and rain.

I looked at her in astonishment.

"I can't go in the building," she said. "Not yet. Maybe not ever. But I wanted to see you, and I was going to leave a note on the car, but your car was running, and . . ."

She was babbling, and then she stopped abruptly, staring at me.

"You're crying," she said, and then, as if it were a command, the first tears found her own eyes.

I reached for her, and she slid across the bench seat and into my arms, and I pulled her onto my lap and held her tightly while she cried into my chest, curled up like a child, her hair soft and damp against my neck. I held her for a long time while the rain drilled off the car, and finally she was still and silent. We sat like that for a little longer before she shifted and leaned back far enough to look me in the eyes. From the surface, it was a fantasy fulfilled, the way I'd wanted to hold Kerri; in reality, it was the worst moment of my life. I'd have rather walked her down the aisle to Jake Crane's waiting hand than have seen the terrible pain in her face.

The security guard van passed by. Rent-a-cops, we called them. This one eyeballed my running car.

"Take me somewhere safe," Kerri said. "Somewhere nobody will bother us."

I was thinking of the state forest—a spot we both knew well, a place of beauty and solitude—before I realized what it now meant to her. I thought then of Lake Griffy . . . but that was even worse, the place where Meredith Sullivan had died. In the end, I drove to Lost Man's Lane and parked at the dead end in front of the massive tract of undeveloped fields, woods, and quarries that Sean Weller's father would someday turn into estate homes. I pulled up to the rusted farm gate that Sean opened before those keg parties and cut the engine. The rain was still falling, but softer now, filtered by the wide red expanse of a sugar maple in full fall color. We had not spoken during the drive. Kerri took a breath and turned to me.

"He is not a murderer," she said.

"I know."

I meant it. I'd hoped it, but I hadn't been sure of it until I heard her voice. Her faith refilled my own.

Then she said, "He is not a healthy man. Psychologically, I mean. He's . . . disturbed. I know that. I didn't know all the details, but I knew he needed help." Her voice broke and she gathered herself before repeating, "He is not a murderer."

"Have you seen him?"

"Not yet. We talked on the phone and it was awful." She put a hand over her face. "He was a wreck. But he kept telling me that he did nothing wrong. He kept saying he could only explain to the right person."

"Who is the right person?"

She lowered her hand. "I have no idea."

"He needs a good lawyer."

"He has a public defender. That will be all he can get because he has no money. He's been lying about work for months, Marshall. Every day he went out and . . . did whatever he did, but he was making *no* money. He was spending money—on guns, on tools, on crazy shit—but he wasn't making a dime. The only way he'll afford bail is to sell our house. His lawyer is working on that with my mom right now."

I stared at her. She'd be moving?

"Mom's destroyed," she said. "Like a shell, all emptied out. She believes he did something terrible. It's like this news came along and validated every fear she had."

"Where are you guys staying?"

"Hiding out with her friend in Brown County. I told Mom I wanted to go to school, said that I had to figure out how to do that or everything was over—college, life, everything. But I can't go in that building. I just needed to see you."

I wish I could tell you that I didn't think of Jake Crane in that moment, that I was able to forget any thought of petty rivalry in the face of peril. But I can't say that because it wasn't as simple or silly as rivalry.

It was love.

Many adults do not think of teenage love as a real thing. They think of it as something sweetly silly at best, or hormonal lust at worst, and they forget how authentic it is, how intensely felt. Maybe they must diminish it in this way, because how awful would it be to admit that your most unguarded, euphoric love might be behind you? I've come close to this response myself as the years have gone by. Then I remind myself of the way I felt about Kerri Flanders on the day her father was arrested, and I make a mental vow that I will never offer a patronizing smile to any sixteen-year-old who tells me she is in love or one who says that he is heartbroken.

"I called you every fifteen minutes," I told Kerri. "You might think that's an exaggeration, but it's the truth."

She squeezed my hand. "Mom took my phone. Reporters had found the number. They didn't stop."

"They're camping outside your house too."

She nodded wearily. "I saw some of the video on the news."

"Is your dad going to get out?"

"They need to free up the money for bail. His lawyer said they can't keep him locked up as a suspect in the Meredith Sullivan case unless they charge him with it, and they haven't done that because there's no evidence." She paused, wet her lips. "He also told us that he thinks they'll impanel a grand jury."

"What does that mean?"

"That six anonymous people will get to listen to the prosecutor's arguments in secrecy and then decide whether to indict my father."

"I thought it all had to be in the open—innocent until proven guilty."

"That's a trial. The next step. The grand jury is a way to get to the trial based largely on circumstantial evidence is what the lawyer told us. I need to read about it. I don't understand enough yet."

"Did your dad . . ." I hesitated. "Did he explain the snakes?"

More color ebbed from her cheeks.

"He said that he was trying to help a man who was catching them to take an inventory for the forest. The man left, and Dad kept on catching them alone, and then he . . . he killed them."

I could tell she was not done. There was more coming, something worse.

"Then he said that they kept coming back to life," she whispered.

"That was why he put them into the barrel. He was trying to figure out a way to make them stay dead."

She looked far too weary for seventeen.

"My mother's lawyer was listening to the call, and he interrupted, told Dad to stop talking about things like that. Shouted it, almost. *Do not say anything about the snakes to her!*' And then my father started to cry."

Words couldn't do any good after a story like that. The wind shivered the car and crimson maple leaves coated the hood. The rusty farm gate creaked. Around us, the fields spread out in shades of defeated browns and grays, the tall grass bent by rain and wind, the sky leaden. It was cold in the car. I turned on the engine and cranked the heater up.

He was trying to figure out a way to make them stay dead, Kerri had said, and I remembered Noah stepping out of his building, gazing around the street as if surprised by what awaited there.

Things that should have stayed dead in Bloomington had uncanny resilience lately.

"I need to go," Kerri said, looking at her watch. "My mom will freak out."

I drove back to the school and dropped her off at her car. She sat staring at the school as if it were someplace remembered only vaguely, a relic of a past life.

"I'll have to go back," she said. "I can't just hide."

I thought about telling her it would be okay, but I didn't. It had been miserable for me, and I was accused only of being a liar. Kerri's situation was another level.

"Maybe I shouldn't believe my dad." She said it slowly and softly, and I was certain it was the first time she'd said it out loud. "I do, though. I still do."

There was a single tear shimmering just beneath her eye, and when I reached for her, all I intended to do was brush it away. She turned toward me when I reached for her, though, and when her cheek slid against my palm, I didn't lower my hand. I didn't know what to do.

Until she reached up with her own hand and pressed it to the back of mine, holding my palm to her cheek, leaning into the touch.

I kissed her. Her lips were not tentative against mine but warm and searching and soft, and as she returned the kiss, I was sure that I hadn't done anything wrong—it was better than right, perfect, and unbelievably long overdue. She slid closer to me, rising a little, and I shifted to let her slide back onto my lap the way she had in the rain in the empty field.

She didn't come that way, though. She broke the kiss abruptly and said, "I'm sorry."

"Sorry? Kerri, what are you—"

But she was already turning from me, opening the passenger door and stepping out into the rain. By the time she reached her own car, I could see that she was crying again.

I watched until her Honda was out of sight and then groaned and dropped my head to the steering wheel.

It had felt right. She'd returned the kiss. What had happened?

She has a boyfriend. Her father was arrested. She didn't want to be kissed.

I waited for a while with futile hopes that she might return, then gave up, left the school, and drove to Raintree Lane. Jerry would be home soon and I wanted to be there when he arrived.

2

JERRY FLANDERS SECURED BAIL with the equity in the home he'd purchased twenty years earlier. Even then the judge added another condition
of release: an ankle bracelet and home detention. He was not to leave the
property, and his location would be monitored twenty-four hours a day.

That night was the first fight I'd had with my mother in years.

We rarely argued. A lot of that was a product of living in isolation;
it was just the two of us, and nobody could find an ally in an argument.
Most of it, though, was a result of Monica Miller's extraordinary patience.
She gave more honest consideration of her son's opinions or plans—even
the ridiculous ones—than any other parent I knew.

Until I said I wanted to welcome Jerry Flanders home.

When Jerry arrived, he was driven by a man I'd never seen before, in
an SUV with *AA Bail Bonds* emblazoned on the side. The press had gotten
a tip, and they were already at the house, waiting to capture the moment.
Cameramen crowded in, and reporters rushed up the driveway with mi-
crophones extended. One stepped directly in Gwen's beloved flower beds.
Jerry looked pale and tired but not frightened, and he kept his composure,
walking with his head high. He said two words, clear as a bell, with that
faint Southern accent that so many native Hoosiers have, as if the Mason-
Dixon Line extended farther north than people realize.

"Not guilty."

It made me swell with excitement and hope, the feeling you get when an athlete on your favorite team shows some swagger. This was hardly Reggie Miller taunting Spike Lee at Madison Square Garden, but that's the way it felt. Jerry had met the enemy, he'd faced them down, and he was confident.

I waited for the TV crews to leave before I headed for the front door.

"Where are you going?" my mother said in an acidic tone. I stopped at the door, surprised. We'd already concluded the *Why did I get a call about your absence?* talk, and she'd been understanding and even supportive, glad that I'd been able to see Kerri. I wasn't expecting any opposition to showing the same support to Jerry.

"To welcome him home."

"No." She shook her head, and her jaw was set, her mouth a hard line.

"*No?* Mom . . . that's Jerry."

"I know who he is. We'll find out more about who he is than we ever wanted to, I think."

I stared at her, speechless.

"Do you not even pause to consider that the deadly snake we had in *our home* might have come from across the street?" she said, voice rising. "That the thing that might have bitten you—might have *killed* you—could have come from our neighbor's house?"

"Mom, there's no way—"

"They found him with twenty-four fucking rattlesnakes!" she shouted, and it was the first time I'd ever heard her say that word except for under her breath when she didn't think I was listening. "You need to be mature enough to consider that."

"I *am* mature enough to consider it. I also know that he has some explanation for it, and we owe it to him to hear that."

She gave a disgusted shake of her head.

"You can speak to Kerri," she said. "You do not need to speak to Jerry."

"That's not fair. That's not right. That's—"

"What if it had bitten *me*, Marshall?" she said, and her voice was her own again, steady and cool, the question so piercing that I almost wished she were shouting again so I could ride the emotion rather than confront the logic. "What if the smoke detector doesn't go off, and you don't come downstairs and see it, and I walk into the house in the dark and step right on that snake? What if it killed me?"

"Mom . . ."

"Would you be so strident in your defense of Jerry Flanders then?"

"He came over here to help!"

"Was he looking for a snake he knew something about?"

"Absolutely not."

"How do you know?"

"Because I know Jerry."

She folded her arms across her chest. "You saw the photographs of those snakes. If he has a quality explanation, it hasn't been offered yet."

I thought of the sketch I'd made in Noah Storm's basement. I thought of Kerri telling me that Jerry had said the snakes wouldn't stay dead. Then I looked at my mother and remembered the therapist, Clint, and I knew that if I offered a word about any of this, I'd be right back in his office, only this time the prescription pad would come out. She trusted me—to a point. I was seeing that point now. Understanding what would happen if I stormed past it.

I went upstairs, closed my bedroom door, and was reaching for my headphones when I heard my mother's footsteps and paused, expecting her to knock. She didn't. She went on to her own bedroom, and her door opened and closed, but I could hear the crying, soft as it was.

I closed my eyes and put on my headphones and tried to disappear into the music. Tried not to think of my mother crying alone in her bedroom, or Jerry doing . . . whatever he was doing over there in his own house, the one that was now going to be sold to keep him out of a jail cell.

Everything solid in my life had once been on Raintree Lane.

That felt like a long time ago.

I would not argue with my mother, though. I didn't have to. Tomorrow she would go to work, and I would be alone, and Jerry would be home.

We all make our choices and keep our secrets. That's the sad truth. My mother didn't want me to talk to Jerry Flanders. I didn't want my father's identity to be a question. Sometimes you make decisions that hurt other people because you want to protect them. It happens.

Just don't expect them to understand.

Meanwhile, Kerri remained in silence, and I couldn't stop replaying our kiss in my mind. When she finally called late that night, I wanted to talk about it. She did not.

"It's fine, Marshall. It was my fault."

"That's not what I meant. Nobody's fault. What I—"

"We've been close for a long time and we have a lot of confused feelings and shit happens when your emotions are intense," she said, cutting me off and rushing her words. "It wasn't the day for that, and I'm sorry."

Wasn't the day.

Did that mean there was a day?

"Did you see my dad?" she asked. Priorities restored. A kiss didn't matter in the face of a murder case.

And yet . . .

The kiss mattered to me. Long after she'd hung up, it was the kiss and not the case that lingered in my mind. Was that wrong, or was it human?

I fell asleep without deciding on an answer to that one.

In the morning I went to school, and Kerri still wasn't back. I ate lunch alone in the library and after school I went to the gym and lifted weights with Sean Weller. It was the first time I'd seen him since Jerry's arrest, and of course he wanted to talk about it.

"The van alone is fucked-up, man," he said, stacking weight plates on the bar he'd positioned on the squat rack. "But the snakes? How does he explain that?"

"People keep snakes. The police are pretending like he's the first one."

"Owning snakes that are kept in an official tarantulum is very different than keeping a barrel of them in the woods."

"Terrarium," I snapped. "And maybe it *isn't* that different. We'll see."

Weller regarded me curiously. "What's up your ass?"

"Nothing. Kerri and her family mean a lot to me, that's all."

His face brightened as if he'd just read the quarterback's eyes and knew the next play.

"You're into that chick."

I started to deny it and tell him to move on, but I needed *someone* to talk to.

"We kissed yesterday," I told him quietly, "and it seemed like it wasn't a mistake—until it was. I'm not sure how to read her. She's got a lot going on, so it was probably the wrong time for—"

"Whoa, whoa, whoa." He lifted his hands, palms out. "Slow down. Catch the Weller up on the play."

" 'Catch the Weller up on the play'?"

"I need to understand the physics of how it went down."

"It was a kiss! There are no physics."

"A kiss is the ultimate example of physics, Marshmallow." He cocked his head, thoughtful. "Well, the second ultimate."

"Penultimate."

"Don't be gross, just explain the situation. I'm here for you. Seriously."

I sighed but did my best to explain, in rapid-fire fashion, the scenario of the kiss. Weller listened thoughtfully while shadowboxing himself in the mirror.

"Question," he said when I was done.

"Yeah?"

"You said she slid toward you."

"Yes."

He sat on the weight bench beside me. "Show me."

"*What?*"

"Her posture. Is she sliding your way hip to hip"—he thumped his massive ass into mine—"or does she *rotate* the hips like so?" Now he turned toward me, wiggling his eyebrows, and I heard laughter from behind us and was acutely aware of how damn loud Weller was and that the room was filled with mirrors.

"Sean . . ."

"It matters!" he barked.

"I don't know! My eyes were closed. I mean, she was kissing me back, and it was all going fine, and then she stopped. But like I said, with everything that—"

"Did you have a boner?"

"Weller!"

"I'm serious, bro. This could be a factor."

"No! It was not a factor, because . . . *no.*"

He regarded me skeptically. "If it were football, I would want to go to the tape on this one."

"That was *not* an issue."

"The body behaves in mysterious ways, Marshmallow. You've already told me, like a total chick, that you were all caught up in your feelings and that your feelings led you to believe a kiss was approved despite an otherwise dubious romantic vibe."

"Can we please just lift?" I begged.

"No. We're getting to the bottom of this first. I think you've got to consider that a kiss in a time of grief is different than a boner in a time of grief."

More laughter around us. I rubbed my forehead, trying to shield my face.

"Weller, shut up," I hissed.

"One cannot have a boner in a time of grief," he proclaimed, then paused and lifted a finger. "One *should* not have a boner in a time of grief. The problem is that one can. And I think you did."

"I think we've talked plenty about—"

But he was catching a rhythm he liked now, which meant he got louder, like a player giving a locker-room speech. He stepped astride a weight bench to face the crowd.

"As Ben Franklin said to the troops at Gettysburg, there is a time for grief and a time to mourn, a season for sexing and years for tears."

I bolted from the room, making it to the door just as he boomed, "Ask not what I can do for your country, gentlemen, but what *we* can do for mankind," to loud applause.

So much for seeking Sean Weller's counsel. By the time I got home, the Bravada was gone and there was food in the fridge and a three-word note on the table:

Thank you, Marshall.

I read it and closed my eyes and sighed. Then I tore it up, threw it in the garbage, and crossed the street to see Jerry.

He didn't answer the door. I wasn't surprised by this; reporters had come and gone frequently, although there were no cars in the drive or on the street now. Not even Jerry's omnipresent van. That was in a police impound yard.

I cupped my hands to my mouth and called, "Jerry, it's Marshall."

The floor creaked. Footsteps on the stairs, a rustle behind the door. The locks clicked, the door cracked, and Jerry Flanders gazed at me warily.

"I wanted to see how you're doing," I said. "And if you need anything."

He gave a tired little laugh. "Your mother raised you right."

"My mother can't know about this."

The laugh died and he looked at me with fresh understanding and nodded sadly.

"Thanks," he said. "I'm good. It was nice of you to check, Marshall."

"Do you have a few minutes?"

He hesitated.

"I think I understand some things," I said. "I know what I saw in Noah Storm's office. Nobody can believe that what I saw was real, but I know that it was. He was dead and then he wasn't. Kerri told me that's what you said about the snakes."

Jerry wet his lips and shot an uneasy glance up the street. "I can't talk about that shit, Marshall."

"Then you might go to prison. Because even if they never charge you with anything to do with Meredith Sull—"

"I never *saw* that girl! Never knew her name until the night you needed the police!"

I let him gather himself, then said, "Even if they never charge you with anything else, they've charged you with the snakes. You've got to explain that."

"I can't."

"I know. I'm the one who reported the murder that nobody thinks happened."

"It is a very different situation."

"I'm not so sure it is."

"Go home, Marshall." He was starting to close the door on me when I unrolled the blueprint and presented him with the sketch I'd made in Noah Storm's office.

Jerry recoiled as if the drawing could hurt him.

"I drew that in a trance in Noah's office," I said. "He'd asked me to draw Maddox. This is what I did instead. We both laughed about it back then. You see what it is, though. I can tell you do."

"Roll that thing back up," he said, head still turned to the side.

I rolled it up, and Jerry took a breath and checked the empty street and then pushed the door wide enough for me to slip through. That was the first time I saw the tracking bracelet clamped around his ankle.

"All right, Marshall. I'll tell it once."

3

WE WENT INTO THE BASEMENT, which still felt natural, although there would be no Ping-Pong game played tonight. The stereo was on but the volume was low, the Kenny Wayne Shepherd Band, Kenny Wayne ripping through his dirty guitar licks and Noah Hunt singing that he was in too deep. Jerry sat on one of the stools below the granite-inlaid bar he'd built beneath the dartboards. I'd helped him that day, handing him tools when he asked for them, balancing the framing pieces as he zipped in screws. I'd thought it was the coolest place in the world: Ping-Pong, darts, big speakers blasting Van Halen and Fleetwood Mac. Kerri hadn't moved into the basement yet; it was Jerry's man cave. I was in sixth grade and Jerry was on his first job after being laid off. Maybe his second. Still in good spirits, though.

Now we sat together at the bar, and he opened a beer and gave me a Dr Pepper, the house-arrest monitor tracking his every step. He looked about a thousand years old, soft and sallow. I might have outweighed him by then. The physical decline had been slow but seemed stark to me because you never look at someone with the same scrutiny as you do after a tragedy. Jerry Flanders was the author of someone's tragedy—maybe Meredith Sullivan's, as half the town believed, or maybe simply his own.

"You really drew that picture before seeing . . . what they showed on TV?" he asked.

"I drew that in May. I'd seen one snake. The one you went looking for."

He suppressed another shiver, and when he grimaced, the bags under his eyes darkened.

"First one I saw too," he whispered. "First rattler, anyhow. After that . . . well, after that, things changed."

"You talked about seeing them in basements and crawl spaces. But you weren't really in anyone's basement or crawl space."

"That's not true. The police made it out to seem like the whole business was a lie."

"It wasn't?"

"No! There's money to be made in that game. This whole region, sitting on top of karst bedrock, has radon everywhere, and that shit is dangerous. Second-leading cause of lung cancer in the country." He pushed the pack of cigarettes farther down the bar. "There's a moneymaker there, and it could help people, and I was getting close to making it happen."

"But the company isn't real?"

"It was going to be! I came up with all that on my own, from the name to the logo, but then Gwen was getting, you know, tense about money, because I'd told her I was full-time at the car lot when I'd really gone down to part-time. But I knew she didn't want me going out on my own, 'cause when I talked about ideas like that, she always said I was an employee and not an entrepreneur."

He drank some beer and looked aside. "Maybe she's not wrong. Point is, I was putting it together. I thought I'd take a few months to prove the thing was working and then break the news in success. She'd be pissed off about what I hadn't told her, sure, but nobody can stay angry when the champagne corks are popping. What I figured, anyhow. Then, once she left, I wasn't going to say, 'Hey, you were right about everything, and I've been lying to boot.' I planned to get the business up and running and then once it was making consistent money, I could explain that the whole damn deal was mine, and we were in high cotton. When she came home, it would be a different scenario."

When she came home.

I heard those words and realized I'd never heard anything approximating the same idea from Kerri; the notion of Gwen Flanders returning to Raintree Lane wasn't on the table. I couldn't look at Jerry. His wife had left him over an accumulation of little lies and he intended to win her back with a bigger one?

"Did you ever have real clients?"

"I gave real estimates. Plenty of them."

"But you didn't do any work? You just went into the people's houses?" I didn't intend for it to sound as menacing as it did, but Jerry blanched.

"I made my bids and let folks know I'd be ready to work in the fall. That was when I figured I'd have my equipment ready. It's hard to build a business without much capital, and I hadn't expected all the trouble with Gwen, and once she was gone and I knew there would be lawyers looking at money . . . well, that was all problematic. And then I got a bit distracted."

Jerry sighed and rubbed his eyes. The Kenny Wayne Shepherd Band was playing a cover of the Buddy Miles song "Them Changes."

"Well, my mind's been / going through them changes / I feel like I could go out / and commit a crime . . ."

Jerry grabbed the remote from the bar and muted the music, but the silence acted as punctuation for the line and made it more awkward. I sipped my Dr Pepper and wondered if my mother had been right. Maybe I shouldn't be there. Maybe I didn't know what Jerry was capable of at all.

"I saw the snake in your house," he said.

"The skin."

"No. I saw the actual *snake*, Marshall."

"You never said that!"

"I got reasons," he said, and gave a low, shaky laugh and wiped at his eyes. When he spoke again his voice was ragged. "Heard it rattle—not sure why they call it a rattle, because it's more of a buzz, closer to a cicada on steroids than any rattle I've ever heard—and I looked left and there it was, big as a damned boa, strangest colors I've ever seen, and it had its head raised and tip of the tail up and . . ." He let his words trail off and took a long swallow of beer. "I'm watching him and trying to figure out how to hit him with the shovel and not get bit, right? But while I'm watching him . . . he dissolved."

I stared. Jerry drank more beer, not even chancing a look in my direction.

"It was like watching the last log in a bonfire. It was there, solid and undeniable, and then it kind of . . . withered, I guess you could say. Then the snake lifted his head, and when it opened its mouth, smoke came out, a thin line, like steam from a radiator that needs coolant. Only I know it was smoke because I could *smell* it. And I heard a laugh, Marshall. I heard a *man's laugh*, deep and clear as a bell. Then the smoke faded, and the snake became ash, just crumbled on itself. Then there was nothing left but that skin, dry and brittle as a cornstalk in September, like it had been there the whole time, sitting empty."

Another swallow of beer.

"I couldn't very well walk outside and tell you and your mother and my daughter that story, could I?"

He finally looked at me. I shook my head.

"So I didn't," he said. "I just brought the skin out and then went home and tried to forget what I'd seen. Told myself it was imagination. I'd been sound asleep and then I was awake and holding a damn shovel and a flashlight and looking for a fuckin' rattlesnake in a house that wasn't my own? The mind can play tricks on you."

Silence.

"Trouble was, I couldn't unsee it. And then I started seeing more of them. Or thinking I did. I'm honestly not sure. Under houses, crawling around on my belly; with that memory in my mind, it's possible I imagined them. But it got me so frozen up that I couldn't go under houses anymore. I was out of a job and a plan, and Gwen was gone, and I didn't know how to fill my days. I wanted to stay active. I got to thinking about how people were ignoring this Y2K deal, which is *real* and it is coming *fast*, and I . . . I suppose you could say I rededicated myself to that. But I still had the snakes on my mind too. You understand that."

He said it hopefully and seemed relieved to see my emphatic nodding. I absolutely did understand that.

"That's where the guns came from," he said. "I was trying to get ready to help. I hate to say it, Marshall, but when the madness starts, you'll need to be ready to shoot back."

I didn't reply. He took a breath and refocused.

"I'd go out to the state forest time to time, just to get some peace. It occurred to me that when the shit hit the fan, the forest was going to be a real good place to be. You got fresh water, you got wild game, and so many good places to build. I didn't want to scare Kerri, not even with the truth, but I wanted to be prepared to help her when the trouble came. That's how I ended up building the pit house out there. Sure, I knew it was public property; that's why I *chose* the damn spot. I didn't want to trespass. The state forest, way I figure it, belongs to the taxpayers."

I tried to imagine being one of Jerry's lawyers, hearing that explanation. They would earn their money on this one.

"I've never been a big gun guy, but the sad fact is, we're gonna need 'em here shortly. For hunting at best. At worst?" He took a breath and faced me and for a flicker I saw the old Jerry in his face. "I'm on this earth to protect my daughter, Marshall. And I intend to do it."

Then his face broke, as if he didn't like what he'd said or didn't believe that he could deliver on it, and he turned away again.

"Anyhow, that was how I ended up in the state forest. I'll be the first to admit I got a little distracted. Should I have been looking for another job? Sure. But will anyone be able to even look up a credit card bill come New Year's Day 2000? I doubt it."

I was twisting my fingers together, so uneasy listening to him that I needed some physical outlet, and he glanced at my hands. I flattened them against my thighs.

"Tell me about the snakes," I said. "Please."

He nodded dismally, and I had the sense that he'd been trying to talk about anything other than the snakes.

"Was the snake hunter who got me started," he said. "Until I came across him, I was just hiking and thinking."

"The snake hunter?"

"One I told you about in the summer, man who did the inventory."

"Oh, right."

"I came out of the Three Lakes Trail one day, end of July, hot and humid as a bastard, and a guy was in the parking lot, dressed in camo and heavy leather boots like he was right out of the military. You know, official. It was just the two of us, and we exchanged a nod and hello, and I was almost to my van when he asked if I'd seen any snakes. Well, as you might expect, that stopped me cold."

I nodded.

"We got to talking, and he told me about the rattlers," Jerry said. "I asked him if he'd ever seen one like the one in your house, that black-and-white deal. And I swear, Marshall, I thought the man's knees were going to buckle. I was damn near ready to reach out to catch him. Then he leans back and puts his hand on the car hood and tries to shrug it off, like it didn't mean a thing to him. Said, nah, he'd never heard of one like that, but he knew timber snakes. That's when he told me about the population numbers, how we have so many of the bastards right under our noses. Then he pops the trunk and comes out with this pole that looks like a golf ball retriever, you know the kind you use to pull one out of the water hazard?"

"Sure."

"That kind of thing, thin and telescoping, only it's got a set of serrated grippers on the end that look like the teeth on channel-lock pliers. Had a flashlight mounted on the pole, same way they'll fix one onto a rifle barrel. You just reach out and grab 'em and can hold the snake at a safe distance while you move it. So he's showing me this, and I kind of shudder and say, 'I'd rather shoot them.' And he told me that you can't do that, or shouldn't do that, what have you. Again, he seems official. I said, 'Well, that snake-catching work ain't for me, brother.' And he says it's easier than it looks and if I follow him, he'll show me."

He reached for his beer, but his hand was shaking so much, his wedding ring rattled against the can, so he set it down.

"What kind of fool follows a man into the forest to look for snakes, Marshall? I don't know why I went. I truly don't. He was . . . a compelling guy, I suppose you'd say. And I was interested in the tool simply because I thought, *Hey, maybe this thing can help me get over my fear.* My phobia. Anyhow, what matters is, I went."

He drank some beer.

"For a time we followed the trail, the one that goes out to Stepp Cemetery. You know it?"

"Yeah."

"Then we branched off that, and we're bushwhacking along, and I'm making conversation just to fill the silence, telling him about Y2K and my pit house idea." His eyes brightened with such intensity that it alarmed me. "He got it! I mean, he got the whole damn deal, the first person I'd talked to all year who took the situation seriously. That was nice."

I looked away.

"We finally came out to this cliff," Jerry continued. "It's got to be the highest cliff in all of Morgan-Monroe, two hundred feet if it's an inch, sheer. The snake hunter—by then he'd told me his name was Wyatt—pointed down to a ledge and said that was where they had a den. Said it was a bad den, the mean ones congregated there, and if you go there in winter, you might find a whole nest of them, snarled up on top of one another, just like you drew it."

He gave a grim nod, watching my face.

"Took him no more than five minutes to find the first one," he said. "I never would've seen it unless I stepped on it. It was tucked behind a fallen tree, which he said was typical, and blended right in. He showed me how the tool worked then. He was so slick with it—grab and twist and then he had this big bastard up and writhing around and I damn near ran for the trailhead. He pitched it down into a sinkhole and said, 'I bet there are more,' just as cheerful as if we were hunting four-leaf clovers instead of snakes. Then he found another. And another."

Jerry rubbed his stubbled jaw, his eyes glassy.

"We found six before he convinced me to try using the pole. I still can't believe he talked me into that, because I'd had the willies since we saw the first one, but . . . he made it look so easy. And, as I said, he was a compelling guy. So I tried it. Wasn't hard at all. Grab and twist and lift. And once I'd done that, once I'd gotten ahold of one, I felt"—he searched for the word—"control. For the first time in a long time, I had a sense of being in control again."

He went for his beer, realized it was empty, and set it down.

"We hiked back out and kept talking, and Wyatt explained he needed some help. He was supposed to have some fella from Texas come in to do the inventory for him. Just collecting and counting the snakes. This guy had bailed out, and now Wyatt was working solo, trying to do the whole damn forest and get down to Deam Wilderness and out to Brown County. Too much ground to cover. He kind of laughed and said, considering how well I'd done, he'd hire me if he could. I went along with it, as a joke, and asked how much he paid. He said he'd give me a hundred bucks for each snake. That gave me pause. I mean, we'd grabbed seven or eight that afternoon hardly trying. So I ask, 'Do I just catch 'em and fling 'em and keep count?' And he chuckled and said he was a trusting man but not *that* trusting. Told me if I was serious, he'd bring out a barrel and I could put them in there, and then he'd come back, count them, and microchip them. He was all excited about that. I'm thinking, I've got no job, no money, and moreover I'm sick of being scared of the fucking snakes, you know? I'm remembering how it felt to catch one and hold it up and know that I was *in control*. So different from being in a crawl space and freezing, wondering whether there might be one coming up on me."

Another lift of the empty beer can. He set it down and wiped his eyes.

"So I took him up on it. He didn't take me seriously, I don't think. But he let me keep the pole, and he gave me a hundred bucks in twenties, and said he'd put a barrel out there, and if I was legitimate, so was he. I asked how was I to get ahold of him, and he said if I was in the forest, he'd find me. And he did. The next week I went back and caught two. Took a hell of a lot longer without him, but I did it. I was on my way back to the parking lot when he came along, and we chatted a bit, and he seemed, you know, pleasantly surprised. Paid me and said he'd chip them and release them, and sure enough, when I came back, they were gone. That was how it went through August and into September. I made fourteen hundred bucks. He kept showing up and he kept paying. Always cash. I should've wondered about that, I suppose—government types don't deal in cash.

But I saw the bills and I needed them. That was the problem. And he was such an agreeable guy, easy talking, I just trusted him."

He rotated the empty beer can.

"Each time we talked, he'd bring up the black-and-white snake. He'd grin like I was a fool or someone telling a fairy tale and tell me that if I ever got a black-and-white he'd pay me ten thousand bucks for it. I could tell he was making fun of me, and I wished he'd stop bringing it up—not because I minded the joke, but because I didn't like to remember that snake. I still *don't* like to remember it."

"Me neither," I said, and he nodded.

"So each time he mentioned it, he acted like it was a joke. But I never forgot his first reaction, either. He wasn't amused then; he was afraid."

"Did you see another like it?" I asked.

Jerry shook his head. "No. I never did."

"I don't understand how the police charged you with this if you were working for another guy, Jerry. Someone official."

He gave a bitter, broken smile.

"Because Wyatt stopped coming around. He'd been clockwork for two months, like he lived in those woods. He could vouch for every word I said. But I can't prove the son of a bitch existed. All I've got is a name—a first name—and a description of the most average-looking man you've ever seen and the tool he gave me. The forest office claims they don't know him and never commissioned any kind of rattlesnake inventory. My lawyers are looking for him, of course, and maybe they'll find him, but until then . . ."

He spread his hands. "It's just me and a barrel full of rattlesnakes, Marshall. If they can't find him, then I'm left with the first part of the story. The part I told you, about the one I saw in your house that started it all. And *that* ain't gonna help me, is it?"

I thought about what he'd said about the smoke: *Then the snake lifted his head, and when it opened its mouth, smoke came out, a thin line, like steam from a radiator that needs coolant. Only I know it was smoke because I could smell it.*

"No, it isn't. What did the snake hunter look like?"

"Shade taller than me, maybe ten years younger, muscular, redheaded, with green eyes, always wearing brown and green or camo and those heavy leather boots. A ball cap that said *Indiana Department of Natural Resources.* Like I said, official—until you really think about it. Then nothing holds together the way it should. He'll be hard to find if he isn't dressed right."

I understood his challenge, having spent so much time that spring trying to depict Maddox for other people.

"Kerri told me that you said the snakes wouldn't stay dead."

He grimaced.

"But you haven't told me about that," I prodded gently.

"And I shouldn't. It's the kind of talk that will get me locked up."

"I'm already this far into it with you."

He sighed and nodded.

"I said I'd tell it once, didn't I? Okay. I had six snakes and I'd been waiting on Wyatt for a couple weeks. I didn't want him to show up and find a barrel of dead snakes; figured that could get me in trouble. Funny, right, to worry about that kind of trouble? But I did. Also, their sounds were creeping me out. I was getting farther along with the pit house, and as the air got warmer, one of those Indian-summer stretches, the snakes got louder. Buzzing, buzzing, buzzing. Maybe because they were hungry? I don't know. I just got to the point where I couldn't take the sound anymore, and the man in charge hadn't shown his face in weeks. So I decided to kill them."

He closed his eyes as if the memory pained him.

"I used the shotgun and peppered them right there in the barrel, and as soon as it was done, I felt awful, because what had they done to deserve that? They were loud and I was afraid of them, that was all. But it was too late then. They were dead." He swallowed. "For a while."

I wished, suddenly and sharply, that I had listened to my mother and stayed on my side of the street.

"What happened?" I asked in a whisper.

He stared at the wall with that troubling, unfocused gaze, as if he'd downed a dozen beers when I wasn't looking, instead of the one that was still in his hand. A hand that had now begun to tremble.

"I hauled them up to the top of that high cliff and dumped them down onto the ledge where he'd said they denned in the winter. I watched those snakes fall, bodies twisting and whipping around like kite strings on a gusty day, tight one second, slack the next."

There was a sheen of sweat on his forehead.

"The rattles started not long after I turned my back," he said. "I had pitched all six down to the bottom. Now the rattles were back, only they were even louder than they had been when the barrel was right beside me, and it seemed as if there were even more of them. The whole woods drowning in that sound, like wind ahead of a storm, all you could hear. I went back to the cliff, looked down . . ."

He stopped talking but his chin shook, his lips still parted. He wiped his mouth and closed his eyes.

"They were coming back up that cliff wall. Slithering up that wall like it was horizontal and not vertical, just cruising along. Only there were more of them. Six had gone over, and there were at least twice as many coming back. I ran for my gun then."

His forehead was bright with sweat.

"Shot them at the top of the cliff. I used the AR-15, and I opened that fucker up, pardon my French. I lacerated those boys, Marshall, turned them to ribbons, and watched them fall." He swallowed. "Then I watched them climb back up. The ones I'd tossed were all different sizes, but these boys, they were like clones, four feet long and thick as a flagpole."

His whole body was trembling now, the shake from his mouth and hands working through his torso, all of him seeming palsied.

"The ones I'd caught before all looked mean. How else can they look? They're evolved to scare. And, kid, they *do*. I've never been more scared of anything in my life than a rattlesnake. But the ones that came back up the cliff face were worse. They had a different quality. First ones *looked* mean. These *were* mean. It sounds the same, but it isn't. There are big kids and there are bullies, right? And you know the difference before they say a word."

He opened his eyes and looked at me for confirmation. I nodded. I knew the difference he meant. We all do. There was Sean Weller and there was Kenny Glass. One guy could break you in half; the other one wanted to. In my experience, most of the bigger guys didn't want to. The ones who did tended to be smaller, or average, or . . .

The first face who came to my mind then wasn't anyone I knew. It was Eric Harris, grinning with the guns in his hands, the oversized trench coat flapping around him.

"Something happened to those snakes I thought I'd killed," Jerry said. "They came back meaner. I'd tossed them from the highest spot I could find, and they'd found their way right back, only they were meaner, and there were more of them. I couldn't figure what the hell to do then. They didn't stay dead, and they didn't run, either. What choice did I have then? I suppose running was my option. But by then I felt like I was doing too much running, too much hiding, too much lying. I wanted to stand my ground."

Sweat was all over his face now, his skin as damp as if he'd run through the rain.

"So I decided to catch 'em. I was good at it by then. Had the right tool and knew how to use it. They were big and they were fast, but the sons of bitches still had to stay on the ground. Whatever rules *didn't* apply to them, that one did. They weren't growing wings down there. I caught them, and into the barrel they went, and onto the barrel went the lid."

My stomach roiled and my throat tightened, picturing the tangle of knotted snakes I'd seen on the news.

"There were twenty-four of them," Jerry whispered. "They were doubling. I killed six, then twelve came back. I killed those, and then . . . twenty-four. I did not know what in the hell to do. I started feeding them. It seemed easier to keep an eye on them. So long as I knew where they were, they couldn't hurt anyone, right? That's how they came to be in the barrel when the police found them. That's the story I cannot tell. You know it, Marshall. You damn well understand that part."

"Yeah," I managed, my own voice a croak. "I do."

Silence built, and then Jerry finished his beer, bent the can in his still-trembling hand, and said, "Well, kid, got any ideas? Any solutions?"

"I can tell them that I saw the snake. That will help. I can testify that it looked the way you said it did."

His smile was heartbreak-song sad.

"I love you, bud, but you aren't exactly the best witness in town."

After that, nobody spoke for a while. Jerry picked up the remote and pressed Play. Kenny Wayne's guitar whined back to life. We sat together with our backs to the beloved room of my childhood and his marriage, and neither of us said a word.

CHAPTER TEN

SPEED QUEENS IN THE NIGHT COUNTRY

October–November 1999

"I'm not a real person, I'm a ghost trapped in a beat"

EMINEM
"BAD MEETS EVIL"

1

THAT FALL WAS MY season of secrets.

I didn't tell my mother that I'd seen Jerry, and I didn't tell anyone, not even Kerri, what Jerry had told me. He was right—it wouldn't help.

But I kept sneaking over to talk in the evenings, trying not to stare at the tracking bracelet on his ankle. I'd watch the news with him so I could report back to my mother that I'd seen the broadcast, and I'd ask about his court case, which was progressing slowly and opaquely. It was always just the two of us. Kerri wasn't allowed to visit her father at home, although they met for approved sessions in a lawyer's office. Jerry was in agreement with Gwen on this approach.

"I don't want my daughter around this crap," he would say, and tap the ankle monitor.

Kerri wasn't around *anyone*, and it was driving me insane.

She hadn't returned to school, negotiating instead to finish via correspondence courses. The school administration backed her on this, but she thought they were more interested in avoiding the media attention than in helping her, a suspicion deepened when she was informed that she wouldn't qualify as class valedictorian if she finished through correspondence.

"That's bullshit!" I snapped when she told me on the phone. Kerri had been so far ahead of the rest of our class for so long, taking college-level classes at IU since she was a sophomore, that she'd already lapped the field.

"It is what it is," she said, with an awful fatigue that now seemed common.

"Will you come back in the spring, when he's cleared?" I asked.

"I'll have my degree by December. I'm not worried about the spring."

And just like that, I had to contend with the notion that all the signature ceremonies of senior year would be conducted without my best friend.

"It's a big choice to make now," I said. "Give it time."

She laughed humorlessly. "Wait until the grand jury fun begins?"

The calls went like that most nights. We tried to be ourselves. Sometimes we succeeded. We never spoke of our kiss. To my great disappointment, Jake Crane hadn't folded up in his role as World's Most Loyal Boyfriend. I'd expected him to head for the hills, a college student who would want no part of a high school girlfriend whose father was portrayed as a snake-handling lunatic, maybe a murderer. Instead, he remained at her side, steadfast. I'd never hated him more.

Unable to spend time alone with Kerri, I filled it by spending time with her father. That time wasn't all about Kerri, though, not by a long stretch. Jerry and I shared the matter of the snakes, and I was the only person in Bloomington who could listen to his story and believe it, because I had seen not only Noah Storm's impossible murder but the black-and-white snake that had started it all.

And Maddox, of course. I told Jerry the story I'd told no one else, of my encounter with Maddox and the snake at the lake. We talked in circles, each wanting desperately to help the other. Jerry was fascinated—and frightened—by the sketch I'd drawn and I thought that if I could generate more of them, it might be evidence of . . . *something.*

My efforts were terrible. I tried again and again, with different types of pencils and different papers, tried in the dark and in the daylight and in the dead of night, tried with my eyes closed and my memory in overdrive.

Not only did my drawings yield nothing tangible; I felt as if the memory of Maddox receded with each one, as if I were driving him away from me with the sheer force of my effort.

I didn't tell Jerry about this when we talked. Mostly I listened. He needed that.

"I trust you, Jerry," I told him once, when he seemed to be striving to convince me of the same story that he told on repeat.

"I don't need *your* trust, I need *their* trust!" he snapped, and while he apologized, he didn't need to. I understood. Jerry provided the best lesson about telling ghost stories: the task isn't to convince someone who already believes in ghosts; it's to sell a skeptic on the same story.

I understood the problem. I'd lived it, after all. And it was because of that unique understanding that on an October afternoon I found myself driving back to the place of my worst terror in search of help for Jerry Flanders.

If I couldn't help, perhaps Noah Storm could.

2

THE HOUSE LOOKED MORE Gothic than ever on this gray October day with the massive elms shedding mustard-colored leaves in a chilled rain. There were no lights on, but I rang the bell anyway.

No answer. Beyond the transom window, the house was dark. I dialed his landline, the only number I had for him, expecting to hear the phone ring in the house. Instead, a robotic voice intoned, "The voice mail box is full."

Noah checked his messages with diligence. Maybe he was gone? But he'd answered this number only a few weeks earlier, in September, when he'd reached out to tell me that Meredith Sullivan had been found. I hadn't called him since.

I also hadn't heard his name, I realized. As the media reports flooded in, none so much as mentioned Noah Storm. Even the police barely discussed him. He was, to most of the world, a nonentity in the Meredith Sullivan case.

I pocketed the phone, shielded my eyes with my hands, and put my face to the window. The hallway was dark and empty and the door to the office was closed. The stairs looked empty, but it was hard to tell in the shadows.

I thought of the last words he'd shared with me: *If you need me, you know where the office is. You've still got a key.*

I pulled my Stephens Oldsmobile dealership key chain from my pocket before I could chicken out. The heavy lock rolled back with an audible click and then the door was open and I was stepping inside for the first time since I'd seen the murdered man who'd returned from the dead.

"Noah?" My voice echoed in the empty house.

I went down the hall.

There was a single yellow Post-it Note stuck to the door. Written on it in Noah Storm's hand were three words:

Good luck, Marshall.

Looking back on that moment, it seems inexplicable that I didn't view the note as a threat or a warning. I was, after all, standing in the same office where I'd witnessed the single most terrifying sight of my life. And yet I read the words as encouragement. Reassurance, even. Noah Storm—dead or alive or whatever he was now—was in control again. He had anticipated my arrival. In our early days together, his casual confidence in me had meant the world. He treated me like a grown man and trusted me to honor my word like one. The note, somehow, held the same promise. I took it down and pushed open the door.

When I put the light on, the first thing I saw was the snake on the desk.

I took a fast step back, a cry rising in my throat, before I realized that the snake was one-dimensional, nothing more than an image on a book cover. I stepped closer. The book on Noah Storm's desk was titled *Rattlesnakes: Their Habits, Life Histories, and Influence on Mankind*. Dozens of Post-it Notes protruded from the pages.

Of course, Noah was researching rattlesnakes. Any detective working the case was.

So what had he learned?

You don't get answers to questions you don't ask.

I crossed the room and sat down behind the desk to see what he'd been working on. Invasive, maybe, but between the unsettling quietude of the house and the personal note left on the door, I felt as if I'd been given permission.

Beneath the book on rattlesnakes were two legal pads, one filled with Noah's notes, one blank, everything stacked up in a tidy pile, as if waiting on me.

I thought of Noah's mantras, all those little reminders—*Nobody can focus for you . . . It's a detail-oriented business . . . Every construction site has a guy who says "measure twice, cut once" and a guy named Stumpy. Which one do you want to be?*—and suddenly I felt eerily certain that he'd known a day would come when I would be left alone at this desk.

With *this* case.

Beneath the snake book were the legal pads filled with his meticulous printing. The notes seemed to have been compiled from old newspaper articles—in some cases very old.

> February 27, 1938. Eloise Martindale-16-reported missing following a picnic at Peden's Bluffs northwest of Ellettsville. Search party formed. Documentation of this case is limited. Weather-snowmelt following three warm, sunny days preceding heavy spring rains that produced damaging floods.
> Distance from den: 22 miles.

A prickle of intensifying unease spread through my body like a fever. It was hard to focus on the details beyond the phrase "distance from den."

> October 12, 1938. Penelope "Penny" Howard-17-last seen in orchard southeast of Martinsville. Left by friends who had to be home by sunset. Reported missing by her parents when she did not return for dinner. Apple basket found in orchard. Howard was never seen again. Case captured national attention briefly when folk singer "Silver John" composed a ballad of her story in 1939. Weather-Indian summer, temperatures exceeding 70 degrees, followed by evening storms. Frost the following morning.
> Distance from den: 9 miles.

April 12, 1949. Robin McGrath-19-last seen walking home from her job in Bloomington, a four-block walk. Police were not notified for nearly a full day as she had been feeling ill and parents believed she'd gone to bed early. Some locals believed she ran away to follow a boyfriend to Cooke City, Montana. Montana police unable to find any leads. Little to no national attention. Unsolved, body never located. Weather-warm and windy, temperatures exceeding 80 degrees, thunderstorms. Temperatures dropped to below freezing within 48 hours.
Distance from den: 14 miles.

March 14, 1967. Elizabeth "Becky" Cox-18-last seen leaving a roller-skating rink in Martinsville. Walked because car failed to start. Reported missing by parents at midnight. Police investigation focused on the boyfriend of an older sister who had come around the house intoxicated on several occasions. No charges filed. Body located in 1970 in Beanblossom Creek, confirmed by dental records. No cause of death determined. Weather-warm and windy, temperatures exceeding 70 degrees, evening thunderstorms with damaging hail.
Distance from den: 8 miles.

November 1, 1976. Caroline Merriman-16-last seen walking home from breakfast shift at café in Nashville. Reported missing shortly after dinner, police responded quickly. Search efforts involved dogs. Dogs were hampered by severe storms but initially led searchers into hills on northwestern track. Investigation focused on two transient men who had recently harassed another girl in town. Arrested but not charged. Body never found. Weather-unseasonably warm ahead of severe storms that hindered search. Tornadoes.
Distance from den: 19 miles.

March 9, 1988. Summer Chastain—19—last seen walking on Low Gap Road in Morgan-Monroe State Forest. Had hitchhiked to the forest to meet a boyfriend known only as "Ben" whom she'd met at a party the week prior. Investigation initially focused on Ben Dobyns, 20, an Indiana University student who had attended the party and had lied about his age and occupation, claiming to be a 25-year-old soldier back from Vietnam. Dobyns was arrested and charged. Charges dropped when prosecutor acknowledged evidence supporting Dobyns' alibi. Chastain's remains were found by a hiker in 1992. Identified through dental records. No cause of death reported. Unsolved. Weather-record highs for March. Tornado warning. Significant temperature drop (52 degrees) within two days. Distance from den: 7 miles.

That was the end of the list. It might have read like the logical work of a detective seeking a serial predator. He was trying to identify similar patterns, that much was clear. But why take it back to 1938?

Because somehow he knows what you didn't tell him, I thought. *He knows that Maddox does not fit this time.*

Not just his uniform—Maddox himself.

Noah had been obsessing over patterns, distances from the den, and . . . the weather.

Why the weather?

The day I'd seen Meredith Sullivan, I'd been driving with the window down—in February. A day that felt like something stolen from another season and dropped into ours like a gift. Or a mistake. On every day of disappearance that Noah had cataloged, the same was true. Sharp temperature spikes ahead of a plummet, beauty followed by brutality.

Did it matter?

I wanted to ask the man himself. The emptiness of the office loomed like a taunt.

I pushed back from the desk and stepped into the hall. The house was silent, surrounded by those thick limestone walls. I had been in only three rooms of the big place: the office, the half bathroom on the ground floor, and, of course, the cellar. I walked up the stairs now, every muscle tensed, memories of Maddox's heavy footsteps crowding my mind.

"Noah?" I craved the comfort of hearing any human voice, even if it was only my own.

I opened one door after another, revealing dust-coated floors and antiquated furniture. It felt as if nothing had changed in the house in many, many years. There was no sign of Noah. I checked every room. Well, every room except for the cellar.

Don't need to check that one, I told myself, but I knew that I did.

The door was locked. Held shut by two new dead bolts, big and solid and gleaming. Why had he added those for a room that contained nothing but dusty old boxes and unused blueprints?

The gun safe, maybe. That made sense. My key didn't work in the new locks.

I walked back to the front staircase and sat on the bottom step, took my cell phone out, and called Ron Walters.

"Hi, Lieutenant Walters. This is Marshall Miller."

"Hello, Marshall." He sounded immediately wary. "What can I do for you?"

"I had a quick question."

"Shoot."

"When was the last time you heard from Noah Storm?"

"Who?"

For a moment I was stunned to silence, sure that Walters was about to dismiss Noah's existence entirely, another slice of my life carved out as a lie.

"Oh, oh, the PI," he said. "The one with the flyers? The one you . . ."

I rushed to fill the silence before he settled on phrasing for that memorable day in July: "Yes, that's him."

"I haven't spoken to him in months. Not since he went back east."

"What do you mean, 'back east'?"

"New York, isn't it? He went home. Why? Has he been calling you again?"

"Not lately. He found her body, though, and I was surprised that no one—"

"What are you talking about? Noah Storm didn't find Meredith's body."

"I thought he recommended the spot," I said. "And hired the guys with the sonar stuff."

"I don't know how you concluded that, but he certainly wasn't involved with our search at Lake Griffy." Walters had shifted from wary to outright suspicion. "Son, what—"

"You haven't talked to him in all that time?"

"No. He was an interloper, not a part of the police investigation."

"That was my question," I said. "I was wondering if you knew who his client was. He never told me."

"He didn't have one, kid."

"What?"

"He's a hustler, same as half the guys in that profession. He approached the Sullivan family to offer his services pro bono. Which was bullshit, because you better believe the bill would've come due if they'd been foolish enough to let him in the door. But they didn't, and so he commenced with his little crusade, no doubt looking to generate notoriety, and when that didn't pan out, he bailed. Manhattan can have him, as far as I'm concerned."

I was stunned. Noah had told me that his client's identity was confidential, but I'd always believed there was one.

"You didn't talk to him about Lake Griffy?"

"No!" Walters's voice rose. "Marshall, I haven't seen the man since your fiasco, I have no reason to call him, and he's made *no* contribution to this case other than headaches for the real investigators."

His anger told me not to press, but I couldn't help it. Noah had known they were going to find the body before they found it. How?

"You did get a tip, right? You were out at Griffy because of a tip; that was on the news. Could he have—"

"I'm not repeating myself. Do you have a question that is worth my time?"

"Sorry," I said. "I shouldn't have bothered you."

"It's fine," Walters told me curtly, and then he disconnected before I could thank him.

I lowered the phone and stared at the front door of the empty detective agency that had never had a client.

Good luck, Marshall.

Maybe that message wasn't nearly as sincere as I'd hoped. The big stone house felt frightening again, the way it probably should have since I'd entered. I needed to get the hell out of there, and I did—but I took his notes and the rattlesnake book with me.

3

JERRY DIDN'T RESPOND with the enthusiasm I'd expected when I presented him with the rattlesnake book and the notes about disappearances
and distances from a den.

"Coincidence," said the only man on earth I'd never expected to hear
it from.

I put a map of Morgan-Monroe State Forest on the Ping-Pong table.

"You said it wasn't far from the cemetery. Right? I figured if you looked
at the map, you could show me how to find it."

"And what will you do then?"

"I'm not sure yet. But I know that finding the spot matters. Look at all
those disappearances Noah found!"

"And where is Noah?"

"New York is what Walters told me."

"Then he left for a reason, and it wasn't because he'd cracked his case."

"If you would just show me on the map where you—"

"It's a bad place."

"That's my *point*. The place is important."

"Let it sit, Marshall."

"Let it sit! This could be the thing that—"

"That what?" He spun to face me. "Convinces people I'm not crazy?

Makes the cops stop looking at me like a sociopath? Brings my daughter back home?"

I stared at him. My discovery had felt guaranteed to excite him. Instead, he was angry.

Jerry folded up the map methodically, smoothing each crease as if tamping down his anger, and then handed it over to me.

"Do not go there," he said. "That's the end of it. I appreciate what you're trying to do. I'd be losing my damn mind without you, to be frank. But you need to remember who's the adult here. I'm still the man of the house."

I looked at his ankle monitor then. Couldn't help myself. He followed my eyes, and he sagged as if I'd diminished him with a single glance.

"Yeah," he said. "I get it. Man *in* the house, that's all I am."

"That's not what I—"

"But my point stands. The spot is damn dangerous. It's not a place where you should go alone. I'm asking you, friend to friend, man to man, to respect that. Honor my wish, okay?"

"If they impanel a grand jury," I said, "you're going to need a way to explain the place."

"I'm not worried about a grand jury."

"How can you *not* be?"

"Because of the timeline," he said. "It's almost November. Even if they do impanel a grand jury, the process will take months. That puts us into 2000, well past New Year's Eve. Won't be a soul worried about Jerry Flanders and some snakes by then."

I couldn't listen to more of his Y2K talk. I told him goodbye and then I went home.

The next morning I got to school early and went directly to the library.

"Mr. Doig?"

"Yes, Marshall?" He was using a letter opener to chisel a wad of gum off the back of a copy of *Ethan Frome*.

"Do we have county maps here?"

"Roads or topographical?"

"I don't know the difference."

Mr. Doig wedged the letter opener under the gum and levered it down and then there was a soft smacking sound as the gum shot into the air. He used his foot to move the wastebasket into position beneath, and the gum plopped directly into the center. He regarded it somberly.

"Heathens," he said. "I do my best, but we must acknowledge that some souls will simply not be saved."

"Mr. Doig . . ."

"Yes, yes, the maps. Topographical maps show terrain conditions and elevations, while road maps show—brace yourself—roads. We have ample supplies of both."

"I just need, like, the street names, I think."

"I shall translate your words into English and determine that you require only the road map." He rose from his desk and went to a cabinet with wide, flat drawers, slid one open, and withdrew a map. "Monroe County roads, circa 1997. There have been some changes, as construction never ceases, but, alas, cartography takes time—at least until computers run the show completely. The machines are coming for us, Marshall, at least until midnight on New Year's Eve. Then the books will rise once more, unbothered by binary-code errors. Bring on the millennium. Everything old will be new again!"

He was joking, but any reference to Y2K made me think of Jerry, and I suppressed a grimace.

"Thanks. What about Morgan and Brown Counties?"

"Check and check." He eyed me curiously. "Are we finally writing the novel?"

I had no intention of writing a novel, but this was the white lie that had convinced him to let me hide out in the library. In fairness, I *was* writing a story; it didn't matter that Mr. Doig thought it was fiction and I didn't.

"Maybe," I said, extending that white lie a little further. "I want to get the facts right."

"Good. A writer who relies purely on talent isn't going nearly as far as the one who pairs a curious mind with an imaginative mind. Facts are the fuel of fiction."

He was being so kind that I ended up telling him more than I'd intended.

"I'd like to research the Morgan-Monroe State Forest."

"Stepp Cemetery?" he asked with a grin.

Everyone knew Stepp Cemetery. It was an ancient graveyard deep in a forest, the sort of place where ghost stories almost told themselves, a place everyone laughed about until they were out there in the dark. There was one simple stone bearing nothing but the name "Baby Lester" and the date of death, 1937, and people believed his grieving mother haunted his grave and cursed a stump called the Warlock's Chair. Some people left toys on his grave, like offerings. Others believed there was the ghost of a dog that a group of frat boys had hanged in the '50s. Stepp Cemetery was the quintessential destination for kids looking for a Halloween trip.

"Not about the cemetery, necessarily," I said. "There are some crazy stories about a rattlesnake den near there, and I . . . I'd like to know more about it."

"You're thinking of the Sullivan story as well, then," he said calmly. "With the snakes."

"Yes, sir."

"It's an area rich with folklore."

"The forest is?"

"I was referring to the topic of rattlesnakes, actually. Let me do a little digging for you, and don't hesitate to make a request. I can interlibrary loan any materials you need."

"Thank you."

"I live to serve." He winked and turned away. I took the map back into the office, closed the door, and spread it out on the desk, then did my best to measure off the locations in Noah Storm's notes against the forest, using Stepp Cemetery as my generic reference point.

They were close. So close that I could see the den would be nearer Jerry's pit house than the cemetery. From there, it was only a matter of locating the cliff.

I stepped back out of the office.

"Mr. Doig, can I see the maps that have the altitude?"

"I presume you mean the *elevation*, which refers to the ground conditions, and not the geopotential height that is represented by altitude." He looked at me with a hint of a smile, then saw my face and said, "Take a breath, Marshall. I'll get the map."

He found a topographic map of the state forest and made me a photocopy. I left the library confident that I could find Jerry's cliff. The only problem was the one promise I'd made to him: I'd said that I wouldn't go alone.

Truth be told, I also didn't *want* to go alone.

My first instinct was to ask Kerri to go, but I respected Jerry's fear of the spot enough to keep his daughter away from it. Dom told me he had two soccer games that weekend, both on the road. But I did know someone who might be up for the trip.

He just wasn't in my school.

4

"*FUCK, YES,*" SEAN WELLER said when I told him my plan between sets. He sucked furiously on a protein shake that was so thick, it pulled his cheeks in and puckered his lips. He made the shakes himself, a blend of protein, creatine, banana, and malt balls, the latter being what he called the "coop de grace" ingredient, a pronunciation I never bothered to correct. While he swore by the shake as a potent power enhancer, he had never figured out that a little more patience with the blender might make it easier to consume.

"Dude, I love rolling out to Stepp Cemetery at Halloween. That place is wild, spooky as hell, and chicks love it. I got half a hand job from Courtney Robbins out there junior year before some assholes screamed in the woods and scared her."

"You knew them?"

"Nah. They were hiding and let out a scream at the *worst* time, I assure you." He winced with the memory. "Courtney thought it was a ghost. She was terrified."

"It didn't scare you?"

"The spirit of blue balls haunted me long after I left Stepp Cemetery that night, but it was definitely not a ghost."

"How do you know?"

"Why would a ghost cockblock? Just because they're dead doesn't mean they don't have memories of getting their rocks off. A ghost would respect it."

"Interesting theory."

"I'm sure of it. Another time, we left a bottle of SoCo there as an offering for the ghosties. Well, not a whole bottle. Just a taste." He eyed the ceiling. "Actually, I think I killed the booze. But we left the bottle, and with ghosts I'm pretty sure it's the gesture that counts."

"No doubt," I said, loading another plate on the bar for him as he belched malt-scented protein. "But I don't want to go to Stepp Cemetery, exactly. Just hang out in that vicinity."

His broad face brightened. "You talking kegger? It's last-minute. But maybe—"

"No," I said, and I was surprised by his evident disappointment. What did Sean Weller want with a kegger in the woods now that he was in college, when the only real challenge was finding a night *without* a fraternity party. "All I want to do is go out there and . . . look around."

"Look around?" He frowned. "Just two dudes? And we're not bringing any booze?"

I sighed. "I want to see the place where Jerry Flanders had his pit house."

"You mean that wannabe Waco?"

I started to object, then settled for a shrug and a nod.

Weller nodded. "Yeah, I'd check that shit out. Why not?"

"When can you go?" I asked. "Sooner the better to me, but I know—"

"Tonight," he said, dipping beneath the squat rack and settling the bar on his shoulders.

"Seriously?"

"Why not?"

"You have the Michigan game tomorrow."

"Best part of being a redshirt? They don't notice whether I'm in the locker room or not." He glared into the mirror, and I couldn't tell if he was looking at me or himself. "Now let's make sure they *do* notice me on the field next year, Marshmallow. Stop twiddling your twat and spot this shit."

With that, he hoisted the bar and began another set.

———

What supplies do you bring to a place where venomous snakes are known to rise from the dead? I spent an hour in the garage, considering various weapons, before deciding that my mother and I were going to be out-gunned if Jerry's predictions for Y2K came true. The best options I found were a five iron and a can of wasp spray. The wasp spray didn't advertise itself as a deterrent against snakes, but I figured they wouldn't *like* it.

I changed the batteries in our two brightest flashlights and sat at the kitchen island, waiting for Sean Weller and watching my mother on television doing the Halloween night forecast. She was wearing a black dress and a witch's hat, and unless you knew her, you wouldn't have any idea how much she hated the station's mandate to dress up for holidays. She was predicting a spooky evening, cautioning parents to be aware of fog and rain. Our doorbell was ringing regularly, and I handed out candy to the trick-or-treaters. Harry Potter costumes were big, but not as popular as the trench-coat-and-shades look of Neo from *The Matrix*.

I looked at the clock. Weller was already ten minutes late.

The weather broadcast ended and newscasters moved to footage of Coast Guard ships searching the waters off Nantucket, where a plane out of John F. Kennedy Airport had crashed with 217 people on board. Some of the Navy ships being used in the search, the newscasters informed us, were the same crafts that had found John F. Kennedy Jr.'s private plane in the waters off Martha's Vineyard earlier that summer and located the wreckage of TWA Flight 800 three years earlier off the coast of Long Island. The latest plane to require the search was Egypt-Air Flight 990, which had been bound from New York to Cairo before entering a steep, inexplicable dive. No one was sure what had happened yet. All they seemed to agree on was that everyone on board was dead. The mayor of New York City, Rudy Giuliani, was shown arriving at a Ramada Plaza hotel near the airport where the families of the crew and passengers were assembling, the same hotel where Bill Clinton had visited families after TWA 800 crashed. It was a sad scene. I changed the channel.

Weller arrived twenty minutes late, and as soon as I pulled open the passenger door of his Chevy Silverado, I smelled booze.

"Sorry, bro," Weller said. "I could *not* find a sign for Sweetgrass Lane."

"That's because it's called Raintree Lane."

"Well, shit. I was close. Here, have a snort." He offered me a bottle of Southern Comfort, and my stomach recoiled immediately.

"No, thanks."

"Liquid courage for the land of the undead."

"Weller, I'm trying to take this seriously."

He made an apologetic gesture with the bottle, took another swallow, and nestled it into the cup holder. He stared across the street.

"That's where the dude lives. Flanders?"

He was looking at the wrong house, but I was fine with that.

"Yeah."

"You really don't think he did it?"

"Hurt Meredith Sullivan? No way."

"Everyone I've talked to says he's deeply weird."

"I'm not arguing that. I'm saying he didn't have anything to do with Meredith."

Weller nodded, then glanced at my supplies. The grip of the five iron, which I'd spray-painted bright blue so I knew it wasn't a snake, jutted out of the duffel bag.

"You brought a golf club?"

"Just drive, man."

He chuckled and put the truck into gear. We drove to the state forest as a light rain began to fall. I didn't mind the rain; I figured the weather would keep Halloween partiers away. I had a decent sense of where Jerry's pit house had been, and the topographic map suggested the steepest slopes were to the southeast. A lot of people think of Indiana as flat country, but the southern half is undulating, heavily forested hill country more similar to Kentucky than Kansas.

"What are you actually expecting to find, Marshmallow?" Weller asked.

"I have no idea. I just want to see the spot."

"With a golf club."

"He said there were snakes."

"No shit there were snakes. He had a barrel of them."

"He says he caught them out there."

Weller nodded. "Possible. My dad's land abuts the forest. It's snake central. Copperheads, mostly, but when my granddad bought it, the old-timers told him this story about when they were quarrying near there, and they blasted a den of rattlesnakes. When it detonated?" He took both hands off the wheel to make a falling gesture with fluttering fingers. "Fourth of fucking July, raining snakes. A bunch of guys never came back, too shaken up."

"This is real?"

"What Granddad said." Weller unscrewed the SoCo. "Sure you don't want a little pop?"

"I'm fine."

He drank and belched and screwed the top back on. We were going about twenty miles per hour above the speed limit on the winding roads and in the rain, and I had to resist the urge to tell him to slow down. He was doing me a favor.

"What era was this?" I asked. "Your grandfather's generation, or his father's?"

"I don't know the whole family tree. I'm not a friggin' geologist."

I let that one slide by, lost in thought.

"Wouldn't be a coincidence," Weller said abruptly.

"Huh?"

"If Flanders really did catch them out there, it wouldn't be the first time someone was doing weird shit with snakes in that place. The Crabbites beat him to it."

"The what?"

"It was a cult." He glanced at me, frowning. "Did you not even pay attention in fourth-grade history?"

"I don't remember cults coming up in fourth grade."

"I think they did. Or maybe it was on the field trip to that one-room schoolhouse. What was it called? Honey Creek? They had the outhouses?

We locked Scotty Macomber inside and he cried—I mean, he was legit sobbing—and when he—"

"Weller, what in the hell were you saying about the snakes?"

He looked dismayed to have been cut off during a good reminiscence of elementary school bullying, but he circled back.

"The Crabbites are the only reason Stepp Cemetery ever became a draw. They moved out there in . . . I don't know, some olden-time year. They made a little village in the woods, built shacks, and the one named Crabb was their priest or whatever. Maybe my granddad told me that. Come to think of it, you might be right—this shit wasn't in school. It's family stuff. This is what the Wellers do, man, talk about land, buy land, build on—"

"The snakes," I implored.

"Well, the Crabbites were snake handlers," he said simply.

We whipped around a series of S curves, the truck's tires fighting for traction on the wet pavement, tendrils of white fog reaching through the bare tree limbs.

"You're serious?"

"Dude, look in a history book. Stepp Cemetery didn't have any ghost stories for, like, a hundred years. Not the Warlock Chair, not Baby Lester, none of it. All that came later, after the Crabbites. They freaked the locals out with the snake-handling shit, and then the police came with a posse, and they chased them out of the forest, and that was the end of it. The real problem at Stepp Cemetery started with a group of sad, weird people. The ghosts and legends came later. I think that's because people would rather be scared than sad, you know? We'd rather be almost *anything* than sad. So the stories changed."

"But they handled snakes," I said. "Rattlesnakes."

"People did that back then. It was how they knew God was stronger than the devil. Like how a witch can't float. They thought you needed to battle-test these things, so they sank witches and handled snakes."

"What?"

"Look, I'm not getting an MBA in religion; I just know the gist."

We were deep into the state forest now, and Weller slowed. When he alternated between high beams and fog lights, there seemed to be little difference.

"If you were a total pussy," Sean Weller said, "tonight would not be for you."

I nodded and tapped the handle of my five iron.

Weller parked at the trailhead nearest the cemetery. It was a short walk from there to the gravestones, but I wasn't interested in those. I turned on the dome light and showed him the map. It looked like hard hiking, and I was considering suggesting we come back in daylight when Weller produced a compass and put it on the map.

"You know how to use that?" I asked.

He looked at me with surprise. "Have you never been deer hunting?"

"No."

"Well, get a permit. I'll help you pack it out, but you've got to gut it yourself."

"Uh . . ."

"Let's roll," he said, taking the map and opening the truck door.

We left the trail and walked into the night woods. The trees were densely packed, the terrain rough and uneven, briars raking my jeans and boulders or loose logs doing their best to break an ankle. I was grateful for the five iron because it gave me a walking stick. The fog knocked the flashlight beam down so I couldn't even get a horizon view. The idea of Jerry coming out here day after day was haunting in a way that ghosts weren't.

The real problem at Stepp Cemetery started with a group of sad, weird people, Weller had said.

I wondered if Jerry was already a part of that lineage. It wasn't hard to imagine a group of kids coming out here in fifty years to scare each other while searching for the kidnapper's bunker or whatever they would call it then.

"There ya go," Weller said, pulling up short. I sidestepped to see around him.

His flashlight beam played over a hollowed-out stretch of earth between towering oak trees. Police tape draped over the limbs and encircled some of the trunks. The soil appeared to have been recently turned over with a backhoe or excavator.

"They busted it up," Weller said, stepping closer. "Dug it all out and filled it back in and drove over it, trying to flatten it like it never existed."

"Why would they do that?"

"Because of people like us. They wouldn't have wanted anyone coming out here to treat a crime scene like a game."

I didn't like the way he'd said *people like us*. It was hardly a game to me.

The rain had stopped but there was the sound of moving water in the woods nearby. I imagined the place the way Jerry had described it, alive with rattling snakes, a sound like the wind ahead of a storm. I shivered and checked the ground at my feet. Every stick and shadow seemed worth a second look.

"Let's find that cliff," Weller said, and walked ahead, leaving me to follow.

It took us much longer to find the cliff than it had to find the pit house. The rain started again while we checked the map and ambled first in one direction and then another, fighting up over downed trees and ducking beneath low limbs or twisting around lacerating thorns. I was dirty and sweating and the rain was falling harder and I was about to tell Weller we should give up for the night when he summoned me with a shrill whistle. All I could see was his silhouette in the fog. When I finally fought my way up through the brush to join him, I saw that he was facing a cliff, ribbons of broken stone culminating in a smooth, long stone face that reached for the night sky.

"Old quarry site," Weller said.

"How can you tell?"

"Because stone doesn't break off into neat squares by itself." He shined the beam around. "Limestone, but it's weird. Look at that black veining."

I wouldn't have noticed until he pointed it out, but now I saw that the pale stone was shot through with thin black lines. He'd grown up around this, walking woodlands or fields with his father, discussing the terrain, what was valuable and what wasn't. All I saw was rock.

"That's a hell of a climb," Weller said. "Every bit of a hundred feet. Probably more."

"Jerry thought it was two hundred."

"He's probably right."

I could see the ledge more than halfway up. That was the snake den.

"What do *you* want to do out here?" Weller asked.

Another hesitation. "I guess I want to climb up and . . . look around."

Weller's laugh echoed. "No way you're climbing up this. It's sheer except for that ledge in the middle. *I* couldn't make it. Your buddy Jake Crane is probably the only person in Monroe County who has a chance."

Just what I wanted to hear.

"What if you started from above and used a long rope?" I suggested. "Could you lower yourself down?"

He tilted the flashlight, studying the angles. "Possibly, but you'd need good equipment to anchor with. You could use a crane."

"Like you could drive a crane up there," I said.

"You could *build* one, numb nuts. You know, a gantry crane."

I did not have the faintest idea what he was talking about.

Weller looked at me. "Why does it matter? You think Jerry left something up there?"

He left a bunch of dead snakes that wouldn't stay dead, I thought, then said, "I was curious, that's all."

"Well, you're going to stay curious. There's no way to climb that cliff."

He was right. The climb was impossible. I pictured Jake's tutorial lesson on the Terminal Tower and thought that, yes, he could do it. What would the point be, though? I panned my light over the stone wall.

The place matters. I know it does. But how?

"Come on," Weller said. "It's starting to pour."

I followed him from the base of the old quarry cliff. Listening to the rain on the dead leaves, it was easy to imagine the rustling of rattlesnakes. It was also easy to imagine that a man who spent a lot of time out here alone could become very nervous, very fast. If that man was already afraid of a world that seemed always beyond his control . . .

Maybe he snapped, I thought. *Maybe whatever was holding Jerry Flanders together just broke out here. Maybe there was never a snake hunter at all.*

He needed help, and all I had to offer were snake sketches, legends, and a track record of lying to police. Without more than that, Jerry Flanders was going to prison. They'd get him for the snakes and the pit house even if they couldn't get him for worse.

Over the course of the year, I'd gotten older and stronger and tried to get smarter. It did not seem to be worth much when the world pushed back, though. I'd lost a job, lost friends, lost girlfriends, lost respect, and was about to lose the closest thing I had to a father—which was the one thing I'd never had to begin with.

I was lost to my own depressed thoughts when Weller said, "Think we should play ghost?"

I didn't understand what he meant for a moment, then realized that there were flashlights bobbing up ahead and a few faint laughs.

"Is that at the cemetery?"

"Parking spot for it, yeah. People smarter than us came out here to laugh and get laid, not hike around looking for inspiration." He didn't seem nonplussed, though, just happy to have sighted strangers. He clicked his flashlight off and pushed mine down so the beam was angled at the ground. "Come on, Marshmallow, let's give 'em a scare."

But I wasn't feeling it. I was in a defeated spirit and wanted to be home, out of the rain.

"I'm done out here, Sean," I said, and then I walked ahead, making no attempt to conceal my flashlight beam or the sound of my approach.

The group in the cemetery parking area fell silent as we neared, and someone angled a light at us. I lifted the hand with the five iron in it, shielding my eyes, as we broke out of the trees. Two cars and another truck were parked beside Weller's truck now, and a cluster of kids were busy hiding beer cans in case we were police.

"You gotta be kidding me! Look who's been having a little Miller Time in the woods!"

I turned to see Kenny Glass. Wonderful.

I recognized the others: guys named Andrew and Clay, both on the South football team; a stoner named Marcus from North; and three girls, all from North, all in my class, all with reputations for feats of sexual prowess that were either created by or enhanced by locker-room retellings. Nikki, Tina, Tammy.

"What in the hell is in Miller's hand?" Andrew said. "A *golf club*? Did you win a putter from some hobo for giving sexual favors in the bushes?"

"It's a five iron," I said, as if that redeemed me.

"How does that matter? That's the . . ."

His voice trailed off when Sean Weller stepped close enough to be recognized. The whole group stopped laughing then. They all seemed surprised and intimidated, and I was duly pleased, until Kenny Glass smiled.

"Look, it's the big man on campus! Thought you were gonna be a star, Weller. Now it's Friday night and you're in the woods crossing shafts with Marshall Miller?"

I was stunned. To hear *anyone* talk to Weller like that was amazing, let alone someone who'd already been thrown into a fire by him.

"I will beat your ass, Kenny," Weller said, but there was something missing from his tone.

"No you won't," Kenny said casually. "But I will shoot yours."

Only when Tammy said, "Kenny . . ." in a warning voice did I realize what Weller had already seen: Kenny Glass was sitting on the tailgate of his truck with a shotgun across his lap.

"Put the gun down and say that," Weller said. "The hell are you even doing out here with a gun, you idiot?"

"I need to protect the ladies from perverts like you two."

"You're a loser," Weller told him, moving toward his own truck.

"Says the walk-on reject."

Weller kept going for the truck.

"You guys hear about this?" Kenny said, louder now. "Weller told everyone he was going to play football for IU, which is sad enough as it is, but at least they're a Big Ten school, right? Guy made everybody call him the 'Speed King' in high school, he thought he was such a badass. But Big Ten football took a look and said, 'Uh, no. He's the Speed Queen, at best.' They were going to let him walk on, but he's so stupid that he couldn't academically qualify as a walk-on. Think about that! He fucking flunked off a team he couldn't even *make*!"

Kenny laughed wildly, and one of the girls and one of the guys tittered, but I felt as if the rest of the group seemed awkward and maybe even a little sad. I looked from Weller to Kenny and back. I had never understood Weller's redshirt year, but was Kenny telling the truth?

He was, I realized as Weller unlocked his door, refusing to look back. Kenny was being allowed to get away with this not because of the shotgun but because he was telling the truth.

"How dumb must you be to be academically ineligible for a practice squad?" Kenny said, and I was about to ask him if he knew what a gantry crane was—even though I sure as hell didn't—when Weller finally turned back to him.

"I'm gonna see you when you don't have the gun in your hand," he said calmly. "Guarantee it."

"I'm gonna see you when you don't have the diploma in your hand," Kenny said, mocking Weller's deep voice. "Guarantee it."

Weller's hand flexed against the door handle as if he were considering ripping the door off the truck.

"Come on, Marshall," he said.

"Yeah, Marshall," Kenny said. "Hope you boys had fun in the bushes."

I got into the truck, and Weller had it in reverse before I was even in the seat. He peeled out, showering mud into the air, and cranked the stereo up. Limp Bizkit blasted through the speakers. Weller unscrewed the top of the Southern Comfort and took a long drink. Neither of us spoke for a few miles. There was real pain in his eyes.

"Kenny's an asshole," I said.

"Yeah." Weller took another drink.

"He's lucky you didn't take that gun from him and bust it over his head."

Weller didn't respond. We drove on, speeding dangerously now, as he chugged his whiskey and sulked, and I thought of every teenage cliché we could become on the next S curve—two guys dead in a wreck after leaving a graveyard on a rainy Halloween, an object lesson for guidance counselors, an inspiration for ghost hunters.

"Ignore him," I said.

Another sip of SoCo, another S curve taken without a graze of the brake pedal. This time the back end of the truck fishtailed. Weller responded by pressing on the gas. We screamed out of the skid.

He needs direction, I thought. *It's just like in the gym. He needs the next set, the next challenge, the next thing to hit.*

"We can egg his house," I said, and Weller grimaced with disgust and accelerated.

"We can burn his house down!" I offered.

Another shake of the head, another shot of whiskey, another ten miles per hour. The night woods whipping past us, the fog devouring the headlights, the truck tires shedding rain.

We are going to die. All because of some asshole who pushed the right button with the wrong guy on the wrong night. There's no one to rescue me this time. I'm trapped now because of Kenny Glass, trapped like his—

"Sean," I said. "We should set their panther loose."

A pause. An easing of acceleration. Weller's face turning to mine in the dark cab of the truck, the SoCo bottle lit by the dashboard lights.

"Marshmallow," he said, "you are a genius."

5

THE GLASS FAMILY LIVED on land near the parcel Sean Weller's father had purchased for development off Lost Man's Lane. They'd been in the area for generations—"All of them big football players, except for the girls, who were just big," Weller informed me. According to him, the panther was housed in a pole barn that Kenny's uncle, Vic, owned.

He was still driving like we were in the Indy 500, and I suggested that he slow down, but once presented with an idea as good as freeing a hundred-pound carnivore from a cage, Sean Weller wasn't one to drag his feet.

Despite the madness, it was good to see his face light up with a touch of the old confidence. I'd always known that he seemed oddly disconnected even for a redshirt—no practices or meetings—so the revelation that he wasn't with the team didn't surprise me. Learning that he'd never been offered a scholarship did. Sean Weller had seemed like a big deal in high school, so it had never occurred to me that he wouldn't be good enough to cut it there. His constant availability made sense now—and made me sad. Just last spring, he'd been a star, beyond reproach from anyone, let alone the likes of Kenny Glass. Now he was adrift, free on a Halloween weekend to hang out with . . . well, the likes of Marshmallow Miller.

"You ever been out to his place?" Weller asked as he turned onto a winding road made into a narrow tunnel by crowding trees.

"No. We're not exactly friends."

"Weird family. One of them cooked meth. They're always in trouble. Lucky there's a cop in the family. Covers shit up."

"There's a cop in the family?"

"Big Vic." Weller belched whiskey. "Same one who stands there with the cat at the football games. Or who *used* to, because that cat is about to be free-ranging."

My expanding knowledge of the Glass family was rapidly diminishing my desire to go near their property. Meth cooks and cops, you say? Maybe, just maybe, this was not a great idea.

"*Yes, I'm freeeee, freeee-raaangin'!*" Weller wailed in his best Tom Petty voice. "Hell, yeah, this is a brilliant night!"

"Maybe they'll know it's us, considering you guys had an altercation."

"An altercation. Marshmallow, you sound like a lawyer."

"I'm afraid we're going to get a chance to compare that in real time very soon."

Weller laughed and punched me in the arm as he reached for his SoCo. "Good thing I'm in my dad's truck," he said.

"Wait, what? How is that good?"

"The toolbox in the bed has a reciprocating saw. I hope it's enough to cut through the bars on that cage. I can grab a butane torch if it's not."

"Sean, we seriously might want to come another night. Maybe—"

"Dude, are you pussing out on me?" He glanced my way, face furious.

"No. What? Never. I'm suggesting, for planning purposes—strategy— we could benefit from treating tonight more like a reconnaissance mission."

"No way. Practice sucks. We came to play the game."

Oh, boy.

I should have protested louder. I should have made more persuasive arguments. It was, after all, my objectively stupid idea. We were intending to trespass on a cop's property with the intention of releasing an apex predator. I'd seen that cat before, at very close range, and if anyone on earth should be smart enough to take the hint to stay away, it was me.

And yet . . .

I touched the bridge of my nose, which still had—still has today—the wide, flat divot that Kenny's fist had left there. I remembered the way the blood had tasted as it poured down my throat, and how Leslie Carter screamed at me with tears in her eyes as I held Jake Crane's cologne-scented shirt to my face. I remembered the way Kerri had stood face-to-face with Kenny and told him what everyone thought but nobody else was brave enough to say about the poor cougar in the cage.

"All right," I said. "Let's do it."

"Thatta boy! *Woooo!*" Weller threw his head back and howled, I managed a weak smile, and when he pressed the SoCo bottle in my palm, I took a sip. I nearly gagged, but at least I held it down.

"We'll show Kenny who the speed queens are now," I said, passing the bottle back.

Weller frowned. "Work on that one."

"Right."

Weller turned onto a narrow road pocked with potholes and then slowed, leaning over the steering wheel, peering into the trees.

"There's gonna be a farm lane before the driveway. We want that. Going down the driveway would be ballsy but probably not smart."

"Probably not."

We went about a quarter mile before he slammed on the brakes and jerked the wheel left. We bounced off the pavement and came to a stop in front of a cattle gate.

"Give it a minute," I said. "Make sure nobody else comes along."

I wanted someone else to come along. No one did, though. The trees weaved in the wind above us, shedding rain, and a low ground fog cloaked the hills. I could see the metal roofs of two pole barns reflecting what little moonlight there was.

"Where's the house?" I whispered.

"Other side of the hill. They had hundreds of acres, but they sold most of it off for timber. They never realized it was zoned for residential and agriculture. You could pay assessment on aggie rates while planning a residential development. They had a perfect situation. Idiots."

I stared at him. Gantry cranes and aggie rates. Maybe Sean Weller would do just fine without Indiana University—or any university. You didn't need to know the difference between a geologist and a genealogist to make money if you understood zoning and taxes.

We left the truck and advanced into the fog carrying a reciprocating saw.

It was so quiet that every footfall sounded like an exploding land mine, and I was certain that a floodlight would come on and pin us in its beam like prison escapees. The path wound past a pond and then parted from the tree line and left us out in an open field, begging to be noticed. The house was visible now, a rambling structure with a sagging porch and an assortment of vehicles parked haphazardly in the front lawn, like dice scattered from an indifferent hand. The newest was a green Jeep that sat facing the barns.

"I bet they've got the cat in the barn that's farthest away from the house," Weller whispered.

"Why would they do that?"

"Did you hear it scream at that party?"

Fair point.

We reached the rear of the pole barn just as a light came on in an upstairs window in the house. Weller gestured for me to stop walking. We stood stock-still, our breath fogging the misty air, until the light went back off.

"Bathroom," Weller whispered. "Kenny's uncle pissing out some Pabst."

He moved away from me, the heavy saw dangling in his hand, and tried the handle on the pedestrian door of the pole barn.

Please, don't open, I pleaded silently.

It swung open, and the cougar growled from the darkness.

"Ho-ly shit!" Weller gave a nervous chuckle. "Guess she doesn't know we're here to help."

I looked over my shoulder, considering the winding roads that led here and the highway waiting a few miles beyond. *Were* we there to help? It was bullshit that the cougar was locked in a cage and stowed in a barn, but was the animal prepared for freedom? Could it survive out there, or would it be hit by a car? Hell, would it just pace around the barnyard, looking for human help?

"Weller," I whispered, but he was already gone.

The rain began to fall in earnest as I followed him across the mud-and-gravel track that led to the door. Weller turned his flashlight on but shielded the beam with his palm as he stepped inside the barn. The floor was wooden, but bits of straw crunched underfoot. As Weller assessed his surroundings, all I could see was his cherubic face lit from beneath like the villain in a horror movie. Another growl came, low and warning and so primal that it lifted the hairs along my neck. I took a step back as Weller removed his hand from the flashlight lens and let the beam blossom, exposing the interior of the building and the cougar in the cage at the back.

The cat's front paws hit the cage, rattling the steel bars as it pinned its ears and spread its jaw, exposing those formidable fangs.

"Yikes," Weller said, and for the first time he seemed aware of what should have been obvious from the start: releasing the cat required removing the protection between us and the cat.

"She's got to hit the door running," Weller said. "If she has, like, bad eyesight or whatever, misses the open door and spins back, then she's freaking out, and we're trapped here."

"Kind of what I was thinking," I said, relieved that he'd come to his senses.

"So we'll have to open the big door," Weller continued. "She can't miss that."

This was not the solution I'd had in mind.

"Come on," he said, setting his saw down and moving to the doors.

He got the first door to rattle open, revealing the dark night on the other side and letting a burst of windswept rain in. The rain speckled the old wooden floor planks. It made me think of the dream I'd had about the blood drops on the floor of the old barn. Instinctively, I turned and put the light on the floor, sweeping the beam across the room. The cougar hissed and smacked one massive paw off the cage in a lightning-quick strike, as if it couldn't wait to get a piece of me.

"You wanna help me, Marshmallow?" Weller grunted, pushing at the other door, which groaned as it shuddered down its track. A high, harsh buzz cut the air, and he stopped moving, thinking that he had caused the sound.

The sound didn't stop. He cocked his head.

"The hell is that?" he asked, just as I moved the flashlight to my left and illuminated the snake cages.

They filled half the wall at the rear of the barn. They were stacked one on top of another, made of molded plastic, and looked like any garage shelving unit—except that these had glass panels lining the front, and coiled serpents on the other side.

While I stared, one of the snakes struck at the glass, and another lifted the tip of its vibrating, rattle-lined tail. A mouse scampered back and forth, trapped.

"Weller . . ."

"I see it." His voice was low and calm.

"He's got so many of them."

"We gotta get out of here."

"I want to take a picture," I said.

"Well, we're shit out of luck there," he answered, and he was right.

I can't tell you how many times in the years since I've lifted my phone to take a casual snapshot and wondered what might have happened if we'd been armed with iPhones when we walked into that barn outside Bloomington. But it was 1999, and unless you were carrying a real camera, the only picture you could leave with was the one in your mind.

We fled in a hurry. Too much of a hurry. Weller had the presence of mind to turn his flashlight off, but I didn't. When I went through the door, I tripped and hit the metal wall, and then the cougar let out a scream that ripped the night as I sprawled into the mud. When the front door of the Glass house opened, my flashlight beam was on the barn.

"Turn it off!" Sean Weller hissed, and I hit the button, finally, but still too late.

"HEY!" someone bellowed from the porch, and then I was back on my feet and Weller and I were sprinting all out, slipping and sliding through the wet grass. I imagined the Jeep roaring to life behind us. If our pursuer had thought of it at the same time, he'd have had us cold. But he didn't think, he just ran, the way we had, and we had a good head start on him and we were young and in shape, each of us having spent the summer and fall training hard for different, unspoken reasons, seeking to change our fates.

Change ourselves.

That Halloween night, it paid off. I ran harder than I ever had, outpacing even Sean Weller, the original Speed King of the Bloomington South secondary, who'd been a free safety until he'd gotten so damn big that they moved him to linebacker. I was out in front of him when we reached the truck, which was locked, and I had to wait, gasping and jerking at the door handle as if it might suddenly pop open, until he joined me and unlocked the doors and threw himself behind the wheel. He started the engine but didn't turn the headlights on, just dropped the gearshift into reverse and floored it. The rear tires spun mud and then caught traction and slammed us backward, out of the dirt and onto the pavement. Weller cut the wheel and shifted into drive and hit the accelerator again, and I twisted in the seat and looked back in time to see the Jeep's headlights blink on at the top of the hill.

"They're coming," I warned.

Weller didn't say a word, but he turned on the Silverado's headlights and pounded the gas pedal. We roared forward. The oaks and walnuts and maples whipped past, and sycamores and beeches that shone bone white in the headlight beams, and behind us the Jeep's lights appeared on the road, then vanished from the mirror as Weller screeched around a curve.

"They're gonna catch us," I said.

Still no answer. Weller blew down the winding road with the truck bed fishtailing wildly, and he let off the gas only long enough to get the truck straightened out again. We were approaching the highway, and the stop sign ahead gleamed red and wet with rain, and I realized that Weller had no intention of braking for it. If a car was coming down the highway, it was going to tattoo us on the passenger side.

My side.

We roared through the intersection. A horn blared and I closed my eyes and braced for impact. Then we were across the road and the horn was still shrieking, a male voice screaming along with it, but the car was past, missing us by a whisper. Weller kept driving, but he was scanning the houses on both sides of the road.

"Sean—"

"Shut up."

I shut up. He picked a house with darkened windows and no cars in the driveway and then he turned off the road and into the drive, pulling all the way up to the farthest reaches of the pavement, nearly hidden behind the house, cut the engine, and turned off the headlights.

"Get down low, Marshmallow."

I scooted down, mimicking his posture, so that the only things visible from behind the truck were the seatbacks. Weller adjusted the mirrors, tilting them so they weren't reflecting the cab.

The sound of an engine came on, loud and muscular and throaty. Then headlights set high.

The Jeep.

Neither of us spoke. I don't think either of us breathed. The Jeep reached the house Weller had picked and then it slowed. The white glare from the lights seemed to fill the cab and surround us. We seemed so obvious, I felt as if I were being illuminated from the inside out.

Then the Jeep roared away.

The next sound was the SoCo bottle opening. Weller drank, offered the bottle to me, then drank again when I shook my head. I slumped against the doorframe, waiting for my heartbeat to resume something approximating normal human function.

"Damn, that was close," Weller said. "You see those fucking snakes? Holy shit, man."

"We've gotta call the police."

"The police?"

I turned to him, stunned. "Yes! That guy has as many snakes as Jerry, and they're trying to put him in prison!"

Weller didn't respond right away. I straightened in the seat.

"Sean, that's evidence that could help clear Jerry Flanders!"

"That we found while breaking and entering," he said softly. "Which is a confession that could put us in jail."

"Nobody's locking us up for that."

"I'm nineteen. You're going to get juvenile court; I'm not."

"All we did was . . . walk in."

"Residential entry, yeah. A crime. And maybe he's allowed to have those snakes."

"It's illegal! They said that when they arrested Jerry!"

"I think there might be permits."

"That's bullshit."

"Is it?" His question was genuine. "I don't know what kind of permits there are for wild animals. Do you?"

I shook my head. "I can't just . . . ignore it, though. I mean, it might help Jerry."

"Owning a bunch of snakes that are kept in an official tarantulum is very different than keeping a barrel of them in the woods."

"Terrarium. And I don't think it is that different. The police said rattlesnakes are protected and keeping them is a federal crime."

"There are different kinds of rattlesnakes. It looked like a pretty legit setup." He lifted a hand against my protestations. "I'm just wondering: Is it *possible* that Big Vic has a permit for them? He's a cop. He knows the law."

"Anything is possible, I guess. But right now, if there is any chance of that helping Jerry, I have to take it. I can leave you out of it and say I went in alone."

"That's not going to work. They'll break your story in five minutes. And I'm not letting you do that. We were partners in crime." He rubbed his jaw. "What if we call it in unanimously?"

"Anonymously?"

"Right."

I thought about it. Why not? It was going to be easier to send the police out there without us than with us, in some ways. Also, how many times had Jerry and I agreed that I wasn't an ideal witness on his behalf, considering the murder I'd reported in July?

"All right," I said. "Let's do that." I reached for my phone, but Weller put his hand on my arm.

"Pay phone. They'll trace it."

"Good call."

So we drove back into town and picked a pay phone close to Nick's English Hut and Kilroy's on Kirkwood where college students would summon taxis. Hopefully, two more kids wouldn't stand out to anyone. I called 911 and told the operator that I'd been playing a Halloween prank on a kid and when I opened his barn door, I found a cougar in a cage and a stack of rattlesnakes along the wall. The operator seemed skeptical at best.

"I'm serious," I said. "There are a lot of them in there. And maybe you've heard of the dead girl who was killed from snake venom?"

"Son, give me your name."

"I'm not doing that. Just go to Vic Glass's house and check. You're going to find exactly what I said."

I hung up then.

Weller dropped me off outside my house and told me to find him in the weight room the next day.

"We can figure out next steps. By then it'll be in the newspaper and on TV," he said.

But it wasn't. Not by morning, not by noon. I couldn't believe it. After all the coverage of Jerry Flanders, they couldn't get so much as a picture out there for Vic Glass? Weller didn't show up at the weight room, either, leaving me alone with my concerns.

I was back in the car, sweaty and nervous, when my cell phone rang. It was Ron Walters with the Indiana State Police.

"Hello, Marshall." He said my name in a tone most people reserved for words like "sewage" or "vomit." "You got time for a quick question?"

"Uh, sure."

"I need an ear to the ground with the local youth. Heard any rumors about a break-in at a barn owned by a police officer named Vic Glass last night?"

I couldn't speak.

"Marshall?"

"Uh, I heard some people saying that they've got illegal animals out there."

"Oh?"

"Yeah, a cougar and a bunch of rattlesnakes."

"This is in the rumor mill, eh?"

"Yes, sir."

Walters laughed. It wasn't a pleasant sound.

"Well, the rumor mill led to officers wasting their time visiting Officer Glass last night, following an instance of false reporting that seems to be oddly common when you're around."

"*False reporting?*" I croaked the words out.

"That's right," he said. "A search of the property—the results of which I'm under no obligation to disclose to you, Marshall, except of course for our close friendship—revealed that Officer Glass does, in fact, have boa constrictors and pythons, for which he has the proper permits. There are no rattlesnakes."

I was so shocked, I couldn't answer. Not out of fear—not yet, anyhow—but because I simply didn't believe what he was telling me. We had seen the snakes. Seen them and heard them. They were real and they were there and this time I had not been alone.

"It wasn't an entirely fruitless search," Walters continued. "We were able to identify the young man who broke into the barn because he happened to leave behind a reciprocating saw with his father's name on it. Real criminal mastermind at work. Now, he swears he traveled alone on this little joyride, but I've listened to the tape of the 911 call and, boy, I tell ya . . . there's a familiarity to the voice. I can't quite place it yet. Tip of my tongue, though. I'll keep at it. Be good, Marshall."

He hung up before I could respond.

CHAPTER ELEVEN

CHASING THE FISH

November–December 1999

"Fear not of men because men must die
Mind over matter and soul before flesh"

MOS DEF
"FEAR NOT OF MAN"

1

WELLER TOOK THE FALL for both of us without a blink. I called him as soon as Walters hung up on me, saying I was ready to confess, only to have Sean shoot me down.

"Chill for a minute. There's no gain to you getting in trouble, too, is there?"

"But I was there with you. We went together. I was the one who called the police."

"And I left the saw. Two dumbasses went into the barn and one dumbass got caught is the way we need to look at this."

Sanguine Sean Weller.

"Bite your tongue for twenty-four hours, okay?" he said. "Let me sort things out and see what it looks like tomorrow. It's not as bad as you think. Let's reconnaissance at the gym tomorrow."

"Reconnoiter."

"You and your words. Right on. Later."

It was a long day, but when I saw him in the weight room after school on Monday, he seemed in oddly good spirits.

"There won't be any charges," he said. "Vic hid the snakes, which was smart, but he doesn't want to spend more time talking to cops than I do, because he told them to drop it. It's a brotherhood with those guys; we should've known they wouldn't press one of their own based on nothing but a unanimous phone call."

"Anon . . ." I waved it off. "Whatever."

"Oh, yeah. Vic has his balls in a vise over the cat now."

"What?"

Weller grinned and slapped a second forty-five-pound plate on the incline press. "Turns out he had an exhibitor's permit that requires regular inspections. He hasn't had the inspections. So maybe it worked out!"

"Except for the police."

"Ya know, even that was kind of good. I mean, not at first, when I thought I'd be going to jail." He slipped onto the bench, flexed his hands, then gripped the bar. "That part sucked, because it would've made my mom cry, and I don't care what Hollywood shows you with cons working out in the movies: you simply can't get the same workout from body weight exercises as you do with free weights."

Exercise regimen was not a concern I had considered about jail. Weller hefted the bar, brought it to his chest, and held it there, talking now in a slightly strained voice.

"But in the end I didn't go to jail, and the whole thing forced me to have a head-to-head with my old man. He was righteously pissed, Marshmallow. Holy shit, you should've seen him."

I could not fathom how lighthearted he seemed, but it was the Weller way. He banged out ten reps with 225 pounds, then slammed the bar back into place and resumed conversation as if the set had been no more distracting than a sneeze.

"Between my flunking out of school and not really having my collective shit together, he wasn't wrong to be upset. So we went at it for a while, and then I figured out what I need to do."

He stood and removed the plates so we could load my weight on.

"What's that?"

"Join the Marines."

"You're kidding."

"I'm serious. I miss football, but even if I got my grades in shape, I'm not good enough to cut it at the next level. Kenny Glass is a douchebag, but he's not wrong. I'm not a Big Ten–caliber football player. I kept growing is the thing. That should've helped, right? But it didn't. Funny." A rueful look crossed his face. "When I started varsity as a freshman, it was a big deal. They were all projecting me as a free safety back then. Speed and strength, right? But I kept getting bigger and I got slower. Weller genetics. This big ass is hard to move fast. The game is more about speed now, and I don't have that." He clanged a single thirty-five-pound plate on the bar so I could do my own set of incline presses. "I miss the identity of it, though, of being on a team, having that spirit, that gang of guys."

"You could go to a smaller school and start. Hell, go to D2 and be the stud."

He shook his head. "It's time for the next thing. I've never really been a classroom guy. I don't have your brains."

"I've got a 3.4 GPA, Sean. It's not impressive."

"That's because you're smart enough to coast, and your mom is easy to please." He grinned. "That's a good punch line, but for once it is not what I meant. She's so happy you're alive and staying out of trouble that a 3.4 is plenty to her. But you're smarter than that. Agile—that's what they'd call it if you played sports. You're agile. That's cool. But it ain't the Weller. So I'm getting into all this with my old man, and he was saying how my grandpa would be disappointed in me, and suddenly I had an eee . . ." He looked to me.

"Epiphany?"

"Yes! I had one of them. Grandpa was a marine. He figured out his tribe. I think it's the right call. I don't want to start working for my dad like one of these trust fund bitches from New York who come out here to dick off on campus for four years and then go back home to take over Daddy's empire like friggin' Tommy Boy. I want to earn my way before I come back here. No handouts, right? I asked myself: What *deserves* the power of the Weller? The United States of America is about the closest thing I can imagine."

"I don't know, man. What if you get killed?"

"Dude." He gave a patient sigh and shake of his head. "The Air Force is doing all the fighting like video games, *Star Wars* shit. The Soviet Union is gone. Where's the threat? Mexico? Gimme a break. China? Nah. You think a billion Chinese can handle the Weller? Please. Next year we'll either have a draft dodger or a tree hugger for a president. Nobody's starting a war. Besides, do you have any idea how much pussy a marine gets?"

It sounded like a rhetorical question, but his expression indicated he wanted an answer.

"Plenty?" I ventured.

"Damn right, plenty!" he said, slapping the weight plate. "Now do your set, Marshmallow. I'm getting weaker just looking at you."

I did my set and was on the bench, breathing hard, when I turned back to him.

"You saw the rattlesnakes."

"Hell yes, I did."

"The police didn't."

"Because we waited too long to call. Big Vic hustled home, hid the rattlesnakes, and left the boa constrictors and whatever else. Made us look like idiots."

"But you saw them."

He sighed. "You aren't crazy. I saw them."

"Maybe if we go back out there, they'll have put them back—"

Weller was already shaking his massive head. "No way. Only chance I have of making the Marines is with a clean criminal record."

"I can go alone."

"Don't. I'm serious. We'll figure something else out."

"How many do you think he had?" I asked.

"Five, six? I wasn't counting, I was running. Get off the bench. I gotta keep my pump."

I slid off the bench and helped him rack his weight plates while wondering what in the hell could be done. I saw a dead man and it turned out he wasn't dead. I saw real snakes with another witness and the snakes disappeared. I still had no idea what the hell I'd seen or not seen at Lake Griffy, only knew the terror I'd felt. The closest I'd ever come to seeing the truth had been when I was closer to unconscious than conscious, down at Noah Storm's drafting table, pencil in hand, mind transported to a past I had never experienced. I'd drawn the right thing without realizing it.

What would have happened if Noah hadn't brought me out of the trance? If I'd continued to draw, what might have become apparent?

"Can I borrow some tools?" I asked Weller. "To cut through a dead bolt?"

He snorted. "Sure. We just got busted and . . . wait, you're serious?"

"Yeah. I need to try something, Sean. It won't make sense to you, but . . . I need to try it."

He was silent, studying me.

"You want help?" he asked at last.

When I thought of the cellar door in that limestone house, I *did* want help, or at least companionship, but Weller had gotten in enough trouble on my behalf.

"I'll be fine," I said. "It's Noah's house. I can handle him, if he ever even finds out. He's gone."

"You're really cutting through locks?"

"I have to. I can buy new ones and replace them, probably before Noah even gets back."

"What do you think you're going to find?"

I didn't think I was going to find anything . . . but I just might *create* something. My efforts at home had been useless; I couldn't even call back a clear memory, let alone sketch anything. Most likely, Noah's guidance had been the key to that hypnotic experience, but maybe it had been the place itself. That much, at least, I could replicate. Last time, Noah had shaken me out of the trance. If I could stay in it longer, there might be answers waiting.

"I don't know what I'm going to find," I said, "and if it works, it will be more of the crazy things that people won't believe."

"Psychic shit," Weller said gravely. "I dig it. There was always something different about you."

"I don't think I'm psychic."

"Ghost bait, then. Call it what you want. Where you go, weird shit follows."

He wasn't wrong. Ever since that February day, weird shit had followed me. The whole year had been a chain of surreal or terrifying events, but nothing like that had ever existed for me before. Why? What had changed?

Where would it end?

"Want my advice?" Weller asked, and I thought it would be related to the supernatural, so I nodded.

"See if you can remove the hinges," he said. "It'll be easy to damage the door with the saw, and harder to fix."

2

THE LIMESTONE HOUSE was as empty as it had been on my last visit. No answer to my knock; no lights on inside. My key still worked, though. I took a quick walk through to see if anything had changed. Nothing had. Then I walked back out to the street to retrieve my tools. I'd put them in my duffel bag, but I was still nervous about being observed by a neighbor, so I took my time in the yard, making a show of checking my watch and phone, as if I were waiting on someone. It was all a pointless routine: the street was empty, the only sound the leaves scattering in a gusting wind. The cold rains of the previous night seemed like a distant memory today, with the sun shining and the temperature closer to September than November.

I got the bag with the bolt cutters, pry bar, and battery-powered reciprocating saw that Weller had given me. Good that he had a backup, considering one saw was already in a police evidence room.

I closed the front door and locked it behind me and then went to the cellar door to study my options. It was solid, heavy wood but over the years the frame had shifted, leaving the steel dead bolts visible in the gap between the door and the frame. There was no way to reach them with the bolt cutters. I would have to use the saw. The thin blade fit into the gap. Weller had recommended taking the door off the hinges, but the door opened inward, meaning the hinges were on the cellar side.

I started the saw, the blade whining as it fired back and forth in the narrow gap between the door and the frame, and then I brought the blade down on the top of the first dead bolt. Immediately, the whine turned to a shriek, as if the saw were protesting the task, and the grip shuddered in my hands. I tightened my hold on it, gritted my teeth, and bore down with everything I had. Tiny bits of metal shredded from the thick dead bolt, barely more than a nick. I could smell smoke and feared I was burning the blade up without getting close to parting the lock. My hands ached from the violent tremor of the saw, and the scream of metal on metal seemed amplified by the high ceilings and stone walls in the empty house.

The lock parted from the frame suddenly and smoothly.

The saw blade dropped and I released the trigger, stepping back to examine my handiwork, elated at how remarkably easy it had been after such a rough start. That was when I saw the second dead bolt rolling back and realized that I hadn't cut through a damn thing.

Someone was on the other side of the door, turning the locks.

I dropped the saw and stumbled backward, my feet tangling in the straps on the duffel bag, as the door opened and Noah Storm said, "Marshall, could you try knocking?"

3

HE WAS PARTIALLY BLOCKED by the door, leaning against the frame and regarding me with a wry grin. He was backlit by one of the bulbs in the cellar, leaving his face shadowed. He wasn't wearing his ever-present starched shirt and blazer but jeans and a baggy, wrinkled chambray shirt with the sleeves rolled to his elbows.

"I was . . . they said . . . you were supposed to be gone," I stammered.

"Sorry to disappoint. Want to tell me why you're breaking into my basement?"

"I thought you were gone," I repeated, as if this were a satisfactory answer.

"I gathered that much when I heard the saw start."

"Sorry."

He gave a little laugh that turned into a cough.

"Let's chat, Marshall. Come join me on the roof. It's a beautiful day."

"The roof?"

"That's right."

He turned and descended the stairs, leaving the door open. I hesitated only a second before I followed. When we passed beneath the light of the bare bulb, I saw that Noah's shirt seemed too big for him because he'd lost weight. A lot of it, judging from the way his clothes draped on his frame.

Even his stride was different; he walked as if each step was an effort. He coughed again as he crossed the cellar, and this time the force of it made him stop and bend over. He took a few shallow breaths and shook his head.

"I'm under the weather," he muttered, and then he turned away from the drafting table and walked to another door in the corner of the room. I had taken it for a closet when I saw it on my first visit, but when he opened it now, it revealed a narrow flight of steps.

"Servants' stairs, back in the day," he said, and then he started up them. He was slow on the ascent, and I could hear each of his breaths, which ended with a little wheeze that seemed to come from deep in his chest. The steps rose steeply through a tight, dimly lit space, thick limestone walls on each side, and I couldn't help thinking that if you got locked in here it would be a long time before anyone found you.

At the top of the stairs, another door was propped open, bright blue sky visible beyond. When we emerged onto the roof, I couldn't believe how high up we were. We were level with the tops of the Dutch elms in the front yard, and if you faced the back of the house, you were looking out across downtown Bloomington. Today there would be a half dozen condo buildings blocking your view, but in 1999 there was a clear view southwest, toward the courthouse. There was a decorative stone lip that rose about two feet above the roof, and the lightning rods that I'd noticed on my first visit were spaced out every ten feet or so, connected by copper wires. The roof itself was covered with old tar paper, and Noah had dragged a lawn chair up and placed it behind the central chimney, which screened him from the street view and faced him directly toward the sun.

"You can take the chair," he said.

"I'm fine."

He didn't argue. He sagged into the chair as if the trip had exhausted him, then wiped his forehead with the back of one hand. In the daylight I could see that he was covered with sweat and so pale that his face matched the limestone.

"Are you okay?"

"Been better," he said. "I have certainly been better. But don't worry about it. I'll bounce back. Meanwhile, you're looking good. A little taller, maybe? You've added some muscle too."

I had such mixed feelings for this man and yet I couldn't help a flush of pride that he'd noticed my physical changes. I sat on the black tar paper. It was warm to the touch. The sun was high and the sky was clear and there were no tall buildings to cast shadows. With the leaves down, there wasn't anything to block the sun at all. Noah faced directly toward it, closed his eyes, and took a deep breath that led to another fierce cough. He cleared his throat—a wet, hacking sound—and then opened his eyes and gave me a crooked smile.

"Sawing through my locks," he said. "Some intern you turned out to be."

"I didn't think you were here. Ron Walters told me you'd gone back to New York."

"Did he, now? How'd that come up?"

"I called him to ask if he knew who your client was."

Noah studied me, waiting.

"He said you didn't have one."

"I bet he said a little more than that, didn't he?"

I gave a slight nod. "He thinks . . . well, he thinks you're a con man, kind of. That you were trying to make money off a tragedy."

Noah kept looking directly into the sun, and he didn't even squint.

"Ron Walters is a decent cop," he said, "but he's not much of a detective. You remember the difference, I hope?"

"Yeah."

He coughed into his hand. "What's the success formula, Marshall?"

"Humility plus curiosity plus effort."

His smile was so genuine that it hurt me. I had missed him. Damn it, I had missed him, and while so much had gone so wrong since my last time with him in this house, I didn't know whether to blame him for any of it. What I knew was that I'd never felt more sure of myself than when he was there, guiding me, offering encouragement or correction. It had been a hell of a nice summer, right up until he'd been murdered.

"I knew you'd remember," he said. "But it still pleases me to hear it.

I'd say Ron brings one of those three elements to the table. Which one, do you think?"

"Effort."

He nodded. "The others? Humility and curiosity? He could probably dig a deeper well on those."

There was something about the way he was sliding so easily into the old patterns that irritated me. He was acting as if nothing had changed when *everything* had changed.

"Well, he's not wrong that you don't have a client," I said. "Is he?"

Noah didn't answer. I pressed on.

"And you left the snake book and the notes on the old cases and that *Good luck, Marshall* thing, but you couldn't pick up the phone when Jerry Flanders got arrested. He might go to prison and he needs help, and you're sitting up here, working on a fucking suntan!"

The look he gave me then reminded me of my mother—a patient, unperturbed gaze that said, *Get the tantrum out of your system, I'll wait.* It was a look that never failed to make me feel like a fool.

I turned away from him, stared out across the town. The courthouse glinted in the sun, the fish weather vane a bright copper line above the rounded roof.

"People are in trouble," I said, "and you quit on the case. Quit on them. So either Ron Walters wasn't wrong about you, or . . ."

"Or what?"

"I don't even know. But it seems like you believe finding Meredith's body was the end of it. That was almost the beginning, as far as I'm concerned. Things are worse now than they ever were. They're accusing the wrong man, an innocent man, and you just disappeared."

"My timeline is unfortunate," he said.

"Timeline?"

"I've got to contend with a pretty serious health condition."

I looked back at him, taking in the way the shirt draped over his thin frame, and the gray-white pallor of his face, and suddenly I was afraid that I understood.

"You're dying," I blurted.

"Nah," he said. "I'll come out the other side."

I didn't believe him, and he saw that.

"I'm not going to die," he said in a soft but firm voice. "That said, I'm . . . not at full strength. Not by a long shot."

"What's wrong?" I asked.

"I have a blood condition, Marshall. It is rare, and it is difficult to treat, and there are times when it forces me to the sidelines. I'm headed for a long winter. Treatment is intense. I'll get through it. But I can't *work* through it. I'm sorry."

I didn't know what to say.

"Why didn't you tell me that, instead of leaving the notes and the book?"

"I thought you might come by," he said, and coughed again. "I was right."

"But why didn't you tell me what was happening?"

He gazed into the sun. Sweat trails ran down his face. It was a warm day but not a *hot* one. He wasn't sweating because of the heat. He was sweating because he was sick.

"You could have left your health out of it," I said when he didn't speak. "But you didn't even explain why you were looking at all those old cases or what you knew about the snake den. You left me with questions but no answers."

My emotions were rolling now. I felt like I had while making the run from the barn, a pounding panic with little sense of control.

"You're always hiding things! Because you also know—damn it, I am *positive* that you know—that something terrible happened that day when I called the police and told them you were dead! You can pretend otherwise and talk about PTSD and whatever, but you're lying!"

He regarded me with a steady gaze, the sun harsh on his pale face.

"I didn't lie about it, Marshall. I didn't *understand* it. I didn't see what you saw."

"You said I hallucinated."

"No I didn't."

"When you came to my house, you said—"

"When I came to your house, I tried to reassure your mother and offer my support to you. I absolutely did not contradict your story. Because I believed you."

I stared at him. "You *believed* that I saw your dead body?"

"Yes," he said simply. He took a breath, choked back a cough, and said, "This place works on you in strange ways. I'm aware of that. Now, as for what you saw and how it came to pass, I don't know how to explain that. But I believe you saw it. And I'm sorry it happened."

"*This place works on you*? What does that even mean? This house?"

He nodded. I looked around the rooftop and then back to him.

"You're telling me the house is . . . haunted?"

"Not exactly." I could see him hesitating, and I was able, finally, to shut up. "There are forces in this town, Marshall—in this world—that I have spent my life trying to understand. I've made some progress, but not enough. Some of these forces are right here." He tapped the limestone chimney with his knuckles. "Some are out there." He spread a hand, indicating our town down below. "And people do not want to believe they exist. Not most people, anyhow. Certainly not the average detective. They seek facts and only facts. I understand that approach; I *share* that approach. But I will also say this: there is a reason that the word 'supernatural' includes 'natural.' Any student of the world should understand that there are inexplicable occurrences. Bloomington has its share of the inexplicable, the mystical, the supernatural, if you wish to call it that."

I pulled my knees up and looped my arms around them, leaning forward.

"What do those old disappearances have to do with Meredith Sullivan?"

"Everything," Noah said. "There's the same cycle, bursts of evil in this area. I'm learning more, but"—he indicated his frail body—"as I said, there are some limitations at the moment. They'll get worse before they get better."

"Then let me help," I said. "It's all I want to do."

He didn't answer.

"Jerry Flanders is like a father to me," I said. "Closest I have, anyhow.

They're going to put a grand jury together, indict him, and he could go to prison for something he *did not do!*"

Noah Storm closed his eyes and breathed shallowly through his nose. I had the sense that he was conserving strength, as if the conversation was almost more than he could endure.

"The grand jury will not move fast," he said. "It is a complex investigation and will demand time. By spring, I'll be able to help. That is a promise, Marshall."

He said it as if he hoped that would be the end of the discussion, but I couldn't accept that. He knew too much, and I had too many questions.

"What happens at that den?" I asked. "Why are you tying everything back to that place?"

He opened his eyes and looked at me wearily.

"You've been through enough now to know that certain stories are not courtroom product. Anecdotal evidence is weak even when it's palatable to the average juror."

"I'm not an average juror," I said, and he smiled then, an authentic smile that made me match it despite myself.

"Truer words," he said. "Okay. I will tell you what I think. I think that snake den was the origin point of . . . call it an ancient evil. The evil lingers. It's here now, and *you* know it, and *I* know it, and probably Jerry knows it. But can you convince most people of that?"

I shook my head.

"You asked why I left only questions and not answers," he continued. "It's because I don't *have* all the answers. What I know is that there are inexplicable patterns that lead back to one quarry site. Daniel Stuart, the man who built this house, opened a new quarry on land that is now in the state forest. When he blasted the site, it destroyed a rattlesnake den. Blew hundreds of them into the air."

The story Sean Weller had told me.

"That bothered some people, as you might expect. Snakes have often been viewed as symbolic, from the Bible to Greek mythology. Pick your civilization and you will find a snake story. But Stuart was unfazed. Dynamiting rock in snake country was bound to produce some snakes,

he reasoned. So he quarried it, and he cut it, and he sold it. Stone from that
site was sold to a company that built headstones and crypts. Homes for the
dead. Middle of the night, one April? The owner of this firm showed up at
Daniel Stuart's door, wild-eyed, panicked, and claiming that these crypts,
well, they don't work so well."

Noah was looking at me, but with the sun hard in his eyes, I couldn't
read his expression.

"They didn't keep the dead in, Marshall. That was his complaint. And
Daniel Stuart did what most men would and summoned the police to take
the crazy man away. Sound familiar?"

It sure did.

"Not long after, though, Daniel Stuart became obsessed with shutting
down the distribution of that stone. People didn't take his fears seriously.
He heard similar things to what you heard this summer. The tolls of stress
on a healthy mind, the breaking point between reality and hallucination.
People believed his obsession with politics and power"—he pointed at the
courthouse roof, where the fish weather vane shifted in the warm wind—
"was a poison to him. That was the most palatable thing to say about a
man who was suddenly afraid of his own stone."

I thought of the carving in Noah's office, the one that said Every Stone
Has A Story.

"He didn't just shut down the quarry, Marshall; he went around buying back the stone. He sent men with red lanterns out to stop trains on the
tracks and paid laborers to unload flatbed cars, tons of stone. He donated
the land to the state under conditions that it never be developed. Then he
locked himself up in this house, ridiculed by his community, and eventually he died here. That was, to most people in Bloomington, the end of the
story. I think they were wrong."

He coughed with such intensity that I could see the tendons in his
gaunt neck and veins in his forehead press against pale skin.

"That much I can prove, but what does it matter?" he said when the
coughing fit had passed. "There is, however, one other thing I can prove,
even to the most cynical of skeptics. The girls on that list I left you—have
you found their photos yet?"

"No." I was embarrassed that it hadn't even occurred to me to look for them.

"Do that," Noah said. "Across nearly seventy years, all the girls who went missing in that area look like they could be sisters. And they all went missing when the weather turned, on a shoulder season day gone mad, a moment when the atmosphere and the calendar couldn't seem to agree on the rules of the game. Super . . . natural."

The sun was still on my back, but I had to suppress a shiver.

"None of this," Noah said, "is any help to Jerry Flanders. But it is true."

"There is something I didn't tell you," I said. "The man I saw, the cop, Maddox? He misspoke once—or at least he seemed to. He didn't say 'corporal'; he said 'corporeal.' I didn't know that word, though. Not back then, anyhow."

Noah's eyes were intense. "What was the full phrase?"

"He called himself 'Corporeal Maddox,' that's all."

Noah gave a slight nod, filing this detail away.

"Another thing," I said, "was the sketch I made. We both thought it was nothing but scribbles and squiggles, right?"

"Yes."

"I drew a picture of a bunch of snakes, all tangled together."

Noah leaned forward. "As they would be in a den."

"Yeah." I looked at him and then said, "When you came to my house, you were afraid of me. Why?"

"I wasn't afraid of . . ." He trailed off, then nodded. "No, that's a good read, an excellent PI observation. I was afraid. But I think I was afraid more *for* you than *of* you. As I said, this house has a strange history. I did not want anyone to suffer because of it. Particularly you."

"What does that mean?"

"Marshall, do you have any thoughts as to why Maddox pulled you over and why the black-and-white snake appeared in your house?"

"Random chance."

He shook his head.

"So your encounter with Maddox was random chance, the snake in your house was random chance, your experience in this house was random chance, your next-door neighbor and friend being accused of the crime and collecting those snakes was random chance. There's a lot of random around you, old buddy, don't you think?"

I had never paused to consider it in this way before: I was the center of the circle rather than someone in a confused orbit.

"What are you saying?"

"I'm *suggesting* that you appear to be drawing energy toward you."

He must have seen the horror on my face, because he rushed ahead.

"This isn't your fault, and it isn't in your control. But we must be aware of it. Attentive to it. An opportunity to help may present itself to you in a way that it would not for other people."

I tried not to look scared by that idea.

We were quiet for a while. The sun was descending, and Noah slid down in the chair as if chasing the light.

"I'm going to be gone for treatment most of the winter," he said. "It's a bitch, but it's necessary. Because I am staying alive, Marshall, I promise. I'm not dying this winter. In the spring, I'll be back. I won't look like this then. I won't be so damn weak. I'll be able to hold my concentration. And then? Then I'll be back at work. You tell Jerry Flanders to hold on and keep his head. With enough time, I'll show the facts of the case—not the ravings I just shared with you, but the facts he must prove. Defending him successfully doesn't require explaining Maddox, although I surely would enjoy it if the two came together."

He sighed, coughed, and said, "I owe you one apology. Maybe more, but at least one. I should've come clean on the client situation. I intended to, but once you were gone . . . well, I thought you'd been through enough trauma courtesy of the Storm Agency. However, Ron Walters is not correct when he says I had no client. My original client was Summer Chastain's family more than twenty years ago. I did not solve the case, clearly. I left town not long after. I was new in the business, and I needed more seasoning. The Chastain case led me toward the inexplicable at a moment in my life when I wasn't ready for such questions, such possibilities. When I saw Meredith Sullivan's face, it chilled me—and I knew I had to dig back in."

"Did you learn about the snake den during the Chastain investigation?"

"Not enough. The one thing I discovered—and the police dismissed—was a roll of undeveloped film Summer shot in the days ahead of her disappearance. She was an amateur photographer, and she was working strictly with black and white. Several of the photographs, Marshall, were of a rattlesnake."

Neither of us said anything for a long time after that.

"Thank you," I murmured at last, and Noah looked confused.

"For?"

"Telling me all that."

He gave that wry, corner-of-the-mouth smile. "It'd be a good campfire story if it weren't the truth. But I don't know that I did you any favors by sharing it."

"Yes, you did. It matters to hear you say that what I saw might be true."

It was quiet for a moment, and then he said, "Son? It *is* true. But we've got to explain it, don't we?"

"Yeah."

"That part," he said, "is not going to be easy."

The sun was sinking, and the wind was cooler now, and when Noah Storm stood, it was with an effort.

"I'll be in touch over winter," he said. "But I can't let you continue pulling stunts like this, walking into my house and trying to cut through dead bolts."

"I won't do it again."

"All the same, until I'm back, I don't think you should be in the house. Not alone. There are things I don't quite trust about this place. So I hope you don't think I'm being an asshole when I say that I want my key back."

I didn't want to be in the house alone, either, but it still hurt to hand my key over. It had meant so much to me in the summer. That trust.

"When I make it through this winter of treatment," he said, emphasizing the "when," "I'd be honored to have you back."

"Maybe if I tried to sketch again, with you doing the hypnosis or guidance or whatever, I might—"

He sighed and put a hand on my shoulder and squeezed.

"Not today. Go home. Be a kid. Enjoy your senior year. And stay the hell out of that forest and this house. I'm asking you to trust me. Will you do that?"

"Yes, sir," I whispered.

"Drop the 'sir.'" He smiled, and I tried to match it, but I didn't think it reached my face.

"We've just got to get through the winter," he said, and then the wind blew and plastered his shirt against his torso, and I saw how withered he looked. He was a very sick man.

"Don't underestimate modern medicine," he said as if reading my mind.

"Sure."

"Keep your head down, be good to your mother and your friends, and wait on me before you start sawing open any locks," he said. "And, Marshall? If you see that black-and-white snake again . . . run like hell."

With that, he walked to the stairs. We went back down to the basement, and I cast a quick glance at the dusty drafting table—Daniel Stuart's drafting table, maybe?—on my way to the steps. I thought about suggesting a drawing session, but I knew he wouldn't back it. Not today, he'd said. I was back in the hallway, gathering my would-be burglar's tools, before I realized that Noah was still in the cellar, breathing hard. He saw me looking down at him with concern, and he waved me off with a dismissive hand.

"Go on. I've got to bring that damn chair down before it blows off the roof."

"I can get it."

"I'll be fine," he said, and his voice was firm. "Take care. We'll talk soon."

"Okay."

I left the house and searched the roof from the yard, but I couldn't see him. The decorative wall blocked some of it from view, and the big central chimney hid the door and the chair. I got into the car and started it but didn't leave, waiting to see if he came up out of the basement to lock the front doors. I'd about given up on him and was thinking of going back inside when he appeared. He was moving very slowly. I thought of Ron Walters calling him a con man, and fury flooded my veins and then found my eyes, leaving them hot and damp. I wiped at them angrily with my fist. When I cleared my eyes, I saw Noah through the glass darkly. He was lifting a hand in the little salute he liked to give at the end of a long day.

I returned it, and then I backed out and headed home.

4

THAT NIGHT I TALKED to Kerri on the phone for an hour, but I didn't tell her anything Noah had said about Daniel Stuart or the snake den, only that Noah was sick but determined to help her father, and that he wanted Jerry to remember it was a long process, and the facts were in his favor.

I didn't think Noah's reassurance meant much to her, and I understood that. She didn't know him. It meant more to me.

"Will I ever see your face again?" I asked.

"Aw, you miss me?"

"Not in the least. I just want to watch your expression of awe when I play the new Jay-Z album for you."

She groaned, I laughed, and then awkward silence filled the void, because we both knew my question had been authentic.

"I'll figure out a way to see you, Marshall. My mom is more of a warden than a mother these days, but I would really like to see you."

"Me too," I said, and I managed to avoid asking if she still saw Jake. Of course she did. Instead, I said, "Is Jake still working at Hoosier High Ground, or did he quit that job when he started at IU?"

"He's still there. He's their best coach." She laughed. "Thinking about a return to the Terminator Tower?"

No—I was thinking of a high cliff in a dark forest.

"Nah," I said. "Just curious. I don't see him much. Nobody waving at me anymore."

"You miss him more than me."

"Exactly."

We talked for a little longer, until Gwen made her hang up, at which point I went to the computer and searched for photographs of the missing girls Noah Storm had identified. I found two: Caroline Merriman and Summer Chastain. Noah wasn't wrong. The resemblance between them and Meredith Sullivan was eerie. There were no photographs on the internet of the other ones, those who had vanished generations ago, but I knew that I could find them in the library.

The next day I told Mr. Doig that I would need his help on my book project. I wanted to know everything that I could about quarries in what was now Morgan-Monroe State Forest.

"We'll put together an archive," he said enthusiastically. "Any other topics of interest?"

I thought about that for a moment and then said yes.

"There was a group in the area called the Crabbites."

"Crabbites?"

"Yeah. With a C. I think that's how it was spelled." Sean Weller was a questionable source on this. "They may not even have been real."

"Well, we can look, can't we?"

"Yes," I said. "Let's do that much."

That afternoon I skipped the weight room and went instead to Hoosier High Ground.

Everyone from Jerry Flanders to Noah Storm had told me to stay the hell away from the snake den, but what did that advice matter if I couldn't even reach it? I thought that someday I might need to reach it. Be attentive for opportunities, Noah had said.

I wanted any other coach on the planet than Jake Crane, but while I searched desperately for some other employee, he came jogging over.

"Didn't you see me waving?"

"Sorry, Jake, I missed you in all the chaos."

There were the standard three or four climbers on the walls and some little kids playing in the corner. The hottest sport in the mountains hadn't quite caught fire in the flatlands yet.

"What's up, Marshall? You looking for Kerri? She doesn't come in much lately."

I took a breath. "I'm here to learn to climb."

I expected hesitation, or possibly even laughter, either of which would've been deserved considering my pants-less plunge from the Terminator Tower in the summer, but Jake's sincerity knew no bounds.

"Bro, I *suspected* you had the hunger back in August. I know there were some technique issues, but I focus on a climber's eyes, because foot-work can be taught, but passion for the rock?" He thumped his chest with a closed fist, then put two fingers to his eyes. "That lives within. And there was one moment—I told Kerri this; you can ask her—when I saw that spark. I told her, 'Marshall is coming back here.' She didn't agree. I said, 'Give it time.'"

He squeezed my shoulder, his face all tan skin and white teeth. "She's gonna have to pay off the bet now, buddy."

"Beautiful," I said, trying not to cringe from the possibilities of what I'd just set in motion. What were the terms of the bet?

"Now, last time you were highly ambitious, which is great," Jake said, "but as a coach, one thing I'd suggest is—"

"Learning how to climb before I try to do it?"

He laughed. "I was going to put it a little differently. Everybody wants to hit the bell on the Terminator Tower. It's not the way to learn the art, though. The wall is all that matters."

"Is there someone here who gives lessons?"

He spread his hands as if the answer were both obvious and awesome.

"We'll get you some climbing shoes and then head over to Kitten's Cradle. The kids will be out of our way in about fifteen minutes."

I followed his eyes to the apparatus known as Kitten's Cradle. A girl of approximately eight years of age was dangling from the top of it.

Success = Humility + Curiosity + Effort, Noah Storm had written on my notepad. Maybe he had misspelled the first ingredient. Was it humiliation?

I looked at the top of the Terminator Tower, where the bell hung, and remembered dangling upside down with my pants sliding off my ass while I shouted *WHIPPER!* at the top of my lungs.

"Let's get those shoes," I told Jake. "And a harness that fits."

5

MR. DOIG'S FIRST HAUL of materials proved that not only was Sean Weller right about the existence of the Crabbites, he'd been accurate with his account. The group was called the Crabbites because they followed a charismatic, snake-handling reverend named William V. Crabb. He rose to attention after the turn of the twentieth century when he began giving sermons from a stump in a field. The Crabbites had indeed passed through what was now the Stepp Cemetery region, but they seemed to have no history before or after their brief and bizarre appearance. It was as if the sect had come from nowhere and vanished swiftly. Mr. Doig was able to find two articles that referenced them in the *Brown County Democrat* newspaper in 1907. The connection between this and Stepp Cemetery was unclear; it seemed as if the lore and legends of the graveyard had absorbed them.

"Very odd," Mr. Doig said while he sorted through the latest of our interlibrary loan materials. "They were written about as if they were an established group, but there's no origin story. Then they disappear from the public consciousness, not to be mentioned again until they began appearing in graveyard ghost stories half a century later. I can see why you want to write this one. It might make for some good, scary reading."

He had no idea.

Meanwhile, nothing in the library was giving me an explanation for the missing snakes in the barn, and the police seemed to trust Vic Glass. Why not? He was one of them, and my credibility was shot.

As November progressed, I shifted several days of my workouts with Weller to trips to the climbing gym, where I was put through embarrassing paces by Jake Crane.

I moved from Kitten's Cradle quickly, but that was a credit to Jake's eye for coaching. He understood that I wanted to prove myself on the big walls and figured maybe the lessons would last longer when the price of failure was higher.

Or maybe he simply enjoyed watching me fall. Many were the minutes I spent dangling from a rope while he belayed me, explaining what had gone wrong and calling out encouragement.

"The wall is a dance! You've got to read your partner. Balance, balance, balance!"

I learned how to optimize rest and focus on economy of movement.

"Smear!" Jake would shout when I started to panic and overreach, and then I'd remember to focus on my footwork, "smearing" as much of my shoe soles as possible on whatever grip they had, taking a breath, and letting the body rest while the mind refocused.

I was terrible at climbing and yet I enjoyed it. I liked the discipline of brain and body working together. In some ways, Jake's reminders were akin to Noah Storm's mantras. I was better at some techniques than others—a foot stack was one, and a mantle was another. Mantling, I learned, was pushing with the upper body rather than pulling, the way you might brace your hands on the deck of a pool and hoist yourself from the water. I discovered that my default grip—a full crimp—cost the hands from fatigue and overuse. I converted these lessons into true progress, and I'd be feeling good, sound in my footwork and intentional in my hand positioning, when I'd glance up at the bell, and my focus would slip—followed by my body.

"You only turn into the Whipper when you look at the bell, bro!" Jake said, bestowing a new nickname on me. "It's like the reverse of Superman's phone booth. You don't *want* to be the Whipper, and you know when you're going to turn into him! So stop walking into the phone booth. The bell does not matter. The wall is all, bro, the wall is all."

One afternoon I made Weller join me, thinking that I'd show off my new skills. Instead—following a delay while they found a harness big enough for him—he headed directly for the Terminator Tower.

"The bell is the point, obviously," he said.

Jake tried to discourage this idea, to no avail.

"He's not exactly a natural," Jake observed as we watched Weller maul the Terminator Tower with a direct frontal assault, "but he's got raw strength and a unique desire."

"FUCK ME SIDEWAYS!" Weller screamed as he missed a foothold and fell.

"Oh, my." Jake went off for a hushed discussion about the language rules. Weller nodded, mimed a lip-zipping motion, and chalked his palms again.

"The Weller wants another try," he announced.

Jake obliged.

"Awful technique," he murmured as Weller made a series of bizarre frog leaps and desperation grabs. He would explode upward like a breaching whale, seeming destined for splashdown, only to hook one hand or the other in a hold. Once he had a grip with either hand, he was strong enough to drag the rest of his body up, find footing, and then catch his breath for another dip-and-lunge. His legs generated extraordinary power, and he routinely snagged a grip that seemed beyond his reach.

It took him five attempts to reach the bell, which he hammered like a cymbal.

Jake winced, but I wasn't sure if his response was from the clanging echo or the sheer disgust in seeing his wall pulverized without consideration of the available rainbow routes.

"I can't believe it," I said as Weller let out a war whoop and flexed his biceps at the top of the Terminator Tower.

"You have to remember," Jake implored, "that it is not about the bell. The wall is all!"

Easy to say if you can reach the bell, I thought, but I nodded.

"That didn't suck," Weller told me as we walked out of the gym together. "The key is being explosive, obviously." He pounded his fists off his quads. "The Weller is built for explosion."

I opted not to tell him that he hadn't executed a single smear or foot stack.

While my climbing improved, my grades were executing a whipper of their own, my GPA plummeting as I ignored homework to obsess over research into the state forest, the Crabbites, and generations of missing girls who looked eerily similar.

On a bright, cold Monday before Thanksgiving, Mr. Doig greeted me with a wide smile and a photocopy in hand.

"I have a friend named Sarkissian who works at the library in Allen County," he said. "He found this in their archives. I was hoping it would get here before the holiday break."

It was a copy of a newspaper from 1907, and this one stopped me cold because of its image: a man in a suit, vest, and tie standing atop a stump, a book in his right hand, his left arm upraised—and encircled by a coiled snake.

"It's the most detailed piece about William Crabb that I've found," Mr. Doig said. "Take a look. It even has a list of their beliefs." He chuckled. "They were quite something."

I read the list. The snake-handling elements were what I'd expected—church elders couldn't be harmed by the bites, etc.—but what grabbed my eye was what followed:

> *Imprisonment must be borne for the faith's sake, insurance and lightning rods are of Satan's devising, the simple life defeats the devil's purpose, and the millennium is near at hand.*

"What does that mean?" I said, pointing at "millennium." "It was 1907. They were more than ninety years away."

"The word was once used as a synonym for Armageddon or the apocalypse," Mr. Doig said casually.

I thought of Jerry's ankle bracelet and returned to the first belief: *Imprisonment must be borne for the faith's sake . . .*

This had to be a coincidence, but in the face of Jerry's blasé reaction to his own charges, it didn't feel like one. Then there was that strange bit about insurance and lightning rods being of Satan's devising, which called to mind Noah Storm's house and its ancient lightning rods.

"Marshall?" Mr. Doig said, his voice registering some concern.

"Huh? Oh, sorry. I was zoning out. This is cool, Mr. Doig. Thank you."

I took the printout into the back office of the library, closed the door, and read the rest of it. I was very grateful that I was alone by then, because it was on the second page that the writer discussed "the rituals of the snake," and if Mr. Doig had seen my face then, he might have had more serious concerns.

Some are said to believe that Crabb is capable of casting evil human souls into the bodies of snakes. Such dark rituals have attracted the outrage of prominent locals, most notably Bloomington limestone magnate and mayoral candidate Daniel Stuart, who attended a service. Stuart deemed the threat "no different than that of a fire; it requires oxygen that I shall not grant."

Others are less sanguine. Two locals who watched the ceremonies insist they saw Crabb and another man, Silas Vesey, place a dried snakeskin into a fire, only to watch two living snakes emerge from the embers. Astonishing as this account may seem, both men swear to it.

At present, the Crabbites are said to be in search of new grounds following hostilities in Brown County that included the destruction with dynamite of a church building near Gose Creek. Their open-air services guarantee they will not be so easily silenced, but merely scattered.

I thought of the snake Jerry had described finding in my house.

It was there, solid and undeniable, and then it kind of . . . withered, I guess you could say. Then the snake lifted his head, and when it opened its mouth, smoke came out, a thin line, like steam from a radiator that needs coolant. Only I know it was smoke because I could smell it. And I heard a laugh, Marshall. I heard a man's laugh, deep and clear as a bell. Then the smoke faded, and the snake became ash, just crumbled on itself. Then there was nothing left but that skin, dry and brittle as a cornstalk in September, like it had been there the whole time, sitting empty.

Mr. Doig cracked the door and looked in at me appraisingly.

"What do you think? Wild stuff, isn't it?"

"Yeah." My eyes were on the sketch of the preacher on the stump with the snake coiled around his upraised left arm. It was impossible to say with a pen-and-ink sketch, but I was almost certain the snake was shaded to look as if it had a white body and black bands.

"Do you think your friend at the Allen County library would help more?" I asked.

"I know he will." Mr. Doig opened a notebook and clicked his pen. "What do you want?"

"I'd like to know as much as possible about the house Daniel Stuart built in Bloomington. It is at 712 Lockridge Lane. It's all limestone, and it was built in 1907."

"A big year for the boogeymen of Bloomington," he said. "I'll call Alex today, and we'll hear back from him after the holiday."

Ah, yes. The holiday.

Thanksgiving. For nearly two decades, a day shared between two families on Raintree Lane. My mother and Gwen divided cooking duties. Jerry and Kerri and I would play games and music. They were great days.

This year, nobody had said a word about Thanksgiving. On Wednesday morning before the holiday, my mother finally broke the silence.

"I would love to believe that you've had no communication with Jerry, but instinct tells me otherwise," she said. She was making oatmeal while I sat at the kitchen island, and she kept her back to me as if she didn't need— or didn't want—to see my reaction. "Tomorrow's Thanksgiving. Will he be seeing his daughter?"

"No."

This much I knew from a phone call, which was my only communication with Kerri. I hadn't seen her in weeks.

"That's terrible," my mother said softly. "The whole situation, for everyone involved. But if his own his family isn't going to visit him, then the least we could do is bring some food by."

I was torn between delight and dismay. I wanted my mother to give Jerry the benefit of the doubt, or at least some compassion, but I also was nervous about them being together. He could say some strange things.

At least, they would seem strange to her.

"No comment?" she asked.

"I think it's a good idea. A nice one, I mean."

"I'm worried about him. What lies ahead."

"So am I. But I'm not going to just give up on him. He's closer to . . ."

She looked at me.

"Family than not," I said.

"A father than not," she said quietly. "That's what you meant."

"I don't confuse Jerry for a dad," I said, and I didn't.

She pulled the steaming oatmeal from the microwave and slid the bowl across the island to me.

"If it's his last holiday at home," she said, "we will bring him a meal."

"Thank you," I said, and I meant it as much as I'd ever meant those words.

My mother's face told me she wasn't completely sure of her own decision.

"They were good to me when I needed help," she said, as if trying to convince herself. "They were good to you."

I ate the oatmeal as she flipped through the newspaper without seeming to register the words.

"How is Dom?" she asked abruptly.

"Fine. Why?"

"Because I used to find that kid asleep on my living room floor on a regular basis, and now I haven't seen him in months. Did you have a fight?"

"No. He had soccer, and he's got a girlfriend." I shrugged. "He's busy."

She was watching me with intense eyes, and I wished I hadn't finished the oatmeal, because I didn't have an excuse to look down at the bowl.

"No girlfriend for you this year."

"Nope."

"I liked Leslie."

"I did too. But it's over."

"That's fine. I'm just wondering . . ."

"What?" I said, pushing the bowl aside, on guard now.

"What it is you do with your time," she said softly. "You were such a social kid, Marshall. It's your senior year. I feel like you're not having any *fun*. This should be the year I worry about you having too *much* fun, but instead—"

"I'm fine," I snapped. "I have friends. I'm happy."

"I didn't mean to imply that you don't have friends. I just . . ." She touched her hair and adjusted her blouse in the self-conscious way she did right before the cameras went live, as if she were aware that the stakes were about to go up.

"You just what?"

"There are so many things you don't talk about. Dom, Leslie, college, or the world ahead. These are big months, requiring big decisions. I have no concept of what you're planning."

"I took the SAT," I said, the only evidence of any future planning I could offer.

"I know that. But what do you want to *do* with it?"

I shrugged. "I've got time."

"Not so much," she said. "It's going by fast, kiddo."

She ruffled my hair then to indicate she was done interrogating me, but the questions lingered in my mind, as she'd intended.

What did I want to do? Not worry about college applications or prom dates. I wanted to solve a murder, explain a ghost, and exonerate a neighbor. I wanted to ring the damn bell at Hoosier High Ground and then climb a cliff in the state forest, looking for a black-and-white rattlesnake.

Except, of course, I didn't want to do the last part at all.

I was just certain that I would have to.

How do you care about precalculus when a real cliff is waiting?

6

WE BROUGHT THE FOOD across the street at noon on Thanksgiving.

When Jerry opened the door, I was relieved to see he'd shaved, combed his hair, and dressed in khaki slacks and a button-down shirt instead of the same sweatpants and grimy T-shirt that he'd worn day after day. The khakis were loose at the ankle and hid his monitoring bracelet.

"This is above and beyond, Monica," he said as he showed us in.

"Don't be silly," my mother responded, as if she hadn't avoided his house for months. "It's Thanksgiving."

Jerry had straightened up the house ahead of our arrival, although everything was developing a sour odor. I tried to remember how long it had been since Gwen was inside and couldn't. Kerri's last day had been in September. The dining room table was set with bone china and crystal glasses; it was wedding china, I knew, a gift from Gwen's parents, who were both dead now. It meant a lot to Gwen to get it out at least once a year. Seeing it there, set for three instead of six, put a lump in my throat.

A bottle of sparkling apple cider sat in the center of the table.

"I'm not supposed to have alcohol," Jerry said with an awkward laugh. "Conditions of . . . you know."

He had a few beers every time I saw him, but I wasn't going to say that.

"Where do you want me to put the potatoes?" Mom said, and the tension broke as we busied ourselves with the sorting and sharing of dishes. For a little while things were fine, small talk and silly jokes. It couldn't last, though, not when a third of the usual group was MIA. Gwen Flanders had always handled half the Thanksgiving duties. My mother would do the turkey, Gwen would do the pies, that sort of thing. Today my mother kept starting and stopping references to the past. Jerry would compliment the cranberry sauce, and my mother would say, "I forgot to zest it with the orange peel the way Gwen always . . ." and then drift off or abruptly change the subject. She was a tuning fork of tension, and I wished that Jerry had stuck with real wine; a glass or two would help them both.

I sought refuge in the safe topic of a Thanksgiving table: sports.

"The Colts need some help from Dallas today," I said. The Dallas Cowboys were playing the Miami Dolphins, an AFC East rival of the Colts.

"Nah," Jerry said. "Indy is locked in. Six straight. Manning is the real deal. Lot of critics last year, but he was a rookie."

"This year's rookie is pretty good too," my mother said. "Edgerrin James."

"That was a good trade," Jerry agreed, and I felt relieved. My mother loved sports, Jerry loved sports, we could coast along on this.

"Think they could actually win the Super Bowl?" my mother asked.

"Team is good enough," Jerry said, wiping his mouth with a napkin, "but there won't be a Super Bowl."

There was a pause, and then my mother said, "You think they need more playoff experience?"

"No, I mean there won't be a Super Bowl, period. League knows it too."

My mother set her fork down. Her eyes were on her plate.

"I hate to be a buzzkill," Jerry said, "but this is the truth. The NFL changed the league schedule by a whole week this year. Did you know that?"

"They started later," my mother said in a strained voice.

"Exactly. But why? Because they know better than to have team planes in the air when the clock strikes midnight on New Year's Day."

Nobody said anything. Jerry looked from my mother to me.

"Fact-check that one. They changed the whole schedule because of

Y2K. It is the truth. Think about all the money that's in that league. Think about how much those owners know that the rest of us do not. Then think about the reality that they *delayed the season* to avoid travel!"

"They've addressed their concerns," my mother said, looking at her plate.

I desperately wanted to redirect the conversation.

"Tough year for the Browns," I said, "but at least they got a team back. It wasn't fair, the way Art Modell moved—"

"Monica," Jerry said in a grave voice that finally drew her eyes to his, "I don't like talking about this any more than you like listening to it. But the problem is nobody wants to face the facts, and we need to. Because we are five weeks away from reality smacking this country—this *world*—in the face."

"There might be some headaches," my mother said, her mouth so tight her lips seemed to scarcely part as she spoke, "but—"

"Headaches!" Jerry bellowed. "Headaches?" He slapped both palms on the table and leaned forward, wide-eyed, and in the moment I was afraid for him.

Or of him?

I'm not sure. I know my mother was both.

"We're going to be *praying* for headaches by the second day of January," Jerry said. "By the second week? Headaches will seem like the Garden of Eden. If it's a mild winter, folks in the Northeast and Midwest will have a chance. Plenty of fresh water, plenty of game. Southwest is too dry and the Rockies too damn cold, although folks out there are better prepared. Panic in the cities is where the shooting will start first. And once people take to the road, they'll head for comfort. That won't be north of the Ohio River until spring. But they'll come. And all this is assuming that the Soviet nuclear system doesn't fail at the stroke of midnight, in which case—"

"Shut up!" my mother shouted. "Just shut up!"

I was stunned, but Jerry seemed unsurprised, nodding with weary resignation.

"This is a sickness," my mother said, throwing her napkin on the table. "Your paranoia is sad but it is also a *sickness*, and I will not let it infect my family! For all I know, it already has. Your paranoia may be the reason my son had the . . ." She looked at me, hot red spots flaring on her cheeks, as if she had just remembered that I was there. ". . . the summer that he had. Fear is poison, do you not see that? Poison! You're spreading it."

"Preparation is salvation," Jerry said. "That's what I'm trying to spread."

My mother closed her hands into fists. Her jaw trembled as she fought to regain composure.

"The people who need to prepare are doing that. They've spent millions—*billions*—of dollars to ensure that nothing will—"

"The people who need to prepare are the ones at this table," Jerry shot back. "Because if you're counting on some sonuvabitch in the Pentagon or the White House to shelter your family, Monica, you are in for a world of heartbreak."

My mother started to respond, then stopped, shook her head, and stood up.

"I tried," she said. "I tried, but I can't do this."

She left the table with a calm, practiced stride, graceful, her on-camera walk. You wouldn't have known a thing was wrong until she made the turn at the top of the stairs. Then the tears on her cheeks became visible. She went down the stairs and the door opened and the door closed and Jerry Flanders and I were alone at the dining room table.

"I hate that she can't see it," he said, and his voice broke and he wiped his face with the back of one hand. "I hate that none of them can see it."

I didn't say anything. I felt numb and sick.

"I'll need to go home now," I told Jerry.

"Yeah," he said sadly. "I'm sorry, damn it. I am. I just . . ."

"I know," I told him, and then I said that I'd see him soon, and I left. When I stepped inside my own house, my mother was sitting on the couch, legs crossed, hands folded in her lap, eyes distant.

"That is not me," she said.

"I know," I said again, the same words to another adult in another house, and I meant them both times.

Raintree Lane was different. The street was the same, but nothing else was.

"You're angry with me," she said. "I don't blame you. I shouldn't have shouted."

"I'm not angry," I said. "I'm just sad."

"Me too," she said, and then she wiped at her eyes the way Jerry had.

Do you know why movie theaters do a good business on Thanksgiving Day? Because sometimes people don't know how to talk to each other. Because sometimes people are sad or scared or angry or alone—or all those at once.

That afternoon, my mother and I went to see *Toy Story 2*, the biggest movie on the planet on Thanksgiving 1999. I don't remember much about the film. It was hard for me to concentrate. But it was good for me to be with her, sitting quietly and in the dark but still together.

7

THEY IMPANELED the grand jury on the first week of December.

Officially, Jerry Flanders wasn't named as a suspect, because that wasn't allowed. It was fair game for the media to speculate, though.

They were happy to do it.

I was watching a TV reporter explain that the process usually took several months but could stretch to as long as two years when my phone rang. My mother.

"I saw the news," I said. "It's okay, though. He was expecting this."

"That's not why I'm calling." She sounded a little breathless. "Marshall, someone just came to the station to serve me a subpoena—for you. You're not eighteen yet, so they served me instead. I already spoke with Ron Walters."

"Why him?"

"Because I know him! He told me that he's not allowed to comment on the process—"

"I bet."

"—but he imagines you will be asked to testify under oath about your conversations with Jerry."

The idea of testifying in front of jurors about my conversations with Jerry made my stomach knot.

"He mentioned the ticket," my mother said.

"What?"

"The ticket from Maddox. He said the only fingerprints on it were yours and Jerry's, and the grand jury might have questions about that."

"I *handed* the ticket to Jerry! I went to him for help!"

"I know, hon."

"When do I have to do this?"

"There's no timetable yet. I'm hiring a lawyer to offer guidance."

We talked more, but the conversation barely registered as I imagined sitting in a courtroom, under oath, answering questions about what Jerry Flanders had shared with me.

Then the snake lifted his head, and when it opened its mouth, smoke came out, a thin line, like steam from a radiator that needs coolant . . . I heard a man's laugh, *deep and clear as a bell.*

I couldn't tell a grand jury that.

But what if Jerry did?

I had a sick certainty that he would. Being under oath would matter to him; sounding like a madman wouldn't. Not anymore. The conversation he'd started at Thanksgiving wasn't one he would have had with my mother in the summer. He seemed determined to look people in the eye and tell them what he believed—ordinarily a good thing. Now I wasn't so sure.

Sometimes it's easier to share the truth if you tell the world that it's fiction. I hadn't finished my first story yet, but already I understood that much.

"The snow," my mother said. "Marshall? Are you there?"

"Huh?" I had completely tuned out.

"I said be careful driving tonight, even though you have the Bravada, because there's definitely going to be snow, and in the south, it might be ice."

I couldn't believe she was worrying about weather.

"I'll be fine," I told her. She'd driven my car to Indy, leaving her beloved all-wheel-drive Bravada in my hands, because I'd not yet driven in snow.

We hung up, and my first call was to Noah Storm. He didn't answer. I left a message, updating him. I wondered where he was, pictured a hospital somewhere on the East Coast.

I will not die, he'd said.

Most patients probably said that when they began treatment. Not all of them made it out.

I called Kerri next. She sounded hollowed out.

"Dad thinks it will all be irrelevant by January," she said wearily. "I don't know what to do. I keep telling Mom that I need to see him. Maybe if I have a couple days alone with him . . ."

I didn't think anyone was going to convince Jerry that Y2K was not an apocalyptic event, but I didn't want to discourage her.

"Will you ever come back?" I asked. I hadn't laid eyes on Kerri since we'd kissed in my car—before she'd run crying into the rain.

"I'm insisting on spending a couple days with him at Christmas. It turned into a big fight, of course—Mom doesn't give up easily—but I'll be eighteen by Christmas and I told her that I'm either visiting him on my own or on a schedule she can live with. Nothing like a good threat."

"Can I see you on your birthday?" I asked. It was only one week away.

"Probably not. Mom is treating this like witness protection. She keeps talking about moving out of state. She doesn't want to be anywhere near him when the trial begins."

"And you'll have graduated by then."

"Yes."

Silence built and lingered.

"Then what?" My throat was dry, making my voice hoarse.

"Not sure. But I'm kind of . . . over Bloomington."

"IU is massive, Kerri. It won't feel like North. You can be anonymous."

"I don't want to be anonymous, I want to be free," she said. "It's different. I keep going back to the brochures from places out west. Colorado. Montana."

"*Montana?*"

"Or maybe Bennington, in Vermont. Colby, in Maine? I don't know. I was supposed to be visiting schools this fall. Instead, I'm in hiding. You blame me for looking at a picture of the campus in Missoula and thinking it looks appealing?"

I didn't blame her. That didn't make it any easier to hear.

"How do Jerry's lawyers feel about the grand jury?" I asked, trying not to be selfish.

"Well, there is no physical evidence to connect Dad to Meredith Sullivan, but the prosecutor will be able to make him seem pretty crazy. I mean, they're going to subpoena people who saw him going into houses under the guise of a fake business, or saw him buying guns and stockpiling ammunition, and then they'll talk about the snakes. For an indictment, that might be enough."

That night I tried to lose myself in music. Napster had a bootleg of Sheryl Crow's live album from Central Park, and she was one of Kerri's favorites. I put it on, and then, even though I knew better, I looked up the University of Montana. The website showed a stunning brick building with a clock tower in front of a lush green mountain, a rainbow arcing across.

I don't want to be anonymous; I want to free, Kerri had said.

I wanted her to be free too. I wanted her father to be free. I wanted to put it all back the way it had been, in any other year.

This wasn't any other year, though—it was 1999—and whatever could go wrong seemed to go wrong. So somehow it felt unsurprising when the phone rang just before 2 a.m. with the news that my mother was in the emergency room.

CHAPTER TWELVE

WINTER TAKES ALL

December 1999

"Even the sun goes down, heroes eventually die"

OUTKAST
"AQUEMINI"

1

THE PAVEMENT WAS SLICK from the season's first dusting of snow, but it wasn't the weather that had gotten Monica Miller; it was fatigue. She'd fallen asleep at the wheel two miles south of the county line, ten minutes from home. If she'd been driving her own car, maybe it would have gone differently. She'd left the best bad-weather vehicle to protect me, though, and my massive Olds Ninety Eight didn't fare well on the snowy road. The car skidded off 37, bounced through a ditch, and met the walnut trees waiting on the other side. It was late at night, as it always was when she made that drive, and by the time a passerby spotted her, she'd been in the trees for fifteen or twenty minutes. It was hard to say, because she'd been unconscious for much of it.

When they got ahold of me, she'd already been transported by ambulance to the Bloomington hospital, and she must have been delirious, because the nurse who called said my mom wanted to have Jerry Flanders drive me.

Problem was, Jerry couldn't leave the house.

I drove alone, with a cold clutch of panic in my chest.

She was my mother and she was all that I had.

It was a ten-minute drive from Raintree Lane to the hospital. You can imagine a lot of terrible things in ten minutes.

By the time I entered the emergency room, I was already expecting the worst news—*We lost her in surgery,* or *She was dead on arrival,* or *There's nothing more we can do.* It didn't matter that the nurse had told me my mother was stable; you try trusting that at 2 a.m. while you drive to the ER.

No one greeted me with the worst, though. She was in surgery—the doctor was setting her arm and ankle, which were both broken. I'd have to wait to see her.

Those were long hours.

The hospital staff kept suggesting that I call someone. I had no one to call. It was just us, I kept explaining, and that seemed to shock them. Where was the rest of the family?

Damn good question, but not one I wanted to get into tonight.

"It is just the two of us," I said on repeat, and finally they left me alone.

It was seven hours before I saw her, and when I finally did, the first words out of her mouth were "I'm sorry."

I teared up a little then. Couldn't help it. I'd never seen her look so helpless. She was bulletproof; from her walk to her wardrobe, Monica Miller was in control. She was younger than all my classmates' mothers and she was prettier and she was stronger. It had always been this way. I had never imagined that it might change. Seeing her under the white sheet, tubes trailing from the arm that wasn't in a cast, her face bruised and scraped from the airbag that had saved her life, I was forced to see what I'd always known and refused to acknowledge: she was mortal.

"It's a big cast for your ankle," I said, looking at her leg, which was elevated and encased in plaster from the toes to the knee.

"Be fine," she slurred, giving a dreamy, feeling-no-pain smile.

I held her free hand. "They said you fell asleep at the wheel?"

"No." She tried to shake her head.

"Did you slide on the snow?"

"No. The police car came up behind me; I remember that . . . and I remember a little of the ambulance. I wanted them to tell you but not scare you."

I didn't bother to tell her that the police car didn't pull up behind her until long after the wreck. I could hear her voice, and that was enough.

I had my head down, my attention focused on her hand because I couldn't stand looking at the tubes running from her arms, when she said, "Heard it first. Right there, so loud. Heard it, and then, in the mirror, saw it."

I looked up. "Saw what?"

Her eyes were closed, painkillers coursing through her bloodstream. "The snake."

All my muscles went liquid, a chill blooming in my gut.

"You saw a snake?"

"In my car," she murmured. "Real. Like you said. Black and white."

Even then, even as the cold spread through my body, I was aware of a crucial slip: she called it her car, but it wasn't.

The snake had been in my car.

2

THE DOCTOR TOLD US that my mother had to rest, which was unnecessary because she was already under again, dragged beneath the surface by the drugs. I kissed her dry, cool cheek and whispered that I loved her, and then I followed the doctor out the door. The doctor kept the smile on his face until the door was closed.

"Her arm and leg will heal," he said, "but it's going to take some time. The concussion is the more pressing concern."

"I didn't know there was a concussion."

"She presents all the symptoms: confusion, dizziness, nausea, light sensitivity. There's no bleeding on the brain, but I want her monitored."

I nodded numbly. "You said leg. In the waiting room, they said ankle."

"Also correct," he said. "Her ankle is pulverized and the reconstruction will be extensive. The leg is broken in two places below the knee, but those are polite, clean breaks."

There is no stranger juxtaposition of words and tone than in the medical world, in which broken bones are "polite" and "clean" and an ankle "pulverized" and all of it is said in the same neutral manner.

"How long before she can . . ." I let the question drift, suddenly struck by the overwhelming fear that she might not be able to walk again, but he anticipated it.

"Two to three weeks in the hospital while the bones set and assisted rehab begins, then another eight to ten weeks at home. She's fit and she's strong and she'll bounce back nicely. By next Christmas, she won't notice anything different. This Christmas, though, she will need to be in a hospital."

I couldn't find words. I simply stared at him.

"There is no one you can call?" he asked, looking at me gravely.

"No, sir."

"The family is . . ."

"Right here. All of it."

He didn't look pleased, but he nodded.

"We'll have a rehab coordinator get in touch with you. In the meantime . . ." He assessed me, then said, "How old are you?" in a forced-casual tone that didn't come close to the nonchalance with which he'd described my mother's ankle as "pulverized."

"Eighteen," I lied. I was afraid of what they might force on me if they realized I was a minor.

"All right. You're a mature young man, but you need to understand that your mother has a long and difficult road ahead."

"Yes, sir."

"Take it a day at a time," he said. "Our rehab coordinator will guide you."

He walked me down the sterile corridor, explaining medications and physical therapies, and I nodded all the while, but I wasn't registering much.

Heard it first, she had said, . . . *and then, in the mirror, saw it.*

"Where is the car?" I asked.

The doctor blinked at me. "The police would have towed it."

"Where?"

"Let's find out."

We went into the lobby and he spoke with a woman behind the desk. Outside, the sky was lightening. A dusting of snow covered the parking lot and swirled in miniature funnel clouds when the wind gusted. The doctor returned to me with names scrawled on a notepad. They were tow yards the police used, he explained, but he wasn't sure which one had the Oldsmobile. I thanked him, assured him one more time that I was fine and didn't need to call anyone to come get me, and then I left. When I got behind the wheel of the Bravada, I couldn't bring myself to lift my eyes to the rearview mirror.

Heard it first . . . and then, in the mirror, saw it.

"Just *look*, pussy," I hissed at myself, trying to will my eyes to the mirror. But I could remember the snake with the wedge-shaped head and the black-and-white-banded body and the flicking black tongue, and I could not check the mirror, convinced that if I looked, the snake would sink fangs into my face.

I got out and opened all the doors and the tailgate and circled the car in the snowy parking lot, kneeling to check beneath the seats.

Unlike me, my mother kept an exquisitely clean vehicle, easy to search. No snake. I found a brush for the snow in the back and used that to clean the windshield while the defroster ran. When I put the brush back in the car, I found a book tucked into the pocket behind the driver's seat. It was titled *Operating Instructions: A Journal of My Son's First Year* by Anne Lamott, and the jacket description made it clear that it was written by a single mother. I put the book back and drove away, trying not to wonder if my mother would be in the hospital if she hadn't left her best vehicle at home just in case her child was going to drive in bad weather.

When I got home, I called the three tow yards that the ER staff had written down for me. The third one was the hit.

"That big Olds? Yeah, we pulled it out."

"Can I pick it up?"

"Son, it's totaled."

"Can you tow it back here?"

"Shit, kid, I can tow it wherever you want it, but I'm telling you, the thing is junked. Might want to talk to your parents before you rack up foolish charges."

He softened when I said my mom had been driving the vehicle and was in the hospital, then warned me that it would be more expensive to tow the car than store it. I said that was fine. It was three hours before they arrived, and I was still at the kitchen island, drinking coffee, my Noah Storm–introduced habit. When the wrecker appeared, I almost dropped the mug.

The Oldsmobile wasn't simply wrecked; it was devastated. The passenger side was crushed into the center of the car, the hood was balled up, the windshield webbed with cracks. The airbag dangled from the steering wheel.

I put Alva and Haldora on their leashes and walked out into the cold December air, trying not to look at the splashes of rust-colored blood on the remains of the airbag. I counted out cash to the driver with shaking hands, dropping two of the bills into the snow before he took mercy on me and said he was sure it was plenty. He unhooked the demolished car and left.

I didn't want to put the dogs up. I liked their alertness; I craved their enhanced senses. Instead of putting them in the house, I unclipped their leashes and let them play in the snow while I went into the garage, put on a jacket, gloves, and boots, and then found a shovel.

I circled the car cautiously, watching every shadowed angle, before I pulled the rear driver's-side door open. It was the only one that still opened. I stood there, shovel held high, poised for a strike.

No motion.

No sound.

My breath fogged the cold air. I tried to draw some saliva into my mouth. I couldn't help chancing a glance across the street at Jerry's house, hoping he might come out to help.

It was still and silent and I was alone.

"Girls! Alva, Haldora!" I whistled, and the dogs came running, tails wagging. When Haldora leaned into the driver's seat to sniff near the bloodstains, I lunged for her, sure that the snake would strike.

She was fine, though, and as I watched her take in the rest of the car, her nose twitching in overdrive as she cataloged the fresh scents and accepted the known ones, I felt better. She knew more than I did. I was somehow certain that the dogs would be aware of the snake.

I leaned into the vehicle and rattled the shovel around, trying to scare up anything that was coiled up under a seat. Glass fell from the wind-shield and something snapped under the seat, but nothing moved.

The only undamaged part of the car was the trunk. I used the key to unlock that. It was empty except for jumper cables and a bag of gym clothes that I should have washed days ago.

No snake.

No snakeskin.

My mother had been doped to the gills with strong painkillers, mut-tering and not making much sense. Maybe she had no idea what she was saying. Maybe it wasn't a memory at all.

But I knew better.

There's a lot of random chance around you, Noah had said.

I stayed at home, trying unsuccessfully to concentrate on precalc homework while the day dragged on and my mother's promised snow began to fall in earnest. It was early for a serious snow in Bloomington, but there were a couple inches by noon, and I went out and shoveled the drive while the dogs played. I kept thinking of my mother pinned inside of my car in a stand of trees alongside the highway.

She called a little after one, and she sounded better, lucid and with a touch of her parental tone. No apologies this time, no mention of a snake, just clear questions about what I was doing. She was in the ICU until the next morning, she said, and then she'd be moved to a different depart-ment, where her rehab would begin. If the doctor had already told her that she wouldn't be home before Christmas, she didn't betray it, and I didn't mention the timeline to her.

"Can I visit?" I asked, and her response, while frustrating, was also reassuring, the first real Mom Moment of the day.

"It is snowing and will continue to snow," she said. "I think we've had more than enough excitement on the roads for one day. Stay home, order a pizza, and do not worry about me. I'll call you later, Marshall. I love you."

I told her that I loved her, too, and almost as soon as I hung up the phone, I felt the exhaustion of the sleepless, stress-filled night and day sweep over me, as if my brain had finally given my body permission to relax. I put the stereo on, then stretched out on the floor in the living room, tucked a pillow under my head, and was asleep before I heard the first verse of the song.

I was out cold when Jerry Flanders looked out of his window for the first time that day and saw the car—*my* car—in its demolished condition in the driveway. I didn't hear his phone call. The music was loud, and I was exhausted. The first thing I heard other than Outkast was a loud, frantic knocking on the front door, followed by the barking of the dogs. I staggered to my feet, pillow lines embedded in my cheek, hurried to the door, skidding once in my socks on the wood floor, and then jerked open the door to see Kerri for the first time in more than a month.

She looked terrified. She stared from me back to the car and then hugged me. It was fierce contact, not affectionate—a stranglehold, as if she were tearing me back from someone else.

"You . . . asshole," she whispered in my ear, and then she pushed off the ground and wrapped her legs tightly around my hips, a full-body clench now. I couldn't breathe, but I damn sure did not mind. At last she unwrapped her legs and dropped back to the porch and punched me in the chest, three times, each one emphasizing a fresh word.

"You . . . are . . . okay."

"Yes. Stop hitting me."

She hit me again, harder. There were tears in her eyes.

"Kerri, what—"

"How in the hell are you *okay* with a car that looks like *that?"*

That was the first time I understood why she was there and what she must have thought.

"My mom was driving," I said.

Her fury shifted to a fresh fear, but I was already shaking my head.

"She's okay. I mean, it's bad, she's in the hospital, but she's . . . she'll be fine."

Kerri looked at the car again, and when she shivered, I knew it had nothing to do with the snow.

"Inside, and explain," she said.

I opened the door and let her in, looking down the street at her house.

Night was settling and there was a light on in the living room, so I could see a silhouetted figure. Jerry. I waved at him and he made a sort of pray-and-bow gesture, clasping his hands together before lowering his forehead to meet them. It might have meant *Thank you* to a stranger, but I wasn't a stranger, so I understood: it meant relief.

He was happy to see me upright and unharmed. Maybe to see me alive, period.

I gave Jerry a thumbs-up as the snow pelted my face, and then his daughter grabbed me by the arm and pulled me across the threshold and into the safe warmth of my house.

3

IT'S STRANGE TO SAY, but that night was the closest anything had felt to normal in a long time. My mother was in the hospital, but I was used to her being gone at night. Those absences had been offset on many nights by Kerri's presence. For the first time in months, Kerri was herself, pestering me for details, asking questions, correcting mistakes in that can't-help-myself way she had, even laughing.

I think there was a mutual fatigue point that broke that night. Yes, my mother was in the hospital, and, yes, her father was under house arrest, but there are different ways to bear up under that emotional weight, and one of them is to laugh.

Hell, it might be the only good one.

We tried too hard sometimes. Once, talking about my mother's accident, Kerri said, "She did not honk," and while I knew she was trying for a smile, and I even managed to find one as I said, "She did not proceed with caution," on the inside I was cringing. But that wasn't as bad as when we were discussing what the weeks of rehab looked like and how all the bedrooms in my house were upstairs, and I said, "You know what she'll need . . ." in the hushed voice that was a patented setup for an old joke.

"An elevator," Kerri delivered on cue. "A machine of simple genius."

The words were right but the moment wasn't, and I think we both knew that the moment probably wouldn't be right ever again. We were getting a glimpse of something many people don't have to confront until they're much older—someday, the roles reverse, and the kids become the caretakers. It's a hell of a lot more fun to tease the adult bosses while basking in the knowledge that they are in control. That was gone for us now, albeit in very different ways.

"I'm going to see him," Kerri declared then, as if it was time to address the elephant in the room. We hadn't spoken yet of Jerry.

"Tonight?" I asked.

"I'll say hi at least. Give him a hug. Let him know that I will figure something out for Christmas so he's not alone." She leaned forward, removed the tie that held her hair back, then shook her hair out and retied it, a classic nervous Kerri gesture. When she was flustered, rings changed fingers, bracelets swapped wrists, hair ties were removed and replaced. Any attempt to reassert control over something, no matter how small.

"I'm worried about Christmas," I said. "Mom's still going to be in the hospital. I lied to the doctor and told him I was eighteen because I'm afraid they'll try to make me stay in some kind of dorm or something."

"I don't think hospitals have dorms."

"You know what I mean. Do they let a minor stay at home if his only parent is in the hospital? I know she'd let me do it, but maybe they won't."

"You'll need a guardian who's over eighteen," Kerri said, and then a familiar and oh-so-missed evil smile slid across her face. "Marshall! You will need a—"

"Don't say it."

"Babysitter!" She shifted on the couch, rising on her knees, palms on her thighs, looking at me with a delighted tormentor's grin. "An *adult* who can care for your childish needs. You know, make you take baths and keep you from putting the small toys in your mouth. Just because they look like candies doesn't mean they aren't choking hazards."

"Hilarious."

"I'm serious!"

"Serious about *what?*"

"I'll stay here. It's perfect. I want to see my dad but I can't stay with my dad. I am losing my mind with my mom and with her friend Elaine, and if we don't get some space soon, it'll . . ." She made an exploding gesture with her hands. "This is the solution. I will become the adult presence in your child's existence."

"I'm sure they won't require me to have a guardian," I said, although I wasn't.

"Who cares? It gives me an excuse. I'm graduating this month, and nobody knows or gives a shit, and my father is over there alone with a grand jury investigating him, and it is *Christmas*."

I was afraid she might be on the verge of tears, but then the wicked light returned to her eyes, called back with an effort.

"Meanwhile, I have an old family friend who is a child—"

"A legal minor. Less than a year younger than you; a classmate since kindergarten."

"Classmate?" She tapped her chin, made a show of trying to recall me. "I don't remember you in many AP classes in high school. Or the ALPS classes in middle school. Or the GT classes in elementary school. Or—"

"That's because the Miller family prioritizes modesty. We stay humble and avoid the arrogance of advanced classes. Same reason you're not going to see me at Harvard."

"Rejection and modesty are the same thing?"

"Matter of perspective."

She laughed, then flopped back against the arm of the couch and looked out the window in the direction of her father's house.

"Seriously, this is good. I mean, it sucks for everyone, especially your mom and my dad, but . . . it feels right, you know? He's so damn stressed, and you're alone, and I'm about to strangle my mother."

"You really want to stay here?"

"Yes."

She was wearing jeans and a fitted black sweater that hugged her slim torso, and it was very hard to look at her and not remember the way she'd slid onto my lap in the car, how perfect her breath had felt against my neck, as if her face had always belonged that close to mine, and always would. We were together on the couch, Kerri curled up in one corner, me with my feet on the ottoman in the other, enough distance between us for the invisible but ever-present Jake Crane. I was about to ask what Jake would say when Kerri stood abruptly, as if anticipating the question.

"So let it be written, so let it be done. Talk to your mother. Offer my condolences and my pledge to take responsibility for her child."

"Minor."

"And I will talk to my parents and explain that there is a child in need, much like—"

"A seventeen-year-old minor."

"—in the Christmas story itself. And verily, I will say unto them, there's a babe in the manger this season." She pointed at herself with both thumbs. "And it's this babe."

With that, she strutted out of the room, grabbing her coat off a chair as she headed for the front door.

"Oh, and, Marshall—one last thing."

"What?"

She turned back with a too-bright smile on her face.

"If something like your mom's car wreck ever happens again and you don't call me? I will hang you by your thumbs in the downtown square, then replace that dumb fish on top of the courthouse with your skull as a message to all other thoughtless morons. Deal?"

"Deal," I said.

"Love you," she said, but her tone was breezy and her back was to me and before I could respond she was out the door and into the snow.

I watched her get into her Honda and drive to her father's house—*her* house once; how had it already become his alone?—and then I turned away because watching such a private moment felt invasive.

Love you, she'd said.

You have no idea, I wished I'd said.

Meanwhile *I* had no idea if she was serious about moving in for the holidays or if anyone would allow it, but I didn't care. It had been wonderful having her back for a few hours. I had missed her more than I'd ever missed anyone, and it meant something to see her anger and fear over my wrecked car, to know—to *feel*—how much she cared. We shouldn't need those awful reassurances, but that doesn't mean they don't resonate. I thought about her promise to impale me on top of the courthouse as a message to other morons, and I started to smile, but lost it fast. The fish weather vane made me think of Noah Storm, telling me to run like hell if I saw the black-and-white snake.

Heard it first, my mother had said, . . . *and then, in the mirror, saw it.*

4

MR. DOIG CALLED my house on Sunday afternoon, full of apologies for
bothering me on the weekend and at home and explaining—as if I cared—
that our number was listed in the phone book, so he wasn't using private
school records. He was a debonair guy, always poised, so it was strange
to hear him flustered. I anticipated he was reaching out with well-wishes
for my mother.

He wasn't.

"You remember my friend Alex? The one who specializes in folklore?"

"Sarkissian, right? He found the old newspaper stories."

"Yes. Well, he sent some more material along. For your, uh, for the
book."

"Okay. Great."

There was a pause.

"I've tried to respect your privacy," Mr. Doig said. "It's none of my
business, of course, what you're working on. I just want to encourage. To
be a resource."

"I appreciate it." Why in the world was he being so strange?

"I hope you don't mind my asking, then . . . how much of what you're
searching for are things that you already know?"

"I don't follow."

"Nor should you: the question was a grammatical catastrophe. Allow me to restate." He took a beat, then said, "Are you seeking to confirm elements of a story that you already know?"

"I guess so. A little bit. I've heard stories about the snake-handling group, the Crabbites. I'm getting new details from your friend's stuff, though."

"Marshall, do you know of the abduction of Daniel Stuart's daughter, Melody?"

"No," I said, suddenly aware of the quiet in my empty house. "When did that happen?"

"In 1907. The same year many things in your research seem to have happened."

"I didn't know about that one."

"You're sure?"

"Yeah I'm sure." I couldn't tell if he was pressing me because he thought I was lying. "What's the problem, Mr. Doig?"

Another pause. I could hear him breathing.

"I have been cautious about addressing the elephant in the room," he said. "It is obvious that elements of your unfortunate summer experiences overlap with your current research, with the house at 712 Lockridge Lane being a prime example. But I try to keep my own counsel."

"Okay," I said, still confused as to why he seemed so shaken. Noah Storm might have been brought up short by news of another missing girl from nearly a century ago, but my high school librarian shouldn't have been. He didn't know enough of the details.

"If I am breaking news to you, this next piece may feel significant," he said. "If I'm confirming something for you . . . well, I hope you'll talk to me about why it matters. The man who was implicated in the 1907 abduction of Melody Stuart was named Harlan Maddox."

I was too stunned to speak, but Mr. Doig took my silence for a lack of surprise.

"I recall your use of the name in the police reports you made last spring," he said, "so if this story is something you've been, I don't know, playing around with for that long, I need you to tell me. I need you to—"

"I've never heard that name," I said, my voice sounding like a stranger's. "You're serious?"

"I'm serious, Mr. Doig. I have never heard the name Harlan Maddox, I had no idea that Daniel Stuart's daughter was a victim of any crime—I didn't even know she existed, in fact—and I hadn't heard the name Maddox until I was pulled over by the police last February."

Neither of us said anything for a while. There was a faint buzz on the line, and I could hear Mr. Doig's breaths, which seemed to come a little faster and shallower than they should have.

The way someone breathes when he is scared.

"Well," he said, and forced a laugh that sounded harsh and false, "I apologize for bothering you at home, but at least we will both be prepared for this . . . rather remarkable coincidence when I share the latest round of documents tomorrow."

Rather remarkable coincidence. That was an understatement.

"Random chance," I murmured.

"Exactly," Mr. Doig said with a measure of relief, as if he wanted to know that I was capable of believing in coincidence rather than in ghosts.

We said our goodbyes, and then I hung up and called Noah Storm. He didn't answer. I left a message explaining what I understood from Mr. Doig and promising to bring photocopies by the office the next day. It was only then that I remembered I no longer had a key.

"I'll put them in the mail slot," I said, then added, "I hope you're feeling better, wherever you are."

5

I GOT TO SCHOOL early Monday morning so I could check in with Mr. Doig. By then I had already searched for information on Harlan Maddox and come up empty. It was an old story, though, and back then—and, I would argue, still today—the internet couldn't match a librarian.

Mr. Doig seemed to be his usual self, betraying none of the nervousness that he had during our phone call.

"You are a magnet for the bizarre," he said, and that made me think of Noah's comment about my "energy," and I tried to smile and not think of the way the events had accumulated since that first February drive, or the fact that Jerry Flanders was under house arrest and my mother was in the hospital. If I was a magnet for energy, it seemed to be the kind that hurt the people I loved.

Mr. Doig passed me a manila folder.

"Sarkissian's archive results."

I sat down across the desk from him, and he waited in silence while I read the articles. There were about a dozen of them, beginning with newspaper clippings from August 1907.

DANIEL STUART'S DAUGHTER MISSING was the first headline, and it took the writer three paragraphs to establish the daughter's first name, as if all that mattered were her father.

Melody Stuart, nineteen years old, the only child of the widower Daniel, had been reported missing late in the evening of August 24 after failing to return home. Home for Melody was still 712 Lockridge Lane, her father's house. They lived there alone, her mother having passed when Melody was a child. Daniel Stuart had not remarried. Upon discovering his daughter missing, he immediately leveraged his political clout, gathering searchers on the first night and offering a $10,000 reward by the second, which was no doubt a fortune in 1907.

There was a picture of the missing girl on the front page, and I was unsurprised to see that Melody Stuart looked a great deal like Meredith Sullivan. Their names even seemed to echo. I opted not to mention this to Mr. Doig, but I had a feeling he knew it too. I kept my eyes away from his and continued reading, taking my time, committing it all to memory.

It was not until the third article that I encountered the name Harlan Maddox.

"Police investigators have interrogated Miss Stuart's former fiancé, Harlan Maddox, who was a foreman with her father's stone company. The engagement had been called off, and many suggest that Maddox was deeply angered by Miss Stuart's decision."

I turned the page, and there, in the low-resolution quality of a reproduction from another era, was a photograph of Harlan Maddox.

I could not draw a breath.

"It's him," Mr. Doig whispered, watching me.

It was most certainly him. That was Maddox, the same man who'd swaggered down to my car with a gun on his belt and Meredith Sullivan in his back seat on an unseasonably warm February day in 1999, nearly a hundred years after this photograph had been taken. Unlike Melody Stuart and Meredith Sullivan, these two were not merely similar. They were identical.

I looked up at Mr. Doig.

"You don't need to believe it," I said.

"I told myself I wouldn't," he answered, still speaking in a whisper, but one that was tinged with wonder rather than doubt or fear. "I spent the weekend telling myself that under no circumstances would I let you convince me of . . . whatever in the world you wish to call this situation."

He cleared his throat and looked chagrined. "In fact, Marshall, I spent a good deal of time trying to convince myself that you might be a dangerous kind of liar."

"A sociopath," I said, and he nodded.

"But I *know* you," he said, "and so I could not believe that. Then, watching you now . . . you had no idea what you were going to see. That was clear when you turned the page. And yet you knew him instantly."

I wet my lips and looked back down at the picture of Harlan Maddox.

"I know him," I said, and then neither of us spoke while I read the rest of the articles.

Two days had passed before Melody Stuart was located. She had been found by unidentified men, referred to only as "locals who would prefer to remain anonymous" in a barn not far from Lost Man's Lane. This should have shocked me, too, I suppose, but by then my capacity for shock was altered. The read no longer felt revelatory, simply inevitable. Of course, she had been found in a barn.

She said she had been driven to the isolated place by Harlan Maddox, savagely attacked, beaten, shot once in the chest, and then left for dead.

"A single bullet from a .38-caliber revolver was removed from her back," the article reported, and I winced, remembering the dream I'd had that night in Weller's field when Maddox had looked at me, lifted the gun, and fired.

"Don't blame the snake when you choose to walk off the path. I won't listen to that shit. I simply will not. The snake has no role here. Your choices are all that matter."

Melody Stuart had no memory of the men who found her, those locals who insisted on anonymity, and she gave no direct interviews to the press, although it appeared she had spoken with the police.

Daniel Stuart also stopped giving interviews. He protected the anonymity requested by the men who'd found his daughter, and he refused to disclose whether he had paid the promised reward. An attorney representing Stuart implored the public to respect the family's privacy.

Meanwhile, the police had a fresh problem: Harlan Maddox, the alleged perpetrator, had gone missing. No sooner had the abductor been identified than he'd vanished.

"Rumors of vigilante justice abound," the newspaper noted.

There were a few more articles in May, and two in June, and one in July, and then that was that. Neither Daniel nor Melody Stuart offered any words to the media. Her rescuers remained anonymous. Harlan Maddox remained missing.

The world moved on.

I closed the folder and looked at Mr. Doig. He was watching me closely, a tentative fascination alive in his eyes.

"Does it help?" he asked.

"I don't know," I said, which was true, but then I remembered that he had put in the time and called in the favors to find all this, and added, "It will, I'm sure. I just don't know how yet."

"Of course not. It is a name and a picture from generations ago."

"Do you know what happened to Maddox?"

"He was never found."

"Rumors of vigilante justice abounded," I said.

"Indeed."

"There's nothing about his limestone," I said.

"Pardon?"

I shook my head. "Sorry. I was thinking of . . . another story I heard. Again, not one on the record. There was a lot of detail as to why he closed his business, and his fear about a specific quarry in what is now the state forest. There's no mention of that in the articles, though."

"Who told you that one?"

"Noah Storm. The private investigator who . . ."

But Mr. Doig was already nodding, and I appreciated him not making me go through it again. I'd made Noah Storm briefly famous in the summer, after all.

We sat there in silence for a while. Beyond the glass wall the halls were filling with students, and soon the bell would ring and the day would begin. The sane day of a sane school, most of whose students had never been pulled over by an alleged criminal from 1907.

"I don't know what to tell you," Mr. Doig said at last. "I don't know what to tell myself. At first, I thought you might be having some fun with the name, lost in some story world."

"I guess I am," I said. "Lost in a story is what it feels like. The problem is the story is real, and it can't be."

"Share as much of it as you want, Marshall," he said. "Please."

I thought about telling him what had happened to my mother and how she'd referenced the snake, or what Jerry Flanders had told me about his time in the state forest, or of what Noah Storm had shared about Daniel Stuart that somehow hadn't made the newspapers of the day. In the end, I kept all that to myself.

"I will, someday," I said. "Not today."

"Keep your word on that," Mr. Doig told me, and I promised him that I would.

I am finally living up to that promise. It has taken me a long time to do it—too long—and the story will be shelved in fiction in most libraries.

Mr. Doig's won't be one of them. I'm sure of that.

I took his photocopies and shook his hand and thanked him, and then I went to the school guidance office to tell them what had happened to my mother and explain that I needed to be with her in the hospital that day. They agreed to excuse the absence if a doctor would call. That was no problem, because I did spend most of the day at the hospital—other than a few minutes on Lockridge Lane, dropping off photocopies and a note for Noah Storm.

THIS IS HIM, I wrote on a Post-it that I stuck beneath the photograph of Harlan Maddox. CALL ME.

I didn't think I would show anyone else the picture of Harlan Maddox, circa 1907. I didn't see whom it would help, or how. Just because I knew him did not mean that I could summon him. He was no more tangible simply because I had a full name and a photograph, and certainly no easier to understand or defeat.

The haunting power of any ghost relies not on entrances into our world but on almighty absences from it.

I hadn't needed to encounter Harlan Maddox to learn that, of course.

That's what fathers are for.

6

THEY MOVED MY MOTHER into the rehab unit the next week. It was hard to watch her in pain, and I never knew where to look when I visited—at the casts, which made me hurt, or into her eyes, which made me hurt worse. She was trying to keep up her usual spirit but she'd lose it from time to time, and I suspected she'd experienced some level of what I had on the drive to the hospital, becoming keenly aware of her own vulnerability. No, that wasn't the right word.

Mortality.

Neither of us wanted to look that one in the eye. Who does?

She was coming back nicely, the doctors said, her healing on course. She wanted to begin physical therapy, but the body dictated that timeline. I brought her books and DVDs and assured her that I was doing my homework. For the first time that semester, it wasn't a lie. I was desperate to bring my grades up so she wouldn't have more disappointment to end her year.

When she told me that Kerri had visited her, I tried to keep my face impassive.

"She explained her plan to stay at the house for Christmas," my mother said. "I don't care, Marshall. I love that girl; you know that. She needs to see her father. Her mother is the one who has to make that decision, not me. But Kerri is eighteen, a point she made repeatedly. Either way, it is not my purview."

She watched me with the cool assessment she would use on the golf course when standing over a tricky lie.

"Kerri has a boyfriend, correct?"

"Yes. Jake."

"Does he know about her holiday plan?"

"I'm not sure."

"I think you should be."

We looked at each other, unspoken understanding in the room between us, and it occurred to me then that while I envied my friends who had two parents, a lot of them would have envied me this kind of moment, because while they might have two parents, they didn't have one who could share the silence with them in the right way.

I left the hospital and went to the climbing gym with my mother's words on my mind. Was it up to me to tell Jake that Kerri would be staying with me, or was that Kerri's news to break? Either way, I figured I should talk to her first. If it caused any trouble, she should know it was coming.

"Let's terminate this tower, bro!" Jake yelled when I entered, and as I looked at his beaming face, I had a crushing realization: Kerri staying at my house would be no trouble to Jake. He was that confident, that secure. Hell, he'd probably praise the plan.

It was just the two of us in the cavernous space, the way it always was for lessons, when I arrived an hour before the gym opened.

"How's your mom doing?" Jake asked, and I updated him as I put on my climbing shoes and tied into the harness and chalked my palms.

"I like her attitude," he announced. "The hunger for rehab is righteous. You'll have to tell me what exercises they make her do. End of the day, it'll all be about balance. Strength is overrated; balance is survival."

I nodded, by now very used to the Tao of Crane.

"Orange route?" he asked.

"Yes."

The orange route was the easiest path to the top, and I still hadn't made it, although I was getting closer. Jake made the initial ascent to set the rope for me, free-climbing with grace and ease, then clipped the carabiner into place and ran a rope through. That was the rope that would be tied onto my harness, keeping me secured.

"Today is the day!" he yelled, and then he climbed back down rather than call for me to belay, evidently wanting to work on his technique. He *always* wanted to work on his technique. "You ready to answer?"

Answer was an acronym in Jake's language. It stood for *"Awareness* of anxiety, *Normalize* your breathing, *Scan* for tension, *Wave* of relaxation, *Erase* the past, *Reset* posture."

I knew how to define it. Executing it was another matter. I assured him that I would try.

"Climber on!" Jake yelled, and then I was off.

I felt confident about the required techniques. It was always my mind that ultimately kept me from the top. When I got near the place where I'd failed before, I inevitably would tell Jake that I was ready for a *take*, and then descend under his power, not my own.

"Cock the lunge, bro, cock the lunge!" Jake shouted.

The lunge was a leap for an out-of-reach hold. By "cocking" for it, or sagging downward to relax your muscles before making the explosive leap, you could get your mind right and concentrate on driving upward. I had not attempted a lunge yet, despite Jake's encouragement. It seemed like disaster, while the static climbing was slower but more practical. Safer.

Static climbing was also, Jake informed me, an energy sapper. A lunge could conserve your mental and physical resources. All of that sounded well and good until you fell.

I made my slow and steady way up the wall.

"Let's play a little 'send me,' bro!" Jake called.

"Send me" was a game in which he used a laser pointer to indicate which route I should take, allowing him to create a Jake Crane–endorsed rainbow. Before I could answer, the red dot from the laser pointer appeared before me, tantalizingly close but higher than I'd ever gone before.

"Next time," I said.

"This time, bro!"

I shook my head and was about to yell out for a take when he cut me off.

"If you can kiss my girl, you can reach that hold."

I stared down at him. He gazed back, blank-faced. He was chewing gum, and I could see his jaw muscles flex as he regarded me.

"Jake . . . ," I started, but before I could think of the right words, he made a flicking gesture, and the coil of blue rope that secured me to the wall snaked out and fell free.

I was still tied to the rope, and it still ran through the carabiner above me, but without Jake holding the other end, there was nothing stopping me from plummeting straight down if I fell.

"What the hell, man! Pick up the rope! We'll talk it out."

"If you can kiss my girl," he said slowly and distinctly, "you can reach that hold. Would take some kind of badass courage to do either one, right? So go ring the bell, Marshall. Be the badass that you apparently are. And do it in front of me this time."

The fear of falling was always within me when I climbed, but it was much easier to ignore when I had a partner belaying me. Without that, the wide room swam and I felt sick and dizzy. I stacked my feet the way Jake had taught me and tried to stop the shaking that was threatening my grip.

"This is not you," I said. "You are too good of a person to do this, Jake."

I didn't care about the fear in my voice. Ego fades in the face of survival.

"You want me to belay you after you made out with my girlfriend?"

"Yes!" I looked down at him, desperate. He kept his head down, and he nudged the loose rope with the toe of his climbing shoe.

"Ring the bell, Marshall."

"Jake . . ."

"RING THE BELL, BITCH!"

I was terrified. Of him, and of falling.

One thing about the wall, though? You run out of options. Climb or fall. I wasn't going to be able to hang on to the wall for forty minutes, waiting for more people to join us. That left climbing for salvation, the only option.

If you *could* reach the bell, you also reached a wide ledge built out along the steel girders of the old warehouse. If I made it there, I could wait for Jake's fury to fade or for someone else to enter the building.

Jake had made one mistake in using the laser—he'd inadvertently shown me the path that could buy me time. I'd have to leave the orange route, but it would be easier to go to the place he'd tagged with the laser. I hadn't reached that hold before, but I knew *how* to reach it. The maneuver was called a twist lock. You twisted toward the wall with a hip turn while drawing yourself up, shifting your center of gravity as close to the wall as possible while you reached. I'd performed the twist lock a hundred times by now.

Always with a belay rope.

I looked at the hold, visualized the move, took a breath, and executed it.

Done. Done well, though that meant nothing today. It should have been a victory, but the higher I got, the worse the impact would be if I fell.

"Way to go," Jake called in that disturbingly toneless voice. I didn't look at him. *Couldn't* look. I had to make the ledge at the top of the wall now simply to survive. The ledge was wide and safe.

And so far away.

I could not believe he'd done this. Punch me in the face? Fair. Kick me in the balls? Fine. But this was different. This was madness. I could literally die if I fell from this height. I couldn't fathom Jake Crane having so much rage.

Maybe he loves Kerri that much. People do crazy things for love. Like killing.

I focused on the ledge, and I let the advice of my potential murderer float through my mind: *Answer.*

Aware of my anxiety? Check.

Normalize breathing. In through the nose, hold, then exhale through the mouth.

Scan for tension. Check, check, and check. Plenty of tension.

Wave of relaxation. Wasn't happening, but the breathing focus helped.

Erase the past. No problem. There was no past. I had one shot at a future.

Reset posture.

I slid my hands closer together and then drooped, letting my legs absorb most of my weight. Cocking for the lunge. I looked up at the ledge. The bell was right there but I didn't even register it. The ledge was every-thing.

Salvation required the leap.

Explode, I told myself, but I couldn't move. I was too scared. My body refused my brain's instruction. I breathed, stared at the ledge, and remem-bered the way Sean Weller had done it, battling up the wall with no tech-nical understanding at all, nothing but a furious willpower. His approach had pissed Jake off, but it had also *worked*. Technique wasn't everything. Heart counted.

Explode! I thought once more, but it was in Weller's voice now, not mine, and this time my body answered the command. I drove off the balls of my feet, airborne, unconnected to the wall by hands, feet, or rope.

You free-climb or you free-fall.

Those are the only choices.

I caught the ledge.

Still alive, still climbing. I caught the ledge squarely and firmly, and then I was chinning myself up and over, pushing my torso above the ledge and swinging my hips onto it, into a seated position, finally able to rest.

To live.

I panted, adrenaline sparking like a downed electrical wire in my bloodstream, and stared at Jake. He gazed at me placidly, as if he hadn't watched me defy death.

"You're insane," I said, my voice shaking. "You really are."

"Hit the bell, Marshall, and then untie that knot so I can belay you."

I had no interest in the bell, but I looked at the carabiner where he'd clipped me in and saw that he hadn't run the belay rope through it. In-stead, he'd tied it off on an adjacent bolt. If I'd fallen, it would have hurt like a bastard, the harness jarring and jolting, but I wouldn't have hit the floor.

"This was a . . ." *game to you*, I started, but then I remembered his empty voice saying, *If you can kiss my girl, you can reach that hold.* He wasn't going to kill me, but he wasn't playing games, either.

I leaned over, untied the rope, and threaded it through the carabiner.

"Congratulations," Jake said. "You officially lead climbed. Nobody was responsible for anchoring that rope but you. Do you trust it?"

I couldn't speak.

"Do you trust it?" he repeated.

"Yeah," I managed.

He picked up the rope at his feet and drew it taut. I felt it slide through the carabiner and cinch against my harness.

"I've got you. Tell me when you need the take. But first? Hit the bell."

And so I did. I hit the bell, and it echoed through the big room, and then I told him to take, and he held me on belay while I came back down. When my feet touched the mat, the strength went out of my legs, and I sagged and wrapped my arms around my knees and closed my eyes and breathed. When I opened my eyes, Jake was sitting beside me, coiling the rope. He gazed at me without speaking, and I saw nothing hostile there.

I just saw the hurt.

The hurt was real, and it was deep.

"I'm sorry," I said.

"For kissing her?"

I started to say yes, then stopped and shook my head.

"Not that. No. Not with her. But I should have told you."

"Yeah."

"I didn't talk to her today," I said. "So I didn't know that she'd told you."

"She didn't tell me today, Marshall. She told me the night it happened."

He gave a sad smile as he looked at my bewildered face.

"Don't worry, she took all the blame. Not that it matters to me, but it might to you." He shook his head in disbelief. "You did that, and you didn't have the balls to tell me, and then you came in here and asked me to coach you! You seriously did that, bro! How could you do that?"

"Because it was that important," I said.

"Learning to climb?"

"Yes. You won't believe me, but . . . yes. And not just for me."

His hands were tight around the coil of rope, and the muscles in his arms popped, but I wasn't afraid of being hit. Not down here, where I could see his eyes. I'd done the hitting in this conflict. It was clear, and it was an awful feeling.

"Why did you go along with it?" I asked. "You knew the whole time and you went through all this, teaching me. Why?"

"Because I miss home," he said, and his voice was the softest I had ever heard it. "I'm homesick every day, and this place helps, because I miss being with the people I love, doing the thing that I love. That's Colorado, and that's climbing. That's the world I need to go back to. I will in the summer. I tried to stay in Bloomington because of Kerri, and because of my father. He's in a wheelchair, you know. He does well, but does that mean life is easy for him? Hell no. It's hard. It's why I climb, of course. Leaving him is going to be hard."

I didn't know what to say.

"Then there's Kerri," Jake said. "She's all I want. But on the worst day of her life, she came looking for you, not me. Took me a while to process that. But it is the truth. You know who Edward Abbey is?"

"No."

"Look him up sometime. He's the reason I ended up in this town. My dad taught about Abbey in Colorado, and then Indiana hired him to do it here, and I had to cope with a move and a new place, right? Anyhow, Abbey once said, 'Better a cruel truth than a comfortable delusion.' I remind myself of that when I think about Kerri."

"She picked you," I said. "Ultimately."

Jake laughed. It was a genuine sound, a laugh I'd heard many times when I made a mistake on the wall, one that was both warm and tinged with sympathy.

"No," he said. "She did not. You'll figure it out, Marshall. One of these days."

"I'm sorry," I said again, and I was. I hated myself a little, looking at this kid from Colorado I'd envied in so many ways who had just told me that he was homesick every day.

"I get it, bro," he said. "I don't like it, but I get it. Kerri is special."

"Yeah," I said. "She is."

He popped to his feet with that graceful burst that made him so natural on the wall, and then he offered his hand to me. I took it, and he pulled me up.

"Get out," he said.

"Okay."

"But you can come back. If you want. Another day."

I took off my harness and walked out, leaving him alone in the cavernous replica of the place he wanted to be, the one he called home.

7

CHRISTMAS WAS ON a Saturday that year, and Kerri moved into my house on Friday. Her mother hated everything about it, but that had nothing to do with me and everything to do with Kerri's insistence on seeing her father on the holiday.

"Tough titty," Kerri said when she explained it to me. "I'm eighteen. I hung that exit sign a long time ago as a warning. They didn't take it seriously."

She was forcing good humor, but I could see the pain in her deep brown eyes. We were in the guest room, where Kerri was unpacking. She hung a few shirts in the closet, and when she spoke, her back was to me.

"My mother is scared for me, Marshall."

"He's not going to hurt you! He never hurt *anyone*."

"It's not that. She's scared of what might be in me."

"What might be *in* you?" I echoed, confused.

"Sure. She's only half of that." Kerri turned and gave me a crooked, sad smile. "My mom has spent a lot of years bragging about my weird brain. You know that. And now she looks at my dad and . . . his mind has spun out. When I say she's scared, I don't mean of him hurting me. What if I'm like him?"

I didn't know how to respond.

"In the end, it is all about control," Kerri said. "Mom wants to keep it forever, she knows she can't, and that is unacceptable to her."

I sat on the bed and thought about that, and about my own mother sending me to see the therapist that summer, and the way I'd felt driving to the hospital when I'd gotten the call from the emergency room.

Control is a dangerous thing, but it is so very easy to want.

And impossible to hold.

"You know when I think Dad spun out?" Kerri asked softly.

"When he came in here and saw the snake."

She shook her head. "April. The way he watched the footage of Columbine . . . It was too much. Too intense. He would record the news each night and play it back, and my mother hated that. He immersed himself in the news, and there was Columbine, and there was Y2K, and . . . I don't know. There was the *world*. With all its threats. And he wanted to shield us from them."

I thought of the nonstop blue-light glow that I'd seen all summer and fall in Jerry's house. She wasn't wrong. For a man who never left his house, he spent a lot of time marinating in the menaces outside his door.

Kerri adjusted a stray hair and smoothed her shirt and looked out the window at her lifelong home, and I could see that she was steeling herself to return to it.

"You're going to the hospital at five?" she asked.

"Yeah."

"I'll go over to see him at the same time, then. Meet back here?"

"Sure. It's supposed to snow. White Christmas. That's nice," I offered lamely, and she forced a smile that didn't reach her eyes.

It was too quiet, and there was no normalcy between us, let alone the intimacy I dreamed of. I hadn't told her about my encounter with Jake. He'd temporarily lost a part of himself that day that I didn't want her to imagine him ever being without. A strange thing to say about your romantic rival, and yet it was true.

"Put on some music," Kerri said. "And pick something good."

"DMX put out a new album this week. It's like a Christmas miracle."

She groaned and put her head in her hands and we managed a laugh. The laugh helped. It always does.

At a quarter to five, as a light snow began ahead of the descending dusk, I left for the hospital, and Kerri walked across the street to see her father. I watched her in the rearview mirror. She was standing tall, shoulders back, chin up, smile on her face, wrapped gift in her hands. She reminded me of my mother, crossing the street on that awful Thanksgiving. I thought Kerri could keep the smile on with Jerry for longer than my mother had, and that would matter more than the gift. I also thought that it would take a lot out of her. The whole year had.

Bring on the millennium. I was ready to say so long, see you, to 1999.

I picked up carryout from Janko's Little Zagreb, my mother's favorite steak house, and then drove to the hospital. She was in good spirits, and she'd had some help from the hospital staff in arranging for my visit— there was a small tree in the room and wrapped presents around it. The highlight was a new set of Ping irons.

"To give you a chance at beating me," she said, and winked.

The idea of seeing her back on the golf course, walking and carrying her own bag the way she always did, scorning a cart, mattered to me far more than the clubs did. I had some books for her and a weather radio that broadcast the National Weather Service forecasts 24/7. That gift made her laugh.

All in all, it was as good a visit as you could have in a hospital on Christmas Eve. She didn't let me stay long, though. It was snowing, and she didn't want me to drive in that. I knew better than to argue. Town was quiet, ample parking available on the square, the way it always is when the students are gone. Christmas lights were strung from the courthouse roof down to the streets in all directions, turning the downtown blocks into a bucolic setting. With the light snow falling, the town looked impossibly quaint, the quintessential college town. And I supposed that it was. When you grow up there, it's easy to want to leave, but the more you travel, the more people you'll meet whose eyes brighten at the mention of Bloomington. If they've seen it. If not? Well, our little secret.

I beat Kerri back to the house, made a fire, and waited. An hour passed, and then another, before the door opened and she stepped inside, exhausted, her auburn hair dusted with snow.

"How'd it go?" I asked.

"It went."

"Did he want to talk about the grand jury?"

"Not a bit." She flopped down on the couch beside me. "Because, ya know . . . January."

"Right. We'll be taking to the caves and counting our bullets."

"You got it." She stared at the TV without seeming to register it. I was playing an episode of *The Sopranos*, her favorite new show. I wanted to be close to her but didn't want to screw it up again, the way I had in the car. I wanted to make her laugh, but that seemed impossible tonight. I wanted to put her family back together the way they should be on Christmas Eve, but that was *definitely* impossible.

"Snowing pretty good," she said distantly, and that gave me an idea. A dumb one, maybe, but better than nothing.

"We should go swinging."

Her eyes brightened and she tilted her chin toward me. Not a full-on smile, but a hint of one.

"Swinging at night in the snow," she said. "Yes. Your first good idea of the decade arrives in the nick of time. Sand was running out of the timer."

"I had a good one in '91 too."

"But it was the same one: swinging at an elementary school. The only difference is we were in the elementary school."

"Fair point."

We pulled on our jackets and put on boots and Kerri made fun of my red-and-white IU stocking cap and I made fun of the way her fleece gloves fuzzed out her hair with static when she tried to smooth it, and then we jogged through the snow and the dark to the elementary school playground, slipping and laughing.

Have you ever seen snow fall on a clear night? A night when you can see the stars and the moon?

I have three times now. I know because I watch for it, always remembering the way it was that night, Christmas Eve of 1999, when Kerri and I rode the pendulums with our faces tilted to the night sky, gazing into the holy blend of darkness and the brightness. The snow came down furiously, the last efforts of a passing squall, and I'm sure if you looked to the northeast, you'd have seen blackness from the cloud cover.

We weren't facing that way, that night.

The sky before us had cleared and the stars were high and bright and the moon was a perfect crescent, all of it presented just beyond that wall of fat, spitting snow, flakes that emerged as if from within the starlight itself.

Neither of us talked. We rode the arcs of the too-small swings with our feet held high so we could clear the same ground we'd once struggled to reach. If we stopped swinging and looked back at the direction from which we'd come, we could have seen my house, empty now, and Kerri's house, lit with waning and waxing blue light from Jerry's television.

We kept swinging, kept our faces to the snow and the stars. I wasn't wearing gloves, and the chains on the swings were cold and slick under my palms. Kerri tried to catch snowflakes on her tongue, failing each time, even when there were so many of them descending. We laughed about that, softly and without words, just watched each other and laughed. It was wonderful, so I was disappointed when Kerri stopped swinging. I held on a little longer, riding that long arc and wishing that Kerri hadn't gotten cold or tired or bored so fast. I wanted to linger here.

She stood up, though, and walked to stand beside my swing, and I let my momentum slow, winding down like a clock. When the momentum was all but dead, I lowered my feet to the snow-covered cinders and started to rise. Kerri put her palm on my chest and pushed me back. I looked up at her, confused, and she put her gloved hands on the chains above mine, then pulled herself up in a swift, graceful motion and settled down on my lap, her face close to mine. The swing drifted and the snow fell and when I started to speak she put her gloved fingertip to my lips.

I stayed quiet. Kerri rested her forehead on mine. We didn't speak, didn't kiss. We floated like that, suspended and silent beneath the starlight and the snow. I waited on her. I was good at that by then.

When we finally kissed, she led the way, and it was so much better than it had been that day in the car. So, so much better. Her hands traced my face, then my chest, and then she unzipped my jacket and I followed suit with hers and the first words uttered were Kerri's:

"Holy shit, your hands are cold!"

"Sorry." I lowered my hands but she laughed and guided them back— inside the unzipped jacket, and under the sweater. Her skin felt unbelievably warm, and when she shivered, she laughed, and when she said, "Give it a minute," her lips were against my neck.

We swung, and we kissed, and my hands warmed against her, and if she was freezing, she didn't show it. Everything was perfect for a long time—and then she stood up, stepped back, and looked at the night sky. Snowflakes and stars. I watched her study it all.

She nodded as if something had been confirmed and then said, "Memorable is good."

I was a foolish kid who talked too much, but I was smart enough to stay silent that night. Credit the stars, I guess. When she stepped back toward me, she said, "Be a gentleman, and cover me with your coat."

I fumbled out of my jacket and reached up to wrap it around her shoulders. She gave a low laugh and shook her head.

"Not the idea."

That was when I realized she'd slipped out of her boots and her hands had descended to the button of her jeans.

Memorable is good, she had said.

She was right about that.

I covered her with my coat, and the night was cold but she was warm, so exquisitely warm, and we rode the slight sway of the swing together while the snow fell.

Now you see why I remember to check the sky whenever it snows at night.

I've heard a few jokes about having sex in the snow in the years since that Christmas Eve, dumb punch lines about frostbite, you know the kind. My advice?

Don't knock it until you've tried it.

We stayed there for a few minutes after, Kerri's face nestled in the hollow between my neck and collarbone. The snow had stopped falling by then and the wind rose and she shivered against me and then lifted her face to mine.

"Maybe we try again by the fire? That could be good."

We did, and it was.

Merry Christmas.

8

THE LAST WEEK OF the year was the best of the year—and the strangest.

It was as if Kerri and I had accelerated time in a dizzying way, moving from friendship to romance to the cohabitation of adults in a blink. Our first time together hadn't been the adolescent standard of a stolen hour or a cut curfew; following a full night we woke and went about our days and returned to the same house, same bed. This sense of a shared life was, in its own way, the most romantic element of the experience. Also the most bittersweet, because we were aware of the deadline from the start. After New Year's Eve, Kerri would return to her mother and my mother would return to me and we'd be children again in the eyes of the world.

But those days before the New Year? Those were special. We were in a bubble, isolated from the outside world. We made dinner together, slept together, woke together. One thing we never did: discuss what any of it meant for the future. Nobody mentioned college in Montana or Maine or in between. Nobody spoke of long-distance relationships, pro or con. We were active in our silence, aligned in an unspoken but understood desire to hold the world at bay.

Meanwhile, I learned that you can fall deeper in love by the hour. The physical relationship was wonderful but not revelatory: It was *supposed* to feel amazing, right? And it did. But I hadn't imagined, at seventeen years old, the joy in the domestic moments that our week afforded. Hearing Kerri hum to herself when she was in another room, or watching the way she rose up on her toes and stretched to test the water temperature as close to the showerhead as possible, as if it might be different from the water below. The way she looked with her hair wet and tangled in the few precious minutes before she dried it. The fact that she never let the toaster complete a cycle before popping the slices up to check on the progress.

"I don't want to burn it," she said when I laughed at her.

"The toaster has settings. You're the valedictorian. You should be able to solve this."

"I want plenty of data before I turn my back on this one," she told me as she sent the toast back in for another round.

It was so unbelievably lovely in our secret existence that it was easy to imagine things were okay out there in the rest of the world. And there *was* positive progress. My mother was healing. Kerri was seeing her father for the first time in months. We were both certain that the stroke of midnight on New Year's Eve would be good for him. Jarring, maybe, to realize that he'd been so wrong about so much, but where was the harm in being wrong about anticipating a disaster that *didn't* arrive?

Neither of us held any fear that the disaster actually would arrive. Most of the world didn't. Jerry wasn't alone but he was certainly an outlier, a member of a small, paranoid tribe who refused to accept the reassurances offered on every broadcast from his relentlessly running television. The only dispute between the talking heads was about how bad things *might* have gone if not for the staggering investments that had gone into preparing for Y2K. The consensus was that there might be some glitches, some headaches, but the systems that mattered—governments and banks, utilities and infrastructure—wouldn't blink. No water faucets would run dry, no planes would fall from the sky.

Jerry was unpersuaded. He begged us not to go out on New Year's Eve. When panic hit, he needed us to be across the street, safe on Raintree Lane.

We acquiesced, but I won't pretend that it had much to do with Jerry's requests. We wanted to remain in our bubble for as long as possible. On the last night of our time together, before Kerri was due to report back to her mother, we would stay at my house and leave Jerry to his own devices.

"We'll let him watch TV over there and give him time to process the situation," Kerri said. "I don't want to have to sit in the house with him when nothing bad happens. I think that would be a cruel 'Told you so' moment."

For his part, Jerry was expecting us to arrive after midnight for a strategizing session.

"Panic won't hit right away," he said. "People will wander around with their champagne flutes and noisemakers, waiting for the lights to come back on. There will be a few hours of giggling. Maybe even a few days. Then the trouble starts. But we're stocked and ready. Don't get caught with your pantry down—that was my advice all year. We won't be."

Kerri and I listened and mostly didn't respond. We were used to this.

My mother was also pleased to learn we would be home for the New Year, although for different, more familiar reasons. She was worried about drunk drivers and wild parties. When I told her that Jerry already had a plan for picking her up at the hospital, she offered a sad smile.

"Tell him we've been assured the backup generators are ready but won't be needed."

She had four days left in what she called the "cordial custody" of the rehab facility and then she would be home. I was glad of that. But I also think she saw exactly how much I was enjoying my week of an alternate life with Kerri.

"Did you talk to the boyfriend?" she asked during one of my visits.

"Yes. They're not together anymore."

"I see. Because of this?"

"Not because she's staying in the house."

"Ah. So the house is innocent, but you might not be."

I nodded grudgingly.

"You're happy," my mother said, and it wasn't a question.

"Not about him. He's a good guy."

"You're happy to be with Kerri again."

"Yes," I said, and although "again" was an inaccurate qualifier for

Kerri and me in our current status, it wasn't one I intended to clarify for my mother.

I *was* happy. It seems selfish now; it felt selfish then. And yet . . . not unearned. It had been a long, hard year, and we deserved our week.

I didn't hear from Noah Storm, and I didn't reach out to him. I didn't search for information on the mysterious Harlan Maddox, or Melody Stuart, or anything else related to 712 Lockridge Lane or the ancient quarry in the Morgan-Monroe State Forest. Not that week. There was a whole year on the other side and I knew that it was loaded for bear when it came to unresolved problems. I had no desire to rush toward the trouble.

On Thursday, December 30, Kerri and I brought a pizza from Cafe Pizzaria—Jerry's favorite—over to his house. She also brought two newspapers, the *Bloomington Herald-Times* and the *New York Times*. It was her personal crusade against the constant television talking heads, which she viewed as marginally better than the talk radio he'd begun to gravitate to, a medium that seemed more inclined to indulge the wilder predictions of what they called the Year 2000 Problem. She wanted to show him that neither local nor national newspapers believed Y2K remained a pressing threat.

Most of the *Times* was focused on political news—John McCain jockeying with George W. Bush for the Republican nomination, Al Gore already presumed to be the Democratic pick—alongside a small mention of a bizarre situation in Afghanistan, where a hijacked plane sat on an airstrip in a place called Kandahar, more than one hundred people held hostage inside, the hijackers negotiating for the release of terrorists imprisoned in India.

The government of Afghanistan, a militant group called the Taliban, was pressuring the Indian government for cooperation. I had never heard of the Taliban and honestly wasn't clear on where Afghanistan was, let alone Kandahar. Kerri skimmed over that story—we all did—and focused on showing her father that the *New York Times* had positive news for the year's end, an above-the-fold story about the Nasdaq closing out the year at an all-time high, the best year ever for a major U.S. stock index. I could have told her that the stock market wasn't a way to make Jerry's day, as by then I knew some of his triggers better than she did.

"It'll be fun to watch their fucking money burn, pardon my French," he said.

It did not help that the *Herald-Times* had ranked the year's top local news stories. Meredith Sullivan held the number one spot, followed by Ben Smith's murder spree, with the massive layoffs in Bloomington's manufacturing sector taking the bronze.

"Maybe we don't show him the newspaper tomorrow," I said as we crossed the street again.

"He needs to grapple with reality," Kerri argued, and I supposed that made some sense.

After reviewing the next day's paper, though, she opted against bringing it across the street. George Harrison, of the Beatles, had been stabbed in London; eight people had been shot and five killed at a hotel in Tampa; a bomb plot by an organization called the Armed Islamic Group had been foiled in New York; and the hostages were still on the plane in Afghanistan.

"A lot of disconnected bad news," Kerri said. "Nobody needs that."

The only thing that made her hesitate was a piece on the front page of the *New York Times* explaining that the extra $70 billion in hard currency that had been printed in expectation of a run on cash for Y2K mostly remained with the banks because of a lack of demand—or an abundance of trust in government.

"We're all hoping this will be the biggest nonevent of the century," a bank vice president told the paper.

"That's not going to convince your dad," I said. "It's also literally right next to the headline saying that there are signs of a terrorist group operating in the U.S. He'll fixate on that one."

"And he loves the Beatles, so that George Harrison story won't help," Kerri said. "Okay. No newspaper today."

The last time we saw Jerry Flanders in that millennium was shortly before sundown. Kerri had baked him cookies, which he accepted with a frown.

"There'll soon be better uses for salt and flour."

"Sure," Kerri said. "I forgot. Sorry."

"They look good, though. You guys want dinner?"

We didn't want to be with him for dinner. Not that night.

"Marshall's going to grill burgers," Kerri said. "It's T-shirt weather."

She wasn't wrong about that. The mercury had reached sixty degrees. I meant to ask my mother if that was a New Year's Eve record for Bloomington.

"I can cook one for you too," I offered.

"I'm good," Jerry said. "Do me a favor, though? Cook those burgers on the stove. You'll want to save the propane."

There was a pregnant pause as the warm wind blew down the street, scattering the sand that the road crews had put down for the snow only days earlier—snow that had long since melted. I turned into the wind and squinted as the sand stung my face, so I didn't have to look at Jerry while Kerri assured him that our cars were topped off with gas and we had plenty of bottled water.

We went back to my house, and I prepared the burgers and started out for the back deck and the grill.

"Do you mind using the stove?" Kerri asked, and she looked embarrassed, but I understood. Sometimes it's easier to go along with the people you love even when you know they're wrong. We all make our concessions.

"Sure," I said, and in truth I didn't mind cooking indoors that night. Kerri was right about it being T-shirt weather—and I didn't like that. It called my mind out of our bubble and back to the limestone house on Lockridge Lane, to Noah Storm's meticulously printed notes about ancient, unsolved disappearances in unseasonable warmth.

I didn't want to let my mind go back there yet.

We sat in the living room, alternating between the sounds of the stereo and the TV, as the parties went on around the world. Every now and then, Kerri glanced across the street. Her father's living room glowed blue and white, his own television on. The countdown to the ball drop in Times Square came and went, and the lights stayed on, and the crowds cheered. Kerri and I began the new millennium with a kiss. I played "A Long December," by the Counting Crows, and the lyrics landed in a different way than they ever had before. I knew the smell of hospitals in winter now.

It was very easy to hope that this year would be better than the last.

Across the street, the light from Jerry's TV was still on.

"Want to go over there and talk to him?" I asked.

"Let's give it a little bit. Let him process things."

Imagining Jerry, alone except for his ankle monitor, watching the same shows that we were watching, with the eye-rolling abundance of Y2K jokes, was gloomy. Kerri grew quiet, curled against my side, as a FEMA representative answered a question about his staff's night by saying, "Never have so many been so bored for so long," to the giddy laughter of the news anchors.

"It's sad to mock people who were afraid," I said. "Even if they were wrong."

"It's dangerous, too," Kerri murmured, and while I didn't necessarily know what she meant at the time, I've thought about those words and that moment frequently in the years that have passed since. She said more than she knew, I think, and certainly anticipated more than she knew.

On the first day of 2000, she called her father at about one in the morning, and I gave them privacy. When I came back into the living room, she was already off the call.

"Is he happy, or embarrassed, or what?" I asked.

"Not sure yet. He didn't answer."

We both looked outside, and the flickering television light in the otherwise dark house seemed impossibly sad, lonelier than ever.

"Want to go over?"

Kerri shook her head. "Let's give him some more time."

So we did. I think we were asleep when he passed us, but it's possible we simply missed him because he drove with the headlights off. The ankle monitor that he'd removed with bolt cutters sat on the coffee table, anchoring a note for his daughter explaining that he'd left the house to find out what was real and what wasn't.

I don't trust these people on TV, he wrote, *so I'm going to check it out for myself.*

Kerri didn't get the news of his departure from the note, though. She got it from a phone call at 3:13 in the morning of the first day of the new millennium, when her mother called to tell her that Jerry had been shot by police in the Morgan-Monroe State Forest.

CHAPTER THIRTEEN

MILLENNIAL MIDNIGHT

January 2000

"The days go by quicker and the nights don't seem to differ
It's gettin cold, so I shivered and asked my soul to be delivered"

REFLECTION ETERNAL
"GOOD MOURNING"

1

I DROVE MY MOTHER'S CAR through the silent night while Kerri cried softly in the passenger seat. The windows were down because she felt like she couldn't breathe and said the fresh air helped. The wind was warm, too warm for a December night—wait, it was January now—sickly warm, unsettled, heightening all that was wrong.

Gwen had called when we were asleep on the couch, and Kerri came awake before I did. By the time I understood what was happening, she was on her knees on the floor, one hand holding the phone to her ear, the other clutching her hair as she said, *No, no, no*, in a way that sounded less like words than a howl.

The rest of it came through after I took the phone from her. Gwen gave me details by way of rapid-fire questions—*Can you get her to the hospital, Marshall? Can you drive safely, Marshall? Do you understand he's been shot, Marshall?* Yes, yes, no, wait, what?

Then we were riding through the night, Kerri crying into that warm wind. I stopped at a red light near the hospital, and she unfurled from where she was huddled against the door panel and screamed, "GO!"

The light was still red, but there was nobody coming in any direction. I went through it.

The hospital was chaos. Ambulances and far more police cars than should have been there. No TV vans—yet.

Kerri held on to me as I walked her to the ER, and I had a sudden, strange sensation that the wormhole of aging we'd seemed to have passed through had gone too far, that we were old now, and I was walking my wife into the hospital because she couldn't walk alone.

My wife. Strange, the things you think when you're in shock. When someone you love has been shot in a forest when he wasn't supposed to leave his house, the house he'd been safe in when you saw him only hours earlier, on a night of celebration, a night of too-warm winds, a night of—

"KERRI!"

As we stepped through the doors, Gwen Flanders rose from a chair, shoved past police, and ran to her daughter. Kerri released me and stumbled forward and then they were together, clutching each other as they sank to the floor in a desperate grasp, whispering over the top of each other. I heard some of the words, missed others, but heard one that mattered most: "alive."

"He's alive?" Kerri pulled back as if she didn't believe it, and Gwen nodded.

"For now." Her tears returned then, and Kerri's with them.

I stood above them, numb, feeling as detached as I had in the police station after calling in Noah's murder, everything seeming both slow and confusing. I moved only when Kerri reached for my hand. I took it and started to lower myself to join her, but she used me to pull herself back up.

"Let's get the family out of here," a voice to my right said, and I looked over to see a police officer I hadn't met before. Or maybe I had: she seemed to recognize me, and it wasn't a positive emotion.

We walked toward her as the others parted to make room and let us enter a hallway with high ceilings and bright lights.

"Family only," the female officer said, looking at me.

Kerri said, "He's family."

"No," Gwen said. "Kerri, he is not."

The female officer lifted a hand to silence them and then faced me.

"Is that your father in there?" she asked.

I stared at her, unable to muster a response, and she took the silence for the answer that I suppose it was, ultimately.

"All right, then. You will wait here, young man. Thank you."

I could see Kerri beginning to object again, but I squeezed her shoulder and told her that I would wait. Then they were gone, hidden from me behind a wall of blue uniforms. I stepped back, rubbed my eyes, and tried to calm down, tried to focus on that single word—*alive*—and not the "for now" that had followed it.

A man's voice, loud and familiar, shook me out of my daze.

"Don't know what that crazy bastard was thinking, but he left me no other choice."

The words came from behind me. I lowered my hand from my eyes and turned and saw another trio of officers standing near the doors. They would have been behind us as soon as we entered, when my attention went to Gwen, and I'd never looked back. The speaker was standing with his back to me, but I was sure that I knew him, and I began to walk toward him slowly.

"No other choice," he said again, and his voice was so familiar, yes, undeniable, and I walked faster now. The cop turned.

Corporal Maddox glared down at me, wordless, his blue eyes lit with hate.

"You know me," I said. The others with him now shifted to see me. Maddox didn't move, didn't speak, just glared, the faintest hint of amusement beneath the hostility in his eyes. I remembered that look. I remembered when I had put some hope in it, on the February day when Meredith Sullivan had waited in his back seat, and he'd told me sometimes he didn't file his tickets.

His shirt was old-fashioned and too tight, and the sidearm on his hip was a revolver while the others had semiautomatics. His lip curled with a trace of contempt, eyes hard on mine.

"You know me," I repeated.

"Excuse me?"

"You killed her."

A Black cop to Maddox's right said, "What's wrong with you, kid?"

I didn't glance his way. I kept my eyes on Maddox.

"You killed Meredith Sullivan," I said. "We both know it. I saw you."

"*Hey!*" Now the Black cop sounded pissed, but I barely registered him. "Step back!"

"Harlan Maddox," I said. "That's your name. I know who you are."

Maddox grinned at me, then looked at his colleagues and spread his hands in a gesture of exasperation.

"I've dealt with enough crazies for one night, Chris. You take this one."

Then Maddox was walking away and Chris had his hand hard on my arm, turning me to face him, his eyes filled with a mixture of anger and concern.

"The hell's the matter with you? Calm down."

I pointed at Maddox's broad departing back.

"I know him."

"You don't know a damn thing. That's Officer Glass to you, son, and he's not Harlan Mattis or Mattix or whatever to anyone, understand? What are you talking about, Meredith Sullivan? That's not funny. You think this is funny?"

The single-minded focus I'd had on Maddox dissipated like smoke and I stared at the officer who held my arm.

"Did you say Glass?"

"*Officer* Glass," he snapped. "He's had a tough night without your circus act, all right? Now, you got yourself under control or do you need some help?"

Yes, I most certainly need some help, I thought. *But it is not going to come from you. I'm not sure who it can come from.*

"I'm okay," I said, and then, to get him to release his grip on my arm, "I'm sorry. I was confused."

"I'll say." He let go of me and stepped back, wary. Maddox was into the parking lot now. Headlights flared.

"Did he shoot Jerry Flanders?" I asked.

"That's not your concern."

He did, I thought, and that certainty brought every nerve in my body alive.

"You need to sit down, son? Who are you here with?"

"I'm fine. I'm leaving. I'm sorry."

"You don't seem fine. Where are your parents?"

That question again. Where were my parents? Jerry Flanders had been shot, and Harlan Maddox was alive, and I was being asked about my parents? I felt a sparking rage that was different than any anger I'd known before, a terrible, trapped fury that rode alongside my inability to explain reality to any of these people, the knowledge that if anyone listened, they would not hear.

"Son?" the officer said, and there was a warning note in his voice, almost as if he saw my rising anger—and probably he did.

"Stop calling me that," I snapped.

"Excuse me?" He cocked his head and leaned forward and suddenly I felt certain that if I didn't leave under my own power immediately, the chance to do so might be gone for good.

"I'm sorry," I said, and then I stepped away, pushing past his partner, and to my relief they didn't stop me as I walked out of the emergency room just in time to watch the police cruiser pass by, Harlan Maddox at the wheel, his eyes on mine. I watched him until his taillights were lost to the blackness, as the wind pushed loose paper across the parking lot with a rustle, the night still full dark but warming, the first day of the new century determined to refuse the rules of weather that had come before it.

I looked back at the hospital. The cops by the door were watching me. Beyond them, Kerri and Gwen were long gone, off to wherever they would wait while surgeons either saved Jerry's life or didn't.

He left me no other choice, the man I knew as Harlan Maddox had said, the man the others knew as Officer Glass had said.

Nothing about him fit this era, but the other cops fit it fine, and they saw him, they *knew* him, and the man they knew was not the same one I saw.

How?

Maybe it didn't matter. Not as much as the fact that he'd shot Jerry, at least. I had been raised to respect and even revere the police, but that morning they'd separated me from the girl I loved and then I'd seen a ghost moving among them, a very dangerous ghost that they were concealing—unwittingly or not—in their own ranks, and I suddenly wanted to be away from the rest of those uniforms. I was confused and I was scared and for some reason I could not take my eyes off the guns on their belts.

It was not yet dawn, and I hadn't heard from Noah Storm in weeks, and yet I headed for his house. It didn't matter if he was there or not; there were guns in his office.

Jerry Flanders had been wrong about most everything he'd predicted for this dawning of the new millennium, but maybe he'd been right about one.

I hate to say it, Marshall, but when the madness starts, you'll need to be ready to shoot back.

Did I honestly believe I could kill a ghost with a gun? I don't know. I can recall the steps of that morning but never the goal of it, to the point that I believe I *had* no goal beyond arming myself, nor motivation beyond fear and a sense of futility. I was scared and I could not find anyone who would listen—listen and believe—and I knew exactly one thing about guns: people who carried them commanded attention.

2

THE TOWN WAS STILL AND DARK and the streets empty, the last of the New Year's Eve revelers long gone. I didn't pass a single car on my way to Noah Storm's house, and this time I didn't park at the curb in my customary spot but pulled into the drive and all the way to the back. The alley was empty and the only light fell in a thin cone from a single streetlamp. The back door belonged to the shadows.

I got out of the Bravada and opened the tailgate and tugged the tire iron free. It was shaped like an L, a socket on one end, the other angled like an oversized flathead screwdriver, solid and sleek black, the metal cold in my palm. It felt good, heavy and mean.

I went up the steps, paused at the top, checked behind me. Nothing. I looked at the door and saw only my own silhouette reflected in the glass. It occurred to me that I had never actually broken glass—not on purpose, not by accident. I'd made it nearly eighteen years avoiding that.

For something you weren't supposed to do, it sure was easy.

One blow with the socket end of the tire iron punched a hole through the windowpane just above the dead bolt. The sound seemed like a cannon shot, sure to draw a crowd, and I swore and ducked back into the darkness, waiting for someone to turn on a light or yell.

Nothing happened. Bloomington slumbered, the breaking of a door no louder than a dropped champagne flute to those safe in their homes. I used the angled end of the tire iron to scrape away the glass fragments until I could reach through without getting cut. The dead bolt turned easily, and then the door was open, and I was inside.

I paused for a moment, letting my eyes adjust to the darkness. I was facing the familiar hallway from an unfamiliar direction, the office door down the hall and on the right, the cellar door closer and to my left. I glanced at it only long enough to determine that it was closed and then I made my way down the hall, ran my hand across the office door until my fingers found the knob, and twisted.

When I hit the switch and flooded the room with light, the office was as I remembered it, clean and organized and filled with books. The gun cabinet would be locked but I knew where the keys were, inside that useless stapler that waited in the top drawer.

I walked behind the desk and pushed the chair back and pulled open the drawer, all without bothering to look at the notebook on the desk, a lined tablet filled with Noah's tidy handwriting. I set the dummy stapler on the desktop and lifted the top, revealing the silver key tucked inside.

No, wait—silver *keys*. There were two of them now. I set the tire iron down on the desk and shook the keys into my palm, and it was only then that my eye caught on the notepad long enough to register my own name.

Dear Marshall—

    I'd hoped it wouldn't be necessary to write this letter, having had enough bad experiences writing letters to last a few lifetimes. After I lost that hope, I developed a new, better one: that I would say the words to you directly rather than write them down. The likelihood of that diminishes by the day for reasons that I hope you will soon understand, and forgive.

I reached out and lifted the top sheet to see if there was more written beneath.

There was more: two pages, three, four . . .

I sank into the chair, the keys to the gun cabinet still in my hand, and began to read.

3

BEAR WITH ME, MARSHALL. The hardest stories to tell are the ones that must be told.

Bloomington, Indiana, 1907. Daniel Stuart is preparing for yet another mayoral campaign. The quarry business is good to him, better than politics, and better than health. He lost his wife in 1899 and did not remarry, doing most of the work of raising their only daughter alone. Melody Stuart turns nineteen years old in 1907, the year the troubles begin . . . or at least the year they reach the door of the Stuart house.

Melody has been accepted at Barnard, a prestigious women's college in New York. Melody is, in many ways, out of balance, perhaps the result of having been raised motherless. She has a world-class mind but small-town contentment, dueling aspirations. She has spent as much time around the limestone industry as in the classroom, and she is already engaged to a twenty-five-year-old policeman who soon becomes a foreman in her father's company. He is known for his looks, physicality, and charm. And, in some circles, his temper.

His name is Harlan Maddox.

Daniel Stuart tolerates Maddox's courtship of his daughter—or at least doesn't obstruct it—but he wishes for her to have a taste of life as an independent woman in a city far away. He tells Harlan Maddox that he must wait for her college days to conclude before she weds. Maddox expresses support of this publicly, though in his private moments he exudes bitterness. Even anger.

Thus, the summer of 1907 is to be their final season together before she departs for the city. It is either an irony or a tragedy, depending on your perspective, that Melody is introduced to a snake-handling minister named William Crabb by Harlan Maddox. Harlan anticipates none of Melody's genuine fascination with the group; he brings her to one of their ceremonies out of sport, the opportunity to ridicule the zealots appealing to his cruel sense of humor.

Melody approaches this self-appointed preacher with the depth of curiosity for which she is known, and while Harlan Maddox hoots with derision at Crabb's claims of dark powers—the ability to cast lost souls into the bodies of snakes, to purge human sin with fire and bind earthly evils into the existence of the serpent—Melody is both fascinated and unsettled by the strange practices, the fervor of the few followers, and, above all, Crabb's clinical, detached confidence.

She begins to attend the services regularly, though always at a distance, and to study the snakes themselves, seeking expert explanations for how Crabb can manipulate a rattlesnake with such ease. She learns theories of de-fanging, venom milking, and other possible methods of removing the snake's deadly capacity.

She is not convinced, however. And Melody Stuart is a woman who requires an explanation.

As the summer of 1907 rises from warmth to scorching heat, Melody is devoted to her questions, and Harlan Maddox is disgusted with them—and with her. He cannot tolerate humor at his own expense, and the jokes about his fiancée having "taken up with the snakes" wound a fragile, foolish ego. Harlan's temper rises along with the summer heat, although Melody is unaware of the depth of his rage. It is, after all, a fair question in her mind: If William Crabb is a con, how does he execute the con?

Harlan Maddox would just as soon execute the man. Temper meets opportunity at the site of a new quarry in the Stuart Company empire, an isolated but rich bedrock zone. It is on this ground that William Crabb captures the snakes used in his ceremonies, and when Harlan Maddox acquires the property on behalf of the Stuart Company, Crabb is incensed—and ominous, writing a series of apocalyptic letters. Melody brings her father to observe one of Crabb's services. A decision must be made. On one side of the ledger are politics and popular opinion—Crabb is widely regarded as a lunatic—and on the other is his beloved only child's wish to leave well enough alone with William Crabb.

In the end, Daniel Stuart is swayed by an unexpected source: the stone itself.

It is uniquely beautiful and oddly colored, bright white limestone laced with veins of black. Stuart authorizes work at the site, and Harlan Maddox promptly takes sport with it, instructing laborers to place excessive charges of dynamite in seams where snakes were known to den. The resulting explosions—and the literal rain of snakes that follow—are so disturbing that several workers walk off the job. Maddox taunts them, chiding them for their fear, and reaches for the charred body of a dead snake.

The snake strikes his arm. Or at least its jaws do. Whether it was a reflex action or whether it still clung to life is not known.

But Harlan Maddox feels its bite.

A half dozen more men quit the job after watching that burned snake sink its long fangs into the foreman's arm. Some swear that smoke gusted from the snake when it spread those formidable jaws and struck.

By the time Harlan Maddox reaches the hospital, most have given him up for dead, but he is young and fit. The venom is no match for his blood. He emerges from the hospital pale, thin, and angry—but he emerges.

For a few weeks, that would seem to be the end of it. Crabb has vanished into the forest, and quarrying continues. Daniel Stuart is so struck by the stone's beauty that he claims the first of it to build his own home, with the remainder of that first—and only—season of the quarry's existence sold to a company that specializes in mausoleums and headstones. The mausoleums soon develop a dark reputation, with claims of reanimated dead, phantoms made flesh. To Daniel Stuart, it is nonsense. To his daughter, it is evidence of something inexplicable but deeply troubling.

As the final stones are laid in the Stuarts' own home, Melody convinces her father to cease operations at the quarry in the forest, and even to stop shipment of the stone already blasted and cut.

Harlan Maddox is furious—but that is little concern to Melody, because she is done with him. On a record-hot day in August, she ends their engagement. When he demands a reason, she says only that she has seen something in him that was not there before, and she does not trust it.

It is two weeks before Melody goes missing. On the day she is supposed to board the train that will take her to New York and Barnard's campus, she is nowhere to be found. Search parties are formed, but their efforts prove futile.

Harlan Maddox, questioned repeatedly, denies any knowledge.

For thirteen days, thirteen terrible days in the high heat of a brutal drought, Melody is imprisoned in an abandoned barn in a field not far from the closed quarry site. She is fed nearly nothing and left a pail of rainwater to sustain her between savage beatings. Maddox returns to her only when he is certain he is not being followed. On the thirteenth day, he fires a single bullet into her battered body, locks the barn door, and leaves her for dead.

She doesn't cooperate with her would-be murderer. She stays alive. She fights for escape from the barn. She screams for help.

It is William Crabb who hears her cries and brings her to the hospital.

It is also William Crabb who waits for Harlan Maddox to return to the barn. The locks are gone, the doors now spread wide, the victim missing.

While surgeons set Melody's shattered bones, remove the bullet, and stitch her wounds, a stranger, identified only as Silas, arrives at the hospital to relay a message to Daniel Stuart. Harlan Maddox, he says, is being held by William Crabb at Crabb's camp deep in the forest. Crabb would like to grant Daniel Stuart an option. He can turn Maddox over to the police, or he can offer a more fitting punishment.

No juries, only justice.

Daniel Stuart leaves the hospital and heads into the night with the stranger named Silas. In the flickering firelight and shadowed craters of the closed quarry site, William Crabb awaits, with Harlan Maddox bound and gagged at his feet. Crabb is calm, almost courtly, even as a four-foot-long timber rattlesnake undulates in roiling coils along his forearm.

The snake, he informs Stuart, is called Winterstone.

He brandishes the deadly serpent with all the attention of a bracelet as he offers Daniel Stuart his condolences—and a choice.

At Stuart's wish—and only if it is his wish—Crabb will see that Harlan Maddox endures a "ritual of penance." He will be touched with fire, Crabb explains, his human form cleansed of his earthly evil . . . and his soul will be cast into the body of the snake.

It is precisely the sort of madness that Daniel Stuart scorned only weeks earlier. But now, with his only child fighting for life in the hospital, and the man who left her for dead lying before him, and that terrifying snake rising and falling, rising and falling, along the minister's extended arm, there is not much about Daniel Stuart's world that matches the one he knew before.

He nods his assent.

There is one crucial question, Crabb says. Is there any chance that Melody Stuart is with child?

Her father insists that she is not. Crabb persists: there is already venom within Harlan Maddox, he explains. Snakes from these dens are different. The bite from the summer might not have killed Maddox, and he may seem fit enough to civilians, but those who understand know that the wrong venom from the wrong snake is not simply purged. It endures.

It follows the blood.

Daniel Stuart is not concerned with Harlan Maddox's bloodline.

Shall they proceed then? Crabb asks.

Stuart nods again, sweat dripping along his trembling jaw.

Not enough, Crabb tells him. Say it. Make the choice aloud. I am only an instrument—*you* are the actor.

And so the words are said. The choice is made. Later, Daniel Stuart will recall the smile that passes, swift as a sparrow, across William Crabb's face. He will be haunted more by that smile than by the horror on Harlan Maddox's face as the torch is lowered to him and Harlan screams against the gag while William Crabb chants a strange incantation.

They burn him to death, there on a limestone ledge.

When it is done, Crabb's disciples place Harlan Maddox's corpse on a canvas tarpaulin that is tied off to long ropes. Crabb extends his arm again, and this time the serpent, Winterstone, slides off it, crossing Maddox's body leisurely, slithering from his burned boots to his still-smoking hair, and now the snake is changing colors, the dark green of life fading to an ash white, its tongue and rattling tail turning as black as coal.

The corpse is lowered from the ledge down into a deep seam in the rock below. It is only when the body is gone from view that Daniel Stuart can muster words.

What will become of the snake? he inquires.

William Crabb smiles again.

Winterstone will come and go, he says. That is the way of snakes. Unless you wish to seal it in this tomb? Shall we keep Winterstone behind the rock, Mr. Stuart?

The answer, so obvious, is yes. Of course this terrible snake must be sealed in with the dead. But Stuart understands, in a primal, previously unknown part of his brain—or his soul?—that his opportunity to control the snake has already passed. What he wishes no longer matters in the way it once did, and he knows that Crabb's question isn't an offer at all. It is a taunt.

Daniel Stuart says nothing at all as he leaves the forest to darkness and makes the long walk back to his beloved hometown alone.

It is the last time he—or anyone else in the area—will encounter William Crabb.

It is not the last time they will encounter Winterstone.

In the days ahead, still more surprises. Melody is defying the doctor's predictions. She is recovering. And the doctors have more news, whispered news, horrible news as far as most are concerned.

She is pregnant.

Her father implores her—begs her—to terminate the pregnancy. He will pay any price and find any doctor, licensed or unlicensed, to perform the task.

Melody refuses. Too many have suffered at Harlan Maddox's hand, she says. She will not add to the list.

Her father is faced with another choice. Should he tell his daughter the truth of his actions, that night in the woods with the self-appointed reverend and the snake—or keep the secret? And, with it, his reputation.

He does not tell his daughter of the choices he made in the name of vengeance.

The punishment, if his role in Harlan Maddox's death becomes known, would be severe. Even for a man of his power, a jury's verdict is an unknown. He could go to prison for murder. He would surely never become mayor, let alone governor, let alone—well, there are so many dreams within that limestone house.

Melody heals. She returns home. A nurse is hired, lawyers deployed to turn away prying eyes.

The child is born in the spring. A son. Healthy. Clear lungs and a strong heart. Hope blooms again. Old secrets will not damn this family.

Or so it seems until winter. Then come the troubles. Unexplained lethargy, low body temperatures. The boy is taken from the house and sent to doctors, growing worse with each visit, baffling the specialists. Melody and Daniel bring him home to die with whatever comfort can be provided.

But he does not die. In fact, he recovers. Stronger in spring, fully healthy by summer. Things are promising.

Until winter's return.

It is January when the boy's grandfather voices the terrible truth to Melody: the child is bound by the seasons of the snake. Vengeance has corrupted.

On the day after his confession, Daniel Stuart leaps from the roof of his house. A spectacular suicide, the talk of the town. His daughter does not attend the funeral. She is in Boston, seeking a new doctor for her ill child.

When she returns, it is a quiet affair, as all her life will be. A spinster, the locals call her, in their kinder moments. Others have darker things to say, but time brings fresh tragedies to fill the mouths and ears of those who require them. An influenza. A war in Europe.

The child is seldom seen, but isn't that the way of the ruined and the rich? They hold their heirs at a distance. Melody tells those few people with whom she speaks that he has been sent east, to a prep school. Later, it is the military. No one in Bloomington knows the boy well, and few know him at all. He returns home in the summers and is regarded as pleasant, kind, athletic, the type of child who may well thrive despite those awful early challenges. Those who see him are often struck by how different he looks, year to year. Why, it is as if he sheds his skin, one says casually.

Then the summer visits cease.

A depression comes, and then another war. The world moves on. The Stuart house is no longer a subject of scrutiny. There is not so much as an obituary in the local paper when Melody dies.

The house is put into a trust. It is a complicated arrangement with a firm in New York that pays the taxes and occasionally rents the house. As time goes by, the place falls into the quiet patterns of many a forgotten estate. Many believe it is tied in with the university. Most do not care at all.

And that is as it must be.

Because Daniel Stuart's grandson lives on within the walls of that house—and even outside the walls, though that is harder to keep track of, because he is seldom seen as he acquaints himself with his own impossible rules. For a good portion of the year, he is healthy and happy . . . if he remains close to home. If he wanders far from it, he weakens, tires, becomes disoriented. The hot days of high summer are best for endurance, but his favorite days are those rare, unanticipated bursts of warmth in the shoulder seasons of spring and autumn, gifts of energy. The basking season.

In the winter, he slumbers.

He ages with astonishing slowness. The seasons of the snake are good for a human, if one believes eternal life in a damned existence is good. On many days—most of them, in fact—the man cannot believe that. He is held here as punishment.

The first time he tries to kill himself, it is with pills. The next, with a gun. The third and final time, he leaps from the roof of the house as his grandfather did.

His grandfather's escape is not granted. No escape shall be.

This is the stuff of folklore, usually depicted as a remarkable gift and not a burden. Stories that do not understand the price of outliving all those you loved, let alone the limitations that prevent the man from forming relationships of love.

For most of his life, he avoids forming relationships. There is one notable exception—in 1981. He is seventy-three years old in 1981, but the physical equivalent of a man in his thirties. To say that he sheds his skin in those long winters is not precisely accurate—but closer than not. Each spring brings substantial changes; the mirror is always a surprise. Hair color and texture, skin tone, and eye colors change dramatically. His physical size has peaked and seems unalterable, his metabolism indifferent to diet or exercise—at least until winter.

In the summer of 1981, he has blond hair and green eyes, green as an emerald bottle. It is the first summer of green eyes since the eve of World War II, and he cannot shake a sense that it means trouble ahead. The light hair is a pleasant change, though. His skin takes on a deep tan.

That summer he meets a woman who lives in a rented room four blocks south. A student from Georgia. A romance flourishes, a perfect summer, the first in his life, the only truly good year. She's so lovely, so smart, so effortlessly witty. He intends—he truly does—to end the romance with each passing week, because he loves her too much to hurt her.

But this is the problem with love. It always hides the capacity for the deepest harm.

He does not bring her into his house or even explain where he lives. He claims he's on a short-term grant, common in college towns. She knows from the beginning that he will be gone in the winter. All is well except for what he must tell her. Which he cannot tell her. The summer passes with a fully realized life of the sort he has never known. Long days and lovely nights. She is enchanted by storms, and together they find isolated viewing locations ahead of oncoming thunder and lightning. A fire tower in a forest. A covered ledge above a lake. A hayloft in a barn. On one memorable night at the edge of autumn, a forgotten hilltop cemetery with a bottle of champagne. There is no shelter that night, no protection from the elements. They let the rain fall.

Summer fades so fast.

As autumn comes on, he begins to lose weight, and their excursions become shorter and more infrequent. She is confused by this—hurt—and while he hates to see the pain in her lovely eyes, how on earth can he allay it?

There is no future for them, though it is all he wants. To tell her the truth would be to destroy her.

The crisis seems awful enough even before she comes to him with news.

She is pregnant.

His response is a terrible thing. He begs her to abort the child. When she resists, he becomes firmer. He tells her that there is something evil within him, something venomous, and that he believes any child of his will be poisoned by his blood. She refuses to speak to him after that. Letters go unanswered, maybe even unread.

The child is born.

The father watches from afar. Seasonally, as he must. He never allows himself to come close. He watches a baseball game once, sitting in the outfield. The boy pitches two innings and strikes out three batters and beans the only left-handed hitter he faces, and later the father will remember the concern on the boy's face when he caused pain to another, and the memory will make him weep.

The father sends money. The checks go uncashed. He is heartened to see the boy growing at a normal rate. He is beyond relieved when he finds a photograph in the newspaper of the boy on a sled, embracing winter.

Perhaps the boy's blood is not poisoned after all.

Meanwhile, the man chases the black-and-white snake. Winterstone. By then, you see, he understands so much more. He has heard the legends of the snake and, more importantly, he has seen the girls who look so much like his mother go missing.

Unlike his mother, they do not survive.

It is as if the black-and-white snake exists simply to finish his task, again and again, to kill, to kill, to kill.

Unrelenting cycles of vengeance. That is the nature of Winterstone.

The man becomes a detective. It is a good endeavor for someone of his limitations. There is much that he cannot do, but he is determined to break the cycle of suffering. It will take time, but time? He has time.

Then one spring day a mother calls him. Her son, she says, has seen a kidnapper. The man is devastated by the sound of her voice and the sweetness of her son's name. He knows that he should turn them away, and nearly does, but there's a problem . . . It feels too coincidental, that of all the children in the world to see the kidnapper, it is the one with his blood.

The mother and son walk into his office, and the man is nearly overwhelmed by the emotion of the moment. But he is also troubled, because the boy stands outside the house and points to the lightning rods. His mother cannot see them, straining her eyes against the sun. That's well and good—the lightning rods have been gone for more than fifty years.

How can the boy see into two eras and be unaware of it? And perhaps more pressing: How did the current host of the snake find the boy? He must have some sense of the boy because he has found him and then returned to him, but with what goal, and at what risk? Because in a terrible way the boy is, of course, also the snake's son. But what will happen when the two meet again, or for longer? The snake has passed him by once. It might fear the boy.

But it might not.

The moment feels precarious in a way the man has never known before.

4

THERE SHOULD BE a better word than shock.

I don't know of one, though. There was no preparation for the emotions I felt—or didn't feel—after reading that letter in Noah Storm's office.

I did not read it twice. I didn't even turn back the pages. I read to the last word and then I closed the notepad and sat in the chair in the big empty house.

My father's house.

Grandfather's. Grandmother's.

It was a story that might have been ridiculed as implausible even for fiction in Mr. Doig's writing workshop, and yet I had no doubt that it was true. It had been a long year. I was a credulous reader by then.

I knew who the snake's host was—I'd faced him that morning—but had he known me?

He must have some sense of the boy, but with what goal, and at what risk?

At what risk seemed like a very fucking important question. I could picture Maddox behind the wheel of that police car, eyeing me as he drove away from the hospital.

After I had called him by name.

The house felt larger and emptier then, and I was suddenly reminded of why I'd arrived: to get a gun. That seemed more important now than ever.

I pushed back from the desk and stood on legs that trembled, then made an oddly formal show of leaving the office, as if by straightening the blotter on the desk and pushing the chair in tight I could force some normalcy back into the day. Into the world.

It didn't work.

I left the office with the notepad and gun cabinet keys in one hand and the tire iron in the other and started down the hall. Each step felt disembodied, each breath an effort, each thought like something pulled from a distance.

What shock does.

If I'd been capable of assessing anything, I might have realized that I was operating the way I'd learned to in the climbing gym, shutting off panic and anticipation, stilling my mind and focusing on the problem. The current problem was the cellar door, which was closed and locked.

I set the notepad and the keys on the carpet and gripped the tire iron in both hands and fitted the angled tip into the gap between door and frame. I clenched my teeth and leaned in, driving the steel bar as far into the gap as possible, and just before I levered the bar to the side, my mind caught up to my body, and I stopped and looked at the keys on top of the notepad.

Two of them.

There had been just one hidden in the stapler in the summer. Also, there had not been fresh dead bolts on the cellar door in the summer.

I popped the tire iron loose with a squeak of protest from the door, picked up the keys, and tried the brightest one. It fit. I turned back both dead bolts—*snick, snick*. Noah's letter had been a numbing blow, so the usual prickle of panic that floated over me whenever I approached this cellar was stifled like a drunk's good judgment. I put the dead bolt key in my pocket and held the tire iron and notepad in my left hand and the key to the gun cabinet in my right as I stepped down into the darkness.

The only light was coming from behind me, allowing me to see little beyond each additional descending step, and I knew that the first pull chain for a light socket waited above the bottom step, so I kept my eyes on my feet. The usual cellar smells were there—the cool and the damp, the dust and the stone—but there was an undertone of something different,

a familiar smell but not one that belonged here. Humans are visual crea-
tures, though, and so instead of stopping and focusing—or, better yet,
retreating—I tilted my head as if to search for the smell, peering into the
blackness, which meant that I was facing the wrong way when I stepped
off the stairs and walked directly into something hard, smacking into it
with my shins.

I cried out and stumbled forward, dropping the notepad and the tire
iron. The iron met the stone floor with an echoing clang just as a hand
struck at me and grabbed my throat.

Fingers dug into the back of my neck as a thumb drove into my Adam's apple, strangling me. I fell backward almost silently, the tire iron's
ring still in my ears as I hit the staircase on my back, falling into a shaft of
light from above, choking and gasping. It was only then, when the light
passed over my face, that the hand suddenly released my throat.

"Marshall!" a low voice hissed, and while I couldn't make him out yet,
I knew the voice.

It was Noah Storm.

It was my father.

He pulled the light chain, and the cellar was made whole, and I could
see that he was standing in front of a cot. This was what I'd walked into
at the base of the steps. It was one of those aluminum-framed folding cots
like they show in movies of military barracks, adorned with a single pillow but a thick stack of blankets. The smell of human life was what I'd
registered too late.

In the winter, he slumbers.

Noah stood over me, gaunt and haggard and hollow-eyed, stubble
thin on his cheeks but thick over his jaw, his emaciated chest heaving as
he breathed.

"What in the hell are you . . ."

He stopped talking then, all his attention going to someplace over my
left shoulder. He was looking at the notepad.

"I wasn't done with it," he said, and he sounded impossibly sad. "There
is so much more to say."

I sat up, rubbing my throat, the pain radiating from chest to jaw, and

I was aware that he could have—would have—killed me with one hand if he hadn't recognized me in time.

"The story is true," I half asked, half said.

He nodded distractedly.

"So much more to say," he repeated, and then he sagged down onto the cot and hung his head. His back rose and fell in long, labored breaths. I had no idea what to do or say or feel.

"I know who Maddox is," I blurted at last. "I saw him. Today."

Noah's eyes opened slowly. He stared at me.

"Where?"

"The hospital. He shot Jerry Flanders. We were there to see Jerry, but then I saw the cops, and he—Maddox—was with them. But they don't see him like I do."

"No," he said softly. "They most certainly do not. What do you mean, he shot Jerry Flanders?"

"I don't know what happened. Jerry ran from home, and Maddox—his name is Glass, Vic Glass—shot him. That's what he was telling the other cops, anyhow."

"He is a cop?"

"Yes. He lives near the state forest." I wet my lips. "The den."

"How far?"

"I don't know. Right by it."

"I mean how far is he from us? It matters."

I thought about it. "Maybe fifteen miles?"

Noah winced and then rubbed his face with one emaciated hand.

"That's a lot," he whispered.

I had no idea what to say to that. I couldn't look away from him. There were a million questions and yet I couldn't voice one.

My father.

"How warm is it?" he asked suddenly.

"What?"

He made a weak gesture at the steps. "Outside."

"It's . . . almost like spring."

"Good. We'll need that. *I'll* need that." He rose wearily from the cot, knelt, and picked up the key to the gun cabinet. His hand hovered over the notepad and he reached down and touched it gently.

"You must have so many questions. I will try to answer them all in time, I promise. But is there one you would like to ask me now?"

He turned to me, and in the shadows he appeared less gaunt, could almost have passed for the man I'd met in the spring and worked with in the summer. Looking back at him, I didn't think I could possibly ask enough questions, so why start with one? Why start at all?

But then I had it, the words leaving my lips almost without thought.

"Why do you call yourself Noah Storm?"

It was the least consequential question, confusing identity with a name rather than actions, and yet I saw him smile faintly and approvingly.

"Because my birth name is Noah," he said, "and because your mother's heart belongs to storms, not Stuarts. She watches for them. She waits for them."

Silence. He rose, key in hand.

"All right. Take me to him, Marshall. It won't be easy, but it will be done."

He lingered on the last word, thoughtful, and then he nodded once and turned to the gun cabinet.

5

WATCHING NOAH GET INTO the Bravada and sag back on the passenger seat, I understood how little energy he had. He looked exhausted from the simple walk up the steps and out to the car. He was carrying a backpack and wearing a gun in a shoulder holster, concealed by a black canvas jacket, but that wasn't the only weapon he'd removed from the cabinet.

He also had a long metal pole with a pistol grip at one end and serrated jaws at the other. Once, I might have had to ask what it was for. That was before Jerry Flanders told me his story.

"I don't understand what you think will happen," I said as I drove us out of town. "The man I see as Maddox other people see as Vic Glass. But nobody is seeing a black-and-white snake." I paused, then said tentatively, "Winterstone."

Even the sound of the name was like a hiss.

"Winterstone will be there," Noah said. His voice was soft and low and he kept his head pressed to the seat back, breathing in long, slow breaths, an almost meditative quality.

"It stays with him? In the letter, you called him a 'host.' What does that mean?"

He didn't answer. I glanced over and saw that his eyes were closed.

"Noah?"

"I'm fine." He took another shallow breath. "Mornings are tough. It'll get better when the sun is high."

The dashboard readout showed 58 degrees. The sun was out but not high.

"You look awful," I said.

He gave a wan grin. "I was born in 1908, Marshall. I look better than I should."

Fair enough.

I was heading north, the sun bright to the east, the passenger side. Noah tilted his face toward it.

"The hosts have to choose the snake," he said. "The wrong man discovers the snake and becomes enchanted by it. Where most people see a danger, they see power. And they simply can't let it pass by. Picture a deadly rifle, a fully loaded AR-15, left untended. Many people will be scared to touch it at all. Others will be guarded and cautious with it. But some? Some will be thrilled with the potential of awful power—and in time the results will be tragic. Now grow that emotion exponentially. That is Winterstone. The snake is seductive to this kind of man. Winterstone allows itself to be handled by the hosts, clearly. For a time."

"Then he . . . bites them?"

"Yes, in the end, the hosts are killed. The snake moves on. Another man will be found. The cycle repeats. I'm sure the men feel as if they're in control of the snake in the beginning. They are not."

"So you think it all ends when the snake is killed?"

He made the slightest shake of his head. "You *can't* kill Winterstone any easier than you can kill me, which is no easy task, as you saw this summer. We are two sides of the same coin. So long as one of us exists, the other must. What my mother—what your grandmother—told me was that the snake must be captured and returned to the den. The tomb where Maddox's body is. I will bring it back there, and I will seal it in with him, and it will be done."

Your grandmother. A mile passed before I asked my next question.

"What in the hell *did* happen this summer? I saw you, didn't I? I mean, really saw you, not some hallucination or vision. I saw *you* and you'd been shot. Killed!"

"Shot," he acknowledged. "Not killed. It doesn't go that easily for Maddox—or me." He gave a strange laugh. "Time to time, we both need to prove it to ourselves, I guess. In early July, I began to get phone calls from an anonymous 'source' who promised information about Meredith Sullivan. He would share his privileged information on one condition: that I met him in person, and in the state forest. I suspect you can guess the place."

"The old quarry?"

Noah gave a faint nod.

"That condition was enough to tell me that he'd found me, but that was no challenge; I've never been hiding. I've been in that house, by and large, for nearly a century. My guess is that Maddox—or Vic Glass, call him what you wish—had the same idea that I do now: if he returned me to the den where it started, perhaps he could end it. End me, rather. Our long feud. I'm not sure how much Vic, the man, understands fully—intellectually, that is—but I believe he *feels* things with clarity. His intuition is Maddox's, without a doubt. Certainly he understood that I'm strongest when I'm in my house, surrounded by stone from the quarry where it all began. He was determined to lure me away from it. Get me far enough away, and weaken me enough, and . . . well, I don't know what would've happened. I think I would've ended up in the den, and I'm not sure what that's like, but I know I don't want to find out. I didn't take the bait, and he didn't show patience. He came for me, as I'd suspected he would. That was why I told you to take a few days off. Do you remember that?"

"Yes. You didn't want me around, and I didn't know why."

"I was afraid he'd pose a danger. He certainly did. I wish I could tell you that I remember the scene clearly, but I must confess that being shot in the head can scramble your memories." Again that eerie laugh rose. "What I recall was simple enough: a man in a mask, a gun in his hand, and a thunderclap in my skull."

"You walked out of the house and looked around like it was all confusing to you," I said. "Like the scene on the street was a complete surprise."

"It was."

I glanced over at him. "So you just . . . heal. A man shoots you in the forehead and you *heal*."

"More or less. One hell of a headache, but, considering the circumstances, who can complain about that?"

His wry smile was the one I'd gotten to know so well in the early days of the summer.

"Would I be able to heal like that?" I asked, and the smile faded fast.

"I don't know," he said softly. "Don't take it the wrong way when I tell you that I hope not. There are some underappreciated advantages to mortality, Marshall."

We rode in silence for a time. I could hear him breathing, long and slow, his face to the sun.

"You're not going to be able to return anything to that den, Noah," I said at last. "Not the way you are now."

"I've been waiting almost a century," he responded. "I'll be able to do it. The warm day will help. Crack the window. I want to feel the air."

So I cracked the windows and that eerie, spring-warm air filled the car on the first day of January. Snippets of the letter kept floating through my mind. *His favorite days . . . The basking season. In the winter, he slumbers.*

The dashboard readout said 60 degrees now. I tried to will it higher.

I turned onto Lost Man's Lane, trying to remember exactly where the Glass farm was. On the night I'd come this way, I'd been more worried about Sean Weller killing us on the S curves than in noting which way he turned. We passed the rutted road with the old farm gate where Weller had thrown his parties and where Kenny Glass had punched me in the face, and then wound on, deeper into the woods, the road making a serpentine boundary of the state forest. So much had happened so close to this spot. There was a strange energy out here, I thought—at least for me. When I glanced at Noah, I saw that his eyes were open, as if he felt it too.

"Close?" he said.

"Yeah." I was remembering the way now. "How far away do you want me to park? How far can you walk?"

"I want you to drive right up to the house," he said simply.

"He just shot someone!"

"If he wanted to hurt you, he'd have done it already," Noah said. "I think you trouble him. You have your grandmother's blood, and he hates that, but you also have *his*. He must sense it. He has shown too much interest not to."

I remembered my first encounter with Maddox, when he'd suddenly shouted, asking me what in the fuck was with me and second chances, telling me there was no promise of getting home safely. All while the girl who looked like my grandmother sat in his back seat. The hair on the back of my neck rose and my forearms prickled with gooseflesh. Each word he'd said felt weighted with new menace now. It was as if he'd been speaking not to me but to Melody Stuart.

My grandmother.

The one who'd reached for my hand from the other side of the barn in all those nightmares.

The one who'd taken the bullet and still lived, saving herself, saving her child.

My father.

Me, if you extended the line. I lived because she had survived.

"How does he find the girls who look like her?" I asked. The sun was higher and harsher now, and I had to reach for my sunglasses. Noah stared directly into the light.

"That's what frightens me the most," Noah said. "In the old days, he had to hunt. It took time. But with Meredith, remember, he used the computer. The day the police announced that, I was scared in a new way. I don't think anything will be slowing down with computers in the years ahead, do you?"

I shook my head.

"More and more people will show their faces to the world," he said. "They'll volunteer to do it; they'll *want* to do it, everyone made a movie star of their own life. Maddox won't have to expend much effort to hunt then, so his range? Well, that grows exponentially."

He sounded deeply troubled.

"Why would he have shot Jerry?" I asked. "He's not like all the other victims at all."

"I have no idea," Noah admitted. "But it feels far from coincidental."

Yes, it did. And I kept saying Jerry had been shot, not killed. Was that still true? Or were the ER surgeons talking to Kerri right now, explaining that they'd done all they could, and it wasn't enough?

The farm lane that Weller had used on the night of our disastrous raid on the barn appeared, and I slowed.

"There's a barn behind the house, and two driveways," I said. "It's easier to sneak up on the place from here, but it will be a long walk."

He shook his head decisively. "The walk will be to the den. I can't waste that strength—and I'm not concerned about sneaking up on anyone. Benefits of immortality, Marshall."

He said it the way he'd offered all his little mantras about detective work, and for some reason that rattled me. He must have seen it in my face because he reached out and grasped my shoulder.

"It will go quickly," he said. "I promise you that."

The next driveway appeared on my left, and already I could see the police car through the trees. My pulse triple-timed at the sight of it, and all I wanted to do was pass by.

"Let's end it," Noah Storm said, and my foot found the brake as if of its own volition.

I pulled into the farmhouse drive and up beside the police car. The Jeep that had been used to chase Sean Weller and me was parked in a gravel semicircle beyond the garage. There was no one in sight. A single Miller Lite can blew off the porch and rattled across the driveway, swept by the ever-strengthening wind. On the dash readout, the temperature had reached 63 degrees. Noah unzipped his jacket. His face was damp with sweat but his eyes lasered on the front door.

"When I get to the porch," he said, "lay on the horn."

"Do what?" I said, but he was already opening the door and stepping out into the warm wind. He let the door swing shut behind him and then he drew the gun and held it down beside his leg as he walked with a swift, fluid stride, nothing like the labored motion he'd shown leaving his own house. The sun was high and clear and even the filthy, peeling paint of the old farmhouse looked bright.

Noah never looked back. The last thing in the world that I wanted to do in that moment was hit the horn, but his unwavering stride was a gesture of trust, and so when he reached the first step, my hand moved to the horn.

WAAAAAAAAA!

Noah took the first set of steps, reached the landing, and pivoted, his back to the car again, his face to the house. I kept pressing on the center of the steering wheel.

WAAAAAAAAA!

The front door banged open, and Harlan Maddox burst onto the porch. He was still wearing his uniform pants but not the shirt, only a white T-shirt, no gun belt, and his hands were empty.

Good, I thought, *Noah has control.*

Noah lifted the gun, and I waited to hear him offer some command, telling Maddox to put up his hands or get on the floor.

Noah pulled the trigger and shot him in the forehead.

My hand slipped from the horn and the world went silent except for the rattle of that lone beer can on the pavement as Noah went up the final two steps, stood over Maddox's body, and pulled the trigger again. The shots sounded small in the wake of the horn, but they were real enough.

He'd killed him. Without so much as a word, he'd killed him.

He knelt beside the body, reached into his jacket pocket, and withdrew a set of handcuffs. He clipped one around Maddox's left wrist, then dragged the body to one of the front porch pillars, looped the chain of the cuffs around it, and snapped the second ring around Maddox's right wrist. I stared in disbelief. Then Noah straightened and looked back at me.

"Bring the pole and the pack, Marshall!" he shouted. "And *hurry!*"

I looked at the pole he'd left in the back seat, the one with the pistol grip and the wide, serrated jaws.

"Marshall! There is not much time!"

Not much time? Maddox was dead!

I looked at the porch, saw something glitter in the sunlight, and realized that the chain on the handcuffs was moving. Maddox, dead only seconds ago, was shifting like a man coming out of a deep sleep.

I grabbed the backpack and snake pole and ran for the porch.

6

NOAH WAS ALREADY in the house when I passed by Harlan Maddox, who was moaning and muttering, rolling his head on his neck as if stretching out from a long sleep in a cramped position. There was blood on his forehead, but it was no more than a smear, the kind you get on the back of your hand before you even realize your nose is bleeding. While I watched, his chest wound sealed, fresh flesh layered on as if by a painter's hand.

"Marshall!" Noah barked from inside the house, and I tore my eyes from Harlan Maddox and stepped through the door, backpack in one hand, snake pole in the other.

The old farmhouse stank of sour food and sweat. The kitchen was visible across the living room, stacks of dirty dishes filling one side of the sink and accumulating on the counter. Cardboard cases of beer were overflowing with empty cans. The only evidence of care in the house was on the coffee table, which was lined with bright brass cartridges and tidy mounds of black gunpowder beside a small scale like the one we used in my physics classroom. Noah emerged from the kitchen, pale and sweating, assessing his options.

"He'll have kept the snake close," he said. "Bedroom, I suspect."

He took the backpack from me, knelt, unzipped a pouch, and withdrew a long syringe. It was filled with a pale liquid, like water with the faintest trace of lemon. Before I could ask what it was, he handed the pack back to me and asked for the pole. I passed it over as Harlan Maddox gave a loud groan outside. I looked over my shoulder nervously.

"He can heal," Noah said, "but he can't slip out of handcuffs. Trust me, Marshall, I've learned a little about our rules."

Our rules. The phrase put a shiver through me. Noah was moving toward the stairs. He hadn't told me to follow, but I did simply because I didn't want to be alone in that foul-smelling room with Harlan Maddox awakening on the other side of the door.

We went up the old, creaking steps, and I was struck by how swiftly Noah was moving, such a contrast to what he'd been capable of when he left his own house. It was as if he'd found a deep well of untapped energy.

At the top of the stairs he paused and studied the hallway, three doors to the left, two to the right, all of them closed.

A high, harsh buzz broke the silence, and Noah Storm gave a cold smile.

"Takes the guesswork out of it," he said, and then he followed the sound to the last door on the left and opened it.

I will never forget that bedroom as long as I live. I've seen some disturbing places since, and I've dreamed up others for fiction, but I've never been able to match the bedroom of Vic Glass for skin-crawling impact.

The walls were lined with stacks of VHS tapes. Hundreds of them. Cameras were mounted in all corners of the ceiling. The bed was nothing but a dirty mattress on the floor, no frame, not even a box spring. The mattress was only a twin, but it had to be small, because it had to fit between the wooden support posts that held the glass terrarium above it. The terrarium was massive, maybe seven feet long by three feet wide, and there was no habitat to it, no rocks or molded plastic features. The snake would be the last thing Vic Glass saw before sleep and the first he saw when he woke.

The snake itself was coiled tightly when we entered the room, tail buzzing but head lowered. I recognized its thick body and distinctive black-and-white bands and the ink-black rattles and tongue. I had walked right by it in the night. How had it not bitten me?

It might fear the boy. But it might not, Noah had written.

The boy sure as hell feared it.

When the snake saw us, it shifted immediately, twisting left to right and then elevating its wicked, wedge-shaped head and spreading its jaws. The size of its mouth was stunning—it was like looking at a yawning dog. Except the dog didn't have those long, curving fangs waiting to inject their killing venom.

I backed away, almost out of the room. Even Noah paused, and he hadn't so much as broken stride before shooting Harlan Maddox in the face. Now he adjusted his grip on the snake pole, wet his lips, and said, "Hello, Winterstone."

The buzzing went wild.

"What are you going to do?" I whispered.

"Catch it." Noah used his thumb to flick the plastic cap off the syringe.

"What's that?"

"A sedative. The snake can't be killed, but I believe it can be slowed. I know I can be."

It was so disturbing to hear him speak of the snake and himself as if they were one and the same.

The snake struck at the glass then, a furious *POP* so blazingly fast that I let out a cry, as if it might blast through the glass. And that didn't seem impossible, based on the way the whole tank rattled. The speed was one thing; the strength was another. The buzzing of the rattles intensified to a hyper, crazed hum. The head dipped back toward the coiled body and then shot forward—*POP!*—before sinking down again. The rattle rose again, furious, as if the snake's captivity were driving it mad.

Hello, Winterstone.

Noah reached for the lid.

"Don't!" I shouted.

"We have to," Noah responded. "You know this."

He looked back at me then and there was something deeply personal in his expression, a gaze that suggested we understood each other in a way no one else possibly could.

A father's gaze.

I swallowed and nodded, and then he turned from me and lifted the heavy lid.

The snake struck immediately, bursting up and out so fast that its head was impossible to track, simply a blur.

Had the terrarium been any smaller, I think the snake might have gotten Noah on that first lunge. It was so large, though, and the glass walls so high, that the effort of clearing it vertically limited the snake's ability to extend outward.

Noah caught the snake just behind the head, his hand moving in a flash, and then the serrated teeth of the pole clamped as the snake thrashed, its heavy body pounding off the glass, sounds like a fist pounding a window. Noah grimaced at the effort of holding the jaws shut and balancing the snake's wildly shifting weight as it whipped in all directions. He lifted it straight up out of the tank and stepped close, and I couldn't keep myself from backing up again, because the snake had found me now, Winterstone's left eye locked on me as it spread that impossibly wide mouth and hissed with fury, forked black tongue flicking.

That was when I saw the first wisp of smoke gust from its mouth.

"Noah," I said, but he wasn't listening to me; all his attention was devoted to keeping the jaws of that snake pole clamped shut. The effort of the struggle was taking its toll, and I was afraid he did not have enough strength for the job. If he lost his grip by even a fraction, the jaws would open enough to let the thrashing snake slip loose—and we would be trapped with it.

Noah lifted the pole even higher so the snake was well above his head, the body whipping against the side of his face as he drove the syringe up and into its white belly. Noah depressed the plunger, the sedative flooded in, and the snake's horrible hiss rose to something like a howl. The rattles clattered off the wall of the tank.

Then came the laugh.

It was just as Jerry had described, low and mocking. The snake's jaws snapped shut, hiding the fangs, but its left eye remained fixed on mine as its body withered. The smell of smoke filled the room while the snake seemed to deflate, the powerful body, once as thick as my arm, contracting until it was no bigger than a garden hose. All the while, it dried, the sleek skin going first papery and then brittle. The laugh faded away, and the smoke dissipated, and then the snake called Winterstone was gone and Noah was holding nothing but a long, empty skin.

He sagged, put one hand on the glass tank to steady himself, and then bowed his head, taking long, halting breaths.

"Not easy," he murmured, and then he coughed so violently that the tank and support beams shook.

"Are you okay?"

"Open the pack, Marshall."

I knelt on the filthy floorboards and unzipped the backpack. It was heavy not due to its contents but because the material was so thick, made of multiple layers of coarse, ripstop nylon. The only thing inside the backpack was a piece of red plastic about the size of a package of hot dogs.

"Take that out," Noah instructed.

"What is it?"

"Explosives. To seal the den."

I set the package down carefully, noting the thin fuse cord taped to the underside of it.

"Hold it open, please," Noah said, and when I looked up, I realized that he intended to lower the snakeskin into the bag. It took all the willpower I had to stay there holding the pack open while the dry, scale-lined skin was lowered slowly past my face, foot by foot, inch by inch, with the sound of crunching autumn leaves underfoot. I forced myself to watch the head pass by, but there was not much head to see—no eyes, no fangs.

I remembered them, though.

"Zip it," Noah said, and I zipped the backpack closed with shaking fingers.

He took the pack from me and told me to pick up the explosives, and it was only when I was back on my feet that I got a true sense of how exhausted he was. He looked like a man who'd been marching for many days without pause, a man who might collapse at any moment.

"Takes a lot to move fast in the winter," he whispered, reading my concern. "Once I rest, I'll be able to do it again. The sun will help."

He took an unsteady breath and wiped sweat from his brow and then took the explosives from my hand and gave me the pole.

"You'll have to drive," he said. "Go fast."

"Where?"

"The forest. The den."

"What then?"

"I'll take it up there and seal it in, and this awful thing will finally be done."

He didn't look like he'd be able to stay upright, let alone make a climb that few men could complete in peak condition. I hoped he was right about the restorative powers of the sun.

He damn sure needed to be.

We went downstairs together. Slowly. His steps were labored and he had to clutch the railing. It was only because of the pace that I even bothered to glance at the photographs on the wall. They were an array of family photos as you'd find in my house and most of my friends' houses, high school kids doing high school things. These pictures were twenty years old, maybe thirty. Homecoming dances and graduations and goofing off. The kid in the pictures had to be Vic Glass, I realized, and because I had never seen Vic Glass's face, only Harlan Maddox's, I studied them with interest. He had a broad jawline and green eyes beneath a bristling red crew cut.

I remembered Jerry's description of the snake hunter, the redheaded, green-eyed snake hunter, and I wanted to take one of the pictures down from the wall and bring it to him—if he was still alive to see it.

As Noah limped down the steps, I lingered behind, studying those old images. The same girl was in many of them—holding hands with Vic in the prom photo, laughing at his side at the homecoming dance, mugging for the camera in others. I took another step down, checked the next picture, and froze.

"Noah," I said.

"I'm fine," he answered without looking back.

"*Noah!*"

He finally turned and followed my pointing finger to one of the photographs. In it, a young Vic Glass sat behind the wheel of a Jeep. The top was off, the summer sun was bright, and the blond girl beside him was dressed in the uniform of a Chocolate Goose employee.

"Son of a bitch," Noah whispered. He limped up another step so he could study the rest of the photos. "That's the teenage romance, it would seem."

"Yeah."

"He's certainly alone now, so it didn't work out."

"No. But the shirt . . ."

"He might've kept the shirt," Noah said, nodding. He turned and managed a smile that almost hid his physical pain. "Told you the shirt might matter. And you thought we were wasting time."

Before I could answer, Harlan Maddox let out a bellow of anger from outside.

"Time to roll," Noah said.

It wasn't rolling, exactly—more like limping. But we made it out of the house and past Harlan Maddox, who was not only alive and alert but plenty angry. He glared at us with fury while trying to jerk free of the handcuffs that held him to the porch support.

"*You fuckers!*" he howled. "*Let me go! I will kill you! I will murder your whole families!*"

"Poor incentive to let him go, if you ask me," Noah said.

We went down the porch steps and back to the Bravada. Noah fell into the passenger seat gratefully, holding the backpack on his lap. I started the engine.

"What do we do with him?" I asked, nodding at Harlan, who was still screaming obscenities.

"Get out of here and call it in to police," he said. "I'll update them and tell them about the photograph."

"It's evidence," I said, stating the obvious only because its impact was just landing on me. Evidence could help Jerry. Was Jerry still alive to benefit?

"It is," Noah agreed, "and it matters. But not to us, not right now. All that matters is right here."

He patted the backpack, which caused a muffled rustling from the empty skin within.

"How long will the sedative last?" I asked as I drove away from the farmhouse.

"It *should* last for many hours—on an ordinary snake. But you can kill an ordinary snake too."

"So you have no idea?"

"I have no idea," Noah admitted. "This is why I think we need to hurry."

I pressed hard on the accelerator and tried to keep my eyes on the road and not flicking to the side to ensure that the empty backpack stayed empty.

It was not easy.

7

I DROVE LIKE A MAD BASTARD, pushing the bulky Bravada to its limits, listening as Noah called a detective with the state police named Easton and detailed the scene awaiting them at Vic Glass's house. He was more effective with his anonymous tip than Weller and I had been. When he hung up, he said simply, "We will see," and then he rode with the window down and his face to the sun, trying to find the restorative warmth.

I worried—perhaps foolishly, perhaps not—about the same restorative sun beating down on the backpack on his lap.

I parked at Stepp Cemetery and asked Noah if he was sure he could walk. He didn't answer; he just walked. He couldn't go fast. Twice he fell, and once I thought he was going to stay down. He forced himself up, though, and staggered on. On the trail, screened from the sun by the towering trees, it felt more like the January day it was.

It was clear that Noah had been there before. He led me off the trail well before I would have departed it, and then we were on another path, this one little more than a deer track, but easy to follow. It wound through the trees and then out into the old quarry site. The cliff loomed above us, the ledge with the den every bit of a hundred feet away.

Noah tripped, stumbled, and fell again. This time he didn't get up on his own. When I helped him to his feet, I was terrified by his face, which had taken on a gray pallor and was dripping with sweat and wracked by pain.

"Need to rest," he murmured.

"You can't do this," I said. "You can't make that climb."

"I can," he said, but when his eyes went to the stone wall, I saw the hope go out of them.

"I've done it before," he said.

"In the summer?" I asked.

His silence was affirmation. I helped him ease down onto a wide rock that caught the sunlight, and then I stepped away to study the wall. It was imposing, no doubt, but it wasn't the flat-out impossibility that it had seemed to be when I'd looked with only the flashlight to illuminate it. I'd also learned a lot about climbing since that night. The narrow vertical crack in the limestone that meant nothing to me then now struck me as an opportunity.

"I can do it," I said.

"Can't let you," he wheezed, but he was bent double with pain.

"Then there's no option," I said. "We wait down here for the sedative to wear off and that bag to fill back up with a live snake."

He hated it. That was clear in his eyes; he despised both options.

But I wasn't wrong.

"I don't want to do it, but I'm the one who can."

He straightened, wincing, and studied the wall.

"I had ropes and anchors when I did it," he said. "I forgot today. I wasn't prepared. I can't believe that I do not have a rope."

No ropes, no Noah climbing, and an unknown ticking clock coiled up in that backpack.

"I've got to do it," I said.

He sighed and gave the faintest of nods.

"There are good grips over there to the right," he whispered. "Sturdier than it looks."

I saw what he was talking about, but I shook my head.

"If I were roped in, sure. But I'm not going to be. I want to use that crack." I pointed at the long, vertical fissure in the face of the wall. It ran all the way up to the ledge and continued twenty feet past.

"You will fall if you try that," Noah said.

"No, I won't. I'm better with those techniques, actually—hand and foot jams and arm bars. I know those."

He looked at me with surprise.

"I've been training," I said.

"For this." He gestured at the wall.

I nodded.

He bowed his head. "I can't let you."

"Then it doesn't end," I said. My mouth was dry and my heart raced, but we'd come a long way to get here. Longer than I'd known. I couldn't let it begin all over again.

When I took the backpack from Noah's shoulders, he didn't resist. I felt okay when I put it on my own shoulders, but the moment I fastened the chest strap and heard it snap into place, I had a flash memory of the black-and-white snake thrashing beneath the grips of the pole, and my nerve almost broke. I think I might have torn the pack off and run from it if not for Noah's presence, his watchful eyes. I did not want to fail in front of him without even trying.

"You'll need these," he said, and I looked down to see that he was holding the plastic explosives in one hand and a Zippo lighter in the other. "I wish I had complicated but fail-safe instructions for you. I don't. It is what it looks like—you'll need to light that fuse, and then get the hell out of the way."

I put the explosives and the lighter in my pockets. My hands were shaking, and I saw Noah register that, but he didn't say anything. I wiped my palms on my jeans, wishing desperately for some chalk. Or, for that matter, gloves or tape. This wasn't a synthetic wall; it was real rock, and real rock can be damn painful.

I hurried to the wall. The speed might have suggested confidence, but I really needed to have the problem of the climb ahead of me so that my mind couldn't be drawn back to Winterstone, whose skin was currently coiled up against my spine.

I needed to move forward.

That meant going up.

I took my first grip and brought my left foot up. My sneakers weren't ideal for climbing but at least they were low-profile. A bulky boot would have been disaster. I swung first one hand, then the next, reaching as high as possible. Insert, jam, lock. Then let the feet follow. Left, right, left, right. The limestone that looked so smooth from a distance was brutally rough on contact. After my second hand jam, my knuckles were raw and bleeding.

I did not look up. The den was the bell, and the bell did not matter yet. It was all about the wall, as Jake Crane said, and that had never been truer.

Left, right, left, right.

Higher.

Higher.

Sweating now, breathing hard, but moving well. Insert, twist, lock. I was probably thirty feet off the ground now, high enough that a fall would break bones. I was glad that Noah was watching in silence. I needed all my attention on the wall.

About forty feet up, I found a fist-sized chunk of rock outside the crack, which was a glorious gift because it allowed me to perform a foot stack and rest. I withdrew first my left hand and then my right for inspection. My knuckles were raw and the backs of my hands were lacerated, the fingertips beginning to split and show beads of blood. The pain could be pushed past, but I was worried about the blood making my hands slick.

I did not rest long.

Higher, higher. Fifty feet now, maybe sixty. A fall would certainly kill me. I was aware of that in a distanced way—less afraid than more simply cognizant of it. I was trying to stay focused on the task at hand, but I couldn't help thinking that it would be harder to come down than it was to go up.

None of it mattered if I didn't make it to the ledge first.

My legs were solid, and although my hands were getting battered by the rock, my grips were strong. My overall condition was good, although I knew I had to be getting tired because the backpack that had felt so light at the start seemed heavier now.

Keep going, that was all.

Hand jam, foot smear, foot jam, stretch . . . breathing hard, but moving steadily. The ledge had to be close. Fifteen feet, maybe twenty?

I was reaching with my left hand when I felt something shift against my back.

I froze there, hand extended, going absolutely still as I frantically tried to come up with an explanation for that sensation against the small of my back. It was just the wind, or simply the shifting of the pack.

The pack that was noticeably heavier than it had been.

I managed to exhale, insert my left hand into the crack, twist it, and set a fist jam. Nice and solid. That was good, because when I lifted my foot to follow, there was more movement against my back, and this time it was undeniable, the press and release of something coiling and then straightening. The backpack was alive.

The snake called Winterstone was waking.

I was too scared to scream. I needed both hands to hold the wall and keep me alive; the snake was held to my back by the pack, securely snapped in with chest strap and hip belt.

Go, Marshall, go now, and go fast!

I made it another five feet, aware of the ever-increasing weight of the pack, my breathing going too fast and too shallow, a risk of hyperventilating. Gray rings crowded my field of vision and I blinked them away.

Going to faint. I am going to faint.

"Marshall!"

Noah's voice brought me back. I didn't look down to him but I said, "It is awake."

My voice was so soft that I was sure the words wouldn't reach him, but they must have, because he immediately shouted back.

"Drop the pack! Drop it now!"

I slipped my right hand out of its jam position and fumbled with the snap on the chest strap. I couldn't get it. My hand was shaking and my fingers were slick with blood and I couldn't lean far enough away from the wall to see the clasp. Meanwhile, the backpack was in motion, heavy and undulating, and all I could think of was how impossibly wide those jaws could spread and how long the fangs were. They could puncture the backpack with an inch to spare, easily, and then Winterstone's fangs would find my spinal cord.

My bloody fingers finally closed on the plastic snap. The clasp of the chest strap parted. Halfway there. I needed only to release the hip belt and then I could shrug this terrible thing off my shoulders and send it tumbling away.

The problem was that the hip belt was pressed tight to the rock—and I couldn't fix that without falling.

"DROP THE PACK!" Noah shouted.

"I can't!" I yelled, and then the slithering pressure of the snake touched between my shoulder blades, and that was too much for me: it scared me into motion, and the only motion I could make was climbing or falling, so I climbed.

I climbed with a panic I have never known before or since. I was gasping and sobbing and my hands were slick with blood and my vision was nothing but overlapping gray rings. I could feel the rock, though; the rock was there, hard and cold and undeniable.

I went on up.

I'd gone about ten feet before the snake attempted a strike.

WHUMP!

It hit me hard, like a smack on the back, and I cried out, sure that I'd been bitten.

There was no pain, though, and the weight in the pack tumbled to the bottom, where the snake writhed, its weight thumping against my kidneys.

It is not back to full strength yet, I realized. The bag had stymied it, deflecting that first bite.

It would not do that for long.

As I reached for a handhold, free-climbing ninety-some feet in the air, the backpack seemed to spark, an electric jolt like touching a live battery terminal, and then I realized the rattling had begun.

I began to breathe in wild, ragged gasps, but I kept moving.

Noah shouted about dropping the pack again. I didn't bother to respond. I could not free the hip belt until I was clear of the rock, and I couldn't be clear of the rock until—unless—I reached the ledge.

WHUMP!

Another smack between the shoulder blades, another cry from me, but once more the thick nylon stopped the bite. Based on the wild, frenetic thrashing that ensued, accompanied by a higher and harsher buzz from the rattles, I suspected the snake's fangs were stuck in the ripstop nylon and it was thrashing to free them.

The creature's weight fell to the bottom of the pack again, a pile of rattlesnake just above my hips. I hoped some venom had been lost in that moment when it got hung up on the inside of the bag, stuck by its own fangs. I needed to believe that was possible, because the snake was heavier now than ever, which meant it was getting bigger, stronger, and once it rested for another strike, it would surely puncture the bag and find my flesh.

I looked up.

The ledge was there. Two feet above, no more. Two laborious, hard-earned feet fighting up the crack using hand and foot jams . . . or one lunge.

BUZZZZZZZ.

I had a good hand grip. Now I dipped, smearing as much of my shoe soles on the rock face as possible, as Jake had taught me. I flexed my legs, bouncing on the balls of my feet. The snake pressed against the base of my spine in a hard, tight coil. Cocking to lunge, I thought, and this time I didn't think the bag was going to be a barrier enough to stop it.

So I lunged first.

Caught the ledge. Sharp rock corners bit into my palms. The mantle I performed then was the fastest and most fluid of my life, pressing myself up and over and onto the ledge and then I was rolling over flat rock, rolling on top of the snake in the backpack, fumbling with frantic, bloody fingertips for the clasp on the hip belt.

Found it.

Freed it.

Then, still rolling, I was loose, clear of the snake.

I lay on my back, staring at the high thin clouds scudding across a bright blue sky. I had made the climb and I had not been bitten.

Impossible.

But done.

The piercing sound of a rattle burst my bubble of safety, and I sat up, looking at the backpack. It was shifting as the snake called Winterstone punched left and right, searching for freedom, but the buzz of the rattle wasn't coming from the backpack.

I looked to my right and saw a second snake waiting three feet from my bare hand, coiled tightly on the ledge where the sun baked the stone.

8

THIS SNAKE WAS DARK GREEN, the whirring rattles a pale brown, nothing like the black-and-white beast, but no less intimidating.

I slid backward slowly, using the heels of my hands to draw away without rising. The rattle intensified when I moved, but the snake didn't strike. Yet.

The problem was that I could not go far. I was at the lip of the ledge, and if I slid any farther, it was a long drop down.

"Marshall?" Noah called, a clear note of fear in his voice.

"I'm here! And there is another one!"

"What?"

"There is a snake on the ledge! A different snake!"

A pause. Then: "It is basking, Marshall. This is the right day."

"It can still bite, right?" I yelled.

"Yes."

"What the hell do I do then?"

Another pause. Meanwhile, the backpack was roiling across the stone. Winterstone was fully awake and fully furious. The green one didn't seem to like the chaos, because it broke from its coil and began to slither away.

Toward me.

"NOAH! It's coming at me!"

A muffled response: "Throw it!"

That was the command I heard, and while it struck me as absolutely insane, it was the only advice I had. I rose on trembling legs, crouched, and sidestepped. My motion seemed to confuse the snake, because it stopped and lifted its head to track me. The backpack to its right popped as Winterstone struck again, and this time the upper fangs did puncture the heavy nylon—and got stuck again. The vicious white curves were clear against the black fabric, and the frustration of being stuck enraged the snake, sending it into a fury of thrashing.

And drawing the attention of the green rattler. I watched its head shift toward the chaos, and I knew that I would have no better opportunity. I ducked and grabbed for it, closing my fist around a scaly body that felt like one massive, seamless muscle, and then I threw it into the air.

The snake's speed was astonishing. I had moved quickly, and yet by the time it was airborne it was already whipping back toward me, and I saw the wide jaws spread, the curved fangs arcing toward my face.

Then it was gone, out into the air and falling. I turned to watch it go, and for an instant I thought of the story of the blasting at the quarry, the rain of snakes that had made men walk off the job.

Suddenly a cry from down below: "Holy shit!"

I walked to the ledge and looked down to see Noah Storm scrambling backward, his eyes on a slithering green ribbon that disappeared into the rocks.

"What happened?" Noah bellowed.

"You told me to throw it!"

"I told you to throw a rock *at* it!"

Oh.

"I didn't hear that part!" I said, and then, "Sorry!"—at which point I almost burst into manic laughter. The adrenaline was fading and my body was shaking and I felt high and giddy and exhausted all at once.

The buzzing backpack brought me back to reality.

I was so close. Time to finish the job.

I skirted the backpack and walked to the back of the ledge, wary of another snake. There were no snakes on the ground, but I pulled up short, heart double clutching, when I spotted a long, dangling coil.

It took me a moment to recognize it as a rope. And not just any rope, either: it was Jerry's rope, the bright blue static line on which he'd wasted some of his remaining money. I grasped it and pulled it away from the face of the wall and tugged. It was tied off to some anchor point overhead, not far from the outcropping ledge.

Had this been what he'd come to do in the night? Had he intended to come to the den himself by lowering himself down from above rather than attempting the climb?

I released the rope and stepped farther back, into the hollow where the rock wall curled inward. There I saw the shadow of a crevice that seemed to go on and on into the depths of the earth.

I threw a handful of small rocks into it, sure that a dozen rattlers would come boiling out. Nothing happened. I returned to the sunlit side of the ledge and looked down at Noah.

"I think I found it!"

"Thin gap but deep?" he called up. He was leaning on a tree for support.

"Yes."

"That's it. It goes awfully deep, Marshall, but you need to make sure the bag goes all the way to the bottom, and you need to be *damn sure . . .*" He was interrupted by a coughing fit, and when he spoke again, his voice was hoarse. "You need to be damn sure that the fuse is lit when you drop that packet in. If you don't get the packet down deep enough, you could get badly hurt. We want to seal that snake in, not you!"

"Okay."

I turned from him and eyed the backpack. It had gone still and silent, as if the snake were also listening to Noah's plan. *Assessing*, I thought, and the word seemed to hiss in my brain.

The snake had punctured the bag once but wasn't able to rip through it. The multiple strikes had surely fatigued it, but it was worth remembering that Winterstone was no ordinary snake. I desperately wanted a long pole or stick so I could hold the backpack at a distance as I pushed it into that deep pit, but I wasn't going to find anything like that on this barren ledge.

I would have to pick the backpack up. That was all there was to it.

I took the package of explosives out of one pocket and set it down, put the Zippo beside it, dried my bleeding palms on my jeans as best as I could, and took a few deep breaths. Then I walked swiftly over to the backpack, grabbed it by one strap, and lifted it, holding it as far away from my body as possible.

Immediately, the black-and-white snake struck. Once, twice, three times, pounding the bag with the rhythm and intensity of a piston. On the final strike, fangs opened a gash in the fabric. I saw that one blue eye fixed on mine, an eye that seemed to contain all the rage of an ancient world, and then a wisp of smoke rose from within the bag.

Winterstone.

I ran for the crevice in an awkward hunch, keeping the bag as far from me as possible, and then I dropped it into the blackness. It fell with a rustle of fabric on stone and then a single, sharp snap.

Then silence.

I dropped to my knees, edged closer, and peered into the darkness. I could hear the bag rustling somewhere far down below, but because it was black, I couldn't make it out.

The one thing I could make out, clearly, was a human hand. All the flesh that had covered it was long decayed, but the yellow-white bones caught the daylight. The skeleton hand was curled inward, almost as if beckoning me.

My grandfather's hand.

Harlan Maddox.

I went for the explosives.

"Make sure you get a clean drop!" Noah yelled. "It could go badly wrong if you don't get that charge deep enough!"

"I'll do it," I said. Why he was worried about things going badly wrong *now*, after I'd climbed up here with one rattlesnake on my back and met another on the ledge, was beyond me. Now I was calm. Every hair on my head might have turned white, but I was calm.

I untaped the fuse cord from the base of the plastic packet and un-furled it. The cord was about ten feet long. I knelt above the deep crevice where the snake waited with Harlan Maddox's corpse, lifted the tip of the fuse, and sparked the Zippo. A flame glowed blue and orange, dancing in the wind. I touched it to the fuse, made sure that it was burning steadily, and then lifted the packet and dropped it into the pit. It fell a long way down, and the burning cord brought a faint light to the darkness, and I could see the outstretched, beckoning hand of Harlan Maddox clearly.

The black-and-white snake began to rattle, as if it sensed trouble, and I was no longer sure if all the smoke I smelled came from the fuse cord.

I turned and hurried away.

I went to the edge of the ledge and gave Noah a thumbs-up and then we waited, and I suspect we were both wondering the same thing: What if the charge was too powerful and it blew the ledge right off the lime-stone wall?

So much time went by that I was certain it was a dud and we had ac-complished nothing, giving the snake plenty of time to make its escape.

But then the charge detonated.

It went off with a deep, resonant boom that shook its way up out of the rock and into the pit of my stomach, and the trembling went on for a few seconds before fading away. When I turned back to the crevice, a cloud of dust obscured everything from sight. I waited until it dissipated, and then I went to inspect the results.

The gap was filled in as if it had never existed, packed tight with crushed rock.

The snake called Winterstone, if it still rattled, could not be heard. Harlan Maddox's beckoning hand was gone.

I was suddenly more tired than I had ever been in my life. I still had to get off this damn ledge, though. I took Jerry's rope and yanked on it as hard as I could, testing the security, and it held firm. Then I grabbed the loose coil, walked to the edge of the ledge, and saw Noah sitting with his head bowed.

"Rope coming over!" I yelled, and he looked up. "Let's see if it'll reach."

It was plenty long. That was crucial because I was going to need to cut some of it. I pulled it back up and took out my pocketknife and cut the last ten feet off it.

"Do you know what you're doing?" Noah called. His voice was weak.

"I actually do," I said. Jake Crane had once shown me how to tie an emergency rig called a Swiss seat. On nights when I couldn't sleep, wondering what Kerri was doing, or what would happen to Jerry, or what my mother would be like once she got out of the hospital, I had practiced, over and over. I tied it now with confidence, then ran Jerry's rope through my bloodied hands, wondering whether tossing this rope was the last thing he'd ever done and if I would ever be able to thank him for it.

When I was sure that the makeshift harness was secure, I stepped backward, off the ledge, for what I sincerely hoped would be the last time.

The rappel was the one smooth thing of the day—the first thing in the year 2000 that had gone as planned. When my feet hit the ground below, I smiled. I couldn't help it. Then I looked at Noah and the smile faded fast.

He had fallen over on his side, curled into the fetal position.

"Noah!"

He murmured something unintelligible. I rushed to him, stumbling in the rope harness, and rolled him onto his back. He opened his eyes, which were dull and rheumy, and then said, "You did so well, Marshall. So well."

"I'll call an ambulance."

"No." He managed this one with more force. "Can't . . . explain this." He rattled in a breath before adding, "Can't explain myself."

And I knew what he meant. Boy, did I ever.

"I'll get you home," I promised, and then I hoisted him upright and tried to support his weight while we walked.

He made it all of five feet before he went down again.

He outweighed me, even in his withered state, and I was physically spent from the climb. I looked at him, with his clammy gray pallor and bleary eyes, and I didn't think the 911 call was optional anymore.

I took out my phone, typed in the 9 and the first 1, and then cleared it. I swore under my breath, looked from Noah Storm to the hills and woods, and then I called Sean Weller.

"Happy New Year, pussy," he said.

"Weller, it's me."

"I know that. You think I was talking to my mom? Geez."

"I need help," I said.

"What's up?" he said, and his voice was all business now.

"It has to be no-questions-asked help. Do you understand?"

"Just say it."

So I told him where I was, and whom I was with, and that I had to get Noah Storm to his house, and that no one could know. I said all of this in a torrent of words and Weller listened without saying one of his own. By the end I was almost out of breath, sure that he thought I was having a mental breakdown.

Then he spoke, low and calm.

"Hold fast, Marshmallow. The Weller is en route."

9

HE MUST HAVE DRIVEN like Mario Andretti, because I'd budgeted at least an hour's wait and Weller arrived in thirty minutes flat, bursting out of the woods at a steady run, his Colts hoodie soaked with sweat. He was scouring the quarry for us when I spotted him and shouted. He approached at a jog while I helped Noah into a sitting position. For the last hour he'd been on his back on the ground, shivering and saying nothing, only semiconscious. I'd pulled him into the clearest patch of sunlight.

"What happened to him?" Weller asked.

"He's sick," I said.

Weller shot me a curious glance. "Right before you called, my dad was telling me the news. Said Flanders was shot by police last night in the state forest. He survived but nobody knows what the hell happened. While that was going on, someone else broke into Big Vic Glass's house and cuffed him to his own porch railing, and now it's a big crime scene, police all over the place."

I lifted both hands, palms out. Weller nodded.

"You did say no questions asked. I heard that."

"Thank you," I said. "Really. And you're sure Jerry is alive?"

"What they said on the news, anyhow." He turned his attention to Noah. "Is it safe to move him?"

"We have to. I can't get him to the car alone."

Noah's eyelids opened slowly and he focused on Weller.

"Good day," he said.

First words I'd heard from him in half an hour.

"Good day, indeed," Weller responded, then raised his eyebrows at me in a *What the hell is going on?* gesture.

"I need to get him to the car," I repeated. "I figure with me on one side and you on the other, it won't be so bad."

Weller knelt and picked Noah off the ground as easily as if he were lifting a child, hoisted him onto his shoulder, and looked back to make sure he was situated comfortably. "How's that, bub?"

Noah murmured something unintelligible and closed his eyes again. Weller nodded and patted his back.

"Let's get you home."

"I can help," I said.

"When the Weller needs help, you'll be the first to know." He looked at the high limestone wall where Jerry's rope dangled. "There's no way you climbed that, right?"

"I did."

"With nothing but the rope?" His eyes went wide.

I looked down at my bloody hands and thought about trying to explain it to him, how it had been up there on the wall with no rope to hold me and the snake thrashing on my back. I couldn't come up with a way to begin.

"I wouldn't have believed that was possible," Weller said, and then he turned and walked toward the trail. "How fast do we need to get him out of here?"

"Quick as we can."

"Should I run him is what I mean."

I looked at Noah's dishwater complexion and closed eyes. "Maybe."

Weller ran the whole way. The only stops he made were to adjust Noah and ask him how he was doing. Noah had stopped answering. The last stretch of the trail was the steepest, straight uphill and over rough ground. Weller paused at the base of the hill, his broad face flushed red, breathing hard.

"I can help, Sean," I said, though in truth I was having trouble simply keeping up with him, and I wasn't carrying a damn thing.

He shook his head. "I need to do this," he said, and I didn't understand what he meant by that—Noah was a stranger, and the path ahead was hard—but before I could say more, Weller was running again.

He made it all the way up the hill without stopping. When we broke out of the trees and the Bravada appeared in sight, with Weller's truck beside it, he finally slowed to a walk, then dropped to one knee and lowered Noah Storm carefully into the grass.

"You with us, boss?"

Noah didn't answer. Weller checked his pulse.

"It's damn slow." He looked up. "I'd say hospital, not home."

Can't explain myself, Noah had told me before he lapsed out of consciousness. I looked at him now, swallowed, and shook my head.

"Home is what he wanted. Help me get him in my car, please."

We got him into the Bravada and I thanked Weller again.

"Nobody else would've done this," I said.

"That's the point," he answered, and then he slapped my shoulder and told me to get the hell out of there.

I did.

I had to drive south, so unfortunately not much sun fell on Noah. He stirred for the first time when I pulled into his driveway. His eyes opened and he looked blearily at his house. I came around the passenger side and got him out of the car and into the house. It took me nearly as long to do that as it had taken Sean Weller to run him all the way up from the quarry.

We hadn't been inside those limestone walls for long before Noah spoke again.

"Sorry," he said, "for the scare."

"Are you all right? I mean . . . your heart was barely beating, Noah."

The corner of his mouth tugged up in a faint smile. "It comes back. Trust me."

He told me he wanted to be downstairs. That seemed like a big ask, but by the time we reached the cellar door, he was moving almost under his own power again, albeit slowly.

Range from the den, as he'd said, came at a price. Returning to it seemed to help immensely.

He sat on the cot, took long, slow breaths, and then he said, "A lot to talk about, isn't there?"

There sure was, but my phone had been ringing the whole way down the steps and now it rang again and I finally looked at it. Kerri. I answered.

"Where have you been?" she said, sounding both relieved and angry.

"It's a lot to explain."

"The police are here. They have pictures of another cop. They're asking Dad about him. He's barely conscious and they won't stop shoving pictures in his face."

"That's a good thing," I told her. "That man is Vic Glass. He's your dad's get-out-of-jail card. Keep the police there; I'm on my way."

I disconnected and saw Noah watching with a faintly pleased expression.

"Detective Easton delivered, it seems."

"They're asking Jerry about things, at least. They need me there."

He nodded. "You're sure you sealed the tomb? You checked?"

"I'm sure. Nothing is coming out of that rock, Noah. Nothing."

He closed his eyes, and I thought, *He has been waiting almost a century for this.* When he opened his eyes, he looked tired but not unhappy.

"I know you need to go, but can you help me one more time?" he asked. "I would like to have the sun on my face."

"You want to be on the roof?" I asked, stunned.

He nodded, and when he stood up from the cot, he was able to do it under his own power. He had to lean on me going up the steps, but it was clear he was coming back, and even quicker than I'd expected, so I felt good about things when I got him situated in his chair facing southwest, looking over the town skyline, and directly into the afternoon sun. I didn't fear for him, and even if I had noticed the second syringe in his jacket pocket, I would likely have thought it was just a backup in case he had needed it with the snake.

I have had many years to consider this, to wonder what I might have done and what I might have said.

What I did do was leave to find Kerri. What I did say was "I think we ended it."

What he said—"I think so too. Your climb was remarkable, Marshall." And then: "You made your grandmother proud today. And your father."

I did not know what to say to that. I told him I would come back in the evening, and he told me to give it until morning, and that made sense, because he needed his rest. He was exhausted, even back in his own house and with the sun on his face. His eyes were clear but there was a liquid shine to them, and though no tears fell, it seemed as if they might.

Maybe that is why I had the random thought, walking down the stairs alone, my bruised and bleeding hands tracing the limestone wall, of the first sentence I had written in Mr. Doig's writing workshop.

He cried when he left the boy.

But nobody was crying, and nobody was leaving. There was much to figure out, much left to resolve, but considering the way that day had started and the way it was winding down, it felt like a moment of victory, and all the fires that still needed to be put out were smaller fires, and there was more time to fight them. We had found the snake, and we had sealed it back into its awful tomb beside the body of Harlan Maddox. The police were at Vic Glass's house, and they had plenty to work with there. Jerry Flanders was alive.

You will forgive me, I hope, for thinking that January 1, 2000, was not going to be a day for farewells.

I certainly hope he did.

10

I FOUND HIM AT 9 a.m. the next morning. He had not answered the phone, but I was used to that by then. I was also punch-drunk with fatigue, having spent a long night at the hospital with Kerri, where Jerry was on the mend, and police were on the hunt. We were there when Ron Walters and a BPD detective named Stan Easton showed Jerry a picture of Vic Glass—the redheaded Vic that everyone else knew, and not the sociopath ghost that only I had seen—and Jerry confirmed that was the man he'd known as the snake hunter.

It was this news that I wanted to share with Noah Storm when I drove, bleary-eyed and exhausted and aching, but also excited, to 712 Lockridge Lane. The door was unlocked—although, with the glass broken out, there would have been little point in locking it. I went directly to the cellar, expecting that I would find him on his cot. He wasn't there. The weather had changed, the temperature dropping dramatically overnight and a cold January wind blowing from an overcast sky, so I checked the rest of the house before I even considered the roof.

He was still in his chair, facing southwest, although the sun would've been at his back if there had been any to see.

The empty syringe was in his left hand.

The letter was in his jacket pocket.

11

IT WASN'T A LONG letter. He had been very weak. Very tired. The sun was going down fast, winter reasserting its rightful claim to the season. He would not have had much time to write, regardless of when he took the injection.

Dear Marshall:

So much left to say, I told you. I hate to leave it this way. But I need to act now, while some measure of control remains my own. I do not know how long that will last. I told you that the snake and I are two sides of the same coin. His rhythms affect mine. If the old legend is the truth, then he will be gone soon. He's back inside the stone and he has nowhere to go and that is as it should be. My understanding is that he will fade away, become part of the stone itself.

It is not an appealing future on this side of the coin. I have tried to check out of this life before without success. I suspect it will work this time. If you're reading the letter, it did.

If you're reading the letter, I'm so very sorry.

And so very proud.

It has been the work of multiple lifetimes to return that evil to the place from which it came. Even with the additional time, I hadn't been able to do it alone. I needed the help of a son. Who could have imagined that? I don't know what waits on the other side for anyone—especially for one like me—but I do know that if there is any level of consciousness or semiconsciousness that allows for a single memory, I hope mine is of watching you climb.

I don't deserve pride in your achievements. I haven't earned any. You've thrived despite me, not because of me.

There are things I would like to ask you to tell your mother—so many things!—but that would be unfair at best, cruel at worst. Tell her what you wish. All those choices are yours. I am grateful to have lived alongside you long enough to say with confidence that I trust your judgment.

You owe me no favors, but family have a way of returning with their hands extended.

Go back to the ledge—safely this time!—and ensure that the seal will hold. I think a few layers of concrete would be prudent. Perhaps your friend will help. I regret missing his name in all the excitement. But he is a good friend, and you are lucky to have him. Today I was certainly lucky you had him.

There is a chamber in the cellar, under the desk, beneath a trapdoor. You'll find it easily enough. The door is heavy, but you are strong now. That is where I would like to be left, for reasons more pertinent to your own ease of explanation than any concerns of mine. No one will come looking for me, Marshall. I outlived all my friends long ago. All but you.

The house, the business, and all related assets are yours. There is more there than you might think. Your grandfather had his flaws, but his investment instincts were sharp. On your eighteenth birthday, you will hear from a man named Pine in New York with the details. He will be able to answer all legal or financial questions, and he is a discreet man. His father was a discreet man, as was his grandfather. I knew him the best of the three. I am tired of knowing the past so well. I am tired of avoiding friendship or love simply because I know that I will be left alone in the end. If you ended that cycle for me, you have given me a greater gift than I can possibly express.

Nothing left to do now but find out, is there?

And yet . . . so much to say.

But the sun is setting, and I am tired—and tired of being tired. I believe the tomb is sealed and my work is done, and now I would like to leave this place. It may mean little to you that for the first time in many years, I am conflicted about that desire. You're the reason. The only one.

It was good to know you, son.

You have no idea how good.

Noah

12

I GOT HIM INTO THE CRYPT in the basement. It was scarcely larger than he was, but it was deep, and I suspected he had carved it himself, and with care.

The door, as he had promised, was heavy, and the seal was tight.

When that was done, I called Kerri. She was the first person to know any of it and she remains the only person to know all of it.

Until now.

Sean Weller was the second to know any of it, because, as Noah had predicted, I needed his help. For a guy who never shut up, Sean understood secrets.

He also understood how to build a gantry crane. We worked together in the night, using bright halogen lamps to illuminate the quarry from above, the winch motor growling as it lowered first us and then bucket after bucket of concrete that we mixed above and then layered onto the tomb below.

"A devil snake," Weller said, smoothing my rough work with his masonry trowel. "The shit you get into, Marshmallow."

Each time I decided our work was done, I ended up mixing more concrete. Once, when I was alone on the ledge and Weller was working up above, I thought I heard a faint buzz and a low laugh. I dropped my trowel and scrambled back, but then there was only silence.

The mind can play tricks.

Sure, it can.

We worked until dawn and then, as the sun reddened the eastern sky, we sat on the ledge together and I produced a bottle of Scotch that I'd found in Noah's office. It was called Macallan and it had been aged for twenty-five years. It seemed symbolic and appropriate to drink from Noah's liquor after the job was done. I took a sip, let the smoky whiskey put its pleasant burn through my throat, and then passed it to Weller. He pounded down a few fingers of it, then held the bottle at arm's length, regarding it skeptically.

"It's no SoCo, but it'll drink."

He swigged some more and then passed the bottle back to me and got to his feet. I sat alone on the edge of the ledge, thinking of Noah's letter and tasting the whiskey, and when I finally looked back to see what he was doing, it was too late.

He had used his trowel to carve the words THE WELLER WAS HERE! in the drying concrete above the tomb.

"What the hell is the matter with you?" I shouted.

He turned back, startled. "What?"

"It's a sacred place!" I said, outraged by his child's prank in this spot where so much evil had been born and then battled back.

"I know that," he said indignantly. "But I was here, and I helped, didn't I? And you know what? Fuck that snake!"

How do you argue with that? In the end, I left my initials and the date in tiny script beneath his massive carving: *MM 2000.* It's still out there. If you find yourself deep in the Morgan-Monroe State Forest, hike out to check.

Watch for snakes.

CHAPTER FOURTEEN

GUARDING THE DEAD

After

"You can't kill nothin' that's ready to die"

NAS

"WE WILL SURVIVE"

JERRY FLANDERS WAS STILL in the hospital, recovering from his gunshot wounds, when the Indiana State Police announced that they had DNA evidence tying Vic Glass to the murder of Meredith Sullivan.

They also had video. Those stacks of VHS tapes in Vic Glass's bedroom revealed hundreds of hours of videos that Vic had taken of the snake. I know only a few of the highlight moments—such as the night he brought it to my house, and the night he placed it in my car.

The snake called Winterstone never bit me or my mother. I wonder about that. Was it curious or was it afraid or was it—dare I write this—*proud?* After all, I share its blood.

I will never know the answer to that one. I remember the way it thrashed on my back, though, and the impact of its strikes, and of course I know that many murder victims are killed by their own family members.

No one, as Harlan Maddox once told me, is guaranteed a safe return home.

Some of the other videos involved Meredith Sullivan. I am grateful for her family that the case never went to trial and the public never saw those tapes.

Vic Glass used the sharpened handle of a broken spoon to open his wrists in the Monroe County Jail. He bled out before anyone discovered the wounds.

An inmate in an adjacent cell swore that he heard a laugh that was not Big Vic's in the moments before the blood trail appeared on the floor.

Nobody gave that much credence.

Jerry was cleared of murder, but his existing charges remained. Prosecutors and defense attorneys quietly arranged a plea agreement that was limited to probation if Jerry would decline to sue the city for his shooting by Officer Vic Glass.

He still wasn't sure exactly what had happened that night. He'd been stunned by the failure of Y2K to deliver and set off to see whether it was true, he told me, but after driving through town, he'd found himself heading north. He had his bug-out bag with him, of course, so he had his rope.

"I had this overpowering desire to see the place," he told me in a whisper as I sat beside his hospital bed. "It wasn't a good feeling. It was . . . all-consuming."

Maybe it wasn't a good feeling, I told him, but he did drop the rope, and the person who needed that rope was me.

He never got the chance to lower himself to the den. A flashlight appeared through the woods. Jerry watched it come on, and what he saw then—the last thing he remembered before the gunshots—was a sight that returned to him in nightmares.

The man with the flashlight was illuminating a path for a black-and-white snake. The snake slithered over the rough ground, and the man followed just behind.

"Like someone walking a dog," Jerry said.

The rest was blackness to him. I thought that was probably a good thing.

Mandatory mental health counseling was a condition of Jerry's probation. He accepted it grudgingly, and I don't think he ever knew that the condition hadn't been suggested by a prosecutor but by his daughter.

He's still at it, twenty years later. I'm proud of him.

———

My mother was released from the hospital in early January. The first month was rough, but she was tenacious about rehab. On a warm day in March, she went golfing. We rented a cart, which she despised, and played just three holes. On the third, she hit a sky-high flop shot out of a sand trap to within a foot of the pin.

I loved the way she smiled in that moment. She couldn't make the walk up to the elevated green—not yet—but she would by summer, and we both knew it then.

———

Kerri registered for a few classes at IU and moved into an apartment. I began to spend a lot of time there. My mother didn't say much about that, other than to observe it would be foolish for her to pretend that Kerri and I were still teenagers in the way she'd hoped we would be.

"You lost that," she said. "I don't like it, but I recognize it. You two were forced to grow up faster than most."

That was one way of putting it.

I managed to make it out of North and into IU. It was no sure thing, and graduating required kindness from several teachers. There were good people at Bloomington North. Mr. Doig was the best of them. He kept urging me to write it all down, and while I wasn't ready to do that yet, I did begin to write. The first story was about a private investigator who has a rare cancer that limits his range due to the need for regular, experimental infusions. I expected it to be a short story, but soon I had 305 pages. No one was more surprised than me when Mr. Doig entered it into a national contest and the story won first prize—and a publishing contract.

Librarians change lives. They may even save some.

———

On the morning of my eighteenth birthday, I handed my mother a box.

"Why am *I* getting a gift on *your* birthday?" she asked, bewildered.

"I'm not sure it is a gift," I said.

I watched her read the letters Noah Storm had left to me. That was a long day. That was a long, hard day. A good one, in its own ways. But not an easy one. I watched her disbelief turn to sorrow, and then I watched her cry. I realized, somehow for the first time, or the first time it was truly felt in my heart, that she had spent nearly two decades hating a man she'd once loved—or at least could have loved. Wished to love.

"He looked so different," she whispered. "And yet, when we sat there in his office . . . Marshall, I knew him. It was impossible, of course. He was a stranger. He was in a different body but he wasn't older, or not old enough, and yet . . . I *knew* him." She wiped beneath her eye with one delicate fingertip. "But if I knew him, I shouldn't have liked him. Right? In my core, my mother's intuition, I should have told you to run from that place."

I remembered the way she'd smiled and laughed with him that day, the way the two of them had made small talk before getting to the urgent point of the visit, and I felt my heart break for her, and for him, and maybe a little bit for myself. For what might have been, once.

For a family.

"He was not an evil man," I told her. "And you don't need to worry about anything in my blood, no matter what he told you."

Maybe this was the truth. It felt good to say so, anyhow.

We sat in silence for a long time, and when I saw her smiling faintly, I was surprised.

"What?"

"I remember that fire tower," she said softly. "And the hayloft, and the lake, and . . ." Her voice wavered but the smile didn't break. "The champagne in that cemetery in the rain."

They were moments I didn't wish to consider, in so many ways, and yet I was very glad she remembered them.

I have never told my mother that I saw Harlan Maddox's face when everyone else in the world saw Vic Glass.

As Noah wrote, these decisions are mine. We will see if he was right to be confident in my judgment.

———————

I moved in with Kerri that fall. Sean Weller spent most of two weeks with us after he completed Marine Corps boot camp, an exercise he deemed "not the easiest thing in the world" but summarized as "Parris Island can't handle the Weller."

He was still crazy, the wild man's wild man, but there was a gravitas to him that hadn't been there before, and he told me often that he was happy to have found his purpose. I thought the Marines were probably happy about that too.

We couldn't see each other much, because of the military life, but we didn't waste the days we got. If you measured friendship by the pint, Sean Weller was my brother from another mother. When he left, he would always put two Hallmark cards on the coffee table for Kerri. One would be an apology card, some cute teddy bear asking for forgiveness or the like, which he signed in his own name, with a thank-you for tolerating his presence and restocking the Alka-Seltzer. The other would be the most over-the-top love letter he could find, which he would sign in Jake Crane's name with the same addendum: "Not too late to fix the mistake—call me."

Weller never tired of this joke.

———

He was visiting us on a beautiful September in our sophomore year when two planes struck the World Trade Center. The three of us watched the towers fall together. Weller raged around the apartment, promising vengeance.

"They can't handle the Weller!" he bellowed.

None of us were sure who "they" were yet. All of us were sure that the world had changed. I could not stop thinking about 1999. There were so many plane disasters that year—EgyptAir 990, John F. Kennedy Jr. off the coast not so far from the airport that bore his father's name, and, of course, the hijacked plane that had sat idling on the tarmac in Afghanistan on New Year's Eve while the Taliban negotiated with the hijackers. It's hard to look at the past and not feel as if there are patterns and warnings.

Weller was deployed in December 2001, almost a year to the day after I'd called him to the forest to save my father.

I did not like that timing.

———

For a long time, we lost track of Jake Crane. He left Bloomington and went back to Boulder. I hadn't heard his name in years before I read an article in the *New York Times* interviewing him about summiting Everest without supplemental oxygen. Five years after that, he made a record-breaking free climb of Half Dome in Yosemite, and then he turned his journals of those expeditions into a hybrid adventure memoir and self-help book titled *The Wall Is All.*

To date, it has sold more copies than all my books combined, and the movie version starring Channing Tatum as Jake Crane was a box office smash. A couple years ago, some genius festival organizer learned that we'd attended high school together and decided to pair us at an authors' event in Florida. It was a hell of a good time. I signed thirteen books and then sat beside Jake while he signed hundreds of books with a ballpoint pen, and the tops of a few breasts with a Sharpie. No one has ever asked me to sign their breasts. To go on book tour as Jake Crane is a unique experience.

You better believe I made him sign a book for me too. The inscription reads: *"To Marshall—WHIPPER!!!!! Keep ringing the bell, bro. Your friend and coach, Jake Crane."*

I keep that one on my desk.

———

Dom Kamsing went to Wisconsin to play soccer and then went to med school. People kept drifting away, as they do anywhere, I suppose, but seem to in greater numbers when your hometown is a college town.

I stayed. Even when Kerri went to law school at Northwestern, I stayed. I can't write as easily in another place as I can in my office in the limestone house at 712 Lockridge Lane, above my father's crypt. The words come quicker there, and the camera of the mind is clearer. I don't know why . . . although of course I have some ideas.

———

Sean Weller wrote me letters sporadically, but he was harder to keep in touch with than most. By the time of his fifth deployment in four years, Facebook was the dominant communication means of our generation, but Weller still insisted on using AIM, which was by turns perplexing and hilarious to me, because everyone else had moved on.

"I like it better," he said simply. "Facebook feels like a bunch of people flexing in the mirror, and you know how I feel about that."

Indeed. But since he was rarely in a place with open internet access and he was damn near the only person still using AIM, I rarely logged on. I figured the letters meant more. Granted, I was having trouble remembering to write them. In fact, I had reminded myself to finally sit down and put pen to paper for him on the day that I heard he was dead.

I heard the news on a perfect spring afternoon in Bloomington. April. It was a weekday, and even though I should've been working—or maybe writing overdue letters to old friends—the weather was so seductive that I decided to walk across campus and beneath the Sample Gates to Kirkwood Avenue and grab a cold beer at Nick's. I ducked into the little side bar that's downstairs and to the left, the one where the townies and old-timers tended to congregate. I sat down beside a man who had an open laptop in front of him, nodded and said hello, but I paid his screen no mind until he said, "That kid was from town. His dad comes in. Construction guy, developer. Funny as hell."

I looked at his computer then and saw that he was on Facebook, viewing a post with a side-by-side of Sean Weller in the full-dress Marine uniform paired with one from his senior year of football, decked out in Bloomington South's signature purple and white, all this above a headline that read HOOSIER SERVICEMAN KILLED IN AMBUSH IN KHOST.

"That can't be right," I said. He gave me a strange look and spread his hands like *It is what it is.*

Already, the wall of comments beneath the post was filling with tributes and memories, people saying Sean was the best guy, was the most loyal friend, was the strongest teammate, on and on, *was, was, was.*

The Weller in past tense.

I paid for my beer and left it unfinished on the counter when the tears began, walked out of the bar beneath a crystal-blue sky, the kind of nearly indescribable blue that people who were in Manhattan on the morning of 9/11 will never forget. I found my car and drove to the property at the end of Lost Man's Lane, the place where so much had happened in 1999. I parked in front of the rusty farm gate, beneath the old sugar maple, and let the engine run while I cried for my crazy friend, the one who earnestly believed a ghost would never cockblock, the one who'd leaped

onto a weight bench to shout about Ben Franklin inspiring the troops at
Gettysburg. Not Weller's fault he got the name wrong. He never claimed
to be a geologist.

He also couldn't climb worth a damn, but he rang that bell. And
one New Year's Day, when a friend called him and begged for help—no-
questions-asked help—he did not hesitate.

Hold fast, Marshmallow. The Weller is en route.

A good friend, my dead father had called him.

Yeah, Pops. He sure was. Wonder if he left me a note, like you?

I looked past the old gate, into the spring fields, and remembered my
first encounter with Sean Weller, on this same ground in almost identical
weather, when he'd told the crowd how good my Away message story
was.

He's the bad guy and he doesn't realize it yet. It is funny as hell.

Weller had joined the marines only after getting in trouble with me,
only because I was scared to go into the forest alone.

Now he was gone. The indestructible, indefatigable Sean Weller was
dead in the dust in Afghanistan. Or maybe it was the snow. A mountain
or a desert. A village or a city. I don't think many of us ever had a clear picture of the world we set out to conquer—not nearly as clear as the picture
of the wounds we needed to avenge, at least. I damn well know that not
enough of us had any sense of what it was like to live there or serve there.

He's the bad guy and he doesn't realize it yet. It is funny as hell.

Someone who got you killed in exchange for your friendship seemed
to meet the definition of a bad guy. I was the reason he'd ended up in Afghanistan. Weller had been right about me all along, wrong only about
the back half—it wasn't funny as hell.

It was awful.

I sat numbly in front of the farm gate for a long time, and then I drove
home, booted up my computer, and logged on to AOL Instant Messenger.
One thing about the Weller—he loved his Away messages. There would
be one waiting, a last note from the dead, my father's work on fresh tech.

It took me a while to write my own message. What to say? I settled
for telling him that I was sorry, and I explained where I'd gone that after-

noon, told him that it would be the last time I'd ever see the old property the way it used to be. The way it always should be, if only it could be, but of course it cannot be.

Soon the old farm would fill with winding roads and sidewalks and manicured lawns, beautiful brick houses with oversized garages, and I promised Sean that I would always hate the neighborhood, because the place should be an expanse of overgrown fields with a rusting farm gate on one side and a crazy kid with a crew cut and a keg of piss-water beer and a bottle of Southern Comfort waiting on the other. They could develop the land, I told my dead friend, but they could not destroy it. Memory is a potent magic. The rusty gate would be there forever to me, and I hoped that it would open and let me pass back through.

I'd see him there.

It's hard to press Send on a farewell. I wondered how long my father had held the pen before he set it down and picked up the syringe. The sun was down and the stone house was cold when I finally made myself hit Enter.

The immediate response of an Away message arrived, as I'd known it would.

> **TheWeller:** Marshmallow, my dad is going to do a nice job with that property. Let it go. High school is over! Besides, he'll make a lot of money.

I stared at the screen, disbelieving it. I'd hallucinated in this place before, after all. Then I typed another message to Sean, told him that he was dead, killed in Khost.

> **TheWeller:** Where in the hell did you get that idea?

Facebook, I explained. It was all over Facebook.

> **TheWeller:** I told you that site was bullshit!

Another marine in Sean's unit hadn't been so lucky. Facebook had helpfully rushed to identify the dead. To this day, I am convinced that it would have gone a different way if I'd sent my message from any other place than the limestone house on Lockridge Lane where my father's remains rest. There is a power in there where the words meet the stone—a power I'm scared to fully explore. I'm almost sure of it. Of course, to this day, Sean Weller tells me that's happy horseshit.

I don't care who's right.

I had exactly one day with a father in this life, but that's okay, because on the other days, Jerry was there, and Weller, and Kerri, and my mother. No one has it all. I have been blessed with far more than most.

Kerri and I married young and made it last. Sometimes the high school sweetheart is so much more than that.

We have not had children. This is, as you might have guessed, an issue of some importance to the last surviving member of the Stuart and Maddox families, a man who could see the dead where others saw only the living.

Bloodlines are complicated.

I don't *think* I fear what harm could come to our child if we had one. The snake called Winterstone is sealed in its tomb with Harlan Maddox's corpse, and the cursed blood is diluted by the generations. Perhaps our child would experience nothing unusual.

But it is difficult not to wonder.

I have worked for years to learn the fate of William Crabb, and I have not found success. It is hard to believe there was only one snake that needed to be entombed. I try to believe that—desperately. But the world suggests there are plenty of snakes out there.

Last spring I met a geologist at a dinner party. He told me that Bloomington sits near not one but two major seismic fault lines. The potential for disaster is already with us, he said—it always has been, right under our feet—and we carry on as if unaware because that's how you have to live. But a big quake will come for our town one of these days, he said. It is only a matter of time.

I'm not sure what he saw in my face, but he gave me a strange look and said that he hadn't meant to frighten me, and I assured him that I was not worried about my house collapsing. That much was true.

What worried me was the possibility of a subtle seam opening in a forgotten quarry deep in the forest, a thin shaft of daylight penetrating a limestone tomb.

An escape hatch.

I imagined a black-and-white snake emerging, its wedged head rising, its black tongue tasting a new day.

There is a reason the word "supernatural" includes "natural," my father told me. Earthquakes happen all the time, around twenty thousand each year, or fifty-five per day. Think about that. One day we're going to rattle that tomb in the forest. It's inevitable.

What to do about that?

I can tell my story, at least. They might shelve it in fiction, but if just a few people read it and remember it when a girl goes missing on an eerie, unseasonably warm day and sightings of a black-and-white rattlesnake begin, well, that's better than nothing.

Every stone has a story.

This is one of them.

ACKNOWLEDGMENTS

IT WAS GREAT FUN to wander back in time in Bloomington, and townie readers will notice the liberties I took with reality—and maps—while creating my fictional version of the place. Most of the time, these changes were intended. Mistakes are mine alone.

If I ever shared a laugh with you in Bloomington in 1999, consider yourself thanked.

This book exists because of Emily Bestler, editor and publisher extraordinaire, and I can't adequately thank her for her faith, enthusiasm, keen eye, and good humor. Emily, it is a joy and a privilege to work with you.

The team at Atria and Simon & Schuster has been wonderful—and patient! Special thanks to Lara Jones, Libby McGuire, Dana Trocker, David Brown, Zakiya Jamal, James Iacobelli, Paige Lytle, Dana Sloan, and Hydia Scott-Riley.

Thanks as always to Richard Pine and InkWell Management for piloting the ship, and to Angela Cheng Caplan and Allison Binder for representing my work so well on the film/TV side. Erin Mitchell makes so many things happen that I can't even begin to list them.

Early readers: Christine Koryta, Bob Hammel, Pete Yonkman, Ben Strawn, Jenn Cristy Strawn, Kaleb Ryan, Rich Chizmar, Brian Freeman, Gideon Pine.

One anonymous early reader deserves particularly deep gratitude from the Weller—and from me.

The heartbeat of the book always comes from home: Thank you,

Christine! Pets also deserve notice for enduring the process, in my opinion, so thanks to Lola, John Pryor, and, one last time, to Marlowe, who supervised eighteen of my nineteen published novels before moving on to more interesting projects.

Much gratitude to every reader. This was a fun one. Let's do it again soon!